GW00859025

The House of the Dead; or, Prison Life in Siberia

by Fyodor Dostoyevsky

Copyright © 7/30/2015
Jefferson Publication

ISBN-13: 978-1515295976

Printed in the United States of America

Contents

PART I.

CHAPTER I. TEN YEARS A CONVICT

In the midst of the steppes, of the mountains, of the impenetrable forests of the desert regions of Siberia, one meets from time to time with little towns of a thousand or two inhabitants, built entirely of wood, very ugly, with two churches—one in the centre of the town, the other in the cemetery—in a word, towns which bear much more resemblance to a good-sized village in the suburbs of Moscow than to a town properly so called. In most cases they are abundantly provided with police-master, assessors, and other inferior officials. If it is cold in Siberia, the great advantages of the Government service compensate for it. The inhabitants are simple people, without liberal ideas. Their manners are antique, solid, and unchanged by time. The officials who form, and with reason, the nobility in Siberia, either belong to the country, deeply-rooted Siberians, or they have arrived there from Russia. The latter come straight from the capitals, tempted by the high pay, the extra allowance for travelling expenses, and by hopes not less seductive for the future. Those who know how to resolve the problem of life remain almost always in Siberia; the abundant and richly-flavoured fruit which they gather there recompenses them amply for what they lose.

As for the others, light-minded persons who are unable to deal with the problem, they are soon bored in Siberia, and ask themselves with regret why they committed the folly of coming. They impatiently kill the three years which they are obliged by rule to remain, and as soon as their time is up, they beg to be sent back, and return to their original quarters, running down Siberia, and ridiculing it. They are wrong, for it is a happy country, not only as regards the Government service, but also from many other points of view.

The climate is excellent, the merchants are rich and hospitable, the Europeans in easy circumstances are numerous; as for the young girls, they are like roses and their morality is irreproachable. Game is to be found in the streets, and throws itself upon the sportsman's gun. People drink champagne in prodigious quantities. The caviare is astonishingly good and most abundant. In a word, it is a blessed land, out of which it is only necessary to be able to make profit; and much profit is really made.

It is in one of these little towns—gay and perfectly satisfied with themselves, the population of which has left upon me the most agreeable impression—that I met an exile, Alexander Petrovitch Goriantchikoff, formerly a landed proprietor in Russia. He had been condemned to hard labour of the second class for assassinating his wife. After undergoing his punishment—ten years of hard labour—he lived quietly and unnoticed as a colonist in the little town of K——. To tell the truth, he was inscribed in one of the surrounding districts; but he resided at K——, where he managed to get a living by giving lessons to children. In the towns of Siberia one often meets with exiles who are occupied with instruction. They are not looked down upon, for they teach the French language, so necessary in life, and of which without them one would not, in the distant parts of Siberia, have the least idea.

I saw Alexander Petrovitch the first time at the house of an official, Ivan Ivanitch Gvosdikof, a venerable old man, very hospitable, and the father of five daughters, of whom the greatest hopes were entertained. Four times a week Alexander Petrovitch gave them lessons, at the rate of thirty kopecks silver a lesson. His external appearance interested me. He was excessively pale and thin, still young—about thirty-five years of age—short and weak, always very neatly dressed in the European style. When you spoke to him he looked at you in a very attentive manner, listening to your words with strict politeness, and with a reflective air, as though you had placed before him a problem or wished to extract from him a secret. He replied clearly and shortly; but in doing so, weighed each word, so that one felt ill at ease without knowing why, and was glad when the conversation came to an end. I put some questions to Ivan Gvosdikof in regard to him. He told me that Goriantchikoff was of irreproachable morals, otherwise Gvosdikof would not have entrusted him with the education of his children; but that he was a terrible misanthrope, who kept apart from all society; that he was very learned, a great reader, and that he spoke but little, and never entered freely into a conversation. Certain persons told him that he was mad; but that was not looked upon as a very serious defect. Accordingly, the most important persons in the town were ready to treat Alexander Petrovitch with respect, for he could be useful to them in writing petitions. It was believed that he was well connected in Russia. Perhaps, among his relations, there were some who were highly placed; but it was known that since his exile he had broken off all relations with them. In a word—he injured himself. Every one knew his story, and was aware that he had killed his wife, through jealousy, less than a year after his marriage; and that he had given himself up to justice; which had made his punishment much less severe. Such crimes are always looked upon as misfortunes, which must be treated with pity. Nevertheless, this original kept himself obstinately apart, and never showed himself except to give lessons. In the first instance I paid no attention to him; then, without knowing why, I found myself interested by him. He was rather enigmatic; to talk with him was quite impossible. Certainly he replied to all my questions; he seemed to make it a duty to do so; but when once he had answered, I was afraid to interrogate him any longer.

After such conversations one could observe on his countenance signs of suffering and exhaustion. I remember that, one fine summer evening, I went out with him from the house of Ivan Gvosdikof. It suddenly occurred to me to invite him to come in with me and smoke a cigarette. I can scarcely describe the fright which showed itself in his countenance. He became confused, muttered incoherent words, and suddenly, after looking at me with an angry air, took to flight in an opposite direction. I was very much astonished afterwards, when he met me. He seemed to experience, on seeing me, a sort of terror; but I did not lose courage. There was something in him which attracted me.

A month afterwards I went to see Petrovitch without any pretext. It is evident that, in doing so, I behaved foolishly, and without the least delicacy. He lived at one of the extreme points of the town with an old woman whose daughter was in a consumption. The latter had a little child about ten years old, very pretty and very lively.

When I went in Alexander Petrovitch was seated by her side, and was teaching her to read. When he saw me he became confused, as if I had detected him in a crime. Losing all self-command, he suddenly stood up and looked at me with awe and astonishment. Then we both of us sat down. He followed attentively all my looks, as if I had suspected him of some mysterious intention. I understood he was horribly mistrustful. He looked at me as a sort of spy, and he seemed to be on the point of saying, "Are you not soon going away?"

I spoke to him of our little town, of the news of the day, but he was silent, or smiled with an air of displeasure. I could see that he was absolutely ignorant of all that was taking place in the town, and that he was in no way curious to know. I spoke to him afterwards of the country generally, and of its men. He listened to me still in silence, fixing his eyes upon me in such a strange way that I became ashamed of what I was doing. I was very nearly offending him by offering him some books and newspapers which I had just received by post. He cast a greedy look upon them; he then seemed to alter his mind, and declined my offer, giving his want of leisure as a pretext.

At last I wished him good-bye, and I felt a weight fall from my shoulders as I left the house. I regretted to have harassed a man whose tastes kept him apart from the rest of the world. But the fault had been committed. I had remarked that he possessed very few books. It was not true, then, that he read so much. Nevertheless, on two occasions when I drove past, I saw a light in his lodging. What could make him sit up so late? Was he writing, and if that were so, what was he writing?

I was absent from our town for about three months. When I returned home in the winter, I learned that Petrovitch was dead, and that he had not even sent for a doctor. He was even now already forgotten, and his lodging was unoccupied. I at once made the acquaintance of his landlady, in the hope of learning from her what her lodger had been writing. For twenty kopecks she brought me a basket full of papers left by the defunct, and confessed to me that she had already employed four sheets in lighting her fire. She was a morose and taciturn old woman. I could not get from her anything that was interesting. She could tell me nothing about her lodger. She gave me to understand all the same that he scarcely ever worked, and that he remained for months together without opening a book or touching a pen. On the other hand, he walked all night up and down his room, given up to his reflections. Sometimes, indeed, he spoke aloud. He was very fond of her little grandchild, Katia, above all when he knew her name; on her name's-day—the day of St. Catherine—he always had a requiem said in the church for some one's soul. He detested receiving visits, and never went out except to give lessons. Even his landlady he looked upon with an unfriendly eye when, once a week, she came into his room to put it in order.

During the three years he had passed with her, he had scarcely ever spoken to her. I asked Katia if she remembered him. She looked at me in silence, and turned weeping to the wall. This man, then, was loved by some one! I took away the papers, and passed the day in examining them. They were for the most part of no importance, merely children's exercises. At last I came to a rather thick packet, the sheets of which were covered with delicate handwriting, which abruptly ceased. It had perhaps been forgotten by the writer. It was the narrative—incoherent and fragmentary—of the ten years Alexander Petrovitch had passed in hard labour. This narrative was interrupted, here and there, either by anecdotes, or by strange, terrible recollections thrown in convulsively as if torn from the writer. I read some of these fragments again and again, and I began to doubt whether they had not been written in moments of madness; but these memories of the convict prison—"Recollections of the Dead-House," as he himself called them somewhere in his manuscript—seemed to me not without interest. They revealed quite a new world unknown till then; and in the strangeness of his facts, together with his singular remarks on this fallen people, there was enough to tempt me to go on. I may perhaps be wrong, but I will publish some chapters from this narrative, and the public shall judge for itself.

CHAPTER II. THE DEAD-HOUSE

Our prison was at the end of the citadel behind the ramparts. Looking through the crevices between the palisade in the hope of seeing something, one sees nothing but a little corner of the sky, and a high earthwork, covered with the long grass of the steppe. Night and day sentries walk to and fro upon it. Then one perceives from the first, that whole years will pass during which one will see by the same crevices between the palisades, upon the same earthwork, always the same sentinels and the same little corner of the sky, not just above the prison, but far and far away. Represent to yourself a court-yard, two hundred feet long, and one hundred and fifty feet broad, enclosed by an irregular hexagonal palisade, formed of stakes thrust deep into the earth. So much for the external surroundings of the prison. On one side of the palisade is a great gate, solid, and always shut; watched perpetually by the sentinels, and never opened, except when the convicts go out to work. Beyond this, there are light and liberty, the life of free people! Beyond the palisade, one thought of the marvellous world, fantastic as a fairy tale. It was not the same on our side. Here, there was no resemblance to anything. Habits, customs, laws, were all precisely fixed. It was the house of living death. It is this corner that I undertake to describe.

On penetrating into the enclosure one sees a few buildings. On each side of a vast court are stretched forth two wooden constructions, made of trunks of trees, and only one storey high. These are convicts' barracks. Here the prisoners are confined, divided into several classes. At the end of the enclosure may be seen a house, which serves as a kitchen, divided into two compartments. Behind it is another building, which serves at once as cellar, loft, and barn. The centre of the enclosure, completely barren, is a large open space. Here the prisoners are drawn up in ranks, three times a day. They are identified, and must answer to their names, morning, noon, and evening, besides several times in the course of the day if the soldiers on guard are suspicious and clever at counting. All around, between the palisades and the buildings there remains a sufficiently large space, where some of the prisoners who are misanthropes, or of a sombre turn of mind, like to walk about when they are not at work. There they go turning over their favourite thoughts, shielded from all observation.

When I met them during those walks of theirs, I took pleasure in observing their sad, deeply-marked countenances, and in guessing their thoughts. The favourite occupation of one of the convicts, during the moments of liberty left to him from his hard labour, was to count the palisades. There were fifteen hundred of them. He had counted them all, and knew them nearly by heart. Every one of them represented to him a day of confinement; but, counting them daily in this manner, he knew exactly the number of days that he had still to pass in the prison. He was sincerely happy when he had finished one side of the hexagon; yet he had to wait for his liberation many long years. But one learns patience in a prison.

One day I saw a prisoner, who had undergone his punishment, take leave of his comrades. He had had twenty years' hard labour. More than one convict remembered seeing him arrive, quite young, careless, thinking neither of his crime nor of his punishment. He was now an old man with gray hairs, with a sad and morose countenance. He walked in silence through our six barracks. When he entered each of them he prayed before the holy image, made a deep bow to his former companions, and begged them not to keep a bad recollection of him.

I also remember one evening, a prisoner, who had been formerly a well-to-do Siberian peasant, so called. Six years before he had had news of his wife's remarrying, which had caused him great pain. That very evening she had come to the prison, and had asked for him in order to make him a present! They talked together for two minutes, wept together, and then separated never to meet again. I saw the expression of this prisoner's countenance when he re-entered the barracks. There, indeed, one learns to support everything.

When darkness set in we had to re-enter the barrack, where we were shut up for all the night. It was always painful for me to leave the court-yard for the barrack. Think of a long, low, stifling room, scarcely lighted by tallow candles, and full of heavy and disgusting odours. I cannot now understand how I lived there for ten entire years. My camp bedstead was made of three boards. This was the only place in the room that belonged to me. In one single room we herded together, more than thirty men. It was, above all, no wonder that we were shut up early. Four hours at least passed before every one was asleep, and, until then, there was a tumult and uproar of laughter, oaths, rattling of chains, a poisonous vapour of thick smoke; a confusion of shaved heads, stigmatised foreheads, and ragged clothes disgustingly filthy.

Yes, man is a pliable animal—he must be so defined—a being who gets accustomed to everything! That would be, perhaps, the best definition that could be given of him. There were altogether two hundred and fifty of us in the same prison. This number was almost invariably the same. Whenever some of them had undergone their punishment, other criminals arrived, and a few of them died. Among them there were all sorts of people. I believe that each region of Russia had furnished its representatives. There were foreigners there, and even mountaineers from the Caucasus.

All these people were divided into different classes, according to the importance of the crime; and consequently the duration of the punishment for the crime, whatever it might be, was there represented. The population of the prison was composed for the most part of men condemned to hard labour of the civil class—"strongly condemned," as the prisoners used to say. They were criminals deprived of all civil rights, men rejected by society, vomited forth by it, and whose faces were marked by the iron to testify eternally to their disgrace. They were incarcerated for different periods of time, varying from eight to ten years. At the expiration of their punishment they were sent to the Siberian districts in the character of colonists.

As to the criminals of the military section, they were not deprived of their civil rights—as is generally the case in Russian disciplinary companies—but were punished for a relatively short period. As soon as they had undergone their punishment they had to return to the place whence they had come, and became soldiers in the battalions of the Siberian Line.

Many of them came back to us afterwards, for serious crimes, this time not for a small number of years, but for twenty at least. They then formed part of the section called "for perpetuity." Nevertheless, the perpetuals were not deprived of their right. There was another section sufficiently numerous, composed of the worst malefactors, nearly all veterans in crime, and which was called the special section. There were sent convicts from all the Russias. They looked upon one another with reason as imprisoned for ever, for the term of their confinement had not been indicated. The law required them to receive double and treble tasks. They remained in prison until work of the most painful character had to be undertaken in Siberia.

"You are only here for a fixed time," they said to the other convicts; "we, on the contrary, are here for all our life."

I have heard that this section has since been abolished. At the same time, civil convicts are kept apart, in order that the military convicts may be organised by themselves into a homogeneous "disciplinary company." The administration, too, has naturally been changed; consequently what I describe are the customs and practices of another time, and of things which have since been abolished. Yes, it was a long time ago; it seems to me that it is all a dream. I remember entering the convict prison one December evening, as night was falling. The convicts were returning from work. The roll-call was about to be made. An under officer with large moustaches opened to me the gate of this strange house, where I was to remain so many years, to endure so many emotions, and of which I could not form even an approximate idea, if I had not gone through them. Thus, for example, could I ever have imagined the poignant and terrible suffering of never being alone even for one minute during ten years? Working under escort in the barracks together with two hundred "companions;" never alone, never!

However, I was obliged to get accustomed to it. Among them there were murderers by imprudence, and murderers by profession, simple thieves, masters in the art of finding money in the pockets of the passers-by, or of wiping off no matter what from the table. It would have been difficult, however, to say why and how certain prisoners found themselves among the convicts. Each of them had his history, confused and heavy, painful as the morning after a debauch.

The convicts, as a rule, spoke very little of their past life, which they did not like to think of. They endeavoured, even, to dismiss it from their memory.

Amongst my companions of the chain I have known murderers who were so gay and so free from care, that one might have made a bet that their conscience never made them the least reproach. But there were also men of sombre countenance who remained almost always silent. It was very rarely any one told his history. This sort of thing was not the fashion. Let us say at once that it was not received. Sometimes, however, from time to time, for the sake of change, a prisoner used to tell his life to another prisoner, who would listen coldly to the narrative. No one, to tell the truth, could have said anything to astonish his neighbour. "We are not ignoramuses," they would sometimes say with singular pride.

I remember one day a ruffian who had got drunk—it was sometimes possible for the convicts to get drink—relating how he had killed and cut up a child of five. He had first tempted the child with a plaything, and then taking it to a loft, had cut it up to pieces. The entire barrack, which, generally speaking, laughed at his jokes, uttered one unanimous cry. The ruffian was obliged to be silent. But if the convicts had interrupted him, it was not by any means because his recital had caused their indignation, but because it was not allowed to speak of such things.

I must here observe that the convicts possessed a certain degree of instruction. Half of them, if not more, knew how to read and write. Where in Russia, in no matter what population, could two hundred and fifty men be found able to read and write? Later on I have heard people say, and conclude on the strength of these abuses, that education demoralises the people. This is a mistake. Education has nothing whatever to do with moral deterioration. It must be admitted, nevertheless, that it develops a resolute spirit among the people. But this is far from being a defect.

Each section had a different costume. The uniform of one was a cloth vest, half brown and half gray, and trousers with one leg brown, the other gray. One day while we were at work, a little girl who sold scones of white bread came towards the convicts. She looked at them for a time and then burst into a laugh. "Oh, how ugly they are!" she cried; "they have not even enough gray cloth or brown cloth to make their clothes." Every convict wore a vest made of gray cloth, except the sleeves, which were brown. Their heads, too, were shaved in different styles. The crown was bared sometimes longitudinally, sometimes latitudinally, from the nape of the neck to the forehead, or from one ear to another.

This strange family had a general likeness so pronounced that it could be recognised at a glance.

Even the most striking personalities, those who dominated involuntarily the other convicts, could not help taking the general tone of the house.

Of the convicts—with the exception of a few who enjoyed childish gaiety, and who by that alone drew upon themselves general contempt—all the convicts were morose, envious, frightfully vain, presumptuous, susceptible, and excessively ceremonious. To be astonished at nothing was in their eyes the first and indispensable quality. Accordingly, their first aim was to bear themselves with dignity. But often the most composed demeanour gave way with the rapidity of lightning. With the basest humility some, however, possessed genuine strength; these were naturally all sincere. But strangely enough, they were for the most part excessively and morbidly vain. Vanity was always their salient quality.

The majority of the prisoners were depraved and perverted, so that calumnies and scandal rained amongst them like hail. Our life was a constant hell, a perpetual damnation; but no one would have dared to raise a voice against the internal regulations of the prison, or against established usages. Accordingly, willingly or unwillingly, they had to be submitted to. Certain indomitable characters yielded with difficulty, but they yielded all the same. Prisoners who when at liberty had gone beyond all measure, who, urged by their over-excited vanity, had committed frightful crimes unconsciously, as if in a delirium, and had been the terror of entire towns, were put down in a very short time by the system of our prison. The "new man," when he began to reconnoitre, soon found that he could astonish no one, and insensibly he submitted, took the general tone, and assumed a sort of personal dignity which almost every convict maintained, just as if the denomination of convict had been a title of honour. Not the least sign of shame or of repentance, but a kind of external submission which seemed to have been reasoned out as the line of conduct to be pursued. "We are lost men," they said to themselves. "We were unable to live in liberty; we must now go to Green Street."

"You would not obey your father and mother; you will now obey thongs of leather." "The man who would not sow must now break stones."

These things were said, and repeated in the way of morality, as sentences and proverbs, but without any one taking them seriously. They were but words in the air. There was not one man among them who admitted his iniquity. Let a stranger not a convict endeavour to reproach him with his crime, and the insults directed against him would be endless. And how refined are convicts in the matter of insults! They insult delicately, like artists; insult with the most delicate science. They endeavour not so much to offend by the expression as by the meaning, the spirit of an envenomed phrase. Their incessant quarrels developed greatly this special art.

As they only worked under the threat of an immense stick, they were idle and depraved. Those who were not already corrupt when they arrived at the convict establishment, became perverted very soon. Brought together in spite of themselves, they were perfect strangers to one another. "The devil has worn out three pairs of sandals before he got us together," they would say. Intrigues, calumnies, scandal of all kinds, envy, and hatred reigned above everything else. In this life of sloth, no ordinary spiteful tongue could make head against these murderers, with insults constantly in their mouths.

As I said before, there were found among them men of open character, resolute, intrepid, accustomed to self-command. These were held involuntarily in esteem. Although they were very jealous of their reputation, they endeavoured to annoy no one, and never insulted one another without a motive. Their conduct was on all points full of dignity. They were rational, and almost always obedient, not by principle, or from any respect for duty, but as if in virtue of a mutual convention between themselves and the administration—a convention of which the advantages were plain enough.

The officials, moreover, behaved prudently towards them. I remember that one prisoner of the resolute and intrepid class, known to possess the instincts of a wild beast, was summoned one day to be whipped. It was during the summer, no work was being done. The Adjutant, the direct and immediate chief of the convict prison, was in the orderly-room, by the side of the principal entrance, ready to assist at the punishment. This Major was a fatal being for the prisoners, whom he had brought to such a state that they trembled before him. Severe to the point of insanity, "he threw himself upon them," to use their expression. But it was above all that his look, as penetrating as that of a lynx, was feared. It was impossible to conceal anything from him. He saw, so to say, without looking. On entering the prison, he knew at once what was being done. Accordingly, the convicts, one and all, called him the man with the eight eyes. His system was bad, for it had the effect of irritating men who were already irascible. But for the Commandant, a well-bred and reasonable man, who moderated the savage onslaughts of the Major, the latter would have caused sad misfortunes by his bad administration. I do not understand how he managed to retire from the service safe and sound. It is true that he left after being called before a court-martial.

The prisoner turned pale when he was called; generally speaking, he lay down courageously, and without uttering a word, to receive the terrible rods, after which he got up and shook himself. He bore the misfortune calmly, philosophically, it is true, though he was never punished carelessly, nor without all sorts of precautions. But this time he considered himself innocent. He turned pale, and as he walked quietly towards the escort of soldiers he managed to conceal in his sleeve a shoemaker's awl. The prisoners were severely forbidden to carry sharp instruments about them. Examinations were frequently, minutely, and unexpectedly made, and all infractions of the rule were severely punished. But as it is difficult to take away from the criminal what he is determined to conceal, and as, moreover, sharp instruments are necessarily used in the prison, they were never destroyed. If the official succeeded in taking them away from the convicts, the latter procured new ones very soon.

On the occasion in question, all the convicts had now thrown themselves against the palisade, with palpitating hearts, to look through the crevices. It was known that this time Petroff would not allow himself to be flogged, that the end of the Major had come. But at the critical moment the latter got into his carriage, and went away, leaving the direction of the punishment to a subaltern. "God has saved him!" said the convicts. As for Petroff, he underwent his punishment quietly. Once the Major had gone, his anger fell. The prisoner is submissive and obedient to a certain point, but there is a limit which must not be crossed. Nothing is more curious than these strange outbursts of disobedience and rage. Often a man who has supported for many years the most cruel punishment, will revolt for a trifle, for nothing at all. He might pass for a madman; that, in fact, is what is said of him.

I have already said that during many years I never remarked the least sign of repentance, not even the slightest uneasiness with regard to the crime committed; and that most of the convicts considered neither honour nor conscience, holding that they had a right to act as they thought fit. Certainly vanity, evil examples, deceitfulness, and false shame were responsible for much. On the other hand, who can claim to have sounded the depths of these hearts, given over to perdition, and to have found them closed to all light? It would seem all the same that during so many years I ought to have been able to notice some indication, even the most fugitive, of some regret, some moral suffering. I positively saw nothing of the kind. With ready-made opinions one cannot judge of crime. Its philosophy is a little more complicated than people think. It is acknowledged that neither convict prisons, nor the hulks, nor any system of hard labour ever cured a criminal. These forms of chastisement only punish him and reassure society against the offences he might commit. Confinement, regulation, and excessive work have no effect but to develop with these men profound hatred, a thirst for forbidden enjoyment, and frightful recalcitrations. On the other hand I am convinced that the celebrated cellular system gives results which are specious and deceitful. It deprives a criminal of his force, of his energy, enervates his soul by weakening and frightening it, and at last exhibits a dried up mummy as a model of repentance and amendment.

The criminal who has revolted against society, hates it, and considers himself in the right; society was wrong, not he. Has he not, moreover, undergone his punishment? Accordingly he is absolved, acquitted in his own eyes. In spite of different opinions, every one will acknowledge that there are crimes which everywhere, always, under no matter what legislation, are beyond discussion crimes, and should be regarded as such as long as man is man. It is only at the convict prison that I have heard related, with a childish, unrestrained laugh, the strangest, most atrocious offences. I shall never forget a certain parricide, formerly a nobleman and a public functionary. He had given great grief to his father—a true prodigal son. The old man endeavoured in vain to restrain him by remonstrance on the fatal slope down which he was sliding. As he was loaded with debts, and his father was suspected of having, besides an estate, a sum of ready money, he killed him in order to enter more quickly into his inheritance. This crime was not discovered until a month afterwards. During all this time the murderer, who meanwhile had informed the police of his father's disappearance, continued his debauches. At last, during his absence, the police discovered the old man's corpse in a drain. The gray head was severed from the trunk, but replaced in its original position. The body was entirely dressed. Beneath, as if by derision, the assassin had placed a cushion.

The young man confessed nothing. He was degraded, deprived of his nobiliary privileges, and condemned to twenty years' hard labour. As long as I knew him I always found him to be careless of his position. He was the most light-minded, inconsiderate man that I ever met, although he was far from being a fool. I never observed in him any great tendency to cruelty. The other convicts despised him, not on account of his crime, of which there was never any question, but because he was without dignity. He sometimes spoke of his father. One day for instance, boasting of the hereditary good health of his family, he said: "My father, for example, until his death was never ill."

Animal insensibility carried to such a point is most remarkable—it is, indeed, phenomenal. There must have been in this case an organic defect in the man, some physical and moral monstrosity unknown hitherto to science, and not simply crime. I naturally did not believe in so atrocious a crime; but people of the same town as himself, who knew all the details of his history, related it to me. The facts were so clear that it would have been madness not to accept them. The prisoners once heard him cry out during his sleep: "Hold him! hold him! Cut his head off, his head, his head!"

Nearly all the convicts dreamed aloud, or were delirious in their sleep. Insults, words of slang, knives, hatchets, seemed constantly present in their dreams. "We are crushed!" they would say; "we are without entrails; that is why we shriek in the night."

Hard labour in our fortress was not an occupation, but an obligation. The prisoners accomplished their task, they worked the number of hours fixed by the law, and then returned to the prison. They hated their liberty. If the convict did not do some work on his own account voluntarily, it would be impossible for him to support his confinement. How could these persons, all strongly constituted, who had lived sumptuously, and desired so to live again, who had been brought together against their will, after society had cast them up—how could they live in a normal and natural manner? Man cannot exist without work, without legal, natural property. Depart from these conditions, and he becomes perverted and changed into a wild beast. Accordingly, every convict, through natural requirements and by the instinct of self-preservation, had a trade—an occupation of some kind.

The long days of summer were taken up almost entirely by our hard labour. The night was so short that we had only just time to sleep. It was not the same in winter. According to the regulations, the prisoners had to be shut up in the barracks at nightfall. What was to be done during these long, sad evenings but work? Consequently each barrack, though locked and bolted, assumed the appearance of a large workshop. The work was not, it is true, strictly forbidden, but it was forbidden to have tools, without which work is evidently impossible. But we laboured in secret, and the administration seemed to shut its eyes. Many prisoners arrived without knowing how to make use of their ten fingers; but they learnt a trade from some of their companions, and became excellent workmen.

We had among us cobblers, bootmakers, tailors, masons, locksmiths, and gilders. A Jew named Esau Boumstein was at the same time a jeweller and a usurer. Every one worked, and thus gained a few pence—for many orders came from the town. Money is a tangible resonant liberty, inestimable for a man entirely deprived of true liberty. If he feels some money in his pocket, he consoles himself a little, even though he cannot spend it—but one can always and everywhere spend money, the more so as forbidden fruit is doubly sweet. One can often buy spirits in the convict prison. Although pipes are severely forbidden, every one smokes. Money and tobacco save the convicts from the scurvy, as work saves them from crime—for without work they would mutually have destroyed one another like spiders shut up in a close bottle. Work and money were all the same forbidden. Often during the night severe examinations were made, during which everything that was not legally authorised was confiscated. However successfully the little hoards had been concealed, they were sometimes discovered. That was one of the reasons why they were not kept very long. They were exchanged as soon as possible for drink, which explains how it happened that spirits penetrated into the convict prison. The delinquent was not only deprived of his hoard, but was also cruelly flogged.

A short time after each examination the convicts procured again the objects which had been confiscated, and everything went on as before. The administration knew it; and although the condition of the convicts was a good deal like that of the inhabitants of Vesuvius, they never murmured at the punishment inflicted for these peccadilloes. Those who had no manual skill did business somehow or other. The modes of buying and selling were original enough. Things changed hands which no one expected a convict would ever have thought of selling or buying, or even of regarding as of any value whatever. The least rag had its value, and might be turned to account. In consequence, however, of the poverty of the convicts, money acquired in their eyes a superior value to that really belonging to it.

Long and painful tasks, sometimes of a very complicated kind, brought back a few kopecks. Several of the prisoners lent by the week, and did good business that way. The prisoner who was ruined and insolvent carried to the usurer the few things belonging to him and pledged them for some halfpence, which were lent to him at a fabulous rate of interest. If he did not redeem them at the fixed time the usurer sold them pitilessly by auction, and without the least delay.

Usury flourished so well in our convict prison that money was lent even on things belonging to the Government: linen, boots, etc.—things that were wanted at every moment. When the lender accepted such pledges the affair took an unexpected turn. The proprietor went, immediately after he had received his money, and told the under officer—chief superintendent of the convict prison—that objects belonging to the State were being concealed, on which everything was taken away from the usurer without even the formality of a report to the superior administration. But never was there any quarrel—and that is very curious indeed—between the usurer and the owner. The first gave up in silence, with a morose air, the things demanded from him, as if he had been waiting for the request. Sometimes, perhaps, he confessed to himself that, in the place of the borrower, he would not have acted differently. Accordingly, if he was insulted after this restitution, it was less from hatred than simply as a matter of conscience.

The convicts robbed one another without shame. Each prisoner had his little box fitted with a padlock, in which he kept the things entrusted to him by the administration. Although these boxes were authorised, that did not prevent them from being broken into. The reader can easily imagine what clever thieves were found among us. A prisoner who was sincerely devoted to me—I say it without boasting—stole my Bible from me, the only book allowed in the convict prison. He told me of it the same day, not from repentance, but because he pitied me when he saw me looking for it everywhere. We had among our companions of the chain several convicts called "innkeepers," who sold spirits, and became comparatively rich by doing so. I shall speak of this further on, for the liquor traffic deserves special study.

A great number of prisoners had been deported for smuggling, which explains how it was that drink was brought secretly into the convict prison, under so severe a surveillance as ours was. In passing it may be remarked that smuggling is an offence apart. Would it be believed that money, the solid profit from the affair, possesses often only secondary importance for the smuggler? It is all the same an authentic fact. He works by vocation. In his style he is a poet. He risks all he possesses, exposes himself to terrible dangers, intrigues, invents, gets out of a scrape, and brings everything to a happy end by a sort of inspiration. This passion is as violent as that of play.

I knew a prisoner of colossal stature who was the mildest, the most peaceable, and most manageable man it was possible to see. We often asked one another how he had been deported. He had such a calm, sociable character, that during the whole time that he passed at the convict prison, he never quarrelled with any one. Born in Western Russia, where he lived on the frontier, he had been sent to hard labour for smuggling. Naturally, then, he could not resist his desire to smuggle spirits into the prison. How many times was he not punished for it, and heaven knows how much he feared the rods. This dangerous trade brought him in but slender profits. It was the speculator who got rich at his expense. Each time he was punished he wept like an old woman, and swore by all that was holy that he would never be caught at such things again. He kept his vow for an entire month, but he ended by yielding once more to his passion. Thanks to these amateurs of smuggling, spirits were always to be had in the convict prison.

Another source of income which, without enriching the prisoners, was constantly and beneficently turned to account, was alms-giving. The upper classes of our Russian society do not know to what an extent merchants, shopkeepers, and our people generally, commiserate the "unfortunate!" Alms were always forthcoming, and consisted generally of little white loaves, sometimes of money, but very rarely. Without alms, the existence of the convicts, and above all that of the accused, who are badly fed, would be too painful. These alms are shared equally between all the prisoners. If the gifts are not sufficient, the little loaves are divided into halves, and sometimes into six pieces, so that each convict may have his share. I remember the first alms, a small piece of money, that I received. A short time after my arrival, one morning, as I was coming back from work with a soldier escort, I met a mother and her daughter, a child of ten, as beautiful as an angel. I had already seen them once before.

The mother was the widow of a poor soldier, who, while still young, had been sentenced by a court-martial, and had died in the infirmary of the convict prison while I was there. They wept hot tears when they came to bid him good-bye. On seeing me the little girl blushed, and murmured a few words into her mother's ear, who stopped, and took from a basket a kopeck which she gave to the little girl. The little girl ran after me.

"Here, poor man," she said, "take this in the name of Christ." I took the money which she slipped into my hand. The little girl returned joyfully to her mother. I preserved that kopeck a considerable time.

FOOTNOTES:

Goriantchikoff became himself a soldier in Siberia, when he had finished his term of imprisonment.

An allusion to the two rows of soldiers, armed with green rods, between which convicts condemned to corporal punishment had and still have to pass. But this punishment now exists only for convicts deprived of all their civil rights. This subject will be returned to further on.

Men condemned to hard labour, and exiles generally, are so called by the Russian peasantry.

CHAPTER III. FIRST IMPRESSIONS

During the first weeks, and naturally the early part of my imprisonment, made a deep impression on my imagination. The following years on the other hand are all mixed up together, and leave but a confused recollection. Certain epochs of this life are even effaced from my memory. I have kept one general impression of it, always the same; painful, monotonous, stifling. What I saw in experience during the first days of my imprisonment seems to me as if it had all taken place yesterday. Such was sure to be the case. I remember perfectly that in the first place this life astonished me by the very fact that it offered nothing particular, nothing extraordinary, or to express myself better, nothing unexpected. It was not until later on, when I had lived some time in the convict prison, that I understood all that was exceptional and unforeseen in such a life. I was astonished at the discovery. I will avow that this astonishment remained with me throughout my term of punishment. I could not decidedly reconcile myself to this existence.

First of all, I experienced an invincible repugnance on arriving; but oddly enough the life seemed to me less painful than I had imagined on the journey.

Indeed, prisoners, though embarrassed by their irons went to and fro in the prison freely enough. They insulted one another, sang, worked, smoked pipes, and drank spirits. There were not many drinkers all the same. There were also regular card parties during the night. The labour did not seem to me very trying; I fancied that it could not be the real "hard labour." I did not understand till long afterwards why this labour was really hard and excessive. It was less by reason of its difficulty, than because it was forced, imposed, obligatory; and it was only done through fear of the stick. The peasant works certainly harder than the convict, for, during the summer, he works night and day. But it is in his own interest that he fatigues himself. His aim is reasonable, so that he suffers less than the convict who performs hard labour from which he derives no profit. It once came into my head that if it were desired to reduce a man to nothing—to punish him atrociously, to crush him in such a manner that the most hardened murderer would tremble before such a punishment, and take fright beforehand—it would be necessary to give to his work a character of complete uselessness, even to absurdity.

Hard labour, as it is now carried on, presents no interest to the convict; but it has its utility. The convict makes bricks, digs the earth, builds; and all his occupations have a meaning and an end. Sometimes, even the prisoner takes an interest in what he is doing. He then wishes to work more skilfully, more advantageously. But let him be constrained to pour water from one vessel into another, or to transport a quantity of earth from one place to another, in order to perform the contrary operation immediately afterwards, then I am persuaded that at the end of a few days the prisoner would strangle himself or commit a thousand crimes, punishable with death, rather than live in such an abject condition and endure such torments. It is evident that such punishment would be rather a torture, an atrocious vengeance, than a correction. It would be absurd, for it would have no natural end.

I did not, however, arrive until the winter—in the month of December—and the labour was then unimportant in our fortress. I had no idea of the summer labour—five times as fatiguing. The prisoners, during the winter season, broke up on the Irtitch some old boats belonging to the Government, found occupation in the workshops, took away the snow blown by hurricanes against the buildings, or burned and pounded alabaster. As the day was very short, the work ceased at an early hour, and every one returned to the convict prison, where there was scarcely anything to do, except the supplementary work which the convicts did for themselves.

Scarcely a third of the convicts worked seriously, the others idled their time and wandered about without aim in the barracks, scheming and insulting one another. Those who had a little money got drunk on spirits, or lost what they had saved at gambling. And all this from idleness, weariness, and want of something to do.

I learned, moreover, to know one suffering which is perhaps the sharpest, the most painful that can be experienced in a house of detention apart from laws and liberty. I mean, "forced cohabitation." Cohabitation is more or less forced everywhere and always; but nowhere is it so horrible as in a prison. There are men there with whom no one would consent to live. I am certain that every convict, unconsciously perhaps, has suffered from this.

The food of the prisoners seemed to me passable; some declared even that it was incomparably better than in any Russian prison. I cannot certify to this, for I was never in prison anywhere else. Many of us, besides, were allowed to procure whatever nourishment we wanted. As fresh meat cost only three kopecks a pound, those who always had money allowed themselves the luxury of eating it. The majority of the prisoners were contented with the regular ration.

When they praised the diet of the convict prison, they were thinking only of the bread, which was distributed at the rate of so much per room, and not individually or by weight. This last condition would have frightened the convicts, for a third of them at least would have constantly suffered from hunger; while, with the system in vogue, every one was satisfied. Our bread was particularly nice, and was even renowned in the town. Its good quality was attributed to the excellent construction of the prison ovens. As for our cabbage-soup, it was cooked and thickened with flour. It had not an appetising appearance. On working days it was clear and thin; but what particularly disgusted me was the way it was served. The prisoners, however, paid no attention to that.

During the three days that followed my arrival, I did not go to work. Some respite was always given to prisoners just arrived, in order to allow them to recover from their fatigue. The second day I had to go out of the convict prison in order to be ironed. My chain was not of the regulation pattern; it was composed of rings, which gave forth a clear sound, so I heard other convicts say. I had to wear them externally over my clothes, whereas my companions had chains formed, not of rings, but of four links, as thick as the finger, and fastened together by three links which were worn beneath the trousers. To the central ring was fastened a strip of leather, tied in its turn to a girdle fastened over the shirt.

I can see again the first morning that I passed in the convict prison. The drum sounded in the orderly room, near the principal entrance. Ten minutes afterwards the under officer opened the barracks. The convicts woke up one after another and rose trembling with cold from their plank bedsteads, by the dull light of a tallow candle. Nearly all of them were morose; they yawned and stretched themselves. Their foreheads, marked by the iron, were contracted. Some made the sign of the Cross; others began to talk nonsense. The cold air from outside rushed in as soon as the door was opened. Then the prisoners hurried round the pails full of water, one after another, and took water in their mouths, and, letting it out into their hands, washed their faces. Those pails had been brought in the night before by a prisoner specially appointed, according to the rules, to clean the barracks.

The convicts chose him themselves. He did not work with the others, for it was his business to examine the camp bedsteads and the floors, to fetch and carry water. This water served in the morning for the prisoners' ablutions, and the rest during the day for ordinary drinking. That very morning there were disputes on the subject of one of the pitchers.

"What are you doing there with your marked forehead?" grumbled one of the prisoners, tall, dry, and sallow.

He attracted attention by the strange protuberances with which his skull was covered. He pushed against another convict round and small, with a lively rubicund countenance.

"Just wait."

"What are you crying out about? You know that a fine must be paid when the others are kept waiting. Off with you. What a monument, my brethren!"

"A little calf," he went on muttering. "See, the white bread of the prison has fattened him."

"For what do you take yourself? A fine bird, indeed."

"You are about right."

"What bird do you mean?"

"You don't require to be told."

"How so?"

"Find out."

They devoured one another with their eyes. The little man, waiting for a reply, with clenched fists, was apparently ready to fight. I thought that an encounter would take place. It was all quite new to me; accordingly I watched the scene with curiosity. Later on I learnt that such quarrels were very innocent, that they served for entertainment. Like an amusing comedy, it scarcely ever ended in blows. This characteristic plainly informed me of the manners of the prisoners.

The tall prisoner remained calm and majestic. He felt that some answer was expected from him, if he was not to be dishonoured, covered with ridicule. It was necessary for him to show that he was a wonderful bird, a personage. Accordingly, he cast a side look on his adversary, endeavouring, with inexpressible contempt, to irritate him by looking at him over his shoulders, up and down, as he would have done with an insect. At last the little fat man was so irritated that he would have thrown himself upon his adversary had not his companions surrounded the combatants to prevent a serious quarrel from taking place.

"Fight with your fists, not with your tongues," cried a spectator from a corner of the room.

"No, hold them," answered another, "they are going to fight. We are fine fellows, one against seven is our style."

Fine fighting men! One was here for having sneaked a pound of bread, the other is a pot-stealer; he was whipped by the executioner for stealing a pot of curdled milk from an old woman.

"Enough, keep quiet," cried a retired soldier, whose business it was to keep order in the barrack, and who slept in a corner of the room on a bedstead of his own.

"Water, my children, water for Nevalid Petrovitch, water for our little brother, who has just woke up."

"Your brother! Am I your brother? Did we ever drink a roublesworth of spirits together?" muttered the old soldier as he passed his arms through the sleeves of his great-coat.

The roll was about to be called, for it was already late. The prisoners were hurrying towards the kitchen. They had to put on their pelisses, and were to receive in their bi-coloured caps the bread which one of the cooks—one of the bakers, that is to say—was distributing among them. These cooks, like those who did the household work, were chosen by the prisoners themselves. There were two for the kitchen, making four in all for the convict prison. They had at their disposal the only kitchen-knife authorised in the prison, which was used for cutting up the bread and meat. The prisoners arranged themselves in groups around the tables as best they could in caps and pelisses, with leather girdles round their waists, all ready to begin work. Some of the convicts had kvas before them, in which they steeped pieces of bread. The noise was insupportable. Many of the convicts, however, were talking together in corners with a steady, tranquil air.

"Good-morning and good appetite, Father Antonitch," said a young prisoner, sitting down by the side of an old man, who had lost his teeth.

"If you are not joking, well, good-morning," said the latter, without raising his eyes, and endeavouring to masticate a piece of bread with his toothless gums.

"I declare I fancied you were dead, Antonitch."

"Die first, I will follow you."

I sat down beside them. On my right two convicts were conversing with an attempt at dignity.

"I am not likely to be robbed," said one of them. "I am more afraid of stealing myself."

"It would not be a good idea to rob me. The devil! I should pay the man out."

"But what would you do, you are only a convict? We have no other name. You will see that she will rob you, the wretch, without even saying, 'Thank you.' The money I gave her was wasted. Just fancy, she was here a few days ago! Where were we to go? Shall I ask permission to go into the house of Theodore, the executioner? He has still his house in the suburb, the one he bought from that Solomon, you know, that scurvy Jew who hung himself not long since."

"Yes, I know him, the one who sold liquor here three years ago, and who was called Grichka—the secret-drinking shop."

"I know."

"*All* brag. You don't know. In the first place it is another drinking shop."

"What do you mean, another? You don't know what you are talking about. I will bring you as many witnesses as you like."

"Oh, you will bring them, will you? Who are you? Do you know to whom you are speaking?"

"Yes, indeed."

"I have often thrashed you, though I don't boast of it. Do not give yourself airs then."

"You have thrashed me? The man who will thrash me is not yet born; and the man who did thrash me is six feet beneath the ground."

"Plague-stricken rascal of Bender?"

"May the Siberian leprosy devour you with ulcers!"

"May a chopper cleave your dog of a head."

Insults were falling about like rain.

"Come, now, they are going to fight. When men have not been able to conduct themselves properly they should keep silent. They are too glad to come and eat the Government bread, the rascals!"

They were soon separated. Let them fight with the tongue as much as they wish. That is permitted. It is a diversion at the service of every one; but no blows. It is, indeed, only in extraordinary cases that blows were exchanged. If a fight took place, information was given to the Major, who ordered an inquiry or directed one himself; and then woe to the convicts. Accordingly they set their faces against anything like a serious quarrel; besides, they insulted one another chiefly to pass the time, as an oratorical exercise. They get excited; the quarrel takes a furious, ferocious character; they seem about to slaughter one another. Nothing of the kind takes place. As soon as their anger has reached a certain pitch they separate.

That astonished me much, and if I relate some of the conversations between the convicts, I do so with a purpose. Could I have imagined that people could have insulted one another for pleasure, that they could find enjoyment in it?

We must not forget the gratification of vanity. A dialectician, who knows how to insult artistically, is respected. A little more, and he would be applauded like an actor.

Already, the night before, I noticed some glances in my direction. On the other hand, several convicts hung around me as if they had suspected that I had brought money with me. They endeavoured to get into my good graces by teaching me how to carry my irons without being incommoded. They also gave me—of course in return for money—a box with a lock, in order to keep safe the things which had been entrusted to me by the administration, and the few shirts that I had been allowed to bring with me to the convict prison. Not later than next morning these same prisoners stole my box, and drank the money which they had taken out of it.

One of them became afterwards a great friend of mine, though he robbed me whenever an opportunity offered itself. He was, all the same, vexed at what he had done. He committed these thefts almost unconsciously, as if in the way of a duty. Consequently I bore him no grudge.

These convicts let me know that one could have tea, and that I should do well to get myself a teapot. They found me one, which I hired for a certain time. They also recommended me a cook, who, for thirty kopecks a month, would arrange the dishes I might desire, if it was my intention to buy provisions and take my meals apart. Of course they borrowed money from me. The day of my arrival they asked me for some at three different times.

The noblemen degraded from their position, here incarcerated in the convict prison, were badly looked upon by their fellow prisoners; although they had lost all their rights like the other convicts, they were not looked upon as comrades.

In this instinctive repugnance there was a sort of reason. To them we were always gentlemen, although they often laughed at our fall.

"Ah! it's all over now. Mossieu's carriage formerly crushed the passers-by at Moscow. Now Mossieu picks hemp!"

They knew our sufferings, though we hid them as much as possible. It was, above all, when we were all working together that we had most to endure, for our strength was not so great as theirs, and we were really not of much assistance to them. Nothing is more difficult than to gain the confidence of the common people; above all, such people as these!

There were only a few of us who were of noble birth in the whole prison. First, there were five Poles—of whom further on I shall speak in detail—they were detested by the convicts more, perhaps, than the Russian nobles. The Poles—I speak only of the political convicts—always behaved to them with a constrained and offensive politeness, scarcely ever speaking to them, and making no endeavour to conceal the disgust which they experienced in such company. The convicts understood all this, and paid them back in their own coin.

Two years passed before I could gain the good-will of my companions; but the greater part of them were attached to me, and declared that I was a good fellow.

There were altogether—counting myself—five Russian nobles in the convict prison. I had heard of one of them even before my arrival as a vile and base creature, horribly corrupt, doing the work of spy and informer. Accordingly, from the very first day I refused to enter into relations with this man. The second was the parricide of whom I have spoken in these memoirs. The third was Akimitch. I have scarcely ever seen such an original; and I have still a lively recollection of him.

Tall, thin, weak-minded, and terribly ignorant, he was as argumentative and as particular about details as a German. The convicts laughed at him; but they feared him, on account of his susceptible, excitable, and quarrelsome disposition. As soon as he arrived, he was on a footing of perfect equality with them. He insulted them and beat them. Phenomenally just, it was sufficient for him that there was injustice, to interfere in an affair which did not concern him. He was, moreover, exceedingly simple. When he quarrelled with the convicts, he reproached them with being thieves, and exhorted them in all sincerity to steal no more. He had served as a sub-lieutenant in the Caucasus. I made friends with him the first day, and he related to me his "affair." He had begun as a cadet in a Line regiment. After waiting some time to be appointed to his commission as sub-lieutenant, he at last received it, and was sent into the mountains to command a small fort. A small tributary prince in the neighbourhood set fire to the fort, and made a night attack, which had no success.

Akimitch was very cunning, and pretended not to know that he was the author of the attack, which he attributed to some insurgents wandering about the mountains. After a month he invited the prince, in a friendly way, to come and see him. The prince arrived on horseback, without suspecting anything. Akimitch drew up his garrison in line of battle, and exposed to the soldiers the treason and villainy of his visitor. He reproached him with his conduct; proved to him that to set fire to the fort was a shameful crime; explained to him minutely the duties of a tributary prince; and then, by way of peroration to his harangue, had him shot. He at once informed his superior officers of this execution, with all the details necessary. Thereupon Akimitch was brought to trial. He appeared before a court-martial, and was condemned to death; but his sentence was commuted, and he was sent to Siberia as a convict of the second class—condemned, that is to say, to twelve years' hard labour and imprisonment in a fortress. He admitted willingly that he had acted illegally, and that the prince ought to have been tried in a civil court, and not by a court-martial. Nevertheless, he could not understand that his action was a crime.

"He had burned my fort; what was I to do? Was I to thank him for it?" he answered to my objections.

Although the convicts laughed at Akimitch, and pretended that he was a little mad, they esteemed him all the same by reason of his cleverness and his precision.

He knew all possible trades, and could do whatever you wished. He was cobbler, bootmaker, painter, carver, gilder, and locksmith. He had acquired these talents at the convict prison, for it was sufficient for him to see an object, in order to imitate it. He sold in the town, or caused to be sold, baskets, lanterns, and toys. Thanks to his work, he had always some money, which he employed in buying shirts, pillows, and so on. He had himself made a mattress, and as he slept in the same room as myself he was very useful to me at the beginning of my imprisonment. Before leaving prison to go to work, the convicts were drawn up in two ranks before the orderly-room, surrounded by an escort of soldiers with loaded muskets. An officer of Engineers then arrived, with the superintendent of the works and a few soldiers, who watched the operations. The superintendent counted the convicts, and sent them in bands to the places where they were to be occupied.

I went with some other prisoners to the workshop of the Engineers—a low brick house built in the midst of a large court-yard full of materials. There was a forge there, and carpenters', locksmiths', and painters' workshops. Akimitch was assigned to the last. He boiled the oil for the varnish, mixed the colours, and painted tables and other pieces of furniture in imitation walnut.

While I was waiting to have additional irons put on, I communicated to him my first impressions.

"Yes," he said, "they do not like nobles, above all those who have been condemned for political offences, and they take a pleasure in wounding their feelings. Is it not intelligible? We do not belong to them, we do not suit them. They have all been serfs or soldiers. Tell me what sympathy can they have for us. The life here is hard, but it is nothing in comparison with that of the disciplinary companies in Russia. There it is hell. The men who have been in them praise our convict prison. It is paradise compared to their purgatory. Not that the work is harder. It is said that with the convicts of the first class the administration—it is not exclusively military as it is here—acts quite differently from what it does towards us. They have their little houses there I have been told, for I have not seen for myself. They wear no uniform, their heads are not shaved, though, in my opinion, uniforms and shaved heads are not bad things; it is neater, and also it is more agreeable to the eye, only these men do not like it. Oh, what a Babel this place is! Soldiers, Circassians, old believers, peasants who have left their wives and families, Jews, Gypsies, people come from Heaven knows where, and all this variety of men are to live quietly together side by side, eat from the same dish, and sleep on the same planks. Not a moment's liberty, no enjoyment except in secret; they must hide their money in their boots; and then always the convict prison at every moment—perpetually convict prison! Involuntarily wild ideas come to one."

As I already knew all this, I was above all anxious to question Akimitch in regard to our Major. He concealed nothing, and the impression which his story left upon me was far from being an agreeable one.

I had to live for two years under the authority of this officer. All that Akimitch had told me about him was strictly true. He was a spiteful, ill-regulated man, terrible above all things, because he possessed almost absolute power over two hundred human beings. He looked upon the prisoners as his personal enemies—first, and very serious fault. His rare capacities, and, perhaps, even his good qualities, were perverted by his intemperance and his spitefulness. He sometimes fell like a bombshell into the barracks in the middle of the night. If he noticed a prisoner asleep on his back or his left side, he awoke him and said to him: "You must sleep as I ordered!" The convicts detested him and feared him like the plague. His repulsive, crimson countenance made every one tremble. We all knew that the Major was entirely in the hands of his servant Fedka, and that he had nearly gone mad when his dog "Treasure" fell ill. He preferred this dog to every other living creature.

When Fedka told him that a convict, who had picked up some veterinary knowledge, made wonderful cures, he sent for him directly and said to him, "I entrust my dog to your care. If you cure 'Treasure' I will reward you royally." The man, a very intelligent Siberian peasant, was indeed a good veterinary surgeon, but he was above all a cunning peasant. He used to tell his comrades long after the affair had taken place the story of his visit to the Major.

"I looked at 'Treasure,' he was lying down on a sofa with his head on a white cushion. I saw at once that he had inflammation, and that he wanted bleeding. I think I could have cured him, but I said to myself, 'What will happen if the dog dies? It will be my fault.' 'No, your noble highness,' I said to him, 'you have called me too late. If I had seen your dog yesterday or the day before, he would now be restored to health; but at the present moment I can do nothing. He will die.' And 'Treasure' died."

I was told one day that a convict had tried to kill the Major. This prisoner had for several years been noticed for his submissive attitude and also his silence. He was regarded even as a madman. As he possessed some instruction he passed his nights reading the Bible. When everybody was asleep he rose, climbed up on to the stove, lit a church taper, opened his Gospel and began to read. He did this for an entire year.

One fine day he left the ranks and declared that he would not go to work. He was reported to the Major, who flew into a rage, and hurried to the barracks. The convict rushed forward and hurled at him a brick, which he had procured beforehand; but it missed him. The prisoner was seized, tried, and whipped—it was a matter of a few moments—carried to the hospital, and died there three days afterwards. He declared during his last moments that he hated no one; but that he had wished to suffer. He belonged to no sect of fanatics. Afterwards, when people spoke of him in the barracks, it was always with respect.

At last they put new irons on me. While they were being soldered a number of young women, selling little white loaves, came into the forge one after another. They were, for the most part, quite little girls who came to sell the loaves that their mothers had baked. As they got older they still continued to hang about us, but they no longer brought bread. There were always some of them about. There were also married women. Each roll cost two kopecks. Nearly all the prisoners used to have them. I noticed a prisoner who worked as a carpenter. He was already getting gray, but he had a ruddy, smiling complexion. He was joking with the vendors of rolls. Before they arrived he had tied a red handkerchief round his neck. A fat woman, much marked with the small-pox, put down her basket on the carpenter's table. They began to talk.

"Why did you not come yesterday?" said the convict, with a self-satisfied smile.

"I did come; but you had gone," replied the woman boldly.

"Yes; they made us go away, otherwise we should have met. The day before yesterday they all came to see me."

"Who came?"

"Why, Mariashka, Khavroshka, Tchekunda, Dougrochva" (the woman of four kopecks).

"What," I said to Akimitch, "is it possible that——?"

"Yes; it happens sometimes," he replied, lowering his eyes, for he was a very proper man.

Yes; it happened sometimes, but rarely, and with unheard of difficulties. The convicts preferred to spend their money in drink. It was very difficult to meet these women. It was necessary to come to an agreement about the place, and the time; to arrange a meeting, to find solitude, and, what was most difficult of all, to avoid the escorts—almost an impossibility—and to spend relatively prodigious sums. I have sometimes, however, witnessed love scenes. One day three of us were heating a brick-kiln on the banks of the Irtitch. The soldiers of the escort were good-natured fellows. Two "blowers" (they were so-called) soon appeared.

"Where were you staying so long?" said a prisoner to them, who had evidently been expecting them. "Was it at the Zvierkoffs that you were detained?"

"At the Zvierkoffs? It will be fine weather, and the fowls will have teeth, when I go to see them," replied one of the women.

She was the dirtiest woman imaginable. She was called Tchekunda, and had arrived in company with her friend, the "four kopecks," who was beneath all description.

"It's a long time since we have seen anything of you," says the gallant to her of the four kopecks; "you seem to have grown thinner."

"Perhaps; formerly I was good-looking and plump, whereas now one might fancy I had swallowed eels."

"And you still run after the soldiers, is that so?"

"All calumny on the part of wicked people; and after all, if I was to be flogged to death for it, I like soldiers."

"Never mind your soldiers, we're the people to love; we have money."

Imagine this gallant with his shaved crown, with fetters on his ankles, dressed in a coat of two colours, and watched by an escort.

As I was now returning to the prison, my irons had been put on. I wished Akimitch good-bye and went away, escorted by a soldier. Those who do task work return first, and, when I got back to the barracks, a good number of convicts were already there.

As the kitchen could not have held the whole barrack-full at once, we did not all dine together. Those who came in first were first served. I tasted the cabbage soup, but, not being used to it, could not eat it, and I prepared myself some tea. I sat down at one end of the table, with a convict of noble birth like myself. The prisoners were going in and out. There was no want of room, for there were not many of them. Five of them sat down apart from the large table. The cook gave them each two ladles full of soup, and brought them a plate of fried fish. These men were having a holiday. They looked at us in a friendly manner. One of the Poles came in and took his seat by our side.

"I was not with you, but I know that you are having a feast," exclaimed a tall convict who now came in.

He was a man of about fifty years, thin and muscular. His face indicated cunning, and, at the same time, liveliness. His lower lip, fleshy and pendant, gave him a soft expression.

"Well, have you slept well? Why don't you say how do you do? Well, now my friends of Kursk," he said, sitting down by the side of the feasters, "good appetite? Here's a new guest for you."

"We are not from the province of Kursk."

"Then my friends from Tambof, let me say?"

"We are not from Tambof either. You have nothing to claim from us; if you want to enjoy yourself go to some rich peasant."

"I have Maria Ikotishna in my belly, otherwise I should die of hunger. But where is your peasant to be found?"

"Good heavens! we mean Gazin; go to him."

"Gazin is on the drink to-day, he's devouring his capital."

"He has at least twenty roubles," says another convict. "It is profitable to keep a drinking shop."

"You won't have me? Then I must eat the Government food."

"Will you have some tea? If so, ask these noblemen for some."

"Where do you see any noblemen? They're noblemen no longer. They're not a bit better than us," said in a sombre voice a convict who was seated in the corner, who hitherto had not risked a word.

"I should like a cup of tea, but I am ashamed to ask for it. I have self-respect," said the convict with the heavy lip, looking at me with a good-humoured air.

14

"I will give you some if you like," I said. "Will you have some?"

"What do you mean—will I have some? Who would not have some?" he said, coming towards the table.

"Only think! When he was free he ate nothing but cabbage soup and black bread, but now he is in prison he must have tea like a perfect gentleman," continued the convict with the sombre air.

"Does no one here drink tea?" I asked him; but he did not think me worthy of a reply.

"White rolls, white rolls; who'll buy?"

A young prisoner was carrying in a net a load of calachi (scones), which he proposed to sell in the prison. For every ten that he sold, the baker gave him one for his trouble. It was precisely on this tenth scone that he counted for his dinner.

"White rolls, white rolls," he cried, as he entered the kitchen, "white Moscow rolls, all hot. I would eat the whole of them, but I want money, lots of money. Come, lads, there is only one left for any of you who has had a mother."

This appeal to filial love made every one laugh, and several of his white rolls were purchased.

"Well," he said, "Gazin has drunk in such a style, it is quite a sin. He has chosen a nice moment too. If the man with the eight eyes should arrive—we shall hide him."

"Is he very drunk?"

"Yes, and ill-tempered too—unmanageable."

"There will be some fighting, then?"

"Whom are they speaking of?" I said to the Pole, my neighbour.

"Of Gazin. He is a prisoner who sells spirits. When he has gained a little money by his trade, he drinks it to the last kopeck; a cruel, malicious animal when he has been drinking. When sober, he is quiet enough, but when he is in drink he shows himself in his true character. He attacks people with the knife until it is taken from him."

"How do they manage that?"

"Ten men throw themselves upon him and beat him like a sack without mercy until he loses consciousness. When he is half dead with the beating, they lay him down on his plank bedstead, and cover him over with his pelisse."

"But they might kill him."

"Any one else would die of it, but not he. He is excessively robust; he is the strongest of all the convicts. His constitution is so solid, that the day after one of these punishments he gets up perfectly sound."

"Tell me, please," I continued, speaking to the Pole, "why these people keep their food to themselves, and at the same time seem to envy me my tea."

"Your tea has nothing to do with it. They are envious of you. Are you not a gentleman? You in no way resemble them. They would be glad to pick a quarrel with you in order to humiliate you. You don't know what annoyances you will have to undergo. It is martyrdom for men like us to be here. Our life is doubly painful, and great strength of character can alone accustom one to it. You will be vexed and tormented in all sorts of ways on account of your food and your tea. Although the number of men who buy their own food and drink tea daily is large enough, they have a right to do so, you have not."

He got up and left the table a few minutes later. His predictions were already being fulfilled.

CHAPTER IV. FIRST IMPRESSIONS (*continued*).

Hardly had M. —cki—the Pole to whom I had been speaking—gone out when Gazin, completely drunk, threw himself all in a heap into the kitchen.

To see a convict drunk in the middle of the day, when every one was about to be sent out to work—given the well-known severity of the Major, who at any moment might come to the barracks, the watchfulness of the under officer who never left the prison, the presence of the old soldiers and the sentinels—all this quite upset the ideas I had formed of our prison; and a long time passed before I was able to understand and explain to myself the effects, which in the first instance were enigmatic indeed.

I have already said that all the convicts had a private occupation, and that this occupation was for them a natural and imperious one. They are passionately fond of money, and think more of it than of anything else—almost as much as of liberty. The convict is half-consoled if he can ring a few kopecks in his pocket. On the contrary, he is sad, restless, and despondent if he has no money. He is ready then to commit no matter what crime in order to get some. Nevertheless, in spite of the importance it possesses for the convicts, money does not remain long in their pockets. It is difficult to keep it. Sometimes it is confiscated, sometimes stolen. When the Major, in a sudden perquisition, discovered a small sum amassed with great trouble, he confiscated it. It may be that he laid it out in improving the food of the prisoners, for all the money taken from them went into his hands. But generally speaking it was stolen. A means of preserving it was, however, discovered. An old man from Starodoub, one of the "old believers," took upon himself to conceal the convicts' savings.

I cannot resist my desire to say some words about this man, although it takes me away from my story. He was about sixty years old, thin, and getting very gray. He excited my curiosity the first time I saw him, for he was not like any of the others; his look was so tranquil and mild, and I always saw with pleasure his clear and limpid eyes, surrounded by a number of little wrinkles. I often talked with him, and rarely have I met with so kind, so benevolent a being. He had been consigned to hard labour for a serious crime. A certain number of the "old believers" at Starodoub had been converted to the orthodox religion. The Government had done everything to encourage them, and, at the same time, to convert the other dissenters. The old man and some other fanatics had resolved to "defend the faith." When the orthodox church was being constructed in their town they set fire to the building. This offence had brought upon its author the sentence of deportation. This well-to-do shopkeeper—he was in trade—had left a wife and family whom he loved, and had gone off courageously into exile, believing in his blindness that he was "suffering for the faith."

When one had lived some time by the side of this kind old man, one could not help asking the question, how could he have rebelled? I spoke to him several times about his faith. He gave up none of his convictions, but in his answers I never noticed the slightest hatred; and yet he had destroyed a church, and was far from denying it. In his view, the offence he had committed and his martyrdom were things to be proud of.

There were other "old believers" among the convicts—Siberians for the most part—men of well-developed intelligence, and as cunning as all peasants. Dialecticians in their way, they followed blindly their law, and delighted in discussing it. But they had great faults; they were haughty, proud, and very intolerant. The old man in no way resembled them. With full more belief in religious exposition than others of the same faith, he avoided all controversy. As he was of a gay and expansive disposition he often laughed—not with the coarse cynical laugh of the other convicts, but with a laugh of clearness and simplicity, in which there was something of the child, and which harmonised perfectly with his gray head. I may perhaps be in error, but it seems to me that a man may be known by his laugh alone. If the laugh of a man you are acquainted with inspires you with sympathy, be assured that he is an honest man.

The old man had acquired the respect of all the prisoners without exception; but he was not proud of it. The convicts called him grandfather, and he took no offence. I then understood what an influence he must have exercised on his co-religionists.

In spite of the firmness with which he supported his prison life, one felt that he was tormented by a profound, incurable melancholy. I slept in the same barrack with him. One night, towards three o'clock in the morning, I woke up; I heard a slow, stifling sob. The old man was sitting upon the stove—the same place where the convict who had wished to kill the Major was in the habit of praying—and was reading from his manuscript prayer-book. As he wept I heard him repeating: "Lord, do not forsake me. Master, strengthen me. My poor little children, my dear little children, we shall never see one another again." I cannot say how much this moved me.

We used to give our money then to this old man. Heaven knows how the idea got abroad in our barrack that he could not be robbed. It was well known that he hid somewhere the savings deposited with him, but no one had been able to discover his secret. He revealed it to us; to the Poles, and myself. One of the stakes of the palisade bore a branch which apparently belonged to it, but it could be taken away, and then replaced in the stake. When the branch was removed a hole could be seen. This was the hiding-place in question.

I now resume the thread of my narrative. Why does not the convict save up his money? Not only is it difficult for him to keep it, but the prison life, moreover, is so sad that the convict by his very nature thirsts for freedom of action. By his position in society he is so irregular a being that the idea of swallowing up his capital in orgies, of intoxicating himself with revelry, seems to him quite natural if only he can procure himself one moment's forgetfulness. It was strange to see certain individuals bent over their labour only with the object of spending in one day all their gains, even to the last kopeck. Then they would go to work again until a new debauch, looked forward to months beforehand. Certain convicts were fond of new clothes, more or less singular in style, such as fancy trousers and waistcoats; but it was above all for the coloured shirts that the convicts had a pronounced taste; also for belts with metal clasps.

On holidays the dandies of the prison put on their Sunday best. They were worth seeing as they strutted about their part of the barracks. The pleasure of feeling themselves well dressed amounted with them to childishness; indeed, in many things convicts are only children. Their fine clothes disappeared very soon, often the evening of the very day on which they had been bought. Their owners pledged them or sold them again for a trifle.

The feasts were generally held at fixed times. They coincided with religious festivals, or with the name's day of the drunken convict. On getting up in the morning he would place a wax taper before the holy image, then he said his prayer, dressed, and ordered his dinner. He had bought beforehand meat, fish, and little patties; then he gorged like an ox, almost always alone. It was very rare to see a convict invite another convict to share his repast. At dinner the vodka was produced. The convict would suck it up like the sole of a boot, and then walk through the barracks swaggering and tottering. It was his desire to show all his companions that he was drunk, that he was carrying on, and thus obtain their particular esteem.

The Russian people feel always a certain sympathy for a drunken man; among us it amounted really to esteem. In the convict prison intoxication was a sort of aristocratic distinction.

As soon as he felt himself in spirits the convict ordered a musician. We had among us a little fellow—a deserter from the army—very ugly, but who was the happy possessor of a violin on which he could play. As he had no trade he was always ready to follow the festive convict from barrack to barrack grinding him out dance tunes with all his strength. His countenance often expressed the fatigue and disgust which his music—always the same—caused him; but when the prisoner called out to him, "Go on playing, are you not paid for it?" he attacked his violin more violently than ever. These drunkards felt sure that they would be taken care of, and in case of the Major arriving would be concealed from his watchful eyes. This service we rendered in the most disinterested spirit. On their side the under officer, and the old soldiers who remained in the prison to keep order, were perfectly reassured. The drunkard would cause no disturbance. At the least scare of revolt or riot he would have been quieted and then bound. Accordingly the inferior officers closed their eyes; they knew that if vodka was forbidden all would go wrong. How was this vodka procured?

It was bought in the convict prison itself from the drink-sellers, as they were called, who followed this trade—a very lucrative one— although the tipplers were not very numerous, for revelry was expensive, especially when it is considered how hardly money was earned. The drink business was begun, continued, and ended in rather an original manner. The prisoner who knew no trade, would not work, and who, nevertheless, desired to get speedily rich, made up his mind, when he possessed a little money, to buy and sell vodka. The enterprise was risky, it required great daring, for the speculator hazarded his skin as well as liquor. But the drink-seller hesitated before no obstacles. At the outset he brought the vodka himself to the prison and got rid of it on the most advantageous terms. He repeated this operation a second and a third time. If he had not been discovered by the officials, he now possessed a sum which enabled him to extend his business.

He became a capitalist with agents and assistants, he risked much less and gained much more. Then his assistants incurred risk in place of him.

Prisons are always abundantly inhabited by ruined men without the habit of work, but endowed with skill and daring; their only capital is their back. They often decide to put it into circulation, and propose to the drink-seller to introduce vodka into the barracks. There is always in the town a soldier, a shopkeeper, or some loose woman who, for a stipulated sum—rather a small one—buys vodka with the drink-seller's money, hides it in a place known to the convict-smuggler, near the workshop where he is employed. The person who supplies the vodka, tastes the precious liquid almost always as he is carrying it to the hiding-place, and replaces relentlessly what he has drunk by pure water. The purchaser may take it or leave it, but he cannot give himself airs. He thinks himself very lucky that his money has not been stolen from him, and that he has received some kind of vodka in exchange. The man who is to take it into the prison—to whom the drink-seller has indicated the hiding-place—goes to the supplier with bullock's intestines which after being washed, have been filled with water, and which thus preserves their softness and suppleness. When the intestines have been filled with vodka, the smuggler rolls them round his body. Now, all the cunning, the adroitness of this daring convict is shown. The man's honour is at stake. It is necessary for him to take in the escort and the man on guard; and he will take them in. If the carrier is artful, the soldier of the escort—sometimes a recruit—does not notice anything particular; for the prisoner has studied him thoroughly, besides which he has artfully combined the hour and the place of meeting. If the convict—a bricklayer for example—climbs up on the wall that he is building, the escort will certainly not climb up after him to watch his movements. Who then, will see what he is about? On getting near the prison, he gets ready a piece of fifteen or twenty kopecks, and waits at the gate for the corporal on guard.

The corporal examines, feels, and searches each convict on his return to the barracks, and then opens the gate to him. The carrier of the vodka hopes that he will be ashamed to examine him too much in detail; but if the corporal is a cunning fellow, that is just what he will do; and in that case he finds the contraband vodka. The convict has now only one chance of salvation. He slips into the hand of the under officer the piece of money he holds in readiness, and often, thanks to this manœuvre, the vodka arrives safely in the hands of the drink-seller. But sometimes the trick does not succeed, and it is then that the sole capital of the smuggler enters really into circulation. A report is made to the Major, who sentences the unhappy culprit to a thorough flogging. As for the vodka, it is confiscated. The smuggler undergoes his punishment without betraying the speculator, not because such a denunciation would disgrace him, but because it would bring him nothing. He would be flogged all the same, the only consolation he could have would be that the drink-seller would share his punishment; but as he needs him, he does not denounce him, although having allowed himself to be surprised, he will receive no payment from him.

Denunciation, however, flourishes in the convict prison. Far from hating spies or keeping apart from them, the prisoners often make friends of them. If any one had taken it into his head to prove to the convicts all the baseness of mutual denunciation, no one in the prison would have understood. The former nobleman of whom I have already spoken, that cowardly and violent creature with whom I had already broken off all relations immediately after my arrival in the fortress, was the friend of Fedka, the Major's body-servant. He used to tell him everything that took place in the convict prison, and this was naturally carried back to the servant's master. Every one knew it, but no one had the idea of showing any ill-will against the man, or of reproaching him with his conduct. When the vodka arrived without accident at the prison, the speculator paid the smuggler and made up his accounts. His merchandise had already cost him sufficiently dear; and that the profit might be greater, he diluted it by adding fifty per cent. of pure water. He was ready, and had only to wait for customers.

The first holiday, perhaps even on a week-day, a convict would turn up. He had been working like a negro for many months in order to save up, kopeck by kopeck, a small sum which he was resolved to spend all at once. These days of rejoicing had been looked forward to long beforehand. He had dreamt of them during the endless winter nights, during his hardest labour, and the perspective had supported him under his severest trials. The dawn of this day so impatiently awaited, has just appeared. He has some money in his pocket. It has been neither stolen from him nor confiscated. He is free to spend it. Accordingly he takes his savings to the drink-seller, who, to begin with, gives vodka which is almost pure—it has been only twice baptized—but gradually, as the bottle gets more and more empty, he fills it up with water. Accordingly the convict pays for his vodka five or six times as much as he would in a tavern.

It may be imagined how many glasses, and, above all, what sums of money are required before the convict is drunk. However, as he has lost the habit of drinking, the little alcohol which remains in the liquid intoxicates him rapidly enough; he goes on drinking until there is nothing left; he pledges or sells all his new clothes—for the drink-seller is at the same time a pawnbroker. As his personal garments are not very numerous he next pledges the clothes supplied to him by the Government. When the drink has made away with his last shirt, his last rag, he lies down and wakes up the next morning with a bad headache. In vain he begs the drink-seller to give him credit for a drop of vodka in order to remove his depression; he experiences a direct refusal. That very day he sets to work again. For several months together, he will weary himself out while looking forward to such a debauch as the one which has now disappeared in the past. Little by little he regains courage while waiting for such another day, still far off, but which ultimately will arrive. As for the drink-seller, if he has gained a large sum—some dozen of roubles—he procures some more vodka, but this time he does not baptize it, because he intends it for himself. Enough of trade! it is time for him to amuse himself. Accordingly he eats, drinks, pays for a little music—his means allow him to grease the palm of the inferior officers in the convict prison. This festival lasts sometimes for several days. When his stock of vodka is exhausted, he goes and drinks with the other drink-sellers who are waiting for him; he then drinks up his last kopeck.

However careful the convicts may be in watching over their companions in debauchery, it sometimes happens that the Major or the officer on guard notices what is going on. The drunkard is then dragged to the orderly-room, his money is confiscated if he has any left, and he is flogged. The convict shakes himself like a beaten dog, returns to barracks, and, after a few days, resumes his trade as drink-seller.

It sometimes happens that among the convicts there are admirers of the fair sex. For a sufficiently large sum of money they succeed, accompanied by a soldier whom they have corrupted, in getting secretly out of the fortress into a suburb instead of going to work. There in an apparently quiet house a banquet is held at which large sums of money are spent. The convicts' money is not to be despised, accordingly the soldiers will sometimes arrange these temporary escapes beforehand, sure as they are of being generously recompensed. Generally speaking these soldiers are themselves candidates for the convict prison. The escapades are scarcely ever discovered. I must add that they are very rare, for they are very expensive, and the admirers of the fair sex are obliged to have recourse to other less costly means.

At the beginning of my stay, a young convict with very regular features excited my curiosity; his name was Sirotkin, he was in many respects an enigmatic being. His face had struck me, he was not more than twenty-three years of age, and he belonged to the special section; that is to say, he was condemned to hard labour in perpetuity. He accordingly was to be looked upon as one of the most dangerous of military criminals. Mild and tranquil, he spoke little and rarely laughed; his blue eyes, his clear complexion, his fair hair gave him a soft expression, which even his shaven crown did not destroy. Although he had no trade, he managed to get himself money from time to time. He was remarkably lazy, and always dressed like a sloven; but if any one was generous enough to present him with a red shirt, he was beside himself with joy at having a new garment, and he exhibited it everywhere. Sirotkin neither drank nor played, and he scarcely ever quarrelled with the other convicts. He walked about with his hands in his pockets peacefully, and with a pensive air. What he was thinking of I cannot say. When any one called to him, to ask him a question, he replied with deference, precisely, without chattering like the others. He had in his eyes the expression of a child of ten; when he had money he bought nothing of what the others looked upon as indispensable. His vest might be torn, he did not get it mended, any more than he bought himself new boots. What particularly pleased him were the little white rolls and gingerbread, which he would eat with the satisfaction of a child of seven. When he was not at work he wandered about the barracks; when every one else was occupied, he remained with his arms by his sides; if any one joked with him, or laughed at him—which happened often enough—he turned on his heel without speaking and went elsewhere. If the pleasantry was too strong he blushed. I often asked myself for what crime he could have been condemned to hard labour. One day when I was ill, and lying in the hospital, Sirotkin was also there, stretched out on a bedstead not far from me. I entered into conversation with him; he became animated, and told me freely how he had been taken for a soldier, how his mother had followed him in tears, and what treatment he had endured in military service. He added that he had never been able to accustom himself to this life; every one was severe and angry with him about nothing, his officers were always against him.

"But why did they send you here?—and into the special section above all! Ah, Sirotkin!"

"Yes, Alexander Petrovitch, although I was only one year with the battalion, I was sent here for killing my captain, Gregory Petrovitch."

"I heard about that, but I did not believe it; how was it that you killed him?"

"All that was told you was true; my life was insupportable."

"But the other recruits supported it well enough. It is very hard at the beginning, but men get accustomed to it and end by becoming excellent soldiers. Your mother must have pampered you and spoiled you. I am sure that she fed you with gingerbread and with sweet milk until you were eighteen."

"My mother, it is true, was very fond of me. When I left her she took to her bed and remained there. How painful to me everything in my military life was; after that all went wrong. I was perpetually being punished, and why? I obeyed every one, I was exact, careful. I did not drink, I borrowed from no one—it's all up with a man when he begins to borrow—and yet every one around me was harsh and cruel. I sometimes hid myself in a corner and did nothing but sob. One day, or rather one night, I was on guard. It was autumn: there was a strong wind, and it was so dark that you could not see a speck, and I was sad, so sad! I took the bayonet from the end of my musket and placed it by my side. Then I put the barrel to my breast and with my big toe—I had taken my boot off—pressed the trigger. It missed fire. I looked at my musket and loaded it with a charge of fresh powder. Then I broke off the corner of my flint, and once more I placed the muzzle against my breast. Again there was a misfire. What was I to do? I said to myself. I put my boot on, I fastened my bayonet to the barrel, and walked up and down with my musket on my shoulder. Let them do what they like, I said to myself; but I will not be a soldier any longer. Half-an-hour afterwards the captain arrived, making his rounds. He came straight upon me. 'Is that the way you carry yourself when you are on guard?' I seized my musket, and stuck the bayonet into his body. Then I had to walk forty-six versts. That is how I came to be in the special section."

He was telling no falsehood, yet I did not understand how they could have sent him there; such crimes deserve a much less severe punishment. Sirotkin was the only one of the convicts who was really handsome. As for his companions of the special section—to the number of fifteen—they were frightful to behold with their hideous, disgusting physiognomies. Gray heads were plentiful among them. I shall speak of these men further on. Sirotkin was often on good terms with Gazin, the drink-seller, of whom I have already spoken at the beginning of this chapter.

This Gazin was a terrible being; the impression that he produced on every one was confusing or appalling. It seemed to me that a more ferocious, a more monstrous creature could not exist. Yet I have seen at Tobolsk, Kameneff, the brigand, celebrated for his crimes. Later, I saw Sokoloff, the escaped convict, formerly a deserter, who was a ferocious creature; but neither of them inspired me with so much disgust as Gazin. I often fancied that I had before my eyes an enormous, gigantic spider of the size of a man. He was a Tartar, and there was no convict so strong as he was. It was less by his great height and his herculean construction, than by his enormous and deformed head, that he inspired terror. The strangest reports were current about him. Some said that he had been a soldier, others that he had escaped from Nertchinsk, and that he had been exiled several times to Siberia, but had always succeeded in getting away. Landing at last in our convict prison, he belonged there to the special section. It appeared that he had taken a pleasure in killing little children when he had attracted them to some deserted place; then he frightened them, tortured them, and after having fully enjoyed the terror and the convulsions of the poor little things, he killed them resolutely and with delight. These horrors had perhaps been imagined by reason of the painful impression that the monster produced upon us; but they seemed probable, and harmonised with his physiognomy. Nevertheless, when Gazin was not drunk, he conducted himself well enough.

He was always quiet, never quarrelled, avoided all disputes as if from contempt for his companions, just as though he had entertained a high opinion of himself. He spoke very little, all his movements were measured, calm, resolute. His look was not without intelligence, but its expression was cruel and derisive like his smile. Of all the convicts who sold vodka, he was the richest. Twice a year he got completely drunk, and it was then that all his brutal ferocity exhibited itself. Little by little he got excited, and began to tease the prisoners with venomous satire prepared long beforehand. Finally when he was quite drunk, he had attacks of furious rage, and, seizing a knife, would rush upon his companions. The convicts who knew his herculean vigour, avoided him and protected themselves against him, for he would throw himself on the first person he met. A means of disarming him had been discovered. Some dozen prisoners would rush suddenly upon Gazin, and give him violent blows in the pit of the stomach, in the belly, and generally beneath the region of the heart, until he lost consciousness. Any one else would have died under such treatment, but Gazin soon got well. When he had been well beaten they would wrap him up in his pelisse, and throw him upon his plank bedstead, leaving him to digest his drink. The next day he woke up almost well, and went to his work silent and sombre. Every time that Gazin got drunk, all the prisoners knew how his day would finish. He knew also, but he drank all the same. Several years passed in this way. Then it was noticed that Gazin had lost his energy, and that he was beginning to get weak. He did nothing but groan, complaining of all kinds of illnesses. His visits to the hospital became more and more frequent. "He is giving in," said the prisoners.

At one time Gazin had gone into the kitchen followed by the little fellow who scraped the violin, and whom the convicts in their festivities used to hire to play to them. He stopped in the middle of the hall silently examining his companions one after another. No one breathed a word. When he saw me with my companions, he looked at us in his malicious, jeering style, and smiled horribly with the air of a man who was satisfied with a good joke that he had just thought of. He approached our table, tottering.

"Might I ask," he said, "where you get the money which allows you to drink tea?"

I exchanged a look with my neighbour. I understood that the best thing for us was to be silent, and not to answer. The least contradiction would have put Gazin in a passion.

"You must have money," he continued, "you must have a good deal of money to drink tea; but, tell me, are you sent to hard labour to drink tea? I say, did you come here for that purpose? Please answer, I should like to know."

Seeing that we were resolved on silence, and that we had determined not to pay any attention to him, he ran towards us, livid and trembling with rage. At two steps' distance, he saw a heavy box, which served to hold the bread given for the dinner and supper of the convicts. Its contents were sufficient for the meal of half the prisoners. At this moment it was empty. He seized it with both hands and brandished it above our heads. Although murder, or attempted, was an inexhaustible source of trouble for the convicts—examinations, counter-examinations, and inquiries without end would be the natural consequence—and though quarrels were generally cut short, when they did not lead to such serious results, yet every one remained silent and waited.

Not one word in our favour, not one cry against Gazin. The hatred of all the prisoners for all who were of gentle birth was so great that every one of them was evidently pleased to see that we were in danger. But a fortunate incident terminated this scene, which must have become tragic. Gazin was about to let fly the enormous box, which he was turning and twisting above his head, when a convict ran in from the barracks, and cried out:

"Gazin, they have stolen your vodka!"

The horrible brigand let fall the box with a frightful oath, and ran out of the kitchen.

"Well, God has saved them," said the prisoners among themselves, repeating the words several times.

I never knew whether his vodka had been stolen, or whether it was only a stratagem invented to save us.

That same evening, before the closing of the barracks, when it was already dark, I walked to the side of the palisade. A heavy feeling of sadness weighed upon my soul. During all the time that I passed in the convict prison I never felt myself so miserable as on that evening, though the first day is always the hardest, whether at hard labour or in the prison. One thought in particular had left me no respite since my deportation—a question insoluble then and insoluble now. I reflected on the inequality of the punishments inflicted for the same crimes. Often, indeed, one crime cannot be compared even approximately to another. Two murderers kill a man under circumstances which in each case are minutely examined and weighed. They each receive the same punishment; and yet by what an abyss are their two actions separated! One has committed a murder for a trifle—for an onion. He has killed on the high-road a peasant who was passing, and found on him an onion, and nothing else.

"Well, I was sent to hard labour for a peasant who had nothing but an onion!"

"Fool that you are! an onion is worth a kopeck. If you had killed a hundred peasants you would have had a hundred kopecks, or one rouble." The above is a prison joke.

Another criminal has killed a debauchee who was oppressing or dishonouring his wife, his sister, or his daughter.

A third, a vagabond, half dead with hunger, pursued by a whole band of police, was defending his liberty, his life. He is to be regarded as on an equality with the brigand who assassinates children for his amusement, for the pleasure of feeling their warm blood flow over his hands, of seeing them shudder in a last bird-like palpitation beneath the knife which tears their flesh!

They will all alike be sent to hard labour; though the sentence will perhaps not be for the same number of years. But the variations in the punishment are not very numerous, whereas different kinds of crimes may be reckoned by thousands. As many characters, so many crimes.

Let us admit that it is impossible to get rid of this first inequality in punishment, that the problem is insoluble, and that in connection with penal matters it is the squaring of the circle. Let all that be admitted; but even if this inequality cannot be avoided, there is another thing to be thought of—the consequences of the punishment. Here is a man who is wasting away like a candle; there is another one, on the contrary, who had no idea before going into exile that there could be such a gay, such an idle life, where he would find a circle of such agreeable friends. Individuals of this latter class are to be found in the convict prison.

Now take a man of heart, of cultivated mind, and of delicate conscience. What he feels kills him more certainly than the material punishment. The judgment which he himself pronounces on his crime is more pitiless than that of the most severe tribunal, the most Draconian law. He lives by the side of another convict, who has not once reflected on the murder he is expiating, during the whole time of his sojourn in the convict prison. He, perhaps, even considers himself innocent. Are there not, also, poor devils who commit crimes in order to be sent to hard labour, and thus to escape the liberty which is much more painful than confinement? A man's life is miserable, he has never, perhaps, been able to satisfy his hunger. He is worked to death in order to enrich his master. In the convict prison his work will be less severe, less crushing. He will eat as much as he wants, better than he could ever have hoped to eat, had he remained free. On holidays he will have meat, and fine people will give him alms, and his evening's work will bring him in some money. And the society one meets with in the convict prison, is that to be counted for nothing? The convicts are clever, wide-awake people, who are up to everything. The new arrival can scarcely conceal the admiration he feels for his companions in labour. He has seen nothing like it before, and he will consider himself in the best company possible.

Is it possible that men so differently situated can feel in an equal degree the punishment inflicted? But why think about questions that are insoluble? The drum beats, let us go back to barracks.

CHAPTER V. FIRST IMPRESSIONS (*continued*)

We were between walls once more. The doors of the barracks were locked, each with a particular padlock, and the prisoners remained shut up till the next morning.

The verification was made by a non-commissioned officer accompanied by two soldiers. When by chance an officer was present, the convicts were drawn up in the court-yard, but generally speaking they were identified in the buildings. As the soldiers often made mistakes, they went out and came back in order to count us again and again, until their reckoning was satisfactory, then the barracks were closed. Each one contained about thirty prisoners, and we were very closely packed in our camp bedsteads. As it was too soon to go to sleep, the convicts occupied themselves with work.

Besides the old soldier of whom I have spoken, who slept in our dormitory, and represented there the administration of the prison, there was in our barrack another old soldier wearing a medal as rewarded for good conduct. It happened often enough, however, that the good-conduct men themselves committed offences for which they were sentenced to be whipped. They then lost their rank, and were immediately replaced by comrades whose conduct was considered satisfactory.

Our good-conduct man was no other than Akim Akimitch. To my great astonishment, he was very rough with the prisoners, but they only replied by jokes. The other old soldier, more prudent, interfered with no one, and if he opened his mouth, it was only as a matter of form, as an affair of duty. For the most part he remained silent, seated on his little bedstead, occupied in mending his own boots.

That day I could not help making to myself an observation, the accuracy of which became afterwards apparent: that all those who are not convicts and who have to deal with them, whoever they may be—beginning with the soldiers of the escort and the sentinels—look upon the convicts in a false and exaggerated light, expecting that for a yes or a no, these men will throw themselves upon them knife in hand. The prisoners, perfectly conscious of the fear they inspire, show a certain arrogance. Accordingly, the best prison director is the one who experiences no emotion in their presence. In spite of the airs they give themselves, the convicts prefer that confidence should be placed in them. By such means, indeed, they may be conciliated. I have more than once had occasion to notice their astonishment at an official entering their prison without an escort, and certainly their astonishment was not unflattering. A visitor who is intrepid imposes respect. If anything unfortunate happens, it will not be in his presence. The terror inspired by the convicts is general, and yet I saw no foundation for it. Is it the appearance of the prisoner, his brigand-like look, that causes a certain repugnance? Is it not rather the feeling that invades you directly you enter the prison, that in spite of all efforts, all precautions, it is impossible to turn a living man into a corpse, to stifle his feelings, his thirst for vengeance and for life, his passions, and his imperious desire to satisfy them? However that may be, I declare that there is no reason for fearing the convicts. A man does not throw himself so quickly nor so easily upon his fellow-man, knife in hand. Few accidents happen; sometimes they are so rare that the danger may be looked upon as non-existent.

I speak, it must be understood, only of prisoners already condemned, who are undergoing their punishment, and some of whom are almost happy to find themselves in the convict prison; so attractive under all circumstances is a new form of life. These latter live quiet and contented. As for the turbulent ones, the convicts themselves keep them in restraint, and their arrogance never goes too far. The prisoner, audacious and reckless as he may be, is afraid of every official connected with the prison. It is by no means the same with the accused whose fate has not been decided. Such a one is quite capable of attacking, no matter whom, without any motive of hatred, and solely because he is to be whipped the next day. If, indeed, he commits a fresh crime his offence becomes complicated. Punishment is delayed, and he gains time. The act of aggression is explained; it has a cause, an object. The convict wishes at all hazards to change his fate, and that as soon as possible. In connection with this, I myself have witnessed a physiological fact of the strangest kind.

In the section of military convicts was an old soldier who had been condemned to two years' hard labour, a great boaster, and at the same time a coward. Generally speaking, the Russian soldier does not boast. He has no time for doing so, even had he the inclination. When such a one appears among a multitude of others, he is always a coward and a rogue. Dutoff—that was the name of the prisoner of whom I am speaking—underwent his punishment, and then went back to the same battalion in the Line; but, like all who are sent to the convict prison to be corrected, he had been thoroughly corrupted. A "return horse" re-appears in the convict prison after two or three weeks' liberty, not for a comparatively short time, but for fifteen or twenty years. So it happened in the case of Dutoff. Three weeks after he had been set at liberty, he robbed one of his comrades, and was, moreover, mutinous. He was taken before a court-martial and sentenced to a severe form of corporal punishment. Horribly frightened, like the coward that he was, at the prospect of punishment, he threw himself, knife in hand, on to the officer of the guard, as he entered his dungeon on the eve of the day that he was to run the gauntlet through the men of his company. He quite understood that he was aggravating his offence, and that the duration of his punishment would be increased; but all he wanted was to postpone for some days, or at least for some hours, a terrible moment. He was such a coward that he did not even wound the officer whom he had attacked. He had, indeed, only committed this assault in order to add a new crime to the last already against him, and thus defer the sentence.

The moment preceding the punishment is terrible for the man condemned to the rods. I have seen many of them on the eve of the fatal day. I generally met with them in the hospital when I was ill, which happened often enough. In Russia the people who show most compassion for the convicts are certainly the doctors, who never make between the prisoners the distinctions observed by other persons brought into direct relations with them. In this respect the common people can alone be compared with the doctors, for they never reproach a criminal with the crime that he has committed, whatever it may be. They forgive him in consideration of the sentence passed upon him.

Is it not known that the common people throughout Russia call crime a "misfortune," and the criminal an "unfortunate"? This definition is expressive, profound, and, moreover, unconscious, instinctive. To the doctor the convicts have naturally recourse, above all when they are to undergo corporal punishment. The prisoner who has been before a court-martial knows pretty well at what moment his sentence will be executed. To escape it he gets himself sent to the hospital, in order to postpone for some days the terrible moment. When he is declared restored to health, he knows that the day after he leaves the hospital this moment will arrive. Accordingly, on quitting the hospital the convict is always in a state of agitation. Some of them may endeavour from vanity to conceal their anxiety, but no one is taken in by that; every one understands the cruelty of such a moment, and is silent from humane motives.

I knew one young convict, an ex-soldier, sentenced for murder, who was to receive the maximum of rods. The eve of the day on which he was to be flogged, he had resolved to drink a bottle of vodka in which he had infused a quantity of snuff.

The prisoner condemned to the rods always drinks, before the critical moment arrives, a certain amount of spirits which he has procured long beforehand, and often at a fabulous price. He would deprive himself of the necessaries of life for six months rather than not be in a position to swallow half a pint of vodka before the flogging. The convicts are convinced that a drunken man suffers less from the sticks or whip than one who is in cold blood.

I will return to my narrative. The poor devil felt ill a few moments after he had swallowed his bottle of vodka. He vomited blood, and was carried in a state of unconsciousness to the hospital. His lungs were so much injured by this accident that phthisis declared itself, and carried off the soldier in a few months. The doctors who had attended him never knew the origin of his illness.

If examples of cowardice are not rare among the prisoners, it must be added that there are some whose intrepidity is quite astounding. I remember many instances of courage pushed to the extreme. The arrival in the hospital of a terrible bandit remains fixed in my memory.

One fine summer day the report was spread in the infirmary that the famous prisoner, Orloff, was to be flogged the same evening, and that he would be brought afterwards to the hospital. The prisoners who were already there said that the punishment would be a cruel one, and every one—including myself I must admit—was awaiting with curiosity the arrival of this brigand, about whom the most unheard-of things were told. He was a malefactor of a rare kind, capable of assassinating in cold blood old men and children. He possessed an indomitable force of will, and was fully conscious of his power. As he had been guilty of several crimes, they had condemned him to be flogged through the ranks.

He was brought, or, rather carried, in towards evening. The place was already dark. Candles were lighted. Orloff was excessively pale, almost unconscious, with his thick curly hair of dull black without the least brilliancy. His back was skinned and swollen, blue, and stained with blood. The prisoners nursed him throughout the night; they changed his poultices, placed him on his side, prepared for him the lotion ordered by the doctor; in a word, showed as much solicitude for him as for a relation or benefactor.

Next day he had fully recovered his faculties, and took one or two turns round the room. I was much astonished, for he was broken down and powerless when he was brought in. He had received half the number of blows ordered by the sentence. The doctor had stopped the punishment, convinced that if it were continued Orloff's death would inevitably ensue.

This criminal was of a feeble constitution, weakened by long imprisonment. Whoever has seen prisoners after having been flogged, will remember their thin, drawn-out features and their feverish looks. Orloff soon recovered his powerful energy, which enabled him to get over his physical weakness. He was no ordinary man. From curiosity I made his acquaintance, and was able to study him at leisure for an entire week. Never in my life did I meet a man whose will was more firm or inflexible.

I had seen at Tobolsk a celebrity of the same kind—a former chief of brigands. This man was a veritable wild beast; by being near him, without even knowing him, it was impossible not to recognise in him a dangerous creature. What above all frightened me was his stupidity. Matter, in this man, had taken such an ascendant over mind, that one could see at a glance that he cared for nothing in the world but the brutal satisfaction of his physical wants. I was certain, however, that Kareneff—that was his name—would have fainted on being condemned to such rigorous corporal punishment as Orloff had undergone; and that he would have murdered the first man near him without blinking.

Orloff, on the contrary, was a brilliant example of the victory of spirit over matter. He had a perfect command over himself. He despised punishment, and feared nothing in the world. His dominant characteristic was boundless energy, a thirst for vengeance, and an immovable will when he had some object to attain.

I was not astonished at his haughty air. He looked down upon all around him from the height of his grandeur. Not that he took the trouble to pose; his pride was an innate quality. I don't think that anything had the least influence over him. He looked upon everything with the calmest eye, as if nothing in the world could astonish him. He knew well that the other prisoners respected him; but he never took advantage of it to give himself airs.

Nevertheless, vanity and conceit are defects from which scarcely any convict is exempt. He was intelligent and strangely frank in talking too much about himself. He replied point-blank to all the questions I put to him, and confessed to me that he was waiting impatiently for his return to health in order to take the remainder of the punishment he was to undergo.

"Now," he said to me with a wink, "it is all over. I shall have the remainder, and shall be sent to Nertchinsk with a convoy of prisoners. I shall profit by it to escape. I shall get away beyond doubt. If only my back would heal a little quicker!"

21

For five days he was burning with impatience to be in a condition for leaving the hospital At times he was gay and in the best of humours. I profited by these rare occasions to question him about his adventures.

Then he would contract his eyebrows a little; but he always answered my questions in a straightforward manner. When he understood that I was endeavouring to see through him, and to discover in him some trace of repentance, he looked at me with a haughty and contemptuous air, as if I were a foolish little boy, to whom he did too much honour by conversing with him.

I detected in his countenance a sort of compassion for me. After a moment's pause he laughed out loud, but without the least irony. I fancy he must, more than once, have laughed in the same manner, when my words returned to his memory. At last he wrote down his name as cured, although his back was not yet entirely healed. As I also was almost well, we left the infirmary together and returned to the convict prison, while he was shut up in the guard-room, where he had been imprisoned before. When he left me he shook me by the hand, which in his eyes was a great mark of confidence. I fancy he did so, because at that moment he was in a good humour. But in reality he must have despised me, for I was a feeble being, contemptible in all respects, and guilty above all of resignation. The next day he underwent the second half of his punishment.

When the gates of the barracks had been closed, it assumed, in less than no time, quite another aspect—that of a private house, of quite a home. Then only did I see my convict comrades at their ease. During the day the under officers, or some of the other authorities, might suddenly arrive, so that the prisoners were then always on the look-out. They were only half at their ease. As soon, however, as the bolts had been pushed and the gates padlocked, every one sat down in his place and began to work. The barrack was lighted up in an unexpected manner. Each convict had his candle and his wooden candlestick. Some of them stitched boots, others sewed different kinds of garments. The air, already mephitic, became more and more impure.

Some of the prisoners, huddled together in a corner, played at cards on a piece of carpet. In each barrack there was a prisoner who possessed a small piece of carpet, a candle, and a pack of horribly greasy cards. The owner of the cards received from the players fifteen kopecks a night. They generally played at the "three leaves"—Gorka, that is to say: a game of chance. Each player placed before him a pile of copper money—all that he possessed—and did not get up until he had lost it or had broken the bank.

Playing was continued until late at night; sometimes the dawn found the gamblers still at their game. Often, indeed, it did not cease until a few minutes before the opening of the gates. In our room—as in all the others—there were beggars ruined by drink and play, or rather beggars innate—I say innate, and maintain my expression. Indeed, in our country, and in all classes, there are, and always will be, strange easy-going people whose destiny it is to remain always beggars. They are poor devils all their lives; quite broken down, they remain under the domination or guardianship of some one, generally a prodigal, or a man who has suddenly made his fortune. All initiative is for them an insupportable burden. They only exist on condition of undertaking nothing for themselves, and by serving, always living under the will of another. They are destined to act by and through others. Under no circumstances, even of the most unexpected kind, can they get rich; they are always beggars. I have met these persons in all classes of society, in all coteries, in all associations, including the literary world.

As soon as a party was made up, one of these beggars, quite indispensable to the game, was summoned. He received five kopecks for a whole night's employment; and what employment it was! His duty was to keep guard in the vestibule, with thirty degrees (Réaumur) of frost, in total darkness, for six or seven hours. The man on watch had to listen for the slightest noise, for the Major or one of the other officers of the guard would sometimes make a round rather late in the night. They arrived secretly, and sometimes discovered the players and the watchers in the act—thanks to the light of the candles, which could be seen from the court-yard.

When the key was heard grinding in the padlock which closed the gate, it was too late to put the lights out and lie down on the plank bedsteads. Such surprises were, however, rare. Five kopecks was a ridiculous payment even in our convict prison, and the exigency and hardness of the gamblers astonished me in this as in many cases: "You are paid, you must do what you are told." This was the argument, and it admitted of no reply. To have paid a few kopecks to any one gave the right to turn him to the best possible account, and even to claim his gratitude. More than once it happened to me to see the convicts spend their money extravagantly, throwing it away on all sides, and, at the same time, cheat the man employed to watch. I have seen this in several barracks on many occasions.

I have already said that, with the exception of the gamblers, every one worked. Five only of the convicts remained completely idle, and went to bed on the first opportunity. My sleeping place was near the door. Next to me was Akim Akimitch, and when we were lying down our heads touched. He used to work until ten or eleven at making, by pasting together pieces of paper, multicolour lanterns, which some one living in the town had ordered from him, and for which he used to be well paid. He excelled in this kind of work, and did it methodically and regularly. When he had finished he put away carefully his tools, unfolded his mattress, said his prayers, and went to sleep with the sleep of the just. He carried his love of order even to pedantry, and must have thought himself in his inner heart a man of brains, as is generally the case with narrow, mediocre persons. I did not like him the first day, although he gave me much to think of. I was astonished that such a man could be found in a convict prison. I shall speak of Akimitch further on in the course of this book.

But I must now continue to describe the persons with whom I was to live a number of years. Those who surrounded me were to be my companions every minute, and it will be understood that I looked upon them with anxious curiosity.

On my left slept a band of mountaineers from the Caucasus, nearly all exiled for brigandage, but condemned to different punishments. There were two Lesghians, a Circassian, and three Tartars from Daghestan. The Circassian was a morose and sombre person. He scarcely ever spoke, and looked at you sideways with a sly, sulky, wild-beast-like expression. One of the Lesghians, an old man with an aquiline nose, tall and thin, seemed to be a true brigand; but the other Lesghian, Nourra by name, made a most favourable impression upon me. Of middle height, still young, built like a Hercules, with fair hair and violet eyes; he had a slightly turned up nose, while his features were somewhat of a Finnish cast. Like all horsemen, he walked with his toes in. His body was striped with scars, ploughed by bayonet wounds and bullets. Although he belonged to the conquered part of the Caucasus, he had joined the rebels, with whom he used to make continual incursions into our territory. Every one liked him in the prison by reason of his gaiety and affability. He worked without murmuring, always calm and peaceful. Thieving, cheating, and drunkenness filled him with disgust, or put him in a rage—not that he wished to quarrel with any one; he simply turned away with indignation. During his confinement he committed no breach of the rules. Fervently pious, he said his prayers religiously every evening, observed all the Mohammedan fasts like a true fanatic, and passed whole nights in prayer. Every one liked him, and looked upon him as a thoroughly honest man. "Nourra is a lion," said the convicts; and the name of "Lion" stuck to him. He was quite convinced that as soon as he had finished his sentence he would be sent to the Caucasus. Indeed, he only lived by this hope, and I believe he would have died had he been deprived of it. I noticed it the very day of my arrival. How was it possible not to distinguish this calm, honest face in the midst of so many sombre, sardonic, repulsive countenances!

Before I had been half-an-hour in the prison, he passed by my side and touched me gently on the shoulder, smiling at the same time with an innocent air. I did not at first understand what he meant, for he spoke Russian very badly; but soon afterwards he passed again, and, with a friendly smile, again touched me on the shoulder. For three days running he repeated this strange proceeding. As I soon found out, he wanted to show me that he pitied me, and that he felt how painful the first moment of imprisonment must be. He wanted to testify his sympathy, to keep up my spirits, and to assure me of his good-will. Kind and innocent Nourra!

Of the three Tartars from Daghestan, all brothers, the two eldest were well-developed men, while the youngest, Ali, was not more than twenty-two, and looked younger. He slept by my side, and when I observed his frank, intelligent countenance, thoroughly natural, I was at once attracted to him, and thanked my fate that I had him for a neighbour in place of some other prisoner. His whole soul could be read in his beaming countenance. His confident smile had a certain childish simplicity; his large black eyes expressed such friendliness, such tender feeling, that I always took a pleasure in looking at him. It was a relief to me in moments of sadness and anguish. One day his eldest brother—he had five, of whom two were working in the mines of Siberia—had ordered him to take his yataghan, to get on horseback, and follow him. The respect of the mountaineers for their elders is so great that young Ali did not dare to ask the object of the expedition. He probably knew nothing about it, nor did his brothers consider it necessary to tell him. They were going to plunder the caravan of a rich Armenian merchant, and they succeeded in their enterprise. They assassinated the merchant and stole his goods. Unhappily for them, their act of brigandage was discovered. They were tried, flogged, and then sent to hard labour in Siberia. The Court admitted no extenuating circumstances, except in the case of Ali. He was condemned to the minimum punishment—four years' confinement. These brothers loved him, their affection being paternal rather than fraternal. He was the only consolation of their exile. Dull and sad as a rule, they had always a smile for him when they spoke to him, which they rarely did—for they looked upon him as a child to whom it would be useless to speak seriously—their forbidding countenances lightened up. I fancied they always spoke to him in a jocular tone, as to an infant. When he replied, the brothers exchanged glances, and smiled good-naturedly.

He would not have dared to speak to them first by reason of his respect for them. How this young man preserved his tender heart, his native honesty, his frank cordiality without getting perverted and corrupted during his period of hard labour, is quite inexplicable. In spite of his gentleness, he had a strong stoical nature, as I afterwards saw. Chaste as a young girl, everything that was foul, cynical, shameful, or unjust filled his fine black eyes with indignation, and made them finer than ever. Without being a coward, he would allow himself to be insulted with impunity. He avoided quarrels and insults, and preserved all his dignity. With whom, indeed, was he to quarrel? Every one loved him, caressed him.

At first he was only polite to me; but little by little we got into the habit of talking together in the evening, and in a few months he had learnt to speak Russian perfectly, whereas his brothers never gained a correct knowledge of the language. He was intelligent, and at the same time modest and full of delicate feeling.

Ali was an exceptional being, and I always think of my meeting him as one of the lucky things in my life. There are some natures so spontaneously good and endowed by God with such great qualities that the idea of their getting perverted seems absurd. One is always at ease about them. Accordingly I had never any fears about Ali. Where is he now?

One day, a considerable time after my arrival at the convict prison, I was stretched out on my camp-bedstead agitated by painful thoughts. Ali, always industrious, was not working at this moment. His time for going to bed had not arrived. The brothers were celebrating some Mussulman festival, and were not working. Ali was lying down with his head between his hands in a state of reverie. Suddenly he said to me:

"Well, you are very sad!"

I looked at him with curiosity. Such a remark from Ali, always so delicate, so full of tact, seemed strange. But I looked at him more attentively, and saw so much grief, so much repressed suffering in his countenance—of suffering caused no doubt by sudden recollections—that I understood in what pain he must be, and said so to him. He uttered a deep sigh, and smiled with a melancholy air. I always liked his graceful, agreeable smile. When he laughed, he showed two rows of teeth which the first beauty in the world would have envied him.

"You were probably thinking, Ali, how this festival is celebrated in Daghestan. Ah, you were happy there!"

"Yes," he replied with enthusiasm, and his eyes sparkled. "How did you know I was thinking of such things?"

"How was I not to know? You were much better off than you are here."

"Why do you say that?"

"What beautiful flowers there are in your country! Is it not so? It is a true paradise."

"Be silent, please."

He was much agitated.

"Listen, Ali. Had you a sister?"

"Yes; why do you ask me?"

"She must have been very beautiful if she is like you?"

"Oh, there is no comparison to make between us. In all Daghestan no such beautiful girl is to be seen. My sister is, indeed, charming. I am sure that you have never seen any one like her. My mother also is very handsome."

"And your mother was fond of you?"

"What are you saying? Certainly she was. I am sure that she has died of grief, she was so fond of me. I was her favourite child. Yes, she loved me more than my sister, more than all the others. This very night she has appeared to me in a dream, she shed tears for me."

He was silent, and throughout the rest of the night did not open his mouth; but from this very moment he sought my company and my conversation; although very respectful, he never allowed himself to address me first. On the other hand he was happy when I entered into conversation with him. He spoke often of the Caucasus, and of his past life. His brothers did not forbid him to converse with me; I think even that they encouraged him to do so. When they saw that I had formed an attachment to him, they became more affable towards me.

Ali often helped me in my work. In the barrack he did whatever he thought would be agreeable to me, and would save me trouble. In his attentions to me there was neither servility nor the hope of any advantage, but only a warm, cordial feeling, which he did not try to hide. He had an extraordinary aptitude for the mechanical arts. He had learnt to sew very tolerably, and to mend boots; he even understood a little carpentering—everything in short that could be learnt at the convict prison. His brothers were proud of him.

"Listen, Ali," I said to him one day, "why don't you learn to read and write the Russian language, it might be very useful to you here in Siberia?"

"I should like to do so, but who would teach me?"

"There are plenty of people here who can read and write. I myself will teach you if you like."

"Oh, do teach me, I beg of you," said Ali, raising himself up in bed; he joined his hands and looked at me with a suppliant air.

We went to work the very next evening. I had with me a Russian translation of the New Testament, the only book that was not forbidden in the prison. With this book alone, without an alphabet, Ali learnt to read in a few weeks, and after a few months he could read perfectly. He brought to his studies extraordinary zeal and warmth.

One day we were reading together the Sermon on the Mount. I noticed that he read certain passages with much feeling; and I asked him if he was pleased with what he read. He glanced at me, and his face suddenly lighted up.

"Yes, yes, Jesus is a holy prophet. He speaks the language of God. How beautiful it is!"

"But tell me what it is that particularly pleases you."

"The passage in which it is said, 'Forgive those that hate you!' Ah! how divinely He speaks!"

He turned towards his brothers, who were listening to our conversation, and said to them with warmth a few words. They talked together seriously for some time, giving their approval of what their young brother had said by a nodding of the head. Then with a grave, kindly smile, quite a Mussulman smile (I liked the gravity of this smile), they assured me that Isu was a great prophet. He had done great miracles. He had created a bird with a little clay on which he breathed the breath of life, and the bird had then flown away. That, they said, was written in their books. They were convinced that they would please me much by praising Jesus. As for Ali, he was happy to see that his brothers approved of our friendship, and that they were giving me, what he thought would be, grateful words. The success I had with my pupil in teaching him to write, was really extraordinary. Ali had bought paper at his own expense, for he would not allow me to purchase any, also pens and ink; and in less than two months he had learnt to write. His brothers were astonished at such rapid progress. Their satisfaction and their pride were without bounds. They did not know how to show me enough gratitude. At the workshop, if we happened to be together, there were disputes as to which of them should help me. I do not speak of Ali, he felt for me more affection than even for his brothers. I shall never forget the day on which he was liberated. He went with me outside the barracks, threw himself on my neck and sobbed. He had never embraced me before, and had never before wept in my presence.

"You have done so much for me," he said; "neither my father nor my mother have ever been kinder. You have made a man of me. God will bless you, I shall never forget you, never!"

Where is he now, where is my good, kind, dear Ali?

Besides the Circassians, we had a certain number of Poles, who formed a separate group. They had scarcely any relations with the other convicts. I have already said that, thanks to their hatred for the Russian prisoners, they were detested by every one. They were of a restless, morbid disposition: there were six of them, some of them men of education, of whom I shall speak in detail further on. It was from them that during the last days of my imprisonment I obtained a few books. The first work I read made a deep impression upon me. I shall speak further on of these sensations, which I look upon as very curious, though it will be difficult to understand them. Of this I am certain, for there are certain things as to which one cannot judge without having experienced them oneself. It will be enough for me to say that intellectual privations are more difficult to support than the most frightful, physical tortures.

A common man sent to hard labour finds himself in kindred society, perhaps even in a more interesting society than he has been accustomed to. He loses his native place, his family; but his ordinary surroundings are much the same as before. A man of education, condemned by law to the same punishment as the common man, suffers incomparably more. He must stifle all his needs, all his habits, he must descend into a lower sphere, must breathe another air. He is like a fish thrown upon the sand. The punishment that he undergoes, equal for all criminals according to the law, is ten times more severe and more painful for him than for the common man. This is an incontestable truth, even if one thinks only of the material habits that have to be sacrificed.

I was saying that the Poles formed a group by themselves. They lived together, and of all the convicts in the prison, they cared only for a Jew, and for no other reason than because he amused them. Our Jew was generally liked, although every one laughed at him. We only had one, and even now I cannot think of him without laughing. Whenever I looked at him I thought of the Jew Jankel, whom Gogol describes in his Tarass Boulba, and who, when undressed and ready to go to bed with his Jewess in a sort of cupboard, resembled a fowl; but Isaiah Fomitch Bumstein and a plucked fowl were as like one another as two drops of water. He was already of a certain age—about fifty—small, feeble, cunning, and, at the same time, very stupid, bold, and boastful, though a horrible coward. His face was covered with wrinkles, his forehead and cheeks were scarred from the burning he had received in the pillory. I never understood how he had been able to support the sixty strokes he received.

He had been sentenced for murder. He carried on his person a medical prescription which had been given to him by other Jews immediately after his exposure in the pillory. Thanks to the ointment prescribed, the scars were to disappear in less than a fortnight. He had been afraid to use it. He was waiting for the expiration of his twenty years (after which he would become a colonist) in order to utilise his famous remedy.

"Otherwise I shall not be able to get married," he would say; "and I must absolutely marry."

We were great friends: his good-humour was inexhaustible. The life of the convict prison did not seem to disagree with him. A goldsmith by trade, he received more orders than he could execute, for there was no jeweller's shop in our town. He thus escaped his hard labour. As a matter of course, he lent money on pledges to the convicts, who paid him heavy interest. He arrived at the prison before I did. One of the Poles related to me his triumphal entry. It is quite a history, which I shall relate further on, for I shall often have to speak of Isaiah Fomitch Bumstein.

As for the other prisoners there were, first of all, four "old believers," among whom was the old man from Starodoub, two or three Little Russians, very morose persons, and a young convict with delicate features and a finely-chiselled nose, about twenty-three years of age, who had already committed eight murders; besides a band of coiners, one of whom was the buffoon of our barracks; and, finally, some sombre, sour-tempered convicts, shorn and disfigured, always silent, and full of envy. They looked askance at all who came near them, and must have continued to do so during a long course of years. I saw all this superficially on the first night of my arrival, in the midst of thick smoke, in a mephitic atmosphere, amid obscene oaths, accompanied by the rattling of chains, by insults, and cynical laughter. I stretched myself out on the bare planks, my head resting on my coat, rolled up to do duty in lieu of a pillow, not yet supplied to me. Then I covered myself with my sheepskin, but, thanks to the painful impression of this evening, I was unable for some time to get to sleep. My new life was only just beginning. The future reserved for me many things which I had not foreseen, and of which I had never the least idea.

CHAPTER VI. THE FIRST MONTH

Three days after my arrival I was ordered to go to work. The impression left upon me to this day is still very clear, although there was nothing very striking in it, unless one considers that my position was in itself extraordinary. The first sensations count for a good deal, and I as yet looked upon everything with curiosity. My first three days were certainly the most painful of all my terms of imprisonment.

My wandering is at an end, I said to myself every moment. I am now in the convict prison, my resting-place for many years. Here is where I am to live. I come here full of grief, who knows that when I leave it I shall not do so with regret? I said this to myself as one touches a wound, the better to feel its pain. The idea that I might regret my stay was terrible to me. Already I felt to what an intolerable degree man is a creature of habit, but this was a matter of the future. The present, meanwhile, was terrible enough.

The wild curiosity with which my convict companions examined me, their harshness towards a former nobleman now entering into their corporation, a harshness which sometimes took the form of hatred—all this tormented me to such a degree that I felt obliged of my own accord to go to work in order to measure at one stroke the whole extent of my misfortune, that I might at once begin to live like the others, and fall with them into the same abyss.

But convicts differ, and I had not yet disentangled from the general hostility the sympathy here and there manifested towards me.

After a time the affability and good-will shown to me by certain convicts gave me a little courage, and restored my spirits. Most friendly among them was Akim Akimitch. I soon noticed some kind, good-natured faces in the dark and hateful crowd. Bad people are to be found everywhere, but even among the worst there may be something good, I began to think, by way of consolation. Who knows? These persons are perhaps not worse than others who are free. While making these reflections I felt some doubts, and, nevertheless, how much I was in the right!

The convict Suchiloff, for example; a man whose acquaintance I did not make until long afterwards, although he was near me during nearly the whole period of my confinement. Whenever I speak of the convicts who are not worse than other men, my thoughts turn involuntarily to him. He acted as my servant, together with another prisoner named Osip, whom Akim Akimitch had recommended to me immediately after my arrival. For thirty kopecks a month this man agreed to cook me a separate dinner, in case I should not be able to put up with the ordinary prison fare, and should be able to pay for my own food. Osip was one of the four cooks chosen by the prisoners in our two kitchens. I may observe that they were at liberty to refuse these duties, and give them up whenever they might think fit. The cooks were men from whom hard labour was not expected. They had to bake bread and prepare the cabbage soup. They were called "cook-maids," not from contempt, for the men chosen were always the most intelligent, but merely in fun. The name given to them did not annoy them.

For many years past Osip had been constantly selected as "cook-maid." He never refused the duty except when he was out of sorts, or when he saw an opportunity of getting spirits into the barracks. Although he had been sent to the convict prison as a smuggler, he was remarkably honest and good-tempered (I have spoken of him before); at the same time he was a dreadful coward, and feared the rod above all things. Of a peaceful, patient disposition, affable with everybody, he never got into quarrels; but he could never resist the temptation of bringing spirits in, notwithstanding his cowardice, and simply from his love of smuggling. Like all the other cooks he dealt in spirits, but on a much less extensive scale than Gazin, because he was afraid of running the same risks. I always lived on good terms with Osip. To have a separate table it was not necessary to be very rich; it cost me only one rouble a month apart from the bread, which was given to us. Sometimes when I was very hungry I made up my mind to eat the cabbage soup, in spite of the disgust with which it generally filled me. After a time this disgust entirely disappeared. I generally bought one pound of meat a day, which cost me two kopecks—

The old soldiers, who watched over the internal discipline of the barracks, were ready, good-naturedly, to go every day to the market to make purchases for the convicts. For this they received no pay, except from time to time a trifling present. They did it for the sake of their peace; their life in the convict prison would have been a perpetual torment had they refused. They used to bring in tobacco, tea, meat—everything, in short, that was desired, always excepting spirits.

For many years Osip prepared for me every day a piece of roast meat. How he managed to get it cooked was a secret. What was strangest in the matter was, that during all this time I scarcely exchanged two words with him. I tried many times to make him talk, but he was incapable of keeping up a conversation. He would only smile and answer my questions by "yes" or "no." He was a Hercules, but he had no more intelligence than a child of seven.

Suchiloff was also one of those who helped me. I had never asked him to do so, he attached himself to me on his own account, and I scarcely remember when he began to do so. His principal duty consisted in washing my linen. For this purpose there was a basin in the middle of the court-yard, round which the convicts washed their clothes in prison buckets.

Suchiloff had found means for rendering me a number of little services. He boiled my tea-urn, ran right and left to perform various commissions for me, got me all kinds of things, mended my clothes, and greased my boots four times a month. He did all this in a zealous manner, with a business-like air, as if he felt all the weight of the duties he was performing. He seemed quite to have joined his fate to mine, and occupied himself with all my affairs. He never said: "You have so many shirts, or your waistcoat is torn;" but, "We have so many shirts, and our waistcoat is torn." I had somehow inspired him with admiration, and I really believe that I had become his sole care in life. As he knew no trade whatever his only source of income was from me, and it must be understood that I paid him very little; but he was always pleased, whatever he might receive. He would have been without means had he not been a servant of mine, and he gave me the preference because I was more affable than the others, and, above all, more equitable in money matters. He was one of those beings who never get rich, and never know how to manage their affairs; one of those in the prison who were hired by the gamblers to watch all night in the ante-chamber, listening for the least noise that might announce the arrival of the Major. If there was a night visit they received nothing, indeed their back paid for their want of attention. One thing which marks this kind of men is their entire absence of individuality, which they seem entirely to have lost.

Suchiloff was a poor, meek fellow; all the courage seemed to have been beaten out of him, although he had in reality been born meek. For nothing in the world would he have raised his hand against any one in the prison. I always pitied him without knowing why. I could not look at him without feeling the deepest compassion for him. If asked to explain this, I should find it impossible to do so. I could never get him to talk, and he never became animated, except when, to put an end to all attempts at conversation, I gave him something to do, or told him to go somewhere for me. I soon found that he loved to be ordered about. Neither tall nor short, neither ugly nor handsome, neither stupid nor intelligent, neither old nor young, it would be difficult to describe in any definite manner this man, except that his face was slightly pitted with the small-pox, and that he had fair hair. He belonged, as far as I could make out, to the same company as Sirotkin. The prisoners sometimes laughed at him because he had "exchanged." During the march to Siberia he had exchanged for a red shirt and a silver rouble. It was thought comical that he should have sold himself for such a small sum, to take the name of another prisoner in place of his own, and consequently to accept the other's sentence. Strange as it may appear it was nevertheless true. This custom, which had become traditional, and still existed at the time I was sent to Siberia, I, at first, refused to believe, but found afterwards that it really existed. This is how the exchange was effected:

A company of prisoners started for Siberia. Among them there are exiles of all kinds, some condemned to hard labour, others to labour in the mines, others to simple colonisation. On the way out, no matter at what stage of the journey, in the Government of Perm, for instance, a prisoner wishes to exchange with another man, who—we will say he is named Mikhailoff—has been condemned to hard labour for a capital offence, and does not like the prospect of passing long years without his liberty. He knows, in his cunning, what to do. He looks among his comrades for some simple, weak-minded fellow, whose punishment is less severe, who has been condemned to a few years in the mines, or to hard labour, or has perhaps been simply exiled. At last he finds such a man as Suchiloff, a former serf, sentenced only to become a colonist. The man has made fifteen hundred versts without a kopeck, for the good reason that a Suchiloff is always without money; fatigued, exhausted, he can get nothing to eat beyond the fixed rations, nothing to wear in addition to the convict uniform.

Mikhailoff gets into conversation with Suchiloff, they suit one another, and they strike up a friendship. At last at some station Mikhailoff makes his comrade drunk, then he will ask him if he will "exchange."

"My name is Mikhailoff," he says to him, "condemned to what is called hard labour, but which, in my own case, will be nothing of the kind, as I am to enter a particular special section. I am classed with the hard-labour men, but in my special division the labour is not so severe."

Before the special section was abolished, many persons in the official world, even at St. Petersburg, were unaware even of its existence. It was in such a retired corner of one of the most distant regions of Siberia, that it was difficult to know anything about it. It was insignificant, moreover, from the number of persons belonging to it. In my time they numbered altogether only seventy. I have since met men who have served in Siberia, and know the country well, and yet have never heard of the "special section." In the rules and regulations there are only six lines about this institution. Attached to the convict prison of ---- is a special section reserved for the most dangerous criminals, while the severest labours are being prepared for them. The prisoners themselves knew nothing of this special section. Did it exist temporarily or constantly? Neither Suchiloff nor any of the prisoners being sent out, not Mikhailoff himself could guess the significance of those two words. Mikhailoff, however, had his suspicion as to the true character of this section. He formed his opinion from the gravity of the crime for which he was made to march three or four thousand versts on foot. It was certain that he was not being sent to a place where he would be at his ease. Suchiloff was to be a colonist. What could Mikhailoff desire better than that?

"Won't you change?" he asks. Suchiloff is a little drunk, he is a simple-minded man, full of gratitude to the comrade who entertains him, and dare not refuse; he has heard, moreover, from other prisoners, that these exchanges are made, and understands, therefore, that there is nothing extraordinary, unheard-of, in the proposition made to him. An agreement is come to, the cunning Mikhailoff, profiting by

Suchiloff's simplicity, buys his name for a red shirt, and a silver rouble, which are given before witnesses. The next day Suchiloff is sober; but more liquor is given to him. Then he drinks up his own rouble, and after a while the red shirt has the same fate.

"If you don't like the bargain we made, give me back my money," says Mikhailoff. But where is Suchiloff to get a rouble? If he does not give it back, the "artel" will force him to keep his promise. The prisoners are very sensitive on such points: he must keep his promise. The "artel" requires it, and, in case of disobedience, woe to the offender! He will be killed, or at least seriously intimidated. If indeed the "artel" once showed mercy to the men who had broken their word, there would be an end to its existence. If the given word can be recalled, and the bargain put an end to after the stipulated sum has been paid, who would be bound by such an agreement? It is a question of life or death for the "artel." Accordingly the prisoners are very severe on the point.

Suchiloff then finds that it is impossible to go back, that nothing can save him, and he accordingly agrees to all that is demanded of him. The bargain is then made known to all the convoy, and if denunciations are feared, the men looked upon as suspicious are entertained. What, moreover, does it matter to the others whether Mikhailoff or Suchiloff goes to the devil? They have had gratuitous drinks, they have been feasted for nothing, and the secret is kept by all.

At the next station the names are called. When Mikhailoff's turn arrives, Suchiloff answers "present," Mikhailoff replies "present" for Suchiloff, and the journey is continued. The matter is not now even talked about. At Tobolsk the prisoners are told off. Mikhailoff will become a colonist, while Suchiloff is sent to the special section under a double escort. It would be useless now to cry out, to protest, for what proof could be given? How many years would it take to decide the affair, what benefit would the complainant derive? Where, moreover, are the witnesses? They would deny everything, even if they could be found.

That is how Suchiloff, for a silver rouble and a red shirt, came to be sent to the special section. The prisoners laughed at him, not because he had exchanged—though in general they despised those who had been foolish enough to exchange a work that was easy for a work that was hard—but simply because he had received nothing for the bargain except a red shirt and a rouble—certainly a ridiculous compensation.

Generally speaking, the exchanges are made for relatively large sums; several ten-rouble notes sometimes change hands. But Suchiloff was so characterless, so insignificant, so null, that he could scarcely even be laughed at. We lived a considerable time together, he and I; I had got accustomed to him, and he had formed an attachment for me. One day, however—I can never forgive myself for what I did—he had not executed my orders, and when he came to ask me for his money I had the cruelty to say to him, "You don't forget to ask for your money, but you don't do what you are told." Suchiloff remained silent and hastened to do as he was ordered, but he suddenly became very sad. Two days passed. I could not believe that what I had said to him could affect him so much. I knew that a person named Vassilieff was claiming from him in a morose manner payment of a small debt. Suchiloff was probably short of money, and did not dare to ask me for any.

"Suchiloff, you wish, I think, to ask me for some money to pay Vassilieff; take this."

I was seated on my camp-bedstead. Suchiloff remained standing up before me, much astonished that I myself should propose to give him money, and that I remembered his difficult position; the more so as latterly he had asked me several times for money in advance, and could scarcely hope that I should give him any more. He looked at the paper I held out to him, then looked at me, turned sharply on his heel and went out. I was as astonished as I could be. I went out after him, and found him at the back of the barracks. He was standing up with his face against the palisade and his arms resting on the stakes.

"What is the matter, Suchiloff?" I asked him.

He made no reply, and to my stupefaction I saw that he was on the point of bursting into tears.

"You think, Alexander Petrovitch," he said, in a trembling voice, in endeavouring not to look at me, "that I care only for your money, but I——"

He turned away from me, and struck the palisade with his forehead and began to sob. It was the first time in the convict prison that I had seen a man weep. I had much trouble in consoling him; and he afterwards served me, if possible, with more zeal than ever. He watched for my orders, but by almost imperceptible indications I could see that his heart would never forgive me for my reproach. Meanwhile other men laughed at him and teased him whenever the opportunity presented itself, and even insulted him without his losing his temper; on the contrary, he still remained on good terms with them. It is indeed difficult to know a man, even after having lived long years with him.

The convict prison had not at first for me the significance it was afterwards to assume. I was at first, in spite of my attention, unable to understand many facts which were staring me in the face. I was naturally first struck by the most salient points, but I saw them from a false point of view, and the only impression they made upon me was one of unmitigated sadness. What contributed above all to this result was my meeting with A——f, the convict who had come to the prison before me, and who had astonished me in such a painful manner during the first few days. The effect of his baseness was to aggravate my moral suffering, already sufficiently cruel. He offered the most repulsive example of the kind of degradation and baseness to which a man may fall when all feeling of honour has perished within him. This young man of noble birth—I have spoken of him before—used to repeat to the Major all that was done in the barracks, and in doing so through the Major's body-servant Fedka. Here is the man's history.

Arrived at St. Petersburg before he had finished his studies, after a quarrel with his parents, whom his life of debauchery had terrified, he had not shrunk for the sake of money from doing the work of an informer. He did not hesitate to sell the blood of ten men in order to satisfy his insatiable thirst for the grossest and most licentious pleasures. At last he became so completely perverted in the St. Petersburg taverns and houses of ill-fame, that he did not hesitate to take part in an affair which he knew to be conceived in madness—for he was not without intelligence. He was condemned to exile and ten years' hard labour in Siberia. One might have thought that such a frightful blow would have shocked him, that it would have caused some reaction and brought about a crisis; but he accepted his new fate without the least confusion. It did not frighten him; all that he feared in it was the necessity of working, and of giving up for ever his habits of debauchery.

The name of convict had no effect but to prepare him for new acts of baseness, and more hideous villainies than any he had previously perpetrated.

"I am now a convict, and can crawl at ease, without shame."

That was the light in which he looked upon his new position. I think of this disgusting creature as of some monstrous phenomenon. During the many years I have lived in the midst of murderers, debauchees, and proved rascals, never in my life did I meet a case of such complete moral abasement, determined corruption, and shameless baseness. Among us there was a parricide of noble birth. I have already spoken of him; but I could see by several signs that he was much better and more humane than A——f. During the whole time of my punishment, he was never anything more in my eyes than a piece of flesh furnished with teeth and a stomach, greedy for the most offensive and ferocious animal enjoyments, for the satisfaction of which he was ready to assassinate anyone. I do not exaggerate in the least; I recognised in A——f one of the most perfect specimens of animality, restrained by no principles, no rule. How much I was disgusted by his eternal smile! He was a monster—a moral Quasimodo. He was at the same time intelligent, cunning, good-looking, had received some education, and possessed a certain capacity. Fire, plague, famine, no matter what scourge, is preferable to the presence of such a man in human society. I have already said that in the convict prison espionage and denunciation flourished as the natural product of degradation, without the convicts thinking much of it. On the contrary, they maintained friendly relations with A——f. They were more affable with him than with any one else. The kindly attitude towards him of our drunken friend, the Major, gave him a certain importance, and even a certain worth in the eyes of the convicts. Later on, this cowardly wretch ran away with another convict and the soldier in charge of them; but of this I shall speak in proper time and place. At first, he hung about me, thinking I did not know his history. I repeat that he poisoned the first days of my imprisonment so as to drive me nearly to despair. I was terrified by the mass of baseness and cowardice in the midst of which I had been thrown. I imagined that every one else was as foul and cowardly as he. But I made a mistake in supposing that every one resembled A——f.

During the first three days I did nothing but wander about the convict prison, when I did not remain stretched out on my camp-bedstead. I entrusted to a prisoner of whom I was sure, the piece of linen which had been delivered to me by the administration, in order that he might make me some shirts. Always on the advice of Akim Akimitch, I got myself a folding mattress. It was in felt, covered with linen, as thin as a pancake, and very hard to any one who was not accustomed to it. Akim Akimitch promised to get me all the most essential things, and with his own hands made me a blanket out of a piece of old cloth, cut and sewn together from all the old trousers and waistcoats which I had bought from various prisoners. The clothes delivered to them, when they have been worn the regulation time, become the property of the prisoners. They at once sell them, for however much worn an article of clothing may be, it always possesses a certain value. I was very much astonished by all this, above all at the outset, during my first relations with this world. I became as low as my companions, as much a convict as they. Their customs, their habits, their ideas influenced me thoroughly, and externally became my own, without affecting my inner self. I was astonished and confused as though I had never heard or suspected anything of the kind before, and yet I knew what to expect, or at least what had been told me. The thing itself, however, produced on me a different impression from the mere description of it. How could I suppose, for instance, that old rags possessed still some value? And, nevertheless, my blanket was made up entirely of tatters. It would be difficult to describe the cloth out of which the clothes of the convicts were made. It was like the thick, gray cloth manufactured for the soldiers, but as soon as it had been worn some little time it showed the threads and tore with abominable ease. The uniform ought to have lasted for a whole year, but it never went so long as that. The prisoner labours, carries heavy burdens, and the cloth naturally wears out, and gets into holes very quickly. Our sheepskins were intended to be worn for three years. During the whole of that time they served as outer garments, blankets, and pillows, but they were very solid. Nevertheless, at the end of the third year, it was not rare to see them mended with ordinary linen. Although they were now very much worn, it was always possible to sell them at the rate of forty kopecks a piece, the best preserved ones even at the price of sixty kopecks, which was a great sum for the convict prison.

Money, as I have before said, has a sovereign value in such a place. It is certain that a prisoner who has some pecuniary resources suffers ten times less than the one who has nothing.

"When the Government supplies all the wants of the convict, what need can he have for money?" reasoned our chief.

Nevertheless, I repeat that if the prisoners had been deprived of the opportunity of possessing something of their own, they would have lost their reason, or would have died like flies. They would have committed unheard-of crimes; some from wearisomeness or grief, the others, in order to get sooner punished, and, according to their expression, "have a change." If the convict who has gained some kopecks by the sweat of his brow, who has embarked in perilous undertakings in order to conquer them, if he spends this money recklessly, with childish stupidity, that does not the least in the world prove that he does not know its value, as might at first sight be thought. The convict is greedy for money, to the point of losing his reason, and, if he throws it away, he does so in order to procure what he places far above money—liberty, or at least a semblance of liberty.

Convicts are great dreamers; I will speak of that further on with more detail. At present I will confine myself to saying that I have heard men, who had been condemned to twenty years' hard labour, say, with a quiet air, "when I have finished my time, if God wishes, then——" The very words hard labour, or forced labour, indicate that the man has lost his freedom; and when this man spends his money he is carrying out his own will.

In spite of the branding and the chains, in spite of the palisade which hides from his eyes the free world, and encloses him in a cage like a wild beast, he can get himself spirits and other delights; sometimes even (not always), corrupt his immediate superintendents, the old soldiers and non-commissioned officers, and get them to close their eyes to his infractions of discipline within the prison. He can, moreover—what he adores—swagger; that is to say, impress his companions and persuade himself for a time, that he enjoys more liberty than he really possesses. The poor devil wishes, in a word, to convince himself of what he knows to be impossible. This is why the prisoners take such pleasure in boasting and exaggerating in burlesque fashion their own unhappy personality.

Finally, they run some risk when they give themselves up to this boasting; in which again they find a semblance of life and liberty—the only thing they care for. Would not a millionaire with a rope round his neck give all his millions for one breath of air? A prisoner has lived quietly for several years in succession, his conduct has been so exemplary that he has been rewarded by special exemptions. Suddenly, to the great astonishment of his chiefs, this man becomes mutinous, plays the very devil, and does not recoil from a capital crime such as assassination, violation, etc. Every one is astounded at the cause of this unexpected explosion on the part of a man thought incapable of such a thing. It is the convulsive manifestation of his personality, an instinctive melancholia, an uncontrollable desire for self-assertion, all of which obscures his reason. It is a sort of epileptic attack, a spasm. A man buried alive who suddenly wakes up must strike in a similar manner against the lid of his coffin. He tries to rise up, to push it from him, although his reason must convince him of the uselessness of his efforts.

Reason, however, has nothing to do with this convulsion. It must not be forgotten that almost every voluntary manifestation on the part of a convict is looked upon as a crime. Accordingly, it is a perfect matter of indifference to them whether this manifestation be important or insignificant, debauch for debauch, danger for danger. It is just as well to go to the end, even as far as a murder. The only difficulty is the first step. Little by little the man becomes excited, intoxicated, and can no longer contain himself. For that reason it would be better not to drive him to extremities. Everybody would be much better for it.

But how can this be managed?

CHAPTER VII. THE FIRST MONTH (*continued*)

When I entered the convict prison I possessed a small sum of money; but I carried very little of it about with me, lest it should be confiscated. I had gummed some banknotes into the binding of my New Testament—the only book authorised in the convict prison. This New Testament had been given to me at Tobolsk, by a person who had been exiled some dozens of years, and who had got accustomed to see in other "unfortunates" a brother.

There are in Siberia people who pass their lives in giving brotherly assistance to the "unfortunates." They feel the same sympathy for them that they would have for their own children. Their compassion is something sacred and quite disinterested. I cannot help here relating in some words a meeting which I had at this time.

In the town where we were then imprisoned lived a widow, Nastasia Ivanovna. Naturally, none of us were in direct relations with this woman. She had made it the object of her life to come to the assistance of all the exiles; but, above all, of us convicts. Had there been some misfortune in her family? Had some person dear to her undergone a punishment similar to ours? I do not know. In any case, she did for us whatever she could. It is true she could do very little, for she was very poor. But we felt when we were shut up in the convict prison that, outside, we had a devoted friend. She often brought us news, which we were very glad to hear, for nothing of the kind reached us.

When I left the prison to be taken to another town, I had the opportunity of calling upon her and making her acquaintance. She lived in one of the suburbs, at the house of a near relation.

Nastasia Ivanovna was neither old nor young, neither pretty nor ugly. It was difficult, impossible even, to know whether she was intelligent and well-bred. But in her actions could be seen infinite compassion, an irresistible desire to please, to solace, to be in some way agreeable. All this could be read in the sweetness of her smile.

I passed an entire evening at her house, with other companions of my imprisonment. She looked us straight in the face, laughed when we laughed, did everything we asked her, in conversation was always of our opinion, and did her best in every way to entertain us. She gave us tea and various little delicacies. If she had been rich we felt sure she would have been pleased, if only to be able to entertain us better and offer for us some solid consolation.

When we wished her "good-bye," she gave us each a present of a cardboard cigar-case as a souvenir. She had made them herself— Heaven knows how—with coloured paper, the paper with which school-boys' copy-books are covered. All round this cardboard cigar-case she had gummed, by way of ornamentation, a thin edge of gilt paper.

"As you smoke, these cigar-cases will perhaps be of use to you," she said, as if excusing herself for making such a present.

There are people who say, as I have read and heard, that a great love for one's neighbour is only a form of selfishness. What selfishness could there be in this? That I could never understand.

Although I had not much money when I entered the convict prison, I could not nevertheless feel seriously annoyed with convicts who, immediately on my arrival, after having deceived me once, came to borrow of me a second, a third time, and even oftener. But I admitted frankly that what did annoy me was the thought that all these people, with their smiling knavery, must take me for a fool, and laugh at me just because I lent the money for the fifth time. It must have seemed to them that I was the dupe of their tricks and their deceit. If, on the contrary, I had refused them and sent them away, I am certain that they would have had much more respect for me. Still, though it vexed me very much, I could not refuse them.

I was rather anxious during the first days to know what footing I should hold in the convict prison, and what rule of conduct I should follow with my companions. I felt and perfectly understood that the place being in every way new to me, I was walking in darkness, and it would be impossible for me to live for ten years in darkness. I decided to act frankly, according to the dictates of my conscience and my personal feeling. But I also knew that this decision might be very well in theory, and that I should, in practice, be governed by unforeseen events. Accordingly, in addition to all the petty annoyances caused to me by my confinement in the convict prison, one terrible anguish laid hold of me and tormented me more and more.

"The dead-house!" I said to myself when night fell, and I looked from the threshold of our barracks at the prisoners just returned from their labours and walking about in the court-yard, from the kitchen to the barracks, and *vice versâ*. As I examined their movements and their physiognomies I endeavoured to guess what sort of men they were, and what their disposition might be.

They lounged about in front of me, some with lowered brows, others full of gaiety—one of these expressions was seen on every convict's face—exchanged insults or talked on indifferent matters. Sometimes, too, they wandered about in solitude, occupied apparently with their own reflections; some of them with a worn-out, pathetic look, others with a conceited air of superiority. Yes, here, even here!—their cap balanced on the side of their head, their sheepskin coat picturesquely over the shoulder, insolence in their eyes and mockery on their lips.

"Here is the world to which I am condemned, in which, in spite of myself, I must somehow live," I said to myself.

I endeavoured to question Akim Akimitch, with whom I liked to take my tea, in order not to be alone, for I wanted to know something about the different convicts. In parenthesis I must say that the tea, at the beginning of my imprisonment, was almost my only food. Akim Akimitch never refused to take tea with me, and he himself heated our tin tea-urns, made in the convict prison and let out to me by M——.

Akim Akimitch generally drank a glass of tea (he had glasses of his own) calmly and silently, then thanked me when he had finished, and at once went to work on my blanket; but he had not been able to tell me what I wanted to know, and did not even understand my desire to know the dispositions of the people surrounding me. He listened to me with a cunning smile which I have still before my eyes. No, I thought, I must find out for myself; it is useless to interrogate others.

The fourth day, the convicts were drawn up in two ranks, early in the morning, in the court-yard before the guard-house, close to the prison gates. Before and behind them were soldiers with loaded muskets and fixed bayonets.

The soldier has the right to fire on the convict if he tries to escape. But, on the other hand, he is answerable for his shot, if there was no absolute necessity for him to fire. The same thing applies to revolts. But who would think of openly taking to flight?

The Engineer officer arrived accompanied by the so-called "conductor" and by some non-commissioned officers of the Line, together with sappers and soldiers told off to superintend the labours of the convicts.

The roll was called. Then the convicts who were going to the tailors' workshop started first. These men worked inside the prison, and made clothes for all the inmates. The other exiles went into the outer workshops, until at last arrived the turn of the prisoners destined for field labour. I was of this number—there were altogether twenty of us. Behind the fortress on the frozen river were two barges belonging to the Government, which were not worth anything, but which had to be taken to pieces in order that the wood might not be lost. The wood was in itself all but valueless, for firewood can be bought in the town at a nominal price. The whole country is covered with forests.

This work was given to us in order that we might not remain with our arms crossed. This was understood on both sides. Accordingly, we went to it apathetically; though just the contrary happened when work had to be done, which would be profitable, or when a fixed task was assigned to us. In this latter case, although prisoners were to derive no profit from their work, they tried to get it over as soon as possible, and took a pride in doing it quickly. When such work as I am speaking of had to be done as a matter of form, rather than because it was necessary, task work could not be asked for. We had to go on until the beating of the drum at eleven o'clock called back the convicts.

The day was warm and foggy, the snow was on the point of melting. Our entire band walked towards the bank behind the fortress, shaking lightly their chains hid beneath their garments: the sound came forth clear and ringing. Two or three convicts went to get their tools from the dépôt.

I walked on with the others. I had become a little animated, for I wanted to see and know in what this field labour consisted, to what sort of work I was condemned, and how I should do it for the first time in my life.

I remember the smallest particulars. We met, as we were walking along, a townsman with a long beard, who stopped and slipped his hand into his pocket. A prisoner left our party, took off his cap and received alms—to the extent of five kopecks—then came back hurriedly towards us. The townsman made the sign of the cross and went his way. The five kopecks were spent the same morning in buying cakes of white bread which were shared equally among us. In my squad some were gloomy and taciturn, others indifferent and indolent. There were some who talked in an idle manner. One of these men was extremely gay, heaven knows why. He sang and danced as we went along, shaking and ringing his chains at each step. This fat and corpulent convict was the very one who, on the very day of my arrival during the general washing, had a quarrel with one of his companions about the water, and had ventured to compare him to some sort of bird. His name was Scuratoff. He finished by shouting out a lively song of which I remember the burden:

They married me without my consent,

When I was at the mill.

Nothing was wanting but a balalaika .

His extraordinary good-humour was justly reproved by several of the prisoners, who were offended by it.

"Listen to his hallooing," said one of the convicts, "though it doesn't become him."

"The wolf has but one song; this Tuliak is stealing it from him," said another, who could be recognised by his accent as a Little Russian.

"Of course I am from Tula," replied Scuratoff; "but we don't stuff ourselves to bursting as you do in your Pultava."

"Liar! what did you eat yourself? Bark shoes and cabbage soup?"

"You talk as if the devil fed you on sweet almonds," broke in a third.

"I admit, my friend, that I am an effeminate man," said Scuratoff with a gentle sigh, as though he were really reproaching himself for his effeminacy. "From my most tender infancy I was brought up in luxury, fed on plums and delicate cakes. My brothers even now have a large business at Moscow. They are wholesale dealers in the wind that blows; immensely rich men, as you may imagine."

"And what did you sell?"

"I was very successful, and when I received my first two hundred——"

"Roubles? impossible!" interrupted one of the prisoners, struck with amazement at hearing of so large a sum.

"No, my good fellow, not two hundred roubles, two hundred blows of the stick. Luka; I say Luka!"

"Some have the right to call me Luka, but for you I am Luka Kouzmitch," replied rather ill-temperedly a small, feeble convict with a pointed nose.

"The devil take you, you are really not worth speaking to; yet I wanted to be civil to you. But to continue my story; this is how it happened that I did not remain any longer at Moscow. I received my fifteen last strokes and was then sent off, and was at——"

"But what were you sent for?" asked a convict who had been listening attentively.

"Don't ask stupid questions. I was explaining to you how it was I did not make my fortune at Moscow; and yet how anxious I was to be rich, you could scarcely imagine how much."

Many of the prisoners began to laugh. Scuratoff was one of those lively persons, full of animal spirits, who take a pleasure in amusing their graver companions, and who, as a matter of course, received no reward except insults. He belonged to a type of men, to whose characteristics I shall, perhaps, have to return.

"And what a fellow he is now!" observed Luka Kouzmitch. "His clothes alone must be worth a hundred roubles."

Scuratoff had the oldest and greasiest sheepskin that could be seen. It was mended in many different places with pieces that scarcely hung together. He looked at Luka attentively from head to foot.

"It is my head, friend," he said, "my head that is worth money. When I took farewell of Moscow, I was half consoled, because my head was to make the journey on my shoulders. Farewell, Moscow, I shall never forget your free air, nor the tremendous flogging I got. As for my sheepskin, you are not obliged to look at it."

"You would like me, perhaps, to look at your head?"

"If it was really his own natural property, but it was given him in charity," cried Luka Kouzmitch. "It was a gift made to him at Tumen, when the convoy was passing through the town."

"Scuratoff, had you a workshop?"

"What workshop could he have? He was only a cobbler," said one of the convicts.

"It is true," said Scuratoff, without noticing the caustic tone of the speaker. "I tried to mend boots, but I never got beyond a single pair."

"And were you paid for them?"

"Well, I found a fellow who certainly neither feared God nor honoured either his father or his mother, and as a punishment, Providence made him buy the work of my hands."

The men around Scuratoff burst into a laugh.

"I also worked once at the convict prison," continued Scuratoff, with imperturbable coolness. "I did up the boots of Stepan Fedoritch, the lieutenant."

"And was he satisfied?"

"No, my dear fellows, indeed he was not; he blackguarded me enough to last me for the rest of my life. He also pushed me from behind with his knee. What a rage he was in! Ah! my life has deceived me. I see no fun in the convict prison whatever." He began to sing again.

Akolina's husband is in the court-yard.

There he waits.

Again he sang, and again he danced and leaped.

"Most unbecoming!" murmured the Little Russian, who was walking by my side.

"Frivolous man!" said another in a serious, decided tone.

I could not make out why they insulted Scuratoff, nor why they despised those convicts who were light-hearted, as they seemed to do. I attributed the anger of the Little Russian and the others to a feeling of personal hostility, but in this I was wrong. They were vexed that Scuratoff had not that puffed-up air of false dignity with which the whole of the convict prison was impregnated.

They did not, however, get annoyed with all the jokers, nor treat them all like Scuratoff. Some of them were men who would stand no nonsense, and forgive no one voluntarily or involuntarily. It was necessary to treat them with respect. There was in our band a convict of this very kind, a good-natured, lively fellow, whom I did not see in his true light until later on. He was a tall young fellow, with pleasant manners, and not without good looks. There was at the same time a very comic expression on his face.

He was called the Sapper, because he had served in the Engineers. He belonged to the special section.

But all the serious-minded convicts were not so particular as the Little Russian, who could not bear to see people gay.

We had in our prison several men who aimed at a certain pre-eminence, either in virtue of skill at their work, of their general ingenuity, of their character, or their wit. Many of them were intelligent and energetic, and reached the point they were aiming at—pre-eminence, that is to say, and moral influence over their companions. They often hated one another, and they excited general envy. They looked upon other convicts with a dignified air, that was full of condescension; and they never quarrelled without a cause. Favourably looked upon by the administration, they in some measure directed the work, and none of them would have lowered himself so far as to quarrel with a man about his songs. All these men were very polite to me during the whole time of my imprisonment, but not at all communicative.

At last we reached the bank; a little lower down was the old hulk, which we were to break up, stuck fast in the ice. On the other side of the water was the blue steppe and the sad horizon. I expected to see every one go to work at once. Nothing of the kind. Some of the convicts sat down negligently on wooden beams that were lying near the shore, and nearly all took from their pockets pouches containing native tobacco—which was sold in leaf at the market at the rate of three kopecks a pound—and short wooden pipes. They lighted them while the soldiers formed a circle around them, and began to watch us with a tired look.

"Who the devil had the idea of sinking this barque?" asked one of the convicts in a loud voice, without speaking to any one in particular.

"Were they very anxious, then, to have it broken up?"

"The people were not afraid to give us work," said another.

"Where are all those peasants going to work?" said the first, after a short silence.

He had not even heard his companion's answer. He pointed with his finger to the distance, where a troop of peasants were marching in file across the virgin snow.

All the convicts turned negligently towards this side, and began from mere idleness to laugh at the peasants as they approached them. One of them, the last of the line, walked very comically with his arms apart, and his head on one side. He wore a tall pointed cap. His shadow threw itself in clear lines on the white snow.

"Look how our brother Petrovitch is dressed," said one of my companions, imitating the pronunciation of the peasants of the locality. One amusing thing—the convicts looked down on peasants, although they were for the most part peasants by origin.

"The last one, too, above all, looks as if he were planting radishes."

"He is an important personage, he has lots of money," said a third.

They all began to laugh without, however, seeming genuinely amused.

During this time a woman selling cakes came up. She was a brisk, lively person, and it was with her that the five kopecks given by the townsman were spent.

The young fellow who sold white bread in the convict prison took two dozen of her cakes, and had a long discussion with the woman in order to get a reduction in price. She would not, however, agree to his terms.

At last the non-commissioned officer appointed to superintend the work came up with a cane in his hand.

"What are you sitting down for? Begin at once."

"Give us our tasks, Ivan Matveitch," said one of the "foremen" among us, as he slowly got up.

"What more do you want? Take out the barque, that is your task."

Then ultimately the convicts got up and went to the river, but very slowly. Different "directors" appeared, "directors," at least, in words. The barque was not to be broken up anyhow. The latitudinal and longitudinal beams were to be preserved, and this was not an easy thing to manage.

"Draw this beam out, that is the first thing to do," cried a convict who was neither a director nor a foreman, but a simple workman. This man, very quiet and a little stupid, had not previously spoken. He now bent down, took hold of a heavy beam with both hands, and waited for some one to help him. No one, however, seemed inclined to do so.

"Not you, indeed, you will never manage it; not even your grandfather, the bear, could do it," muttered some one between his teeth.

"Well, my friend, are we to begin? As for me, I can do nothing alone," said, with a morose air, the man who had put himself forward, and who now, quitting the beam, held himself upright.

"Unless you are going to do all the work by yourself, what are you in such a hurry about?"

"I was only speaking," said the poor fellow, excusing himself for his forwardness.

"Must you have blankets to keep yourselves warm, or are you to be heated for the winter?" cried a non-commissioned officer to the twenty men who seemed to loathe to begin work. "Go on at once."

"It is never any use being in a hurry, Ivan Matveitch."

"But you are doing nothing at all, Savelieff. What are you casting your eyes about for? Are they for sale, by chance? Come, go on."

"What can I do alone?"

"Set us tasks, Ivan Matveitch."

"I told you before that I had no task to give you. Attack the barque, and when you have finished we will go back to the house. Come, begin."

The prisoners began work, but with no good-will, and very indolently. The irritation of the chief at seeing these vigorous men remain so idle was intelligible enough. While the first rivet was being removed it suddenly snapped.

"It broke to pieces," said the convict in self-justification. It was impossible, then, they suggested, to work in such a manner. What was to be done? A long discussion took place between the prisoners, and little by little they came to insults; nor did this seem likely to be the end of it. The under officer cried out again as he agitated his stick, but the second rivet snapped like the first. It was then agreed that hatchets were of no use, and that other tools must be procured. Accordingly, two prisoners were sent under escort to the fortress to get the proper instruments. Waiting their return, the other convicts sat down on the bank as calmly as possible, pulled out their pipes and began again to smoke. Finally, the under officer spat with contempt.

"Well," he exclaimed, "the work you are doing will not kill you. Oh, what people, what people!" he grumbled, with an ill-natured air. He then made a gesture, and went away to the fortress, brandishing his cane.

After an hour the "conductor" arrived. He listened quietly to what the convicts had to say, declared that the task he gave them was to get off four rivets unbroken, and to demolish a good part of the barque. As soon as this was done the prisoners could go back to the house. The task was a considerable one, but, good heavens! how the convicts now went to work! Where now was their idleness, their want of skill? The hatchets soon began to dance, and soon the rivets were sprung. Those who had no hatchets made use of thick sticks to push beneath the rivets, and thus in due time and in artistic fashion, they got them out. The convicts seemed suddenly to have become intelligent in their conversation. No more insults were heard. Every one knew perfectly what to say, to do, to advise. Just half-an-hour before the beating of the drum, the appointed task was executed, and the prisoners returned to the convict prison fatigued, but pleased to have gained half-an-hour from the working time fixed by the regulations.

As regards myself, I have only one thing to say. Wherever I stood to help the workers I was never in my place; they always drove me away, and generally insulted me. Any one of the ragged lot, any miserable workman who would not have dared to say a syllable to the other convicts, all more intelligent and skilful than he, assumed the right of swearing at me if I went near him, under pretext that I interfered with him in his work. At last one of the best of them said to me frankly, but coarsely:

"What do you want here? Be off with you! Why do you come when no one calls you?"

"That is it," added another.

"You would do better to take a pitcher," said a third, "and carry water to the house that is being built, or go to the tobacco factory. You are no good here."

I was obliged to keep apart. To remain idle while others were working seemed a shame; but when I went to the other end of the barque I was insulted anew.

"What men we have to work!" was the cry. "What can be done with fellows of this kind?"

All this was said spitefully. They were pleased to have the opportunity of laughing at a gentleman.

It will now be understood that my first thought on entering the convict prison was to ask myself how I should ever get on with such people. I foresaw that such incidents would often be repeated; but I resolved not to change my conduct in any way, whatever might be the result. I had decided to live simply and intelligently, without manifesting the least desire to approach my companions; but also without repelling them, if they themselves desired to approach me; in no way to fear their threats or their hatred; and to pretend as much as possible not to be affected by them. Such was my plan. I saw from the first that they would despise me, if I adopted any other course.

When I returned in the evening to the convict prison, having finished my afternoon's work, fatigued and harassed, a deep sadness took possession of me. "How many thousands of days have I to pass like this one?" Always the same thought. I walked about alone and meditated as night fell, when, suddenly, near the palisade behind the barracks, I saw my friend, Bull, who ran towards me.

Bull was the dog of the prison; for the prison has its dog as companies of infantry, batteries of artillery, and squadrons of cavalry have theirs. He had been there for a long time, belonged to no one, looked upon every one as his master, and lived on the remains from the kitchen. He was a good-sized black dog, spotted with white, not very old, with intelligent eyes, and a bushy tail. No one caressed him or paid the least attention to him. As soon as I arrived I made friends with him by giving him a piece of bread. When I patted him on the back he remained motionless, looked at me with a pleased expression, and gently wagged his tail.

That evening, not having seen me the whole day—me, the first person who in so many years had thought of caressing him—he ran towards me, leaping and barking. It had such an effect on me that I could not help embracing him. I placed his head against my body. He placed his paws on my shoulders and looked me in the face.

"Here is a friend sent to me by destiny," I said to myself, and during the first weeks, so full of pain, every time that I came back from work I hastened, before doing anything else, to go to the back of the barracks with Bull, who leaped with joy before me. I took his head in my hands and kissed it. At the same time a troubled, bitter feeling pressed my heart. I well remember thinking—and taking pleasure in the thought—that this was my one, my only friend in the world—my faithful dog, Bull.

CHAPTER VIII. NEW ACQUAINTANCES—PETROFF

Time went on, and little by little I accustomed myself to my new life. The scenes I had daily before me no longer afflicted me so much. In a word, the convict prison, its inhabitants, and its manners, left me indifferent. To get reconciled to this life was impossible, but I had to accept it as an inevitable fact. I had driven entirely away from me all the anxiety by which I had at first been troubled. I no longer wandered through the convict prison like a lost soul, and no longer allowed myself to be subjugated by my anxiety. The wild curiosity of the convicts had had its edge taken off, and I was no longer looked upon with that affectation or insolence previously displayed. They had become indifferent to me, and I was very glad of it. I began to feel at home in the barracks. I knew where to go and sleep at night; gradually I became accustomed to things the very idea of which would formerly have been repugnant to me. I went every week regularly to have my head shaved. We were called every Saturday one after another to the guard-house. The regimental barbers lathered our skulls with cold water and soap, and scraped us afterwards with their saw-like razors.

Merely the thought of this torture gives me a shudder. I soon found a remedy for it—Akim Akimitch pointed it out to me—a prisoner in the military section who for one kopeck shaved those who paid for it with his own razor. This was his trade. Many of the prisoners were his customers merely to avoid the military barbers, yet these were not men of weak nerves. Our barber was called the "major," why, I cannot say. As far as I know he possessed no points of resemblance with any major. As I write these lines I see clearly before me the "major" and his thin face. He was a tall fellow, silent, rather stupid, absorbed entirely by his business; he was never to be seen without a strop in his hand, on which day and night he sharpened a razor, which was always in admirable condition. He had certainly made this work the supreme object of his life; he was really happy when his razor was quite sharp and his services were in request; his soap was always warm, and he had a very light hand—a hand of velvet. He was proud of his skill, and used to take with a careless air the kopeck he received; one might have thought that he worked from love of his art, and not in order to gain money.

A——f was soundly corrected by our real Major one day, because he had the misfortune to say the "major" when he was speaking of the barber who shaved him. The real Major was in a violent rage.

"Blackguard," he cried, "do you know what a major is?" and according to his habit he shook A——f violently. "The idea of calling a scoundrel of a convict a 'major' in my presence."

From the first day of my imprisonment I began to dream of my liberation. My favourite occupation was to count thousands and thousands of times in a thousand different manners the number of days that I should have to pass in prison. I thought of that only, and every one deprived of his liberty for a fixed time does the same; of that I am certain. I cannot say that all the convicts had the same degree of hopefulness, but their sanguine character often astonished me. The hopefulness of a prisoner differs essentially from that of a free man. The latter may desire an amelioration in his position, or a realisation of some enterprise which he has undertaken, but meanwhile he lives, he acts; he is swept away in the whirlwind of real life. Nothing of the kind takes place in the case of the convict for life. He lives also in a way, but not being condemned to a fixed number of years, he takes a vaguer view of his situation than the one who is imprisoned for a definite term. The man condemned for a comparatively short period feels that he is not at home; he looks upon himself, so to say, as on a visit; he regards the twenty years of his punishment as two years at most; he is sure that at fifty, when he has finished his sentence, he will be as young and as lively as at thirty-five. "We have time before us," he thinks, and he strives obstinately to dispel discouraging thoughts. Even a man sentenced for life thinks that some day an order may arrive from St. Petersburg—"Transport such a one to the mines at Nertchinsk and fix a term for his detention." It would be famous, first because it takes six months to get to Nertchinsk, and the life on the road is a hundred times preferable to the convict prison. He would finish his time at Nertchinsk, and then—more than one gray-haired old man speculates in this way.

At Tobolsk I have seen men fastened to the wall by a chain about two yards long; by their side they have their bed. They are thus chained for some terrible crime committed after their transportation to Siberia; they are kept chained up for five, ten years. They are nearly all brigands, and I only saw one of them who looked like a man of good breeding; he had been in some branch of the Civil Service, and spoke in a soft, lisping way; his smile was sweet but sickly; he showed us his chain, and pointed out to us the most convenient way of lying down. He must have been a nice person! All these poor wretches are perfectly well-behaved; they all seem satisfied, and yet their desire to finish their period of chains devours them. Why? it will be asked. Because then they will leave their low, damp, stifling cells for the court-yard of the convict prison, that is all. These last places of confinement they will never leave; they know that those who have once been chained up will never be liberated, and they will die in irons. They know all this, and yet they are very anxious to be no longer chained up. Without this hope could they remain five or six years fastened to a wall, and not die or go mad?

I soon understood that work alone could save me, by fortifying my health and my body, whereas incessant restlessness of mind, nervous irritation, and the close air of the barracks would ruin them completely. I should go out vigorous and full of elasticity. I did not deceive myself, work and movement were very useful to me.

I saw one of my comrades, to my terror, melt away like a piece of wax; and yet, when he was with me in the convict prison, he was young, handsome, and vigorous; when he left his health was ruined, and his legs could no longer support him. His chest, too, was oppressed by asthma.

"No," I said to myself, as I gazed upon him; "I wish to live, and I will live."

My love for work exposed me in the first place to the contempt and bitter laughter of my comrades; but I paid no attention to them, and went away with a light heart wherever I was sent. Sometimes, for instance, to break and pound alabaster. This work, the first that was given to me, is easy. The engineers did their utmost to lighten the task-work of all the gentlemen; this was not indulgence, but simple justice. Would it not have been strange to require the same work from a labourer as from a man whose strength was less by half, and who had never worked with his hands? But we were not "spoilt" in this way for ever, and we were only spared in secret, for we were severely watched. As real severe work was by no means rare, it often happened that the task given to us was beyond the strength of the gentlemen, who thus suffered twice as much as their comrades.

Generally three or four men were sent to pound the alabaster, and nearly always old men or feeble ones were chosen. We were of the latter class. A man skilled in this particular kind of work was sent with us. For several years it was always the same man, Almazoff by name. He was severe, already in years, sunburnt, and very thin, by no means communicative, moreover, and difficult to get on with. He despised us profoundly; but he was of such a reserved disposition that he never broke it sufficient to call us names. The shed in which we calcined the alabaster was built on a sloping and deserted bank of the river. In winter, on a foggy day, the view was sad, both on the river and on the opposite shore, even to a great distance. There was something heartrending in this dull, naked landscape, but it was still sadder when a brilliant sun shone above the boundless white plain. How one would have liked to fly away beyond this steppe, which began on the opposite shore and stretched out for fifteen hundred versts to the south like an immense table-cloth.

Almazoff went to work silently, with a disagreeable air. We were ashamed not to be able to help him more effectually, but he managed to do his work without our assistance, and seemed to wish to make us understand that we were acting unjustly towards him, and that we ought to repent our uselessness. Our work consisted in heating the oven in order to calcine the alabaster that we had got together in a heap.

The day following, when the alabaster was entirely calcined, we turned it out. Each one filled a box of alabaster, which he afterwards crushed. This work was not disagreeable. The fragile alabaster soon became a white, brilliant dust. We brandished our heavy hammers, and dealt such formidable blows, that we admired our own strength. When we were tired we felt lighter, our cheeks were red, the blood circulated more rapidly in our veins. Almazoff would then look at us in a condescending manner, as he would have looked at little children. He smoked his pipe with an indulgent air, unable, however, to prevent himself from grumbling. When he opened his mouth he was never otherwise, and he was the same with every one. At bottom I believe he was a kind man.

They gave me another kind of labour, which consisted in working the turning wheel. This wheel was high and heavy, and great efforts were necessary to make it go round, above all when the workmen from the workshop of the engineers used to make the balustrade of a staircase or the foot of a large table, which required almost the whole trunk. No one man could have done the work alone. To two convicts, B—— (formerly gentleman) and myself, this work was given nearly always for several years, whenever there was anything to turn. B—— was weak, even still young, and somewhat sympathetic. He had been sent to prison a year before me, with two companions who were also of noble birth. One of them, an old man, used to pray day and night. The prisoners respected him greatly for it. He died in prison. The other one was quite a young man, fresh-coloured, strong, and courageous. He had carried his companion B—— for several hundred versts, seeing that at the end of the first half-stage he had fallen down from fatigue. Their friendship for one another was something to see.

B—— was a perfectly well-bred man, of noble and generous disposition, but spoiled and irritated by illness. We used to turn the wheel well together, and the work interested us. As for me, I found the exercise most salutary.

I was very—too—fond of shovelling away the snow, which we generally did after the hurricanes, so frequent in the winter. When the hurricane had been raging for an entire day, more than one house would be buried up to the windows, even if it was not covered over entirely. The hurricane ceased, the sun reappeared, and we were ordered to disengage the houses, barricaded as they were by heaps of snow.

We were sent in large bands, sometimes the whole of the convicts together. Each of us received a shovel and had an appointed task to do, which it sometimes seemed impossible to get through. But we all went to work with a good-will. The light dust-like snow had not yet congealed, and was frozen only on the surface. We removed it in enormous shovelfuls, which were dispersed around us. In the air the snow-dust was as brilliant as diamonds. The shovel sank easily into the white glittering mass. The convicts did this work almost always with gaiety, the cold winter air and the exercise animated them. Every one felt himself in better spirits, laughter and jokes were heard, snowballs were exchanged, which after a time excited the indignation of the serious-minded convicts, who liked neither laughter nor gaiety. Accordingly these scenes finished almost always in showers of insults.

Little by little the circle of my acquaintances increased, although I never thought of making new ones. I was always restless, morose, and mistrustful. Acquaintances, however, were made involuntarily. The first who came to visit me was the convict Petroff. I say visit, and I retain the word, for he lived in the special division which was at the farthest end of the barracks from mine. It seemed as if no relations could exist between him and me, for we had nothing in common.

Nevertheless, during the first period of my stay, Petroff thought it his duty to come towards me nearly every day, or at least to stop me when, after work, I went for a stroll at the back of the barracks as far as possible from observation. His persistence was disagreeable to me; but he managed so well that his visits became at last a pleasing diversion, although he was by no means of a communicative disposition. He was short, strongly built, agile, and skilful. He had rather an agreeable voice, and high cheek-bones, a bold look, and white, regular teeth. He had always a quid of tobacco in his mouth between the lower lip and the gums. Many of the convicts had the habit of chewing. He seemed to me younger than he really was, for he did not appear to be more than thirty, and he was really forty. He spoke to me without any ceremony, and behaved to me on a footing of equality with civility and attention. If, for instance, he saw that I wished to be alone, he would talk to me for about two minutes and then go away. He thanked me, moreover, each time for my kindness in conversing with him, which he never did to any one else. I must add that his relations underwent no change not only during the first period of my story, but for several years, and that they never became more intimate, although he was really my friend. I never could say exactly what he looked for in my society, nor why he came every day to see me. He robbed me sometimes, but almost involuntarily. He never came to me to borrow money; so that what attracted him was not personal interest.

It seemed to me, I know not why, that this man did not live in the same prison with me, but in another house in the town, far away. It appeared as though he had come to the convict prison by chance in order to pick up news, to inquire for me, in short, to see how I was getting on. He was always in a hurry, as though he had left some one for a moment who was waiting for him, or as if he had given up for a time some matter of business. And yet he never hurried himself. His look was strongly fixed, with a slight air of levity and irony. He had a habit of looking into the distance above the objects near him, as though he were endeavouring to distinguish something behind the person to whom he was talking. He always seemed absent-minded. I sometimes asked myself where he went when he left me, where could Petroff be so anxiously expected? He would simply go with a light step to one of the barracks or to the kitchen, and sit down to hear the conversation. He listened attentively, and joined in with animation; after which he would suddenly become silent. But whether he spoke or kept silent, one could always see on his countenance that he had business somewhere else, and that some one was waiting for him in the town, not very far away. The most astonishing thing was that he never had any business—apart, of course, from the hard labour assigned to him. He knew no trade, and had scarcely ever any money. But that did not seem to grieve him. Why did he speak to me? His conversation was as strange as he himself was singular. When he noticed that I was walking alone at the back of the barracks he made a stand, and turned towards me. He walked very fast, and when I turned he was suddenly on his heel. He approached me walking, but so quickly that he seemed to be going at a run.

"Good-morning."

"Good-morning."

"I am not disturbing you?"

"No."

"I wish to ask you something about Napoleon. I wanted to ask you if he is not a relation of the one who came to us in the year 1812."

Petroff was a soldier's son, and knew how to read and write.

"Of course he is."

"People say he is President. What President—and of what?"

His questions were always rapid and abrupt, as though he wished to know as soon as possible what he asked. I explained to him of what Napoleon was President, and I added that perhaps he would become Emperor.

"How will that be?"

I explained it to him as well as I could; Petroff listened with attention. He understood perfectly all I told him, and added, as he leant his ear towards me:

"Hem! Ah, I wished to ask you, Alexander Petrovitch, if there are really monkeys who have hands instead of feet, and are as tall as a man?"

"Yes."

"What are they like?"

I described them to him, and told him what I knew on the subject.

"And where do they live?"

"In warm climates. There are some to be found in the island of Sumatra."

"Is that in America? I have heard that people there walk with their heads downwards."

"No, no; you are thinking of the Antipodes." I explained to him as well as I could what America was, and what the Antipodes. He listened to me as attentively as if the question of the Antipodes had alone caused him to approach me.

"Ah, ah! I read last year the story of the Countess de la Vallière. Arevieff had bought this book from the Adjutant. Is it true or is it an invention? The work is by Dumas."

"It is an invention, no doubt."

"Ah, indeed. Good-bye. I am much obliged to you."

And Petroff disappeared. The above may be taken as a specimen of our ordinary conversation.

I made inquiries about him. M—— thought he had better speak to me on the subject, when he learnt what an acquaintance I had made. He told me that many convicts had excited his horror on their arrival; but not one of them, not even Gazin, had produced upon him such a frightful impression as this Petroff.

"He is the most resolute, most to be feared of all the convicts," said M——. "He is capable of anything, nothing stops him if he has a caprice. He will assassinate you, if the fancy takes him, without hesitation and without the least remorse. I often think he is not in his right senses."

This declaration interested me extremely; but M—— was never able to tell me why he had such an opinion of Petroff. Strangely enough, for many years together I saw this man and talked with him nearly every day. He was always my sincere friend, though I could not at the time tell why, and during the whole time he lived very quietly, and did nothing extreme. I am moreover convinced that M—— was right, and that he was perhaps a most intrepid man and the most difficult to restrain in the whole prison. And why so, I can scarcely explain.

This Petroff was that very convict who, when he was called up to receive his punishment, had wished to kill the Major. I have told you the latter was saved by a miracle—that he had gone away one minute before the punishment was inflicted.

Once when he was still a soldier—before his arrival at the convict prison—his Colonel had struck him on parade. Probably he had often been beaten before, but that day he was not in a humour to bear an insult, in open day, before the battalion drawn up in line. He killed his Colonel. I don't know all the details of the story, for he never told it to me himself. It must be understood that these explosions only took place when the nature within him spoke too loudly, and these occasions were rare; as a rule he was serious and even quiet. His strong, ardent passions were not burnt out, but smouldering, like burning coals beneath ashes.

I never noticed that he was vain, or given to bragging like so many other convicts. He hardly ever quarrelled, but he was on friendly relations with scarcely any one, except, perhaps, Sirotkin, and then only when he had need of him. I saw him, however, one day seriously irritated. Some one had offended him by refusing him something he wanted. He was disputing on the point with a tall convict, as vigorous as an athlete, named Vassili Antonoff, known for his nagging, spiteful disposition. The man, however, who belonged to the class of civil convicts, was far from being a coward. They shouted at one another for some time, and I thought the quarrel would finish like so many others of the same kind, by simple interchange of abuse. The affair took an unexpected turn. Petroff only suddenly turned pale, his lips trembled, and turned blue, his respiration became difficult. He got up, and slowly, very slowly, and with imperceptible steps—he liked to walk about with his feet naked—approached Antonoff; at once the noise of shouting gave place to a death-like silence—a fly passing through the air might have been heard—every one anxiously awaited the event. Antonoff pointed to his adversary. His face was no longer human. I was unable to endure the scene, and I left the prison. I was certain that before I got to the staircase I should hear the shrieks of a man who was being murdered; but nothing of the kind took place. Before Petroff had succeeded in getting up to Antonoff, the latter threw him the object which had caused the quarrel—a miserable rag, a worn-out piece of lining.

Of course afterwards, Antonoff did not fail to call Petroff names, merely as a matter of conscience, and from a feeling of what was right, in order to show that he had not been too much afraid; but Petroff paid no attention to his insults, he did not even answer him. Everything had ended to his advantage, and the insults scarcely affected him; he was glad to have got his piece of rag.

A quarter of an hour later he was strolling about the barracks quite unoccupied, looking for some group whose conversation might possibly gratify his curiosity. Everything seemed to interest him, and yet he remained apparently indifferent to all he heard. He might have been compared to a workman, a vigorous workman, whom the work fears; but who, for the moment, has nothing to do, and condescends meanwhile to put out his strength in playing with his children. I did not understand why he remained in prison, why he did not escape. He would not have hesitated to get away if he had really desired to do so. Reason has no power on people like Petroff unless they are spurred on by will. When they desire something there are no obstacles in their way. I am certain that he would have been clever enough to escape, that he would have deceived every one, that he would have remained for a time without eating, hid in a forest, or in the bulrushes of the river; but the idea had evidently not occurred to him. I never noticed in him much judgment or good sense. People like him are born with one idea, which, without being aware of it, pursues them all their life. They wander until they meet with some object which apparently excites their desire, and then they do not mind risking their head. I was sometimes astonished that a man who had assassinated his Colonel for having been struck, would lie down without opposition beneath the rods, for he was always flogged when he was detected introducing spirits into the prison. Like all those who had no settled occupation, he smuggled in spirits; then, if caught, he would allow himself to be whipped as though he consented to the punishment, and confessed himself in the wrong. Otherwise they would have killed him rather than make him lie down. More than once I was astonished to see that he was robbing me in spite of his affection for me; but he did so from time to time. Thus he stole my Bible, which I had asked him to carry to its place. He had only a few steps to go; but on his way he met with a purchaser, to whom he sold the book, at once spending the money he had received on vodka. Probably he felt that day a violent desire for drink, and when he desired something it was necessary that he should have it. A man like Petroff will assassinate any one for twenty-five kopecks, simply to get himself a pint of vodka. On any other occasion he will disdain hundreds and thousands of roubles. He told me the same evening of the theft he had committed, but without showing the least sign of repentance or confusion, in a perfectly indifferent tone, as though he were speaking of an ordinary incident. I endeavoured to reprove him as he deserved, for I regretted the loss of my Bible. He listened to me without hesitation very calmly. He agreed that the Bible was a very useful book, and sincerely regretted that I had it no longer; but he was not for one moment sorry, though he had stolen it. He looked at me with such assurance that I gave up scolding him. He bore my reproaches because he thought I could not do otherwise than I was doing. He knew that he ought to be punished for such an action, and consequently thought I ought to abuse him for my own satisfaction, and to console myself for my loss. But in his inner heart he considered that it was all nonsense, to which a serious man ought to be ashamed to descend. I believe even that he looked upon me as a child, an infant, who does not yet understand the simplest things in the world. If I spoke to him of anything, except books and matters of knowledge, he would answer me, but only from politeness, and in laconic phrases. I wondered what made him question me so much on the subject of books. I looked at him carefully during our conversation to assure myself that he was not laughing at me; but no, he listened seriously, and with an attention which was genuine, though not always maintained. This latter circumstance irritated me sometimes. The questions he put to me were clear and precise, and he always seemed prepared for the answer. He had made up his mind once for all that it was no use speaking to me as to other matters, and that, apart from books, I understood nothing. I am certain that he was attached to me, and much that fact astonished me; but he looked upon me as a child, or as an imperfect man. He felt for me that sort of compassion which every stronger being feels for a weaker; he took me for—I do not know what he took me for. Although this compassion did not prevent him from robbing me, I am sure that in doing so he pitied me.

"What a strange person!" he must have said to himself, as he lay hands on my property; "he does not even know how to take care of what he possesses." That, I think, is why he liked me. One day he said to me as if involuntarily:

"You are too good-natured, you are so simple, so simple that one cannot help pitying you. Do not be offended at what I was saying to you, Alexander Petrovitch," he added a minute afterwards, "it is not ill-meant."

People like Petroff will sometimes, in times of trouble and excitement, manifest themselves in a forcible manner; then they find the kind of activity which suits them; they are not men of words; they could not be instigators and chiefs of insurrections, but they are the men who execute and act; they act simply without any fuss, and run just to throw themselves against an obstacle with bared breast, neither thinking nor fearing. Every one follows them to the foot of the wall, where they generally leave their life. I do not think Petroff can have ended well, he was marked for a violent end; and if he is not yet dead, that only means that the opportunity has not yet presented itself. Who knows, however? He will, perhaps, die of extreme old age, quite quietly, after having wandered through life, here and there, without an object; but I believe M—— was right, and that Petroff was the most determined man in the whole convict prison.

CHAPTER IX. MEN OF DETERMINATION—LUKA

It is difficult to speak of these men of determination. In the convict prison, as elsewhere, they are rare. They can be known by the fear they inspire; people beware of them. An irresistible feeling urged me first of all to turn away from them, but I afterwards changed my point of view, even in regard to the most frightful murderers. There are men who have never killed any one, and who, nevertheless, are more atrocious than those who have assassinated six persons. It is impossible to form an idea of certain crimes, of so strange a nature are they.

A type of murderers that one often meets with is the following: A man lives calmly and peacefully. His fate is a hard one, but he puts up with it. He is a peasant attached to the soil, a domestic serf, a shopkeeper, or a soldier. Suddenly he finds something give way within him; what he has hitherto suffered he can bear no longer, and he plunges his knife into the breast of his oppressor or his enemy. He then goes beyond all measure. He has killed his oppressor, his enemy. That can be understood—there was cause for that crime; but afterwards he does not assassinate his enemies alone, but the first person he happens to meet he kills for the pleasure of killing—for an abusive word, for a look, to make an equal number, or only because some one is standing in his way. He behaves like a drunken man—a man in a delirium. When once he has passed the fatal line, he is himself astonished to find that nothing sacred exists for him. He breaks through all laws, defies all powers, and gives himself boundless license. He enjoys the agitation of his own heart and the terror that he inspires. He knows all the same that a frightful punishment awaits him. His sensations are probably like those of a man who, looking down from a high tower on to the abyss yawning at his feet, would be happy to throw himself head first into it in order to bring everything to an end. That is what happens with even the most quiet, the most commonplace individuals. There are some even who give themselves airs in this extremity. The more they were quiet, self-effacing before, the more they now swagger and seek to inspire fear. The desperate men enjoy the horror they cause; they take pleasure in the disgust they excite; they perform acts of madness from despair, and care nothing how it must all end, or seem impatient that it should end as soon as possible. The most curious thing is that their excitement, their exaltation, will last until the pillory. After that the thread is cut, the moment is fatal, and the man becomes suddenly calm, or, rather, he becomes extinct, a thing without feeling. In the pillory all his strength fails him, and he begs pardon of the people. Once at the convict prison, he is quite different. No one would ever imagine that this white-livered chicken had killed five or six men.

There are some men whom the convict prison does not easily subdue. They preserve a certain swagger, a spirit of bravado.

"I say, I am not what you take me for; I have sent six fellows out of the world," you will hear them boast; but sooner or later they have all to submit. From time to time, the murderer will amuse himself by recalling his audacity, his lawlessness when he was in a state of despair.

He likes at these moments to have some silly fellow before whom he can brag, and to whom he will relate his heroic deeds, by pretending not to have the least wish to astonish him. "That is the sort of man I am," he says.

And with what a refinement of prudent conceit he watches him while he is delivering his narrative! In his accent, in every word, this can be perceived. Where did he acquire this particular kind of artfulness?

During the long evening of one of the first days of my confinement, I was listening to one of these conversations. Thanks to my inexperience I took the narrator for the malefactor, a man with an iron character, a man to whom Petroff was nothing. The narrator, Luka Kouzmitch, had "knocked over" a Major, for no other reason but that it pleased him to do so. This Luka Kouzmitch was the smallest and thinnest man in all the barracks. He was from the South. He had been a serf, one of those not attached to the soil, but who serve their masters as domestics. There was something cutting and haughty in his demeanour. He was a little bird, but had a beak and nails. The convicts sum up a man instinctively. They thought nothing of this one, he was too susceptible and too full of conceit.

That evening he was stitching a shirt, seated on his camp-bedstead. Close to him was a narrow-minded, stupid, but good-natured and obliging fellow, a sort of Colossus, Kobylin by name. Luka often quarrelled with him in a neighbourly way, and treated him with a haughtiness which, thanks to his good-nature, Kobylin did not notice in the least. He was knitting a stocking, and listening to Luka with an indifferent air. Luka spoke in a loud voice and very distinctly. He wished every one to hear him, though he was apparently speaking only to Kobylin.

"I was sent away," said Luka, sticking his needle in the shirt, "as a brigand."

"How long ago?" asked Kobylin.

"When the peas are ripe it will be just a year. Well, we got to K——v, and I was put into the convict prison. Around me there were a dozen men from Little Russia, well-built, solid, robust fellows, like oxen, and how quiet! The food was bad, the Major of the prison did what he liked. One day passed, then another, and I soon saw that all these fellows were cowards.

"'You are afraid of such an idiot?' I said to them.

"'Go and talk to him yourself,' and they burst out laughing like brutes that they were. I held my tongue.

"There was one fellow so droll, so droll," added the narrator, now leaving Kobylin to address all who chose to listen.

"This droll fellow was telling them how he had been tried, what he had said, and how he had wept with hot tears.

"'There was a dog of a clerk there,' he said, 'who did nothing but write and take down every word I said. I told him I wished him at the devil, and he actually wrote that down. He troubled me so, that I quite lost my head.'"

"Give me some thread, Vasili; the house thread is bad, rotten."

"There is some from the tailor's shop," replied Vasili, handing it over to him.

"Well, but about this Major?" said Kobylin, who had been quite forgotten.

Luka was only waiting for that. He did not go on at once with his story, as though Kobylin were not worth such a mark of attention. He threaded his needle quietly, bent his legs lazily beneath him, and at last continued as follows:

"I excited the fellows to such an extent that they all called out against the Major. That same morning I had borrowed the 'rascal' from my neighbour, and had hid it, so as to be ready for anything. When the Major arrived, he was as furious as a madman. 'Come now, you Little Russians,' I whispered to them, 'this is not the time for fear.' But, dear me, all their courage had slipped down to the soles of their feet, they trembled! The Major came in, he was quite drunk.

"'What is this, how do you dare? I am your Tzar, your God,' he cried.

"When he said that he was the Tzar and God, I went up to him with my knife in my sleeve.

"'No,' I said to him, 'your high nobility,' and I got nearer and nearer to him, 'that cannot be. Your "high nobility" cannot be our Tzar and our God.'

"'Ah, you are the man, it is you,' cried the Major; 'you are the leader of them.'

"'No,' I answered, and I got still nearer to him; 'no, your "high nobility," as every one knows, and as you yourself know, the all-powerful God present everywhere is alone in heaven. And we have only one Tzar placed above every one else by God himself. He is our monarch, your "high nobility." And, your "high nobility," you are as yet only Major, and you are our chief only by the grace of the Tzar, and by your merits.'

"'How? how? how?' stammered the Major. He could not speak, so astounded was he.

"This is how I answered, and I threw myself upon him and thrust my knife into his belly up to the hilt. It had been done very quickly; the Major tottered, turned, and fell.

"I had thrown my life away.

"'Now, you fellows,' I cried, 'it is for you to pick him up.'"

I will here make a digression from my narrative. The expression, "I am the Tzar! I am God!" and other similar ones were once, unfortunately, too often employed in the good old times by many commanders. I must admit that their number has seriously diminished, and perhaps even the last has already disappeared. Let me observe that those who spoke in this way were, above all, men promoted from the ranks. The grade of officer had turned their brain upside down. After having laboured long years beneath the knapsack, they suddenly found themselves officers, commanders, and nobles above all. Thanks to their not being accustomed to it, and to the first excitement caused by their promotion, they contracted an exaggerated idea of their power and importance relatively to their subordinates. Before their superiors such men are revoltingly servile. The most fawning of them will even say to their superiors that they have been common soldiers, and that they do not forget their place. But towards their inferiors they are despots without mercy. Nothing irritates the convicts so much as such abuses. These overweening opinions of their own greatness; this exaggerated idea of their immunity, causes hatred in the hearts of the most submissive men, and drives the most patient to excesses. Fortunately, all this dates from a time that is almost forgotten, and even then the superior authorities used to deal very severely with abuses of power. I know more than one example of it. What exasperates the convicts above all is disdain or repugnance manifested by any one in dealing with them. Those who think that it is only necessary to feed and clothe the prisoner, and to act towards him in all things according to the law, are much mistaken. However much debased he may be, a man exacts instinctively respect for his character as a man. Every prisoner knows perfectly that he is a convict and a reprobate, and knows the distance which separates him from his superiors; but neither the branding irons nor chains will make him forget that he is a man. He must, therefore, be treated with humanity. Humane treatment may raise up one in whom the divine image has long been obscured. It is with the "unfortunate," above all, that humane conduct is necessary. It is their salvation, their only joy. I have met with some chiefs of a kind and noble character, and I have seen what a beneficent influence they exercised over the poor, humiliated men entrusted to their care. A few affable words have a wonderful moral effect upon the prisoners. They render them as happy as children, and make them sincerely grateful towards their chiefs. One other remark—they do not like their chiefs to be familiar and too much hail-fellow-well-met with them. They wish to respect them, and familiarity would prevent this. The prisoners will feel proud, for instance, if their chief has a number of decorations; if he has good manners; if he is well-considered by a powerful superior; if he is severe, but at the same time just, and possesses a consciousness of dignity. The convicts prefer such a man to all others. He knows what he is worth, and does not insult others. Everything then is for the best.

"You got well skinned for that, I suppose," asked Kobylin.

"As for being skinned, indeed, there is no denying it. Ali, give me the scissors. But, what next; are we not going to play at cards to-night?"

"The cards we drank up long ago," remarked Vassili. "If we had not sold them to get drink they would be here now."

"If!—— Ifs fetch a hundred roubles a piece on the Moscow market."

"Well, Luka, what did you get for sticking him?" asked Kobylin.

"It brought me five hundred strokes, my friend. It did indeed. They did all but kill me," said Luka, once more addressing the assembly and without heeding his neighbour Kobylin. "When they gave me those five hundred strokes, I was treated with great ceremony. I had never before been flogged. What a mass of people came to see me! The whole town had assembled to see the brigand, the murderer, receive his punishment. How stupid the populace is!—I cannot tell you to what extent. Timoshka the executioner undressed me and laid me down and cried out, 'Look out, I am going to grill you!' I waited for the first stroke. I wanted to cry out, but could not. It was no use opening my mouth, my voice had gone. When he gave me the second stroke—you need not believe me unless you please—I did not hear when they counted two. I returned to myself and heard them count seventeen. Four times they took me down from the board to let me breathe for half-an-hour, and to souse me with cold water. I stared at them with my eyes starting from my head, and said to myself, 'I shall die here.'"

"But you did not die," remarked Kobylin innocently.

Luka looked at him with disdain, and every one burst out laughing.

"What an idiot! Is he wrong in the upper storey?" said Luka, as if he regretted that he had condescended to speak to such an idiot.

"He is a little mad," said Vassili on his side.

Although Luka had killed six persons, no one was ever afraid of him in the prison. He wished, however, to be looked upon as a terrible person.

CHAPTER X. ISAIAH FOMITCH—THE BATH—BAKLOUCHIN.

But the Christmas holidays were approaching, and the convicts looked forward to them with solemnity. From their mere appearance it was easy to see that something extraordinary was about to arrive. Four days before the holidays they were to be taken to the bath; every one was pleased, and was making preparations. We were to go there after dinner. On this occasion there was no work in the afternoon, and of all the convicts the one who was most pleased, and showed the greatest activity, was a certain Isaiah Fomitch Bumstein, a Jew, of whom I spoke in my fifth chapter. He liked to remain stewing in the bath until he became unconscious. Whenever I think of the prisoner's bath, which is a thing not to be forgotten, the first thought that presents itself to my memory is of that very glorious and eternally to be remembered, Isaiah Fomitch Bumstein, my prison companion. Good Lord! what a strange man he was! I have already said a few words about his face. He was fifty years of age, his face wrinkled, with frightful scars on his cheeks and on his forehead, and the thin, weak body of a fowl. His face expressed perpetual confidence in himself, and, I may almost say, perfect happiness. I do not think he was at all sorry to be condemned to hard labour. He was a jeweller by trade, and as there was no other in the town, he had always plenty of work to do, and was more or less well paid. He wanted nothing, and lived, so to say, sumptuously, without spending all that he gained, for he saved money and lent it out to the other convicts at interest. He possessed a tea-urn, a mattress, a tea-cup, and a blanket. The Jews of the town did not refuse him their patronage. Every Saturday he went under escort to the synagogue (which was authorised by the law); and he lived like a fighting cock. Nevertheless, he looked forward to the expiration of his term of imprisonment in order to get married. He was the most comic mixture of simplicity, stupidity, cunning, timidity, and bashfulness; but the strangest thing was that the convicts never laughed, or seriously mocked him—they only teased him for amusement. Isaiah Fomitch was a subject of distraction and amusement for every one.

"We have only one Isaiah Fomitch, we will take care of him," the convicts seemed to say; and as if he understood this, he was proud of his own importance. From the account given to me it appeared he had entered the convict prison in the most laughable manner (it took place before my arrival). Suddenly one evening a report was spread in the convict prison that a Jew had been brought there, who at that moment was being shaved in the guard-house, and that he was immediately afterwards to be taken to the barracks. As there was not a single Jew in the prison, the convicts looked forward to his entry with impatience, and surrounded him as soon as he passed the great gates. The officer on service took him to the civil prison, and pointed out the place where his plank bedstead was to be.

Isaiah Fomitch held in his hand a bag containing the things given to him, and some other things of his own. He put down his bag, took his place at the plank bedstead, and sat down there with his legs crossed, without daring to raise his eyes. People were laughing all round him. The convicts ridiculed him by reason of his Jewish origin. Suddenly a young convict left the others, and came up to him, carrying in his hand an old pair of summer trousers, dirty, torn, and mended with old rags. He sat down by the side of Isaiah Fomitch, and struck him on the shoulder.

"Well, my dear fellow," said he, "I have been waiting for the last six years; look up and tell me how much you will give for this article," holding up his rags before him.

Isaiah Fomitch was so dumbfounded that he did not dare to look at the mocking crowd, with mutilated and frightful countenances, now grouped around him, and did not speak a single word, so frightened was he. When he saw who was speaking to him he shuddered, and began to examine the rags carefully. Every one waited to hear his first words.

"Well, cannot you give me a silver rouble for it? It is certainly worth that," said the would-be vendor smiling, and looking towards Isaiah Fomitch with a wink.

"A silver rouble! no; but I will give you seven kopecks."

These were the first words pronounced by Isaiah Fomitch in the convict prison. A loud laugh was heard from all sides.

"Seven kopecks! Well, give them to me; you are lucky, you are indeed. Look! Take care of the pledge, you answer for it with your head."

"With three kopecks for interest; that will make ten kopecks you will owe me," said the Jew, at the same time slipping his hand into his pocket to get out the sum agreed upon.

"Three kopecks interest—for a year?"

"No, not for a year, for a month."

"You are a terrible screw, what is your name?"

"Isaiah Fomitch."

"Well, Isaiah Fomitch, you ought to get on. Good-bye."

The Jew examined once more the rags on which he had lent seven kopecks, folded them up, and put them carefully away in his bag. The convicts continued to laugh at him.

In reality every one laughed at him, but, although every prisoner owed him money, no one insulted him; and when he saw that every one was well disposed towards him, he gave himself haughty airs, but so comic that they were at once forgiven.

Luka, who had known many Jews when he was at liberty, often teased him, less from malice than for amusement, as one plays with a dog or a parrot. Isaiah Fomitch knew this and did not take offence.

"You will see, Jew, how I will flog you."

"If you give me one blow I will return you ten," replied Isaiah Fomitch valiantly.

"Scurvy Jew."

"As scurvy as you like; I have in any case plenty of money."

"Bravo! Isaiah Fomitch. We must take care of you. You are the only Jew we have; but they will send you to Siberia all the same."

"I am already in Siberia."

"They will send you farther on."

"Is not the Lord God there?"

"Of course, he is everywhere."

"Well, then! With the Lord God, and money, one has all that is necessary."

"What a fellow he is!" cries every one around him.

The Jew sees that he is being laughed at, but does not lose courage. He gives himself airs. The flattery addressed to him causes him much pleasure, and with a high, squealing falsetto, which is heard throughout the barracks, he begins to sing, "la, la, la, la," to an idiotic and ridiculous tune; the only song he was heard to sing during his stay at the convict prison. When he made my acquaintance, he assured me solemnly that it was the song, and the very air, that was sung by 600,000 Jews, small and great, when they crossed the Red Sea, and that every Israelite was ordered to sing it after a victory gained over an enemy.

The eve of each Saturday the convicts came from the other barracks to ours, expressly to see Isaiah Fomitch celebrating his Sabbath. He was so vain, so innocently conceited, that this general curiosity flattered him immensely. He covered the table in his little corner with a pedantic air of importance, opened a book, lighted two candles, muttered some mysterious words, and clothed himself in a kind of chasuble, striped, and with sleeves, which he preserved carefully at the bottom of his trunk. He fastened to his hands leather bracelets, and finally attached to his forehead, by means of a ribbon, a little box, which made it seem as if a horn were starting from his head. He then began to pray. He read in a drawling voice, cried out, spat, and threw himself about with wild and comic gestures. All this was prescribed by the ceremonies of his religion. There was nothing laughable or strange in it, except the airs which Isaiah Fomitch gave himself before us in performing his ceremonies. Then he suddenly covered his head with both hands, and began to read with many sobs. His tears increased, and in his grief he almost lay down upon the book his head with the ark upon it, howling as he did so; but suddenly in the midst of his despondent sobs he burst into a laugh, and recited with a nasal twang a hymn of triumph, as if he were overcome by an excess of happiness.

"Impossible to understand it," the convicts would sometimes say to one another. One day I asked Isaiah Fomitch what these sobs signified, and why he passed so suddenly from despair to triumphant happiness. Isaiah Fomitch was very pleased when I asked him these questions. He explained to me directly that the sobs and tears were provoked by the loss of Jerusalem, and that the law ordered the pious Jew to groan and strike his breast; but at the moment of his most acute grief he was suddenly to remember that a prophecy had foretold the return of the Jews to Jerusalem, and he was then to manifest overflowing joy, to sing, to laugh, and to recite his prayers with an expression of happiness in his voice and on his countenance. This sudden passage from one phase of feeling to another delighted Isaiah Fomitch, and he explained to me this ingenious prescription of his faith with the greatest satisfaction.

One evening, in the midst of his prayers, the Major entered, followed by the officer of the guard and an escort of soldiers. All the prisoners got immediately into line before their camp-bedsteads. Isaiah Fomitch alone continued to shriek and gesticulate. He knew that his worship was authorised, and that no one could interrupt him, so that in howling in the presence of the Major he ran no risk. It pleased him to throw himself about beneath the eyes of the chief.

The Major approached within a few steps. Isaiah Fomitch turned his back to the table, and just in front of the officer began to sing his hymn of triumph, gesticulating and drawling out certain syllables. When he came to the part where he had to assume an expression of extreme happiness, he did so by blinking with his eyes, at the same time laughing and nodding his head in the direction of the Major. The latter was at first much astonished; then he burst into a laugh, called out, "Idiot!" and went away, while the Jew still continued to shriek. An hour later, when he had finished, I asked him what he would have done if the Major had been wicked enough and foolish enough to lose his temper.

"What Major?"

"What Major! Did you not see him? He was only two steps from you, and was looking at you all the time." But Isaiah Fomitch assured me as seriously as possible that he had not seen the Major, for while he was saying his prayers he was in such a state of ecstasy that he neither saw nor heard anything that was taking place around him.

I can see Isaiah Fomitch wandering about on Saturday throughout the prison, endeavouring to do nothing, as the law prescribes to every Jew. What improbable anecdotes he told me! Every time he returned from the synagogue he always brought me some news of St. Petersburg, and the most absurd rumours imaginable from his fellow Jews of the town, who themselves had received them at first hand. But I have already spoken too much of Isaiah Fomitch.

In the whole town there were only two public baths. The first, kept by a Jew, was divided into compartments, for which one paid fifty kopecks. It was frequented by the aristocracy of the town.

The other bath, old, dirty, and close, was destined for the people. It was there that the convicts were taken. The air was cold and clear. The prisoners were delighted to get out of the fortress and have a walk through the town. During the walk their laughter and jokes never ceased. A platoon of soldiers, with muskets loaded, accompanied us. It was quite a sight for the town's-people. When we had reached our destination, the bath was so small that it did not permit us all to enter at once. We were divided into two bands, one of which waited in the cold room while the other one bathed in the hot one. Even then, so narrow was the room that it was difficult for us to understand how half of the convicts could stand together in it.

Petroff kept close to me. He remained by my side without my having begged him to do so, and offered to rub me down. Baklouchin, a convict of the special section, offered me at the same time his services. I recollect this prisoner, who was called the "Sapper," as the gayest and most agreeable of all my companions. We had become intimate friends. Petroff helped me to undress, because I was generally a long time getting my things off, not being yet accustomed to the operation; and it was almost as cold in the dressing-room as outside the doors.

It is very difficult for a convict who is still a novice to get his things off, for he must know how to undo the leather straps which fasten on the chains. These leather straps are buckled over the shirt, just beneath the ring which encloses the leg. One pair of straps costs sixty kopecks, and each convict is obliged to get himself a pair, for it would be impossible to walk without their assistance. The ring does not enclose the leg too tightly. One can pass the finger between the iron and the flesh; but the ring rubs against the calf, so that in a single day the convict who walks without leather straps, gets his skin broken.

To take off the straps presents no difficulty. It is not the same with the clothes. To get the trousers off is in itself a prodigious operation, and the same may be said of the shirt whenever it has to be changed. The first who gave us lessons in this art was Koreneff, a former chief of brigands, condemned to be chained up for five years. The convicts are very skilful at the work, and do it readily.

I gave a few kopecks to Petroff to buy soap and a bunch of the twigs with which one rubs oneself in the bath. Bits of soap were given to the convicts, but they were not larger than pieces of two kopecks. The soap was sold in the dressing-room, as well as mead, cakes of white flour, and boiling water; for each convict received but one pailful, according to the agreement made between the proprietor of the bath and the administration of the prison. The convicts who wished to make themselves thoroughly clean, could for two kopecks buy another pailful, which the proprietor handed to them through a window pierced in the wall for that purpose. As soon as I was undressed, Petroff took me by the arm and observed to me that I should find it difficult to walk with my chains.

"Drag them up on to your calves," he said to me, holding me by the arms at the same time, as if I were an old man. I was ashamed at his care, and assured him that I could walk well enough by myself, but he did not believe me. He paid me the same attention that one gives to an awkward child. Petroff was not a servant in any sense of the word. If I had offended him, he would have known how to deal with me. I had promised him nothing for his assistance, nor had he asked me for anything. What inspired him with so much solicitude for me?

Represent to yourself a room of twelve feet long by as many broad, in which a hundred men are all crowded together, or at least eighty, for we were in all two hundred divided into two sections. The steam blinded us; the sweat, the dirt, the want of space, were such that we did not know where to put a foot down. I was frightened and wished to go out. Petroff hastened to reassure me. With great trouble we

41

succeeded in raising ourselves on to the benches, by passing over the heads of the convicts, whom we begged to bend down, in order to let us pass; but all the benches were already occupied. Petroff informed me that I must buy a place, and at once entered into negotiations with the convict who was near the window. For a kopeck this man consented to cede me his place. After receiving the money, which Petroff held tight in his hand, and which he had prudently provided himself with beforehand, the man crept just beneath me into a dark and dirty corner. There was there, at least, half an inch of filth; even the places above the benches were occupied, the convicts swarmed everywhere. As for the floor there was not a place as big as the palm of the hand which was not occupied by the convicts. They sent the water in spouts out of their pails. Those who were standing up washed themselves pail in hand, and the dirty water ran all down their body to fall on the shaved heads of those who were sitting down. On the upper bench, and the steps which led to it, were heaped together other convicts who washed themselves more thoroughly, but these were in small number. The populace does not care to wash with soap and water, it prefers stewing in a horrible manner, and then inundating itself with cold water. That is how the common people take their bath. On the floor could be seen fifty bundles of rods rising and falling at the same time, the holders were whipping themselves into a state of intoxication. The steam became thicker and thicker every minute, so that what one now felt was not a warm but a burning sensation, as from boiling pitch. The convicts shouted and howled to the accompaniment of the hundred chains shaking on the floor. Those who wished to pass from one place to another got their chains mixed up with those of their neighbours, and knocked against the heads of the men who were lower down than they. Then there were volleys of oaths as those who fell dragged down the ones whose chains had become entangled in theirs. They were all in a state of intoxication of wild exultation. Cries and shrieks were heard on all sides. There was much crowding and crushing at the window of the dressing-room through which the hot water was delivered, and much of it got spilt over the heads of those who were seated on the floor before it arrived at its destination. We seemed to be fully at liberty; and yet from time to time, behind the window of the dressing-room, or through the open door, could be seen the moustached face of a soldier, with his musket at his feet, watching that no serious disorder took place.

The shaved heads of the convicts, and their red bodies, which the steam made the colour of blood, seemed more monstrous than ever. On their backs, made scarlet by the steam, stood out in striking relief the scars left by the whips and the rods, made long before, but so thoroughly that the flesh seemed to have been quite recently torn. Strange scars. A shudder passed through me at the mere sight of them. Again the volume of steam increased, and the bath-room was now covered with a thick, burning cloud, covering agitation and cries. From this cloud stood out torn backs, shaved heads; and, to complete the picture, Isaiah Fomitch howling with joy on the highest of the benches. He was saturating himself with steam. Any other man would have fainted away, but no temperature is too high for him; he engages the services of a rubber for a kopeck, but after a few moments the latter is unable to continue, throws away his bunch of twigs, and runs to inundate himself with cold water. Isaiah Fomitch does not lose courage, he runs to hire a second rubber, then a third; on these occasions he thinks nothing of expense, and changes his rubber four or five times. "He stews well, the gallant Isaiah Fomitch," cry the convicts from below. The Jew feels that he goes beyond all the others, he has beaten them; he triumphs with his hoarse falsetto voice, and sings out his favourite air which rises above the general hubbub. It seemed to me that if ever we met in hell we should be reminded of the place where we then were. I could not resist a wish to communicate this idea to Petroff. He looked all round him, but made no answer.

I wished to buy a place for him on the bench by my side; but he sat down at my feet and declared that he felt quite at his ease. Baklouchin meanwhile bought us some hot water which he would bring to us as soon as we wanted it. Petroff offered to clean me from head to foot, and he begged me to go through the preliminary stewing process. I could not make up my mind to it. At last he rubbed me all over with soap. I wished to make him understand that I could wash myself, but it was no use contradicting him and I gave myself up to him.

When he had done with me he took me back to the dressing-room, holding me up, and telling me at each step to take care, as if I had been made of porcelain. He helped me to put on my clothes, and when he had finished his kindly work he rushed back to the bath to have a thorough stewing.

When we got back to the barracks I offered him a glass of tea, which he did not refuse. He drank it and thanked me. I wished to go to the expense of a glass of vodka in his honour, and I succeeded in getting it on the spot. Petroff was exceedingly pleased. He swallowed his vodka with a murmur of satisfaction, declared that I had restored him to life, and then suddenly rushed to the kitchen, as if the people who were talking there could not decide anything important without him.

Now another man came up for a talk. This was Baklouchin, of whom I have already spoken, and whom I had also invited to take tea.

I never knew a man of a more agreeable disposition than Baklouchin. It must be admitted that he never forgave a wrong, and that he often got into quarrels. He could not, above all, endure people interfering with his affairs. He knew, in a word, how to take care of himself; but his quarrels never lasted long, and I believe that all the convicts liked him. Wherever he went he was well received. Even in the town he was looked upon as the most amusing man in the world. He was a man of lofty stature, thirty years old, with a frank, determined countenance, and rather good-looking, with his tuft of hair on his chin. He possessed the art of changing his face in such a comic manner by imitating the first person he happened to see, that the people around him were constantly in a roar. He was a professed joker, but he never allowed himself to be slighted by those who did not enjoy his fun. Accordingly, no one spoke disparagingly of him. He was full of life and fire. He made my acquaintance at the very beginning of my imprisonment, and related to me his military career, when he was a sapper in the Engineers, where he had been placed as a favour by people of influence. He put a number of questions to me about St. Petersburg; he even read books when he came to take tea with me. He amused the whole company by relating how roughly Lieutenant K—— had that morning handled the Major. He told me, moreover, with a satisfied air, as he took his seat by my side, that we should probably have a theatrical representation in the prison. The convicts proposed to get up a play during the Christmas holidays. The necessary actors were found, and, little by little, the scenery was prepared. Some persons in the town had promised to lend women's clothes for the performance. Some hopes were even entertained of obtaining, through the medium of an officer's servant, a uniform with epaulettes, provided only the Major did not take it into his head to forbid the performance, as he had done the previous year. He was at that time in ill-humour through having lost at cards, and he had been annoyed at something that had taken place in the prison. Accordingly, in a fit of ill-humour, he had forbidden the performance. It was possible, however, that this year he would not prevent it. Baklouchin was in a state of exultation. It could be seen that he would be one of the principal supporters of the meditated theatre. I made up my mind to be present at the performance. The ingenuous joy which Baklouchin manifested in speaking of the undertaking was quite touching. From whispering, we gradually got to talk of the matter quite openly. He told me, among other things, that he had not served at St. Petersburg alone. He had been sent to R—— with the rank of non-commissioned officer in a garrison battalion.

"From there they sent me on here," added Baklouchin.

"And why?" I asked him.

"Why? You would never guess, Alexander Petrovitch. Because I was in love."

"Come now. A man is not exiled for that," I said, with a laugh.

"I should have added," continued Baklouchin, "that it made me kill a German with a pistol-shot. Was it worth while to send me to hard labour for killing a German? Only think."

"How did it happen? Tell me the story. It must be a strange one."

"An amusing story indeed, Alexander Petrovitch."

"So much the better. Tell me."

"You wish me to do so? Well, then, listen."

And he told me the story of his murder. It was not "amusing," but it was indeed strange.

"This is how it happened," began Baklouchin; "I had been sent to Riga, a fine, handsome city, which has only one fault, there are too many Germans there. I was still a young man, and I had a good character with my officers. I wore my cap cocked on the side of my head, and passed my time in the most agreeable manner. I made love to the German girls. One of them, named Luisa, pleased me very much. She and her aunt were getters-up of fine linen. The old woman was a true caricature; but she had money. First of all I merely passed under the young girl's windows; but I soon made her acquaintance. Luisa spoke Russian well enough, though with a slight accent. She was charming. I never saw any one like her. I was most pressing in my advances; but she only replied that she would preserve her innocence, that as a wife she might prove worthy of me. She was an affectionate, smiling girl, and wonderfully neat. In fact, I assure you, I never saw any one like her. She herself had suggested that I should marry her, and how was I not to marry her? Suddenly Luisa did not come to her appointment. This happened once, then twice, then a third time. I sent her a letter, but she did not reply. 'What is to be done?' I said to myself. If she had been deceiving me she could easily have taken me in. She could have answered my letter and come all the same to the appointment; but she was incapable of falsehood. She had simply broken off with me. 'This is a trick of the aunt,' I said to myself. I was afraid to go to her house.

"Even though she was aware of our engagement, we acted as if she were ignorant of it. I wrote a fine letter in which I said to Luisa, 'If you don't come, I will come to your aunt's for you.' She was afraid and came. Then she began to weep, and told me that a German named Schultz, a distant relation of theirs, a clockmaker by trade, and of a certain age, but rich, had shown a wish to marry her—in order to make her happy, as he said, and that he himself might not remain without a wife in his old age. He had loved her a long time, so she told me, and had been nourishing this idea for years, but he had kept it a secret, and had never ventured to speak out. 'You see, Sasha,' she said to me, 'that it is a question of my happiness; for he is rich, and would you prevent my happiness?' I looked her in the face, she wept, embraced me, clasped me in her arms.

"'Well, she is quite right,' I said to myself, 'what good is there in marrying a soldier—even a non-commissioned officer? Come, farewell, Luisa. God protect you. I have no right to prevent your happiness.'

"'And what sort of a man is he? Is he good-looking?'

"'No, he is old, and he has such a long nose.'

"She here burst into a fit of laughter. I left her. 'It was my destiny,' I said to myself. The next day I passed by Schultz' shop (she had told me where he lived). I looked through the window and saw a German, who was arranging a watch, forty-five years of age, an aquiline nose, swollen eyes, a dress-coat with a very high collar. I spat with contempt as I looked at him. At that moment I was ready to break the shop windows, but 'What is the use of it?' I said to myself; 'there is nothing more to be done: it is over, all over.' I got back to the barracks as the night was falling, and stretched myself out on my bed, and—will you believe it, Alexander Petrovitch?—began to sob—yes, to sob. One day passed, then a second, then a third. I saw Luisa no more. I had learned, however, from an old woman (she was also a washerwoman, and the girl I loved used sometimes to visit her), that this German knew of our relations, and that for that reason he had made up his mind to marry her as soon as possible, otherwise he would have waited two years longer. He had made Luisa swear that she would see me no more. It appeared that on account of me he had refused to loosen his purse-strings, and kept Luisa and her aunt very close. Perhaps he would yet change his idea, for he was not very resolute. The old woman told me that he had invited them to take coffee with him the next day, a Sunday, and that another relation, a former shopkeeper, now very poor, and an assistant in some liquor store, would also come. When I found that the business was to be settled on Sunday, I was so furious that I could not recover my cold blood, and the following day I did nothing but reflect. I believe I could have devoured that German. On Sunday morning I had not come to any decision. As soon as the service was over I ran out, got into my great-coat, and went to the house of this German. I thought I should find them all there. Why I went to the German, and what I meant to say to him, I did not know myself.

"I slipped a pistol into my pocket to be ready for everything; a little pistol which was not worth a curse, with an old-fashioned lock—a thing I had used when I was a boy, and which was really fit for nothing. I loaded it, however, because I thought they would try to kick me out, and that the German would insult me, in which case I would pull out my pistol to frighten them all. I arrived. There was no one on the staircase; they were all in the work-room. No servant. The one girl who waited upon them was absent. I crossed the shop and saw that the door was closed—an old door fastened from the inside. My heart beat; I stopped and listened. They were speaking German. I broke open the door with a kick. I looked round. The table was laid; there was a large coffee-pot on it, with a spirit lamp underneath, and a plate of biscuits. On a tray there was a small decanter of brandy, herrings, sausages, and a bottle of some wine. Luisa and her aunt, both in their Sunday best, were seated on a sofa. Opposite them, the German was exhibiting himself on a chair, got up like a bridegroom, and in his coat with the high collar, and with his hair carefully combed. On the other side, there was another German, old, fat, and gray. He was taking no part in the conversation. When I entered, Luisa turned very pale. The aunt sprang up with a bound and sat down again. The German became angry. What a rage he was in! He got up, and walking towards me, said:

"'What do you want?'

"I should have lost my self-possession if anger had not supported me.

"'What do I want? Is this the way to receive a guest? Why do you not offer him something to drink? I have come to pay you a visit.'

"The German reflected a moment, and then said, 'Sit down.'

"I sat down.

"'Here is some vodka. Help yourself, I beg.'

"'And let it be good,' I cried, getting more and more into a rage.

"'It is good.'

"I was enraged to see him looking at me from top to toe. The most frightful part of it was, that Luisa was looking on. I took a drink and said to him:

"'Look here, German, what business have you to speak rudely to me? Let us be better acquainted. I have come to see you as friends.'

"'I cannot be your friend,' he replied. 'You are a private soldier.'

"Then I lost all self-command.

"'Oh, you German! You sausage-seller! You know how much you are in my power. Look here; do you wish me to break your head with this pistol?'

"I drew out my pistol, got up, and struck him on the forehead. The women were more dead than alive; they were afraid to breathe. The eldest of the two men, quite white, was trembling like a leaf.

"The German seemed much astonished. But he soon recovered himself.

"'I am not afraid of you,' he said, 'and I beg of you, as a well-bred man, to put an end to this pleasantry. I am not afraid of you!'

"'You are afraid! You dare not move while this pistol is presented at you.'

"'You dare not do such a thing!' he cried.

"'And why should I not dare?'

"'Because you would be severely punished.'

"May the devil take that idiot of a German! If he had not urged me on, he would have been alive now.

"'So you think I dare not?'

"'No.'

"'I dare not, you think?'

"'You would not dare!'

"'Wouldn't I, sausage-maker?' I fired the pistol, and down he sank on his chair. The others uttered shrieks. I put back my pistol in my pocket, and when I returned to the fortress, threw it among some weeds near the principal entrance.

"Inside the barracks I laid on my bed, and said to myself, 'I shall be taken away soon.' One hour passed, then another, but I was not arrested.

"Towards evening I felt so sad, I went out at all hazards to see Luisa; I passed before the house of the clockmaker's. There were a number of people there, including the police. I ran on to the old woman's and said:

"'Call Luisa!'

"I had only a moment to wait. She came immediately, and threw herself on my neck in tears.

"'It is my fault,' she said. 'I should not have listened to my aunt.'

"She then told me that her aunt, immediately after the scene, had gone back home. She was in such a fright that she fell and did not speak a word; she had uttered nothing. On the contrary, she ordered her niece to be as silent as herself.

"'No one has seen her since,' said Luisa.

"The clockmaker had previously sent his servant away, for he was afraid of her. She was jealous, and would have scratched his eyes out had she known that he wished to get married.

"There were no workmen in the house, he had sent them all away; he had himself prepared the coffee and collation. As for the relation, who had scarcely spoken a word all his life, he took his hat, and, without opening his mouth, went away.

"'He is quite sure to be silent,' added Luisa.

"So, indeed, he was. For two weeks no one arrested me nor suspected me the least in the world.

"You need not believe me unless you choose, Alexander Petrovitch.

"These two weeks were the happiest in my life. I saw Luisa every day. And how much she had become attached to me!

"She said to me through her tears: 'If you are exiled, I will go with you. I will leave everything to follow you.'

"I thought of making away with myself, so much had she moved me; but after two weeks I was arrested. The old man and the aunt had agreed to denounce me."

"But," I interrupted, "Baklouchin, for that they would only have given you from ten to twelve years' hard labour, and in the civil section; yet you are in the special section. How does that happen?"

"That is another affair," said Baklouchin. "When I was taken before the Council of War, the captain appointed to conduct the case began by insulting me, and calling me names before the Tribunal. I could not stand it, and shouted out to him: 'Why do you insult me? Don't you see, you scoundrel! that you are only looking at yourself in the glass?'

"This brought a new charge against me. I was tried a second time, and for the two things was condemned to four thousand strokes, and to the special section. When I was taken out to receive my punishment in the *Green Street*, the captain was at the same time sent away. He had been degraded from his rank, and was despatched to the Caucasus as a private soldier. Good-bye, Alexander Petrovitch. Don't fail to come to our performance."

CHAPTER XI. THE CHRISTMAS HOLIDAYS

The holidays were approaching. On the eve of the great day the convicts scarcely ever went to work. Those who had been assigned to the sewing workshops, and a few others, went to work as usual; but they went back almost immediately to the convict prison, separately, or in parties. After dinner no one worked. From the early morning the greater part of the convicts were occupied with their own affairs, and not with those of the administration. Some were making arrangements for bringing in spirits, while others were seeking permission to see their friends, or to collect small accounts due to them for the work they had already executed. Baklouchin, and the convicts who were to take part in the performance, were endeavouring to persuade some of their acquaintances, nearly all officers' servants, to procure for them the necessary costumes. Some of them came and went with a business-like air, solely because others were really occupied. They had no money to receive, and yet seemed to expect a payment. Every one, in short, seemed to be looking for a change of some kind. Towards evening the old soldiers, who executed the convicts' commissions, brought them all kinds of victuals—meat, sucking-pigs, and geese. Many prisoners, even the most simple and most economical, after saving up their kopecks throughout the year, thought they ought to spend some of them that day, so as to celebrate Christmas Eve in a worthy manner. The day afterwards was for the convicts a still greater festival, one to which they had a right, as it was recognised by law. The prisoners could not be sent to work that day. There were not three days like it in all the year.

And, moreover, what recollections must have been agitating the souls of those reprobates at the approach of such a solemn day! The common people from their childhood kept the great festival in their memory. They must have remembered with anguish and torments these days which, work being laid aside, are passed in the bosom of the family. The respect of the convicts for that day had something imposing about it. The drunkards were not at all numerous; nearly every one was serious, and, so to say, preoccupied, though they had for the most part nothing to do. Even those who feasted most preserved a serious air. Laughter seemed to be forbidden. A sort of intolerant susceptibility reigned throughout the prison; and if any one interfered with the general repose, even involuntarily, he was soon put in his proper place, with cries and oaths. He was condemned as though he had been wanting in respect to the festival itself.

This disposition of the convicts was remarkable, and even touching. Besides the innate veneration they have for this great day, they foresee that in observing the festival they are in communion with the rest of the world; that they are not altogether reprobates lost and cast off by society. The usual rejoicings took place in the convict prison as well as outside. They felt all that. I saw it, and understood it myself.

Akim Akimitch had made great preparations for the festival. He had no family recollections, being an orphan, born in a strange house, and put into the army at the age of fifteen. He could never have experienced any great joys, having always lived regularly and uniformly in the fear of infringing the rules imposed upon him, nor was he very religious; for his acquired formality had stifled in him all human feeling, all passions and likings, good or bad. He accordingly prepared to keep Christmas without exciting himself about it. He was saddened by no painful, useless recollection. He did everything with the punctuality imposed upon him in the execution of his duties, and in order once for all to get through the ceremony in a becoming manner. Moreover, he did not care to reflect upon the importance of the day, had never troubled his brain about it, even while he was executing his prescribed duties with religious minuteness. If he had been ordered the day following to do contrary to what he had done the evening before he would have done it with equal submission. Once in life, once, and once only, he had wished to act by his own impulse—and he had been sent to hard labour for it.

This lesson had not been lost upon him, although it was written that he was never to understand his fault. He had yet become impressed with this salutary moral principle: never to reason in any matter because his mind was not equal to the task of judging. Blindly devoted to ceremonies, he looked with respect at the sucking-pig which he had stuffed with millet-seed, and which he had roasted himself (for he had some culinary skill), just as if it had not been an ordinary sucking-pig which could have been bought and roasted at any time, but a particular kind of animal born specially for Christmas Day. Perhaps he had been accustomed from his tender infancy to see that day a sucking-pig on the table, and he may have concluded that a sucking-pig was indispensable for the proper celebration of the festival. I am certain that if by ill-luck he had not eaten this particular kind of meat on that day, he would have been troubled with remorse all his life for not having done his duty. Until Christmas morning he wore his old vest and his old trousers, which had long been threadbare. I then learned that he kept carefully in his box his new clothes which had been given to him four months before, and that he had not put them on once, in order that he might wear them for the first time on Christmas Day. He did so. The evening before he took his new clothes out of his trunk, unfolded, examined them, cleaned them, blew on them to remove the dust, and when he was convinced that they were perfect, probably tried them on. The dress became him perfectly; all the different garments suited one another. The waistcoat buttoned up to the neck, the collar, straight and stiff like cardboard, kept his chin in its proper place. There was a military cut about the dress; and Akim Akimitch, as he wore it, smiled with satisfaction, turning himself round and round, not without swagger, before a little mirror adorned with a gilt border.

One of the waistcoat-buttons alone seemed out of place; Akim Akimitch remarked it, and at once set it right. He tried on the vest again and found it irreproachable. Then he folded up his things as before, and with a satisfied mind locked them up in his box until the next day. His skull was sufficiently shaved; but, after careful examination, Akim Akimitch came to the conclusion that it was not in good condition, his hair had imperceptibly sprung up. He accordingly went immediately to the "Major" to be properly shaved according to the rules. In reality no one would have dreamed of looking at him next day, but he was acting conscientiously in order to fulfil all his duties. This care lest the smallest button, the least thread of an epaulette, the slightest string of a tassel should go wrong, was engraved in his mind as an imperious duty, and in his heart as the image of the most perfect order that could possibly be attained. As one of the "old hands" in the barracks, he saw that hay was brought and strewed about on the floor; the same thing was done in the other barracks. I do not know why, but hay was always strewed on the ground at Christmas time.

As soon as Akim Akimitch had finished his work he said his prayers, stretched himself on his bed, and went to sleep, with the sleep of a child, in order to wake up as early as possible the next day. The other convicts did the same. It must be added that all of them went to bed, but sooner than usual. They gave up their ordinary evening work that day. As for playing cards, no one would have dared even to speak of such a thing; every one was anxiously expecting the next morning.

At last this morning arrived. At an early hour, even before it was light, the drum was sounded, and the under officer, whose duty it was to count the convicts, wished them a happy Christmas. The prisoners answered him in an affable and amiable tone by expressing a like wish. Akim Akimitch, and many others, who had their geese and their sucking-pigs, went to the kitchen, after saying their prayers, in a hurried manner to see where their victuals were and how they were being cooked.

Through the little windows of our barracks, half hidden by the snow and the ice, could be seen, flaring in the darkness, the bright fire of the two kitchens where six stoves had been lighted. In the court-yard, where it was still dark, the convicts, each with a half pelisse round his shoulders, or perhaps fully dressed, were hurrying towards the kitchen. Some of them, meanwhile—a very small number—had already visited the drink-sellers. They were the impatient ones, but they behaved becomingly, possibly much better than on ordinary days; neither quarrels nor insults were heard, every one understood that it was a great day, a great festival. The convicts went even to visit the other barracks in order to wish the inmates a happy Christmas; that day a sort of friendship seemed to exist between them all. I will remark in passing that the convicts have scarcely ever any intimate friendships. It was very rare to see a man on confidential terms with any other man, as, in the outer world. We were generally harsh and abrupt in our mutual relations. With some rare exceptions this was the general tone adopted and maintained.

I went out of the barracks like the others. It was beginning to get late. The stars were paling, a light, icy mist was rising from the earth, and spirals of smoke were ascending in curls from the chimneys. Several convicts whom I met wished me, with affability, a happy Christmas. I thanked them and returned their wishes. Some of them had never spoken to me before.

Near the kitchen, a convict from the military barracks, with his sheepskin on his shoulder, came up to me. Recognising me, he called out from the middle of the court-yard, "Alexander Petrovitch." He ran towards me. I waited for him. He was a young fellow, with a round face and soft eyes, and not at all communicative as a rule. He had not spoken to me since my arrival, and seemed never to have noticed me. I did not know on my side what his name was. When he came up, he remained planted before me, smiling with a vacuous smile, but with a happy expression of countenance.

"What do you want?" I asked, not without astonishment.

He remained standing before me, still smiling and staring, but without replying to my question.

"Why, it is Christmas Day," he muttered.

He understood that he had nothing more to say, and now hastened into the kitchen.

I must add that, after this we scarcely ever met, and that we never spoke to one another again.

Round the flaming stoves of the kitchen the convicts were rubbing and pushing against one another. Every one was watching his own property. The cooks were preparing the dinner, which was to take place a little earlier than usual. No one began to eat before the time, though a good many wished to do so; but it was necessary to be well-behaved before the others. We were waiting for the priest, and the fast preceding Christmas would not be at an end until his arrival.

It was not yet perfectly light, when the corporal was already heard shouting out from behind the principal gate of the prison:

"The kitchen; the kitchen."

These calls were repeated without interruption for about two hours. The cooks were wanted in order to receive gifts brought from all parts of the town in enormous numbers; loaves of white bread, scones, rusks, pancakes, and pastry of various kinds. I do not think there was a shop-keeper in the whole town who did not send something to the "unfortunates." Amongst these gifts there were some magnificent ones, including a good many cakes of the finest flour. There were also some very poor ones, such as rolls worth two kopecks a piece, and a couple of brown rolls, covered lightly over with sour cream. These were the offerings of the poor to the poor, on which a last kopeck had often been spent.

All these gifts were accepted with equal gratitude, without reference to the value or the giver. The convicts, on receiving the offerings, took off their caps and thanked the donors with low bows, wishing them a happy Christmas, and then carried the things to the kitchen.

When a number of loaves and cakes had been collected, the elders of each barrack were called, and it was for them to divide the whole in equal portions among all the sections. The division excited neither protest nor annoyance. It was made honestly, equitably. Akim Akimitch, helped by another prisoner, divided between the convicts of our barracks the share assigned to us, and gave to each of us what came to him. Every one was satisfied. No objection was made by any one. There was not the least manifestation of envy, and it occurred to no one to deceive another.

When Akim Akimitch had finished at the kitchen, he proceeded religiously to dress himself, and did so with a solemn air. He buttoned up his waistcoat button by button, in the most punctilious manner. Then, when he had got his new clothes on, he went to pray, which occupied him a considerable time. Numbers of convicts fulfilled their religious duties, but these were for the most part old men. The young men scarcely ever prayed. The most they did was to make the sign of the cross when they rose from table, and that happened only on festival days.

Akim Akimitch came up to me as soon as he had finished his prayer, to express to me the usual good wishes. I invited him to have some tea, and he returned my politeness by offering me some of his sucking-pig. After some time Petroff came up to address to me the usual compliments. I think he had been already drinking, and although he seemed to have much to say, he scarcely spoke. He stood up before me for some seconds, and then went back to the kitchen. The priest was now expected in the military section of the barracks. This section was not constructed like the others. The camp-bedsteads were arranged all along the wall, and not in the middle of the room as in all the others, so that it was the only one in which the middle was not obstructed. It had been probably arranged in this manner so that in case of necessity it might be easier to assemble the convicts. A small table had been prepared in the middle of the room, and a holy image placed upon it, before which burned a little lamp.

At last the priest arrived, with the cross and holy water. He prayed and chanted before the image, and then turned towards the convicts, who one after the other came and kissed the cross. The priest then walked through all the barracks, sprinkling them with holy water. When he got to the kitchen he praised the bread of the convict prison, which had quite a reputation in town. The convicts at once expressed a desire to send him two loaves of new bread, still hot, which an old soldier was ordered to take to his house forthwith. The convicts walked back after the cross with the same respect as they had received it. Almost immediately afterwards, the Major and the Commandant arrived. The Commandant was liked, and even respected. He made the tour of the barracks in company with the Major, wished the convicts a happy Christmas, went into the kitchen, and tasted the cabbage soup. It was excellent that day. Each convict was entitled to nearly a pound of meat, besides which there was millet-seed in it, and certainly the butter had not been spared. The Major saw the Commandant to the door, and then ordered the convicts to begin dinner. Each endeavoured not to be under the Major's eyes. They did not like his spiteful, inquisitorial look from behind his spectacles as he wandered from right to left, seeking apparently some disorder to repress, some crime to punish.

We dined. Akim Akimitch's sucking-pig was admirably roasted. I could never understand how, five minutes after the Major left, there was a mass of drunken prisoners, whereas as long as he remained every one was perfectly calm. Red, radiant faces were now numerous, and the balalaiki soon appeared. Then came the little Pole, playing his violin, a convivial prisoner having engaged him for the whole day to play lively dance-tunes. The conversation became more animated and more noisy, but the dinner ended without great disorders. Every one had had enough. Some of the old men, serious-minded convicts, went immediately to bed. So did Akim Akimitch, who probably thought it was a duty to go to sleep after dinner on festival days.

The "old believer" from Starodoub, after having slumbered a little, climbed up on to the top of the stove, opened his book, and prayed the entire day until late in the evening without interruption. The spectacle of so shameless an orgie was painful to him, he said. All the Circassians left the table. They looked with curiosity, but with a touch of disgust, at this drunken society. I met Nourra.

"Aman, aman," he said, with a burst of honest indignation, and shaking his head. "What an offence to Allah!" Isaiah Fomitch lighted, with an arrogant and obstinate air, a candle in his favourite corner, and went to work in order to show that in his eyes this was no holiday. Here and there card parties were arranged. The convicts did not fear the old soldiers, but men were placed on the look-out in case the under officer should suddenly come in. He made a point, however, of seeing nothing. The officer of the guard made altogether three rounds. The prisoners, if they were drunk, hid themselves at once. The cards disappeared in the twinkling of an eye. I fancy that he had made up his mind not to notice any contraventions of an unimportant kind. Drunkenness was not an offence that day. Little by little every one became more or less gay. Then there were some quarrels. The greater number of the prisoners, however, remained calm, amusing themselves with the spectacle of those who were intoxicated. Some of these drank without limit.

Gazin was triumphant. He walked about with a self-satisfied air, by the side of his camp bedstead, beneath which he had concealed his spirits, previously buried beneath the snow behind the barracks, in a secret place. He smiled knowingly when he saw customers arrive in crowds. He was perfectly calm. He had drunk nothing at all; for it was his intention to regale himself the last day of the holidays, after he had emptied the pockets of the other prisoners. Throughout the barracks the drunkenness was becoming infernal. Singing was heard, and the songs were giving way to tears. Some of the prisoners walked about in bands, sheepskin on shoulder, striking with a haughty air the strings of their balalaiki. A chorus of from eight to ten men had been formed in the special section. The singing here was excellent, with its accompaniments of balalaiki and guitars.

Songs of a truly popular kind were rare. I remember one which was admirably sung:

Yesterday, I, a young girl,

Went to the feast.

A variation was introduced previously unknown to me. At the end of the song these lines were added:

At my house, the house of a young girl,

Everything is in order.

I have washed the spoons,

I have turned out the cabbage-soup,

I have wiped down the panels of the door,

I have cooked the patties.

What they chiefly sang were prison songs; one of them, called "As it happened," was very humorous. It related how a man amused himself, and lived like a prince until he was sent to the convict prison, where he fared very differently. Another song, only too popular, set forth how the hero of it had formerly possessed capital, but had now nothing but captivity. Here is a true convict's song:

The day breaks in the heavens,

We are waked up by the drum.

The old man opens the door,

The warder comes and calls us.

No one sees us behind the prison walls,

Nor how we live in this place.

But God, the Heavenly Creator, is with us

He will not let us perish.

Another still more melancholy, but with a superb melody, was sung to tame and incorrect words. I can remember a few of the verses:

My eyes no more will see the land,

Where I was born;

To suffer torments undeserved,

Will be my punishment.

The owl will shriek upon the roof,

And raise the echoes of the forest.

My heart is broken down with grief.

No, never more shall I return.

This song is often sung; not as a chorus, but always as a solo. When the work is over, a prisoner goes out of the barracks, sits down on the threshold, meditates with his chin resting on his hand, and then drawls out his song in a high falsetto. One listens to him, and the effect is heart-breaking. Some of our convicts had beautiful voices.

Meanwhile it was getting dusk. Wearisomeness and general depression were making themselves felt through the drunkenness and the debauchery. The prisoner, who an hour beforehand was holding his sides with laughter, now sobbed in a corner, exceedingly drunk; others were fighting, or wandering in a tottering manner through the barracks, pale, very pale, and seeking whom to quarrel with. These poor people had wished to pass the great festival in the most joyous manner, but, gracious heaven, how painful the day was for all of them! They had passed it in the vague hope of a happiness that was not to be realised. Petroff came up to me twice. As he had drunk very little he was calm; but until the last moment he expected something which he made sure would happen, something extraordinary, and highly diverting. Although he said nothing about it, this could be seen from his looks. He ran from barrack to barrack without fatigue. Nothing, however, happened; nothing except general intoxication, idiotic insults from drunkards, and general giddiness of heated heads.

Sirotkin wandered about also, dressed in a brand-new red shirt, going from barrack to barrack, and good-looking as usual. He also was on the watch for something to happen. The spectacle became insupportably repulsive, indeed nauseating. There were some laughable things, but I was too sad to be amused by them. I felt a deep pity for all these men, and felt strangled, stifled, in the midst of them. Here two convicts were disputing as to which should treat the other. The dispute lasts a long time; they have almost come to blows. One of them has, for a long time past, had a grudge against the other. He complains, stammering as he does so, and tries to prove to his companion that he acted unjustly when, a year before, he sold a pelisse and concealed the money. There was more than this too. The complainant is a tall young fellow, with good muscular development, quiet, by no means stupid, but who, when he is drunk, wishes to make friends with every one, and to pour out his grief into their bosom. He insults his adversary with the intention of becoming reconciled to him later on. The other man, a big, massive person, with a round face, as cunning as a fox, had perhaps drunk more than his companion, but appeared only slightly intoxicated. This convict has character, and passes for a rich man; he has probably no interest in irritating his companion, and he accordingly leads him to one of the drink-sellers. The expansive friend declares that his companion owes him money, and that he is bound to stand him a drink "if he has any pretensions to be considered an honest man."

The drink-seller, not without some respect for his customer, and with a touch of contempt for the expansive friend (for he was drinking at the expense of another man), took a glass and filled it with vodka.

"No, Stepka, you must pay, because you owe me money."

"I won't tire my tongue talking to you any longer," replied Stepka.

"No, Stepka, you lie," continues his friend, taking up a glass offered to him by the drink-seller. "You owe me money, and you must be without conscience. You have not a thing about you that you have not borrowed, and I don't believe your very eyes are your own. In a word, Stepka, you are a blackguard."

"What are you whining about? Look, you are spilling your vodka."

"If you are being treated, why don't you drink?" cries the drink-seller, to the expansive friend. "I cannot wait here until to-morrow."

"I will drink, don't be frightened. What are you crying out about? My best wishes for the day. My best wishes for the day, Stepan Doroveitch," replies the latter politely, as he bows, glass in hand, towards Stepka, whom the moment before he had called a blackguard. "Good health to you, and may you live a hundred years in addition to what you have lived already." He drinks, gives a grunt of satisfaction, and wipes his mouth. "What quantities of brandy I have drunk," he says, gravely speaking to every one, without addressing any one in particular, "but I have finished now. Thank me, Stepka Doroveitch."

"There is nothing to thank you for."

"Ah! you won't thank me. Then I will tell every one how you have treated me, and, moreover, that you are a blackguard."

"Then I shall have something to tell you, drunkard that you are," interrupts Stepka, who at last loses patience. "Listen and pay attention. Let us divide the world in two. You shall take one half, I the other. Then I shall have peace."

"Then you will not give me back my money?"

"What money do you want, drunkard?"

"My money. It is the sweat of my brow; the labour of my hands. You will be sorry for it in the other world. You will be roasted for those five kopecks."

"Go to the devil."

"What are you driving me for? Am I a horse?"

"Be off, be off."

"Blackguard!"

"Convict!"

And the insults exchanged were worse than they had been before the visit to the drink-seller.

Two friends are seated separately on two camp-bedsteads. One is tall, vigorous, fleshy, with a red face—a regular butcher. He is on the point of weeping; for he has been much moved. The other is tall, thin, conceited, with an immense nose, which always seems to have a cold, and little blue eyes fixed upon the ground. He is a clever, well-bred man, and was formerly a secretary. He treats his friend with a little disdain, which the latter cannot stand. They have been drinking together all day.

"You have taken a liberty with me," cries the stout one, as with his left hand he shakes the head of his companion. To take a liberty signifies, in convict language, to strike. This convict, formerly a non-commissioned officer, envies in secret the elegance of his neighbour, and endeavours to make up for his material grossness by refined conversation.

"I tell you, you are wrong," says the secretary, in a dogmatic tone, with his eyes obstinately fixed on the ground, and without looking at his companion.

"You struck me. Do you hear?" continues the other, still shaking his dear friend. "You are the only man in the world I care for; but you shall not take a liberty with me."

"Confess, my dear fellow," replies the secretary, "that all this is the result of too much drink."

The corpulent friend falls back with a stagger, looks stupidly with his drunken eyes at the secretary, and suddenly, with all his might, sends his fist into the secretary's thin face. Thus terminates the day's friendship.

The dear friend disappears beneath the camp-bedstead unconscious.

One of my acquaintances enters the barracks. He is a convict of the special section, very good-natured, and gay, far from stupid, and jocular without malice. He is the man who, on my arrival at the convict prison, was looking out for a rich peasant, who spoke so much of his self-respect, and ended by drinking my tea. He was forty years old, had enormous lips, and a fat, fleshy, red nose. He held a balalaika, and struck negligently its strings. He was followed by a little convict, with a large head, whom I knew very little, and to whom no one paid any attention. Now that he was drunk he had attached himself to Vermaloff, and followed him like his shadow, at the same time gesticulating and striking with his fist the wall and the camp-bedsteads. He was almost in tears. Vermaloff did not notice him any more than if he had not existed. The most curious point was that these two men in no way resembled one another, neither by their occupations nor by their disposition. They belonged to different sections, and lived in separate barracks. The little convict was named Bulkin.

Vermaloff smiled when he saw me seated by the stove. He stopped at some distance from me, reflected for a moment, tottered, and then came towards me with an affected swagger. Then he swept the strings of his instrument, and sung, or recited, tapping at the same time with his boot on the ground, the following chant:

My darling!

With her full, fair face,

Sings like a nightingale;

In her satin dress,

With its brilliant trimming,

She is very fair.

This song excited Bulkin in an extraordinary manner. He agitated his arms, and shrieked out to every one: "He lies, my friends; he lies like a quack doctor. There is not a shadow of truth in what he sings."

"My respects to the venerable Alexander Petrovitch," said Vermaloff, looking at me with a knowing smile. I fancied even he wished to embrace me. He was drunk. As for the expression, "My respects to the venerable so-and-so," it is employed by the common people throughout Siberia, even when addressed to a young man of twenty. To call a man old is a sign of respect, and may amount even to flattery.

"Well, Vermaloff, how are you?" I replied.

"So, so. Nothing to boast of. Those who really enjoy the holiday have been drinking since early morning."

Vermaloff did not speak very distinctly.

"He lies; he lies again," said Bulkin, striking the camp-bedsteads with a sort of despair.

One might have sworn that Vermaloff had given his word of honour not to pay any attention to him. That was really the most comic thing about it; for Bulkin had not quitted him for one moment since the morning. Always with him, he quarrelled with Vermaloff about every word; wringing his hands, and striking with his fists against the wall and the camp bedsteads till he made them bleed, he suffered visibly from his conviction that Vermaloff "lied like a quack doctor." If Bulkin had had hair on his head, he would certainly have torn it in his grief, in his profound mortification. One might have thought that he had made himself responsible for Vermaloff's actions, and that all Vermaloff's faults troubled his conscience. The amusing part of it was that Vermaloff continued.

"He lies! He lies! He lies!" cried Bulkin.

"What can it matter to you?" replied the convicts, with a laugh.

"I must tell you, Alexander Petrovitch, that I was very good-looking when I was a young man, and the young girls were very fond of me," said Vermaloff suddenly.

"He lies! He lies!" again interrupted Bulkin, with a groan. The convicts burst into a laugh.

"And well I got myself up to please them. I had a red shirt, and broad trousers of cotton velvet. I was happy in those days. I got up when I liked; did whatever I pleased. In fact——"

"He lies," declared Bulkin.

"I inherited from my father a stone house, two storeys high. Within two years I made away with the two storeys; nothing remained to me but the street door. Well, what of that. Money comes and goes like a bird."

"He lies!" declared Bulkin, more resolutely than before.

"Then when I had spent all, I sent a letter to my relations, that they might send me some money. They said that I had set their will at naught, that I was disrespectful. It is now seven years since I sent off my letter."

"And any answer?" I asked, with a smile.

"No," he replied, also laughing, and almost putting his nose in my face.

He then informed me that he had a sweetheart.

"You a sweetheart?"

"Onufriel said to me the other day: 'My young woman is marked with small-pox, and as ugly as you like; but she has plenty of dresses, while yours, though she may be pretty, is a beggar.'"

"Is that true?"

"Certainly, she is a beggar," he answered.

He burst into a laugh, and the others laughed with him. Every one indeed knew that he had a *liaison* with a beggar woman, to whom he gave ten kopecks every six months.

"Well, what do you want with me?" I said to him, wishing at last to get rid of him.

He remained silent, and then, looking at me in the most insinuating manner, said:

"Could not you let me have enough money to buy half-a-pint? I have drunk nothing but tea the whole day," he added, as he took from me the money I offered him; "and tea affects me in such a manner that I am afraid of becoming asthmatic. It gives me the wind."

When he took the money I offered him, the despair of Bulkin went beyond all bounds. He gesticulated like a man possessed.

"Good people all," he cried, "the man lies. Everything he says—everything is a lie."

"What can it matter to you?" cried the convicts, astonished at his goings on. "You are possessed."

"I will not allow him to lie," continued Bulkin, rolling his eyes, and striking his fist with energy on the boards. "He shall not lie."

Every one laughed. Vermaloff bowed to me after receiving the money, and hastened, with many grimaces, to go to the drink-seller. Then only he noticed Bulkin.

"Come!" he said to him, as if the latter were indispensable for the execution of some design. "Idiot!" he added, with contempt, as Bulkin passed before him.

But enough about this tumultuous scene, which, at last, came to an end. The convicts went to sleep heavily on their camp-bedsteads. They spoke and raged during their sleep more than on the other nights. Here and there they still continued to play at cards. The festival looked forward to with such impatience was now over, and to-morrow the daily work, the hard labour, will begin again.

CHAPTER XII. THE PERFORMANCE.

On the evening of the third day of the holidays took place our first theatrical performance. There had been much trouble about organising it. But those who were to act had taken everything upon themselves, and the other convicts knew nothing about the representation except that it was to take place. We did not even know what was to be played. The actors, while they were at work, were always thinking how they could get together the greatest number of costumes. Whenever I met Baklouchin he snapped his fingers with satisfaction, but told me nothing. I think the Major was in a good humour; but we did not know for certain whether he knew what was going on or not, whether he had authorised it, or whether he had determined to shut his eyes and be silent, after assuring himself that everything would take place quietly. He had heard, I fancy, of the meditated representation, and said nothing about it, lest he should spoil everything. The soldiers would be disorderly, or would get drunk, unless they had something to divert them. Thus I think the Major must have reasoned, for it will be only natural to do so. I may add that if the convicts had not got up a performance during the holidays, or done something of the kind, the administration would have been obliged to organise some sort of amusement; but as our Major was distinguished by ideas directly opposed to those of other people, I take a great responsibility on myself in saying that he knew of our project and authorised it. A man like him must always be crushing and stifling some one, taking something away, depriving some one of a right—in a word, for establishing order of this character he was known throughout the town.

It mattered nothing to him that his exactions made the men rebellious. For such offences there were suitable punishments (there are some people who reason in this way), and with these rascals of convicts there was nothing to do but to treat them very severely, deal with them strictly according to law. These incapable executants of the law did not in the least understand that to apply the law without understanding its spirit is to provoke resistance. They are quite astonished that, in addition to the execution of the law, good sense and a sound head should be expected from them. The last condition would appear to them quite superfluous; to require such a thing is vexatious, intolerant.

However this may be, the Sergeant-Major made no objection to the performance, and that was all the convicts wanted. I may say in all truth that if throughout the holidays there were no disorders in the convict prison, no sanguinary quarrels, no robberies, that must be attributed to the convicts being permitted to organise their performance. I saw with my own eyes how they got out of the way of those of their companions who had drunk too much, and how they prevented quarrels on the ground that the representation would be forbidden. The non-commissioned officer made the prisoners give their word of honour that they would behave well, and that all would go off quietly. They gave it with pleasure, and kept their promise religiously. They were much flattered at finding their word of honour accepted. Let me add that the representation cost nothing, absolutely nothing, to the authorities, who were not called upon to spend a farthing. The theatre could be put up and taken down within a quarter of an hour; and, in case an order stopping the performance suddenly arrived, the scenery could have been put away in a second. The costumes were concealed in the convicts' boxes; but first of all let me say how our theatre was constructed, what were the costumes, and what the bill, that is to say, the pieces that were to be played. To tell the truth, there was no written playbill, not, at least, for the first representation. It was ready only for the second and third. Baklouchin composed it for the officers and other distinguished visitors who might deign to honour the performance with their presence, including the officer of the guard, the officer of the watch, and an Engineer officer. It was in honour of these that the playbill was written out.

It was supposed that the reputation of our theatre would extend to the fortress, and even to the town, especially as there was no theatre at N——: a few amateur performances, but nothing more. The convicts delighted in the smallest success, and boasted of it like children.

"Who knows?" they said to one another; "when our chiefs hear of it they will perhaps come and see. Then they will know what convicts are worth, for this is not a performance given by soldiers, but a genuine piece played by genuine actors; nothing like it could be seen anywhere in the town. General Abrosimoff had a representation at his house, and it is said he will have another. Well, they may beat us in the matter of costumes, but as for the dialogue that is a very different thing. The Governor himself will perhaps hear of it, and—who knows?—he may come himself."

They had no theatre in the town. In a word, the imagination of the convicts, above all after their first success, went so far as to make them think that rewards would be distributed to them, and that their period of hard labour would be shortened. A moment afterwards they were the first to laugh at this fancy. In a word, they were children, true children, when they were forty years of age. I knew in a general way the subjects of the pieces that were to be represented, although there was no bill. The title of the first was *Philatka and Miroshka Rivals*. Baklouchin boasted to me, at least a week before the performance, that the part of Philatka, which he had assigned to himself, would be played in such a manner that nothing like it had ever been seen, even on the St. Petersburg stage. He walked about in the barracks puffed up with boundless importance. If now and then he declaimed a speech from his part in the theatrical style, every one burst out laughing, whether the speech was amusing or not; they laughed because he had forgotten himself. It must be admitted that the convicts, as a body, were self-contained and full of dignity; the only ones who got enthusiastic at Baklouchin's tirades were the young ones, who had no false shame, or those who were much looked up to, and whose authority was so firmly established that they were not afraid to commit themselves. The others listened silently, without blaming or contradicting, but they did their best to show that the performance left them indifferent.

It was not until the very last moment, the very day of the representation, that every one manifested genuine interest in what our companions had undertaken. "What," was the general question, "would the Major say? Would the performance succeed as well as the one given two years before?" etc., etc. Baklouchin assured me that all the actors would be quite at home on the stage, and that there would even be a curtain. Sirotkin was to play a woman's part. "You will see how well I look in women's clothes," he said. The Lady Bountiful was to have a dress with skirts and trimmings, besides a parasol; while her husband, the Lord of the Manor, was to wear an officer's uniform, with epaulettes, and a cane in his hand.

The second piece that was to be played was entitled, *Kedril, the Glutton*. The title puzzled me much, but it was useless to ask any questions about it. I could only learn that the piece was not printed; it was a manuscript copy obtained from a retired non-commissioned officer in the town, who had doubtless formerly participated in its representation on some military stage. We have, indeed, in the distant towns and governments, a number of pieces of this kind, which, I believe, are perfectly unknown and have never been printed, but which appear to have grown up of themselves, in connection with the popular theatre, in certain zones of Russia. I have spoken of the popular theatre. It would be a good thing if our investigators of popular literature would take the trouble to make careful researches as to this popular theatre which exists, and which, perhaps, is not so insignificant as may be thought.

I cannot think that everything I saw on the stage of our convict prison was the work of our convicts. It must have sprung from old traditions handed down from generation to generation, and preserved among the soldiers, the workmen in industrial towns, and even the shopkeepers in some poor, out-of-the-way places. These traditions have been preserved in some villages and some Government towns by the servants of the large landed proprietors. I even believe that copies of many old pieces have been multiplied by these servants of the nobility.

The old Muscovite proprietors and nobles had their own theatres, in which their servants used to play. Thence comes our popular theatre, the originals of which are beyond discussion. As for *Kedril, the Glutton*, in spite of my lively curiosity, I could learn nothing about it, except that demons appeared on the stage and carried Kedril away to hell. What did the name of Kedril signify? Why was he called Kedril and not Cyril? Was the name Russian or foreign? I could not resolve this question.

It was announced that the representation would terminate with a musical pantomime. All this promised to be very curious. The actors were fifteen in number, all vivacious men. They were very energetic, got up a number of rehearsals which sometimes took place behind the barracks, kept away from the others, and gave themselves mysterious airs. They evidently wished to surprise us with something extraordinary and unexpected.

On work days the barracks were shut very early as night approached, but an exception was made during the Christmas holidays, when the padlocks were not put to the gates until the evening retreat—nine o'clock. This favour had been granted specially in view of the play. During the whole duration of the holidays a deputation was sent every evening to the officer of the guard very humbly "to permit the representation and not to shut at the usual hour." It was added that there had been previous representations, and that nothing disorderly had occurred at any of them.

The officer of the guard must have reasoned as follows: There was no disorder, no infraction of discipline at the previous performance, and the moment they give their word that to-night's performance shall take place in the same manner, they mean to be their own police—the most rigorous police of all. Moreover, he knew well that if he took it upon himself to forbid the representation, these fellows (who knows, and with convicts?) would have committed some offence which would have placed the officer of the guard in a very difficult position. One final reason insured his consent: To mount guard is horribly tiresome, and if he authorised the performance he would see the play acted, not by soldiers, but by convicts, a curious set of people. It would certainly be interesting, and he had a right to be present at it.

In case the superior officer arrived and asked for the officer of the guard, he would be told that the latter had gone to count the convicts and close the barracks; an answer which could easily be made, and which could not be disproved. That is why our superintendents authorised the performance; and throughout the holidays the barracks were kept open each evening until the retreat. The convicts had known beforehand that they would meet with no opposition from the officer of the guard. They were quite quiet about him.

Towards six o'clock Petroff came to look for me, and we went together to the theatre. Nearly all the prisoners of our barracks were there, with the exception of the "old believer" from Tchernigoff, and the Poles. The latter did not decide to be present until the last day of the representation, the 4th of January, after they had been assured that everything would be managed in a becoming manner. The haughtiness of the Poles irritated our convicts. Accordingly they were received on the 4th of January with formal politeness, and conducted to the best places. As for the Circassians and Isaiah Fomitch, the play was for them a genuine delight. Isaiah Fomitch gave three kopecks each time, except the last, when he placed ten kopecks on the plate; and how happy he looked!

The actors had decided that each spectator should give what he thought fit. The receipts were to cover the expenses, and anything beyond was to go to the actors. Petroff assured me that I should be allowed to have one of the best places, however full the theatre might be; first, because being richer than the others, there was a probability of my giving more; and, secondly, because I knew more about acting than any one else. What he had foreseen took place. But let me first describe the theatre.

The barrack of the military section, which had been turned into the theatre, was fifteen feet long. From the court-yard one entered, first an ante-chamber, and afterwards the barrack itself. The building was arranged, as I have already mentioned, in a particular manner, the beds being placed against the wall, so as to leave an open space in the middle. One half of the barrack was reserved for the spectators, while the other, which communicated with the second building, formed the stage. What astonished me directly I entered, was the curtain, which was about ten feet long, and divided the barrack into two. It was indeed a marvel, for it was painted in oil, and represented trees, tunnels, ponds, and stars.

It was made of pieces of linen, old and new, given by the convicts; shirts, the bandages which our peasants wrap round their feet in lieu of socks, all sewn together well or ill, and forming together an immense sheet. Where there was not enough linen, it had been replaced by writing paper, taken sheet by sheet from the various office bureaus. Our painters (among whom we had our Bruloff) had painted it all over, and the effect was very remarkable.

This luxurious curtain delighted the convicts, even the most sombre and most morose. These, however, like the others, as soon as the play began, showed themselves mere children. They were all pleased and satisfied with a certain satisfaction of vanity. The theatre was lighted with candle ends. Two benches, which had been brought from the kitchen, were placed before the curtain, together with three or four large chairs, borrowed from the non-commissioned officers' room. These chairs were for the officers, should they think fit to honour the performance. As for the benches, they were for the non-commissioned officers, engineers, clerks, directors of the works, and all the immediate superiors of the convicts who had not officer's rank, and who had come perhaps to take a look at the representation. In fact, there was no lack of visitors. According to the days, they came in greater or smaller numbers, while for the last representation there was not a single place unoccupied on the benches.

At the back the convicts stood crowded together; standing up out of respect to the visitors, and dressed in their vests, or in their short pelisses, in spite of the suffocating heat. As might have been expected, the place was too small; so all the prisoners stood up, heaped together—above all in the last rows. The camp-bedsteads were all occupied; and there were some amateurs who disputed constantly behind the stage in the other barrack, and who viewed the performance from the back. I was asked to go forward, and Petroff with me, close to the benches, whence a good view could be obtained. They looked upon me as a good judge, a connoisseur, who had seen many other theatres. The convicts remarked that Baklouchin had often consulted me, and that he had shown deference to my advice. Consequently they thought that I ought to be treated with honour, and to have one of the best places. These men are vain and frivolous, but only on the surface. They laughed at me when I was at work, because I was a poor workman. Almazoff had a right to despise us gentlemen, and to boast of his superior skill in pounding the alabaster. His laughter and raillery were directed against our origin, for we belonged by birth to the caste of his former masters, of whom he could not preserve a good recollection; but here at the theatre these same men made way for me; for they knew that about this matter I knew more than they did. Those, even, who were not at all well disposed towards me, were glad to hear me praise the performance, and gave way to me without the least servility. I judged now by my impressions of that time. I understood that in this new view of theirs there was no lowering of themselves; rather a sentiment of their own dignity.

The most striking characteristic of our people is its conscientiousness, and its love of justice; no false vanity, no sly ambition to reach the first rank without being entitled to do so; such faults are foreign to our people. Take it from its rough shell, and you will perceive, if you study it without prejudice, attentively, and close at hand, qualities which you would never have suspected. Our sages have very little to teach our people. I will even say more; they might take lessons from it.

Petroff had told me innocently, on taking me into the theatre, that they would pass me to the front, because they expected more money from me. There were no fixed prices for the places. Each one gave what he liked, and what he could. Nearly every one placed a piece of money in the plate when it was handed round. Even if they had passed me forward in the hope that I should give more than others, was there not in that a certain feeling of personal dignity?

"You are richer than I am. Go to the first row. We are all equal here, it is true; but you pay more, and the actors prefer a spectator like you. Occupy the first place then, for we are not here with money, and must arrange ourselves anyhow."

What noble pride in this mode of action! In final analysis not love of money, but self-respect. There was little esteem for money among us. I do not remember that one of us ever lowered himself to obtain money. Some men used to make up to me, but from love of cunning and of fun rather than in the hope of obtaining any benefit. I do not know whether I explain myself clearly. I am, in any case, forgetting the performance. Let me return to it.

Before the rise of the curtain, the room presented a strange and animated look. In the first place, the crowd pressed, crushed, jammed together on all sides, but impatient, full of expectation, every face glowing with delight. In the last ranks was the grovelling, confused mass of convicts. Many of them had brought with them logs of wood, which they placed against the wall, on which they climbed up. In this fatiguing position they paused to rest themselves by placing both hands on the shoulders of their companions, who seemed quite at ease. Others stood on their toes, with their heels against the stove, and thus remained throughout the representation, supported by those around them. Massed against the camp-bedsteads was another compact crowd; for here were some of the best places of all. Five convicts had hoisted themselves up to the top of the stove, whence they had a commanding view. These fortunate ones were extremely happy. Elsewhere swarmed the late arrivals, unable to find good places.

Every one conducted himself in a becoming manner, without making any noise. Each one wished to show advantageously before the distinguished persons who were visiting us. Simple and natural was the expression of these red faces, damp with perspiration, as the rise of the curtain was eagerly expected. What a strange look of infinite delight, of unmixed pleasure, was painted on these scarred faces, these branded foreheads, so dark and menacing at ordinary times! They were all without their caps, and as I looked back at them from my place, it seemed to me that their heads were entirely shaved.

Suddenly the signal is given, and the orchestra begins to play. This orchestra deserves a special mention. It consisted of eight musicians: two violins, one of which was the property of a convict, while the other had been borrowed from outside; three balalaiki, made by the convicts themselves; two guitars, and a tambourine. The violins sighed and shrieked, and the guitars were worthless, but the balalaiki were remarkably good; and the agile fingering of the artists would have done honour to the cleverest executant.

They played scarcely anything but dance tunes. At the most exciting passages they struck with their fingers on the body of their instruments. The tone, the execution of the motive, were always original and distinctive. One of the guitarists knew his instrument thoroughly. It was the gentleman who had killed his father. As for the tambourinist, he really did wonders. Now he whirled round the disk, balanced on one of his fingers; now he rubbed the parchment with his thumb, and brought from it a countless multitude of notes, now dull, now brilliant.

At last two harmonigers join the orchestra. I had no idea until then of all that could be done with these popular and vulgar instruments. I was astonished. The harmony, but, above all, the expression, the very conception of the motive, were admirably rendered. I then understood perfectly, and for the first time, the remarkable boldness, the striking abandonment, which are expressed in our popular dance tunes, and our village songs.

At last the curtain rose. Every one made a movement. Those who were at the back raised themselves upon the point of their feet; some one fell down from his log. At once there were looks that enjoined silence. The performance now began.

I was seated not far from Ali, who was in the midst of the group formed by his brothers and the other Circassians. They had a passionate love of the theatre, and did not miss one of our evenings. I have remarked that all the Mohammedans, Circassians, and so on, are fond of all kinds of representations. Near them was Isaiah Fomitch, quite in a state of ecstasy. As soon as the curtain rose he was all ears and eyes; his countenance expressed an expectation of something marvellous. I should have been grieved had he been disappointed. The charming face of Ali shone with a childish joy, so pure that I was quite happy to behold it. Involuntarily, whenever a general laugh echoed an amusing remark, I turned towards him to see his countenance. He did not notice it, he had something else to do.

Near him, placed on the left, was a convict, already old, sombre, discontented, and always grumbling. He also had noticed Ali, and I saw him cast furtive glances more than once towards him, so charming was the young Circassian. The prisoners always called him Ali Simeonitch, without my knowing why.

In the first piece, *Philatka and Miroshka*, Baklouchin, in the part of Philatka, was really marvellous. He played his rôle to perfection. It could be seen that he had weighed each speech, each movement. He managed to give to each word, each gesture, a meaning which responded perfectly to the character of the personage. Apart from the conscientious study he had made of the character, he was gay, simple, natural, irresistible. If you had seen Baklouchin you would certainly have said that he was a genuine actor, an actor by vocation, and of great talent. I have seen Philatka several times at the St. Petersburg and Moscow theatres, and I declare that none of our celebrated actors was equal to Baklouchin in this part. They were peasants, from no matter what country, and not true Russian moujiks. Moreover, their desire to be peasant-like was too apparent. Baklouchin was animated by emulation; for it was known that the convict Potsiakin was to play the part of Kedril in the second piece, and it was assumed—I do not know why—that the latter would show more talent than Baklouchin. The latter was as vexed by this preference as a child. How many times did he not come to me during the last days to tell me all he felt! Two hours before the representation he was attacked by fever. When the audience burst out laughing, and called out "Bravo, Baklouchin! what a fellow you are!" his figure shone with joy, and true inspiration could be read in his eyes. The scene of the kisses between Kiroshka and Philatka, in which the latter calls out to the daughter, "Wife, your mouth," and then wipes his own, was wonderfully comic. Every one burst out laughing.

What interested me was the spectators. They were all at their ease, and gave themselves up frankly to their mirth. Cries of approbation became more and more numerous. A convict nudged his companion with his elbow, and hastily communicated his impressions, without even troubling himself to know who was by his side. When a comic song began, one man might be seen agitating his arms violently, as if to engage his companions to laugh; after which he turned suddenly towards the stage. A third smacked his tongue against his palate, and could not keep quiet a moment; but as there was not room for him to change his position, he hopped first on one leg, then on the other; towards the end of the piece the general gaiety attained its climax. I exaggerate nothing. Imagine the convict prison, chains, captivity, long years of confinement, of task-work, of monotonous life, falling away drop by drop like rain on an autumn day; imagine all this despair in presence of permission given to the convicts to amuse themselves, to breathe freely for an hour, to forget their nightmare, and to organise a play—and what a play! one that excited the envy and admiration of our town.

"Fancy those convicts!" people said: everything interested them, take the costumes for instance. It seemed very strange, but then to see, Nietsvitaeff, or Baklouchin, in a different costume from the one they had worn for so many years.

He is a convict, a genuine convict, whose chains ring when he walks; and there he is, out on the stage with a frock-coat, and a round hat, and a cloak, like any ordinary civilian. He has put on hair, moustaches. He takes a red handkerchief from his pocket and shakes it, like a real nobleman. What enthusiasm is created! The "good landlord" arrives in an aide-de-camp uniform, a very old one, it is true, but with epaulettes, and a cocked hat. The effect produced was indescribable. There had been two candidates for this costume, and—will it be believed?—they had quarrelled like two little schoolboys as to which of them should play the part. Both wanted to appear in military uniform with epaulettes. The other actors separated them, and, by a majority of voices, the part was entrusted to Nietsvitaeff; not because he was more suited to it than the other, and that he bore a greater resemblance to a nobleman, but only because he had assured them all that he would have a cane, and that he would twirl it and rap it out grand, like a true nobleman—a dandy of the latest fashion—which was more than Vanka and Ospiety could do, seeing they have never known any noblemen. In fact, when Nietsvitaeff went to the stage with his wife, he did nothing but draw circles on the floor with his light bamboo cane, evidently thinking that this was the sign of the best breeding, of supreme elegance. Probably in his childhood, when he was still a barefooted child, he had been attracted by the skill of some proprietor in twirling his cane, and this impression had remained in his memory, although thirty years afterwards.

Nietsvitaeff was so occupied with his process that he saw no one, he gave the replies in his dialogue without even raising his eyes. The most important thing for him was the end of his cane, and the circles he drew with it. The Lady Bountiful was also very remarkable; she came on in an old worn-out muslin dress, which looked like a rag. Her arms and neck were bare. She had a little calico cap on her head, with strings under her chin, an umbrella in one hand, and in the other a fan of coloured paper, with which she constantly fanned herself. This great lady was welcomed with a wild laugh; she herself, too, was unable to restrain herself, and burst out more than once. The part was filled by the convict Ivanoff. As for Sirotkin, in his girl's dress, he looked exceedingly well. The couplets were all well sung. In a word, the piece was played to the satisfaction of every one; not the least hostile criticism was passed—who, indeed, was there to criticise? The air, "Sieni moi Sieni," was played again by way of overture, and the curtain again went up.

Kedril, the Glutton, was now to be played. Kedril is a sort of Don Juan. This comparison may justly be made, for the master and the servant are both carried away by devils at the end of the piece; and the piece, as the convicts had it, was played quite correctly; but the beginning and the end must have been lost, for it had neither head nor tail. The scene is laid in an inn somewhere in Russia. The innkeeper introduces into a room a nobleman wearing a cloak and a battered round hat; the valet, Kedril, follows his master; he carries a valise, and a fowl rolled up in blue paper; he wears a short pelisse and a footman's cap. It is this fellow who is the glutton. The convict Potsiakin, the rival of Baklouchin, played this part, while the part of the nobleman was filled by Ivanoff, the same who played the great lady in the first piece. The innkeeper (Nietsvitaeff) warns the nobleman that the room is haunted by demons, and goes away; the nobleman is interested and preoccupied; he murmurs aloud that he has known that for a long time, and orders Kedril to unpack his things and to get supper ready.

Kedril is a glutton and a coward. When he hears of devils he turns pale and trembles like a leaf; he would like to run away, but is afraid of his master; besides, he is hungry, he is voluptuous, he is sensual, stupid, though cunning in his way, and, as before said, a poltroon; he cheats his master every moment, though he fears him like fire. This type of servant is a remarkable one in which may be recognised the principal features of the character of Leporello, but indistinct and confused. The part was played in really superior style by Potsiakin, whose talent was beyond discussion, surpassing as it did in my opinion that of Baklouchin himself. But when the next day I spoke to Baklouchin I concealed my impression from him, knowing that it would give him bitter pain.

As for the convict who played the part of the nobleman, it was not bad. Everything he said was without meaning, incomparable to anything I had ever heard before; but his enunciation was pure and his gestures becoming. While Kedril occupies himself with the valise, his master walks up and down, and announces that from that day forth he means to lead a quiet life. Kedril listens, makes grimaces, and amuses the spectators by his reflections "aside." He has no pity for his master, but he has heard of devils, would like to know what they are like, and thereupon questions him. The nobleman replies that some time ago, being in danger of death, he asked succour from hell. Then the devils aided and delivered him, but the term of his liberty has expired; and if the devils come that evening, it will be to exact his soul, as has been agreed in their compact. Kedril begins to tremble in earnest, but his master does not lose courage, and orders him to prepare the supper. Hearing of victuals, Kedril revives. Taking out a bottle of wine, he taps it on his own account. The audience expands with laughter; but the door grates on its hinges, the winds shakes the shutters, Kedril trembles, and hastily, almost without knowing what he is doing, puts into his mouth an enormous piece of fowl, which he is unable to swallow. There is another gust of wind.

"Is it ready?" cries the master, still walking backwards and forwards in his room.

"Directly, sir. I am preparing it," says Kedril, who sits down, and, taking care that his master does not see him, begins to eat the supper himself. The audience is evidently charmed with the cunning of the servant, who so cleverly makes game of the nobleman; and it must be admitted that Poseikin, the representative of the part, deserved high praise. He pronounced admirably the words: "Directly, sir. I—am—preparing—it."

Kedril eats gradually, and at each mouthful trembles lest his master shall see him. Every time that the nobleman turns round Kedril hides under the table, holding the fowl in his hand. When he has appeased his hunger, he begins to think of his master.

54

"Kedril, will it soon be ready?" cries the nobleman.

"It is ready now," replies Kedril boldly, when all at once he perceives that there is scarcely anything left. Nothing remains but one leg. The master, still sombre and pre-occupied, notices nothing, and takes his seat, while Kedril places himself behind him with a napkin on his arm. Every word, every gesture, every grimace from the servant, as he turns towards the audience to laugh at his master's expense, excites the greatest mirth among the convicts. Just at the moment when the young nobleman begins to eat, the devils arrive. They resemble nothing human or terrestrial. The side-door opens, and the phantom appears dressed entirely in white, with a lighted lantern in lieu of a head, and with a scythe in its hand. Why the white dress, scythe, and lantern? No one could tell me, and the matter did not trouble the convicts. They were sure that this was the way it ought to be done. The master comes forward courageously to meet the apparitions, and calls out to them that he is ready, and that they can take him. But Kedril, as timid as a hare, hides under the table, not forgetting, in spite of his fright, to take a bottle with him. The devils disappear, Kedril comes out of his hiding-place, and the master begins to eat his fowl. Three devils enter the room, and seize him to take him to hell.

"Save me, Kedril," he cries. But Kedril has something else to think of. He has now with him in his hiding-place not only the bottle, but also the plate of fowl and the bread. He is now alone. The demons are far away, and his master also. Kedril gets from under the table, looks all round, and suddenly his face beams with joy. He winks, like the rogue he is, sits down in his master's place, and whispers to the audience: "I have now no master but myself."

Every one laughs at seeing him masterless; and he says, always in an under-tone and with a confidential air: "The devils have carried him off!"

The enthusiasm of the spectators is now without limits. The last phrase was uttered with such roguery, with such a triumphant grimace, that it was impossible not to applaud. But Kedril's happiness does not last long. Hardly has he taken up the bottle of wine, and poured himself out a large glass, which he carries to his lips, than the devils return, slip behind, and seize him. Kedril howls like one possessed, but he dare not turn round. He wishes to defend himself, but cannot, for in his hands he holds the bottle and the glass, from which he will not separate. His eyes starting from his head, his mouth gaping with horror, he remains for a moment looking at the audience with a comic expression of cowardice that might have been painted. At last he is dragged, carried away. His arms and legs are agitated in every direction, but he still sticks to his bottle. He also shrieks, and his cries are still heard when he has been carried from the stage.

The curtain falls amid general laughter, and every one is delighted. The orchestra now attacks the famous dance tune Kamarinskaia. First it is played softly, pianissimo; but little by little, the motive is developed and played more lightly. The time is quickened, and the wood, as well as the strings of the balalaiki, is made to sound. The musicians enter thoroughly into the spirit of the dance. Glinka should have heard it as it was executed in our Convict Prison.

The pantomimic musical accompaniment is begun; and throughout the Kamarinskaia is played. The stage represents the interior of a hut. A miller and his wife are sitting down, one mending clothes, the other spinning flax. Sirotkin plays the part of the wife, and Nietsvitaeff that of the husband. Our scenery was very poor. In this piece, as in the preceding ones, imagination had to supply what was wanting in reality. Instead of a wall at the back of the stage, there was a carpet or a blanket; on the right, shabby screens; while on the left, where the stage was not closed, the camp-bedsteads could be seen; but the spectators were not exacting, and were willing to imagine all that was wanting. It was an easy task for them; all convicts are great dreamers. Directly they are told "this is a garden," it is for them a garden. Informed that "this is a hut," they accept the definition without difficulty. To them it is a hut. Sirotkin was charming in a woman's dress. The miller finishes his work, takes his cap and his whip, goes up to his wife, and gives her to understand by signs, that if during his absence she makes the mistake of receiving any one, she will have to deal with him—and he shows her his whip. The wife listens, and nods affirmatively her head. The whip is evidently known to her; the hussey has often deserved it. The husband goes out. Hardly has he turned upon his heel, than his wife shakes her fist at him. There is a knock; the door opens, and in comes a neighbour, miller also by trade. He wears a beard, is in a kuftan, and he brings as a present a red handkerchief. The woman smiles. Another knock is heard at the door. Where shall she hide him? She conceals him under the table, and takes up her distaff again. Another admirer now presents himself—a farrier in the uniform of a non-commissioned officer.

Until now the pantomime had gone on capitally; the gestures of the actors being irreproachable. It was astounding to see these improvised players going through their parts in so correct a manner; and involuntarily one said to oneself:

"What a deal of talent is lost in our Russia, left without use in our prisons and places of exile!"

The convict who played the part of the farrier had, doubtless, taken part in a performance at some provincial theatre, or had played with amateurs. It seemed to me, in any case, that our actors knew nothing of acting as an art, and bore themselves in the meanest manner. When it was his turn to appear, he came on like one of the classical heroes of the old repertory—taking a long stride with one foot before he raised the other from the ground, throwing back his head on the upper part of his body and casting proud looks around him. If such a gait was ridiculous on the part of classical heroes, still more so was it when the actor was representing a comic character. But the audience thought it quite natural, and accepted the actor's triumphant walk as a necessary fact, without criticising it.

A moment after the entry of the second admirer there is another knock at the door. The wife loses her head. Where is the farrier to be concealed? In her big box. It fortunately is open. The farrier disappears within it and the lid falls upon him.

The new arrival is a Brahmin, in full costume. His entry is hailed by the spectators with a formidable laugh. This Brahmin is represented by the convict Cutchin, who plays the part perfectly, thanks, in a great measure, to a suitable physiognomy. He explains in the pantomime his love of the miller's wife, raises his hands to heaven, and then clasps them on his breast.

There is now another knock at the door—a vigorous one this time. There could be no mistake about it. It is the master of the house. The miller's wife loses her head; the Brahmin runs wildly on all sides, begging to be concealed. She helps him to slip behind the cupboard, and begins to spin, and goes on spinning without thinking of opening the door. In her fright she gets the thread twisted, drops the spindle, and, in her agitation, makes the gesture of turning it when it is lying on the ground. Sirotkin represented perfectly this state of alarm.

Then the miller kicks open the door and approaches his wife, whip in hand. He has seen everything, for he was spying outside; and he indicates by signs to his wife that she has three lovers concealed in the house. Then he searches them out.

First, he finds the neighbour, whom he drives out with his fist. The frightened farrier tries to escape. He raises, with his head, the cover of the chest, and is at once seen. The miller thrashes him with his whip, and for once this gallant does not march in the classical style.

The only one now remaining is the Brahmin, whom the husband seeks for some time without finding him. At last he discovers him in his corner behind the cupboard, bows to him politely, and then draws him by his beard into the middle of the stage. The Brahmin tries to defend himself, and cries out, "Accursed, accursed!"—the only words pronounced throughout the pantomime. But the husband will not listen to him, and, after settling accounts with him, turns to his wife. Seeing that her turn has come, she throws away both wheel and spindle, and runs out, causing an earthen pot to fall as she shakes the room in her fright. The convicts burst into a laugh, and Ali, without looking at me, takes my hand, and calls out, "See, see the Brahmin!" He cannot hold himself upright, so overpowering is his laugh. The curtain falls, and another song begins.

There were two or three more, all broadly humorous and very droll. The convicts had not composed them themselves, but they had contributed something to them. Every actor improvised to such purpose that the part was a different one each evening. The pantomime ended with a ballet, in which there was a burial. The Brahmin went through various incantations over the corpse, and with effect. The dead man returns to life, and, in their joy, all present begin to dance. The Brahmin dances in Brahminical style with the dead man. This was the final scene. The convicts now separated, happy, delighted, and full of praise for the actors and gratitude towards the non-commissioned officers. There was not the least quarrel, and they all went to bed with peaceful hearts, to sleep with a sleep by no means familiar to them.

This is no fantasy of my imagination, but the truth, the very truth. These unhappy men had been permitted to live for some moments in their own way, to amuse themselves in a human manner, to escape for a brief hour from their sad position as convicts; and a moral change was effected, at least for a time.

The night is already quite dark. Something makes me shudder, and I awake. The "old believer" is still on the top of the high porcelain stove praying, and he will continue to pray until dawn. Ali is sleeping peacefully by my side. I remember that when he went to bed he was still laughing and talking about the theatre with his brothers. Little by little I began to remember everything; the preceding day, the Christmas holidays, and the whole month. I raised my head in fright and looked at my companions, who were sleeping by the trembling light of the candle provided by the authorities. I look at their unhappy countenances, their miserable beds; I view this nakedness, the wretchedness, and then convince myself that it is not a frightful night there, but a simple reality. Yes, it is a reality. I hear a groan. Some one has moved his arm and made his chains rattle. Another one is agitated in his dreams and speaks aloud, while the old grandfather is praying for the "Orthodox Christians." I listened to his prayer, uttered with regularity, in soft, rather drawling tones: "Lord Jesus Christ have mercy upon us."

"Well, I am not here for ever, but only for a few years," I said to myself, and I again laid my head down on my pillow.

Part II.

CHAPTER I. THE HOSPITAL

Shortly after the Christmas holidays I felt ill, and had to go to our military hospital, which stood apart at about half a verst (one-third of a mile) from the fortress. It was a one-storey building, very long, and painted yellow. Every summer a great quantity of ochre was expended in brightening it up. In the immense court-yard stood buildings, including those where the chief physicians lived, while the principal building contained only wards intended for the patients. There were a good many of them, but as only two were reserved for the convicts, these latter were nearly always full, above all in summer, so that it was often necessary to bring the beds closer together. These wards were occupied by "unfortunates" of all kinds: first by our own, then by military prisoners, previously incarcerated in the guard-houses. There were others, again, who had not yet been tried, or who were passing through. In this hospital, too, were invalids from the Disciplinary Company, a melancholy institution for bringing together soldiers of bad conduct, with a view to their correction. At the end of a year or two, they come back the most thorough-going rascals that the earth can endure.

When a convict felt that he was ill, he told the non-commissioned officer, who wrote the man's name down on a card, which he then gave to him and sent him to the hospital under the escort of a soldier. On his arrival he was examined by a doctor, who authorised the convict to remain at the hospital if he was really ill. My name was duly written down, and towards one o'clock, when all my companions had started for their afternoon work, I went to the hospital. Every prisoner took with him such money and bread as he could (for food was not to be expected the first day), a little pipe, and pouch containing tobacco, with flint, steel, and match-paper. The convicts concealed these objects in their boots. On entering the hospital I experienced a feeling of curiosity, for a new aspect of life was now presented.

The day was hot, cloudy, sad—one of those days when places like a hospital assume a particularly disagreeable and repulsive look. Myself and the soldier escorting me went into the entrance room, where there were two copper baths. There were two convicts waiting there with their warders. An assistant surgeon came in, looked at us with a careless and patronising air, and went away still more carelessly to announce our arrival to the physician on duty. Soon the physician arrived. He examined me, treating me in a very affable manner, and gave me a paper on which my name was inscribed. The ordinary physician of the wards reserved for the convicts was to make the diagnosis of my illness, to prescribe the fitting remedies, together with the necessary diet. I had already heard the convicts say that their doctors could not be too much praised. "They are fathers to us," they would say.

I took my clothes off to put on another costume. Our clothes and linen were taken away, and we were given hospital linen instead, to which were added long stockings, slippers, cotton nightcaps, and a dressing-gown of a very thick brown cloth, which was lined, not with linen, but with filth. The dressing-gown was indeed very filthy, but I soon understood its utility. We were afterwards taken to the convict wards, which were at the head of a long corridor, very high, and very clean. The external cleanliness was quite satisfactory. Everything that could be seen shone; so, at least, it seemed to me, after the dirtiness of the convict prison.

The two prisoners, whom I had found in the entrance hall, went to the left of the corridor, while I entered a room. Before the padlocked door walked a sentinel, musket on shoulder; and not far off was the soldier who was to replace him. The sergeant of the hospital guard ordered him to let me pass, and suddenly I found myself in the middle of a long narrow room, with beds to the number of twenty-two arranged against the walls. Three or four of them were still unoccupied. These wooden beds were painted green, and, as is notoriously the case with all hospital beds in Russia, were doubtless inhabited by bugs. I went into a corner by the side of the windows. There were very few prisoners dangerously ill and confined to their beds.

The inmates of the hospital were, for the most part, convalescents, or men who were slightly indisposed. My new companions were stretched out on their couches, or walking about up and down between the rows of beds. There was just space enough for them to come and go. The atmosphere of the ward was stifling with the odour peculiar to hospitals. It was composed of various emanations, each more disagreeable than the other, and of the smell of drugs; though the stove was kept well heated all day long, my bed was covered with a counterpane, which I took off. The bed itself consisted of a cloth blanket lined with linen, and coarse sheets of more than doubtful cleanliness. By the side of the bed was a little table with a pitcher and a pewter mug, together with a diminutive napkin, which had been given to me. The table could, moreover, hold a tea-urn for those patients who were rich enough to drink tea. These men of means, however, were not very numerous. The pipes and the tobacco pouches—for all the patients smoked, even the consumptive ones—could be concealed beneath the mattress. The doctors and the other officials scarcely ever made searches, and when they surprised a patient with a pipe in his mouth, they pretended not to see. The patients, however, were very prudent, and smoked always at the back of the stove. They never smoked in their beds except at night, when no rounds were made by the officers commanding the hospital.

Until then I had not been in any hospital in the character of patient, so that everything was quite new to me. I noticed that my entry had mystified some of the prisoners. They had heard of me, and all the inmates now looked upon me with that slight shade of superiority which recognised members of no matter what society show to one newly admitted among them. On my right was lying down a man committed for trial—an ex-secretary and the illegitimate son of a retired captain—accused of having made false money. He had been in the hospital nearly a year. He was not in the least ill, but he assured the doctors that he had an aneurism, and he so thoroughly convinced them that he escaped both the hard labour and the corporal punishment to which he had been sentenced. He was sent a year later to T——k, where he was attached to an asylum. He was a vigorous young fellow of eight-and-twenty, cunning, a self-confessed rogue, and something of a lawyer. He was intelligent, had easy manners, but was very presumptuous, and suffered from morbid self-esteem. Convinced that there was no one in the world a bit more honest or more just than himself, he did not consider himself at all guilty, and never kept this assurance to himself.

This personage was the first to address me, and he questioned me with much curiosity. He initiated me into the ways of the hospital; and, of course, began by telling me that he was the son of a captain. He was very anxious that I should take him for a noble, or at least, for some one connected with the nobility.

Soon afterwards an invalid from the Disciplinary Company came and told me that he knew a great many nobles who had been exiled; and, to convince me, he repeated to me their christian names and their patronymics. It was only necessary to see the face of this soldier to understand that he was lying abominably. He was named Tchekounoff, and came to pay court to me, because he suspected me of having money. When he saw a packet of tea and sugar, he at once offered me his services to make the water boil and to get me a tea-urn. M. D. S. K—— had promised to send me my own by one of the prisoners who worked in the hospital, but Tchekounoff arranged to get me one forthwith. He got me a tin vessel, in which he made the water boil; and, in a word, he showed such extraordinary zeal, that it drew down upon him bitter laughter from one of the patients, a consumptive man, whose bed was just opposite mine, Usteantseff by name. This was the soldier condemned to the rods, who, from fear, had swallowed a bottle of vodka, in which he had infused tobacco, this bringing on lung disease.

I have spoken of him above. He had remained silent until now, stretched out on his bed, and breathing with difficulty. He looked at me all the time with a very serious air. He did not take his eyes from Tchekounoff, whose civility irritated him. His extraordinary gravity rendered his indignation comic. At last he could stand it no longer.

"Look at this fellow! He has found his master," he said, stammering out the words with a voice strangled by weakness, for he had now not long to live.

Tchekounoff, much annoyed, turned round.

"Who is the fellow?" he asked, looking at Usteantseff, with contempt.

"Why, you are a flunkey," replied Usteantseff, as confidently as if he had possessed the right of calling Tchekounoff to order.

"I a fellow?"

"Yes, you are a flunkey; a true flunkey. Listen, my good friends. He won't believe me. He is quite astonished, the brave fellow."

"What can that matter to you? You see when they don't know how to make use of their hands that they are not accustomed to be without servants. Why should I not serve him, buffoon with a hairy snout?"

"Who has a hairy snout?"

"You!"

"I have a hairy snout?"

"Yes; certainly you have."

"You are a nice fellow, you are. If I have a hairy snout, you have a face like a crow's egg."

"Hairy snout! The merciful Lord has settled your account. You would do much better to keep quiet and die."

"Why? I would rather prostrate myself before a boot than before a slipper. My father never prostrated himself, and never made me do so."

He would have continued, but an attack of coughing convulsed him for some minutes. He spat blood, and a cold sweat broke out on his low forehead. If his cough had not prevented him from speaking, he would have continued to declaim. One could see that from his look; but in his powerlessness he could only move his hand, the result of which was that Tchekounoff spoke no more about the matter.

I quite understood that the consumptive patient hated me much more than Tchekounoff. No one would have thought of being angry with him or of looking down upon him by reason of the services he was rendering me, and the few kopecks that he tried to get from me. Every one understood that he did it all in order to get himself a little money.

The Russian people are not at all susceptible on such points, and know perfectly well how to take them.

I had displeased Usteantseff, as my tea had also displeased him. What irritated him was that, in spite of all, I was a gentleman, even with my chains; that I could not do without a servant, though I neither asked for nor desired one. In reality I tried to do everything for myself, in order not to appear a white-handed, effeminate person, and not to play the part which excited so much envy.

I even felt a little pride on this point; but, in spite of every thing—I do not know why—I was always surrounded by officious, complaisant people, who attached themselves to me of their own free will, and who ended by governing me. It was I rather who was their servant; so that, whether I liked it or not, I was made to appear to every one a noble, who could not do without the services of others, and who gave himself airs. This exasperated me.

Usteantseff was consumptive, and, therefore, irascible. The other patients only showed me indifference, tinged with a shade of contempt. They were occupied with a circumstance which now presents itself to my memory.

I learned, as I listened to their conversation, that there was to be brought into the hospital that evening a convict who, at that moment, was receiving the rods. The prisoners were looking forward to this new arrival with some curiosity. They said, however, that his punishment was but slight—only five hundred strokes.

I looked round. The greater number of genuine patients were, as far as I could observe, affected by scurvy and diseases of the eyes—both peculiar to this country. The others suffered from fever, lung disease, and other illnesses. The different illnesses were not separated; all the patients were together in the same room.

I have spoken of genuine patients, for certain convicts had come in merely to get a little rest. The doctors admitted them from pure compassion, above all, if there were any vacant beds. Life in the guard-house and in the prison was so hard compared with that of the hospital, that many persons preferred to remain lying down in spite of the stifling atmosphere and the rules against leaving the room.

There were even men who took pleasure in this kind of life. They belonged nearly all to the Disciplinary Company. I examined my new companions with curiosity. One of them puzzled me very much. He was consumptive, and was dying. His bed was a little further on than that of Usteantseff, and was nearly beside mine. He was named Mikhailoff. I had seen him in the Convict Prison two weeks before, when he was already seriously ill. He ought to have been under treatment long before, but he bore up against his malady with surprising courage. He did not go to the hospital until about the Christmas holidays, to die three weeks afterwards of galloping consumption. He seemed to have burned out like a candle. What astonished me most was the terrible change in his countenance. I had noticed him the very first day of my imprisonment. By his side was lying a soldier of the Disciplinary Company—an old man with a bad expression on his face, whose general appearance was disgusting.

But I am not going to enumerate all the patients. I just remember this old man simply because he made an impression on me, and initiated me at once into certain peculiarities of the ward. He had a severe cold in the head, which made him sneeze at every moment, even during his sleep, as if firing salutes, five or six times running, while each time he called out, "My God, what torture!"

Seated on his bed he stuffed his nose eagerly with snuff, which he took from a paper bag, in order to sneeze more strongly, and with greater regularity. He sneezed into a checked cotton pocket-handkerchief which belonged to him, and which had lost its colour through perpetual washing. His little nose then became wrinkled in a most peculiar manner with a multitude of wrinkles, and his open mouth exhibited broken teeth, decayed and black, and red gums moist with saliva. When he sneezed into his handkerchief he unfolded it and wiped it on the lining of his dressing-gown. His proceedings disgusted me so much that involuntarily I examined the dressing-gown I had just put on myself. It exhaled a most offensive odour, which contact with my body helped to bring out. It smelt of plasters and medicaments of all kinds. It seemed as though it had been worn by patients from time immemorial. The lining had, perhaps, been washed once, but I would not swear to it. Certainly, at the time I put it on, it was saturated with lotions, and stained by contact with poultices and plasters of all imaginable kinds.

The men condemned to the rods, having undergone their punishment, were brought straight to the hospital, their backs still bleeding. As compresses and as poultices were placed on their wounds, the dressing-gown they wore over their wet shirt received and retained the droppings.

During all the time of my hard labour I had to go to the hospital, which often happened, I always put on, with mistrust and abhorrence, the dressing-gown that was delivered to me. As soon as Tchekounoff had given me my tea (I will say, in parenthesis, that the water brought in in the morning, and not renewed throughout the day, was soon corrupted, soon poisoned by the fetid air), the door opened, and the soldier, who had just received the rods, was brought in under a double escort. I saw, for the first time, a man who had just been whipped. Later on many were brought in, and whenever this happened it caused great distress to the patients. These unfortunate men were received with grave composure, but the nature of the reception depended nearly always on the enormity of the crime committed, and, consequently, the number of strokes administered.

The criminals most cruelly whipped, and who were celebrated as brigands of the first order, enjoyed more respect and attention than a simple deserter, a recruit, like the one who had just been brought in. But in neither case was any particular sympathy manifested, nor were any annoying remarks made. The unhappy man was attended to in silence, above all if he was incapable of attending to himself. The assistant-surgeons knew that they were entrusting their patients to skilful and experienced hands. The usual treatment consisted in applying very often to the back of the man who had been whipped a shirt or a piece of linen steeped in cold water. It was also necessary to withdraw skilfully from the wounds the twigs left by the rods which had been broken on the criminal's back. This last operation was particularly painful to the patients. The extraordinary stoicism with which they supported their sufferings astonished me greatly.

I have seen many convicts who had been whipped, and cruelly, I can tell you. Well, I do not remember one of them uttering a groan. Only after such an experience, the countenance becomes pale, decomposed, the eyes glitter, the look wanders, and the lips tremble so that the patient sometimes bites them till they bleed.

The soldier who had just come in was twenty-three years of age; he had a good muscular development, and was rather a fine man, tall, well-made, with a bronzed skin. His back, uncovered down to the waist, had been seriously beaten, and his body now trembled with fever beneath the damp sheet with which his back was covered. For about an hour and a half he did nothing but walk backwards and forwards in the room. I looked at his face: he seemed to be thinking of nothing; his eyes had a strange expression, at once wild and timid; they seemed to fix themselves with difficulty on the various objects. I fancied I saw him looking attentively at my hot tea; the steam was rising from the full cup, and the poor devil was shivering and clattering his teeth. I invited him to have some; he turned towards me without saying a word, and taking up the cup, swallowed the tea at one gulp, without putting sugar in it. He tried not to look at me, and when he had finished he put the cup back in silence without making a sign, and then began to walk up and down as before. He was in too much pain to think of speaking to me or thanking me. As for the other prisoners, they abstained from questioning him; when once they had applied compresses they paid no more attention to him, thinking probably it would be better to leave him alone, and not to worry him by their questions and compassion. The soldier seemed quite satisfied with this view.

Meanwhile, night came on and the lamp was lighted; some of the patients possessed candlesticks of their own, but these were not numerous. In the evening the doctor came round, after which a non-commissioned officer on guard counted the patients and closed the room.

The prisoners could not speak in too high terms of their doctors. They looked upon them truly as fathers and respected them. These doctors had always something pleasant to say, a kind word even for reprobates, who appreciated it all the more because they knew it was said in all sincerity.

Yes, these kind words were really sincere, for no one would have thought of blaming the doctors had they shown themselves cross and inhuman; they were kind purely from humanity. They understood perfectly that a convict who is sick has as much right to breathe pure air as any other person, even though the latter might be a great personage. The convalescents there had a right to walk freely through the corridors to take exercise, and to breathe air less pestilential than that of our infirmary, which was close and saturated with deleterious emanations. In our ward, when once the doors had been closed in the evening, they had to remain closed throughout the night, and under no pretext was one of the inmates allowed to go out.

For many years an inexplicable fact troubled me like an insoluble problem. I must speak of it before going on with my description. I am thinking of the chains which every convict is obliged to wear, however ill he may be; even consumptives have died beneath my eyes with their legs loaded with irons.

Everybody was accustomed to it, and regarded it as an inevitable fact. I do not think any one, even the doctors, would have thought of demanding the removal of the irons from convicts who were seriously ill, not even from the consumptive ones. The chains, it is true, were not exceedingly heavy; they did not in general weigh more than eight or ten pounds, which is a supportable burden for a man in good health. I have been told, however, that after some years the legs of the convicts dry up and waste away. I do not know whether it is true. I am inclined to think it is; the weight, however light it may be (say not more than ten pounds), if it is fixed to the leg for ever, increases the general weight in an abnormal manner, and at the end of a certain time must have a disastrous effect on its development.

For a convict in good health this is nothing, but the same cannot be said of one who is sick. For the convicts who were seriously ill, for the consumptive ones whose arms and legs dry up of themselves, this last straw is insupportable. Even if the medical authorities claimed alleviation for the consumptive patients alone, it would be an immense benefit, I assure you. I shall be told convicts are malefactors, unworthy of compassion; but ought increased severity to be shown towards him on whom the finger of God already weighs? No one will believe that the object of this aggravation is to reform the criminal. The consumptive prisoners are exempted from corporal punishment by the tribunal.

There must be some mysterious, important reason for all this, but what it is, it is impossible to understand. No one believes—it is impossible to believe—that a consumptive man will run away. Who can think of such a thing, especially if the illness has reached a certain degree of intensity? It is impossible to deceive the doctors and make them mistake a convict in good health for one who is in a consumption, for this malady is one that can be recognised at the first glance. Moreover, can the irons prevent the convict not in good health from escaping? Not in the least. The irons are a degradation and shame, a physical and moral burden; but they would not hinder any one attempting to escape. The most awkward and least intelligent convict can saw through them, or break the rivets by hammering at them with a stone. Chains, then, are a useless precaution; and if the convicts wear them as a punishment, should not this punishment be spared to dying men?

As I write these lines, a face stands out from my memory: that of a dying man, a man who died in consumption, this same Mikhailoff, whose bed was nearly opposite me, and who expired, I think, four days after my arrival at the hospital. When I spoke above of the consumptive patients, I was only reproducing involuntarily the sensations and ideas which occurred to me on the occasion of this death. I knew Mikhailoff very little; he was a young man of twenty-five at most, not very tall, thin, and with a fine face; he belonged to the "special section," and was remarkable for his strange, but soft and sad taciturnity; he seemed to have "dried up" in the convict prison, to use an expression employed by the convicts who had a good recollection of him. I remember he had very fine eyes. I really cannot tell why I think of that.

He died at three o'clock in the afternoon on a clear, dry day. The sun was darting its brilliant rays obliquely through the greenish, frozen panes of our room. A torrent of light inundated the unhappy patient, who had lost all consciousness, and was several hours dying. From the early morning his sight became confused; he was unable to recognise those who approached him. The convicts would gladly have done anything to relieve him, for they saw he was in great suffering. His respiration was painful, deep, and irregular; his breast rose and fell violently, as though he were in want of air; he cast his blanket and his clothes far from him. Then he began to tear up his shirt, which seemed to him a terrible burden. It was taken off. Then it was frightful to see this immensely long body, with fleshless arms and legs, with beating breast, and ribs which were as clearly marked as those of a skeleton. There was nothing now on this skeleton but a cross and the irons, from which his dried-up legs might easily have freed themselves. A quarter of an hour before his death everything was silent in our ward, and the inmates spoke only in whispers. The convicts walked on the tips of their toes. From time to time they exchanged remarks on other subjects, and cast a furtive glance at the dying man. The rattling in his throat grew more and more painful. At last, with a trembling hand, he felt the cross on his breast and endeavoured to tear it off; it was also weighing upon him, suffocating him. It was taken off. Ten minutes afterwards, he died. Some one then knocked at the door in order to give notice to the sentinel; the warder entered, looked at the dead man with a vacant air, and went away to get the assistant-surgeon. The assistant-surgeon was a good fellow enough, but a little too much occupied with his personal appearance, otherwise very agreeable; he soon arrived, went up to the corpse with long strides which made a noise in the silent ward, and felt the dead man's pulse with an unconcerned air which seemed to have been put on for the occasion. He then made a vague gesture with his hand and went out.

Information was given at the guard-house; for the criminal was an important one (he belonged to the special section), and in order to register his death it was necessary to go through some formalities. While we were waiting for the hospital guard to come, one of the prisoners said in a whisper, "The eyes of the defunct might as well be closed." Another one profited by this remark, and approaching Mikhailoff in silence, closed his eyes; then perceiving on the pillow the cross which had been taken from his neck, he took it and looked at it, put it down, and crossed himself. The face of the dead man was becoming ossified; a ray of white light was playing on the surface and illuminated two rows of white, good teeth which sparkled between his thin lips, glued to the gums by the mouth.

The non-commissioned officer on guard arrived at last, musket on shoulder, helmet on head, accompanied by two soldiers; he approached the corpse, slackening his pace with an air of uncertainty. Then he examined with a side glance the silent prisoners, who looked at him with a sombre expression. At one step from the dead man he stopped short, as if suddenly nailed to the spot; the naked, dried-up body, loaded with irons, had impressed him; he undid his chin-strap, removed his helmet (which was not at all necessary for him to do), and made the sign of the cross; he had a gray head, the head of a soldier who had seen much service. I remember that by his side stood Tchekounoff, an old man who was also gray. He looked all the time at the non-commissioned officer, and followed all his movements with strange attention. They glanced across, and I saw that Tchekounoff also trembled. He bit and closed his teeth, and said to the non-commissioned officer, as if involuntarily, at the same time nodding his head in the direction of the dead man, "He had a mother, too!"

These words went to my heart. Why had he said them? and how did this idea occur to him? The corpse was raised with the mattress; the straw creaked, the chains dragged along the ground with a sharp ring; they were taken up and the body was carried out. Suddenly all spoke once more in a loud voice. The non-commissioned officer in the corridor could well be heard crying out to some one to go for the blacksmith. It was necessary to take the dead man's irons off. But I have digressed from my subject.

CHAPTER II. THE HOSPITAL (*continued*).

The doctors used to visit the wards in the morning, towards eleven o'clock; they appeared all together, forming a procession, which was headed by the chief physician. An hour and a half before, the ordinary physician had made his round. He was a quiet young man, always affable and kind, much liked by the prisoners, and thoroughly versed in his art; they only found one fault with him, that he was "too soft." He was, in fact, by no means communicative, he seemed confused in our presence, blushed sometimes, and changed the quantity of food at the first representation of the patient. I think he would have consented to give them any medicine they desired: in other respects an excellent young man.

A doctor in Russia often enjoys the affection and respect of the people, and with reason, as far as I have been able to see. I know that my words would seem a paradox, above all when the mistrust of this same people for foreign drugs and foreign doctors is taken into account; in fact, they prefer, even when suffering from a serious illness, to address themselves year after year to a witch, or employ old women's remedies (which, however, ought not to be despised), rather than consult a doctor, or go into the hospital. In truth, these prejudices may be above all attributed to causes which have nothing to do with medicine, namely, the mistrust of the people for anything which bears an official and administrative character; nor must it be forgotten that the common people are frightened and prejudiced in regard to the hospitals, by the stories, often absurd, of fantastic horrors said to take place within them. Perhaps, however, these stories have a basis of truth.

But what repels them above all, is the Germanism of the hospitals, the idea that during their illness they will be attended to by foreigners, the severity of the diet, the heartlessness of the surgeons and doctors, the dissection and autopsy of the bodies, etc. The common people reflect, moreover, that they will be attended by nobles—for in their view the doctors belong to the nobility. Once they have made acquaintance with them (there are exceptions, no doubt, but they are rare), their fears vanish. This success must be attributed to our doctors, especially the young ones, who, for the most part, know how to gain the respect and affection of the people. I speak now of what I myself have seen and experienced in many cases and in different parts, and I think matters are the same everywhere. In some distant localities the doctors receive presents, make profit out of their hospitals, and neglect the patients; sometimes they forget even their art. This happens, no doubt; but I am speaking of the majority, inspired as it is by that spirit, that generous tendency which is regenerating the medical art. As for the apostates, the wolves in the sheep-fold, they may excuse themselves, and cast the blame on the circumstances amid which they live; but they are absurd, inexcusable, especially if they are no longer humane; it is precisely the humanity, affability, and brotherly compassion of the doctor which prove most efficacious remedies for the patients. It is time to stop these apathetic lamentations on the circumstances surrounding us. There may be truth in the lament, but a cunning rogue who knows how to take care of himself never fails to blame the circumstances around him when he wishes his faults to be forgiven—above all, if he writes or speaks with eloquence.

I have again departed from my subject; I wish only to say that the common people mistrust and dislike officialism and the Government doctors, rather than the doctors themselves; but on personal acquaintance many prejudices disappear.

Our doctor generally stopped before the bed of each patient, questioned him seriously and attentively, then prescribed the remedies, potions, etc. He sometimes noticed that the pretended invalid was not ill at all; he had come to take rest after his hard work, and to sleep on a mattress in a warm room, far preferable to the naked planks in a damp guard-house among a mass of pale, broken-down men, waiting for their trial. In Russia the prisoners in the House of Detention are almost always broken down, which shows that their moral and material condition is worse even than those of the convicts.

In cases of feigned sickness our doctor would describe the patient as suffering from *febris catharalis*, and sometimes allowed him to remain a week in the hospital. Every one laughed at this *febris catharalis*, for it was known to be a formula agreed upon between the doctor and the patient to indicate no malady at all. Often the robust invalid who abused the doctor's compassion remained in the hospital until he was turned out by force. Our doctor was worth seeing then. Confused by the prisoner's obstinacy, he did not like to tell him plainly that he was cured and offer him his leaving ticket, although he had the right to send him away without the least explanation on writing the words, *sanat. est.* First he would hint to him that it was time to go, and then would beg him to leave.

"You must go, you know you are cured now, and we have no place for you, we are very much cramped here, etc."

At last, ashamed to remain any longer, the patient would consent to go. The physician-in-chief, although compassionate and just (the patients were much attached to him), was incomparably more severe and more decided than our ordinary physician. In certain cases he showed merciless severity which only gained for him the respect of the convicts. He always came into the room accompanied by all the doctors of the hospital, when his assistants visited all the beds and diagnosed on each particular case; he stopped longest at the beds of those who were seriously ill, and had an encouraging word for them. He never sent back the convicts who arrived with *febris catharalis*; but if one of them was determined to remain in the hospital, he certified that the man was cured. "Come," he would say, "you have had your rest; now go, you must not take liberties."

Those who insisted upon remaining, were, above all, the convicts who were worn out by field labour, performed during the great summer heat, or prisoners who had been sentenced to be whipped. I remember that they were obliged to be particularly severe, merely in order to get rid of one of them. He had come to be cured of some disease of the eyes, which were red all over; he complained of suffering a sharp pain in the eyelids. He was incurable; plasters, blisters, leeches, nothing did him any good; and the diseased organ remained in the same condition.

Then it occurred to the doctors that the illness was feigned, for the inflammation neither became worse nor better; and they soon understood that a comedy was being played, although the patient would not admit it. He was a fine young fellow, not ill-looking, though he produced a disagreeable impression upon all his companions; he was suspicious, sombre, full of dissimulation, and never looked any one straight in the face; he also kept himself apart as if he mistrusted us all. I remember that many persons were afraid that he would do some one harm.

When he was a soldier he had committed some small theft, he had been arrested and condemned to receive a thousand strokes, and afterwards to pass into a disciplinary company.

To put off the moment of punishment, the prisoners, as I have already said, will do incredible things. On the eve of the fatal day, they will stick a knife into one of their chiefs, or into a comrade, in order that they may be tried again for this new offence, which will delay their punishment for a month or two. It matters little to them that their punishment be doubled or tripled, if they can escape this time. What they desire is to put off temporarily the terrible minute at whatever cost, so utterly does their heart fail them.

Many of the patients thought the man with the sore eyes ought to be watched, lest in his despair he should assassinate some one during the night; but no precaution was taken, not even by those who slept next to him. It was remarked, however, that he rubbed his eyes with plaster from the wall, and with something else besides, in order that they might appear red when the doctor came round; at last the doctor-in-chief threatened to cure him by means of a seton.

When the malady resists all ordinary treatment, the doctors determine to try some heroic, however painful, remedy. But the poor devil did not wish to get well, he was either too obstinate or too cowardly; for, however painful the proposed operation may be, it cannot be compared to the punishment of the rods.

The operation consists in seizing the patient by the nape of the neck, taking up the skin, drawing it back as much as possible, and making in it a double incision, through which is passed a skein of cotton about as thick as the finger. Every day at a fixed hour this skein is pulled backwards and forwards in order that the wound may continually suppurate and may not heal; the poor devil endured this torture which caused him horrible suffering, for several days.

At last he consented to quit the hospital. In less than a day his eyes became quite well; and, as soon as his neck was healed, he was sent to the guard-house which he left next day to receive the first thousand strokes.

Painful is the minute which precedes such a punishment; so painful, that perhaps I am wrong in taxing with cowardice those convicts who fear it.

It must be terrible; for the convicts to risk a double or triple punishment, merely to postpone it. I have spoken, however, of convicts who have thus wished to quit the hospital before the wounds caused by the first part of the flogging were healed, in order to receive the last part and make an end of it. For life in a guard-room is certainly worse than in a convict prison.

The habit of receiving floggings helps in some cases to give intrepidity and decision to convicts. Those who have been often flogged, are hardened both in body and mind, and have at last looked upon such a punishment as merely a disagreeable incident no longer to be feared.

One of our convicts of the special section was a converted Tartar, who was named Alexander, or Alexandrina, as they called him in fun at the convict prison; who told me how he had received 4,000 strokes. He never spoke of this punishment except with amusement and laughter; but he swore very seriously that if he had not been brought up in his horde, from his most tender infancy, on whipping and flogging—and as the scars which covered his back, and which refused to disappear, were there to testify—he would never have been able to support those 4,000 strokes. He blessed the education of sticks that he had received.

"I was beaten for the least thing, Alexander Petrovitch," he said one evening, when we were sitting down before the fire. "I was beaten without reason for fifteen years, as long as I can ever remember, and several times a day. Any one who liked beat me; so that, at last, it made no impression upon me."

I do not know how it was he became a soldier, for perhaps he lied, and had always been a deserter and vagabond. But I remember his telling me one day of the fright he was seized with when he was condemned to receive 4,000 strokes for having killed one of his officers.

"I know that they will punish me severely," he said to himself, "that, accustomed as I am to be whipped, I shall perhaps die on the spot. The devil! 4,000 strokes is not a trifle; and then all my officers were in a fearful temper with me on account of this affair. I knew well that it would not be 'rose-water.' I even believed that I should die under the rods. I determined to get baptized. I said to myself, that perhaps they would not then flog me, at any rate it was worth trying, my comrades had told me that it would be of no good. But,' I said to myself, 'who knows? perhaps they will pardon me, they will have more compassion on a Christian than on a Mohammedan. They baptized me, and give me the name of Alexander; but, in spite of that, I had to take my flogging; they did not let me off a single stroke; I was, however, very savage. 'Wait a bit,' I said to myself, 'and I will take you all in'; and, would you believe it, Alexander? I did take them all in. I knew how to look like a dead man; not that I appeared altogether without life, but I looked as if I were on the point of breathing my last. They led me in front of the battalion to receive my first thousand; my skin was burning, I began to howl. They gave me my second thousand, and I said to myself, 'It's all over now.' I had lost my head, my legs seemed broken, so I fell to the ground, with the eyes of a dead man. My face blue, my mouth full of froth, I no longer breathed. When the doctor came he said I was on the point of death. I was carried to the hospital, and at once returned to life. Twice again they flogged me. What a rage they were in! I took them all in on each occasion. I received my third thousand, and died again. On my word, when they gave me the last thousand each stroke ought to have counted for three, it was like a knife in my heart. Oh, how they did beat me! They were so severe with me. Oh, that cursed fourth thousand! it was well worth three firsts put together. If I had pretended to be dead when I had still 200 to receive, I think they would have finished me; but they did not get the better of me. I had them again and again, for they always thought it was all over with me, and how could they have thought otherwise? The doctor was sure of it. But as for the 200 which I had still to receive, they might have struck as hard as they liked—they were worth 2,000; I only laughed at them. Why? Because, when I was a youngster, I had grown up under the whip. Well, I am well, and alive now; but I have been beaten in the course of my life," he repeated, with a passive air, as he brought his story to an end. As he did so, he seemed to recollect and count anew the blows he had received.

After a brief silence, he said: "I cannot count them, nor can any one else; there are not figures enough." He looked at me, and burst into a laugh, so simple and natural, that I could not help smiling in return.

"Do you know, Alexander Petrovitch, when I dream at night, I always dream that I am being flogged. I dream of nothing else." He, in fact, talked in his sleep, and woke up the other prisoners.

"What are you yelling about, you demon?" they would say to him.

This strong, robust fellow, short in stature, about forty-four years of age, active, good-looking, lived on good terms with every one, though he was very fond of taking what did not belong to him, and afterwards got beaten for it. But each of our convicts who stole got beaten for their thefts.

I will add to these remarks that I was always surprised at the extraordinary good-nature, the absence of rancour with which these unhappy men spoke of their punishment, and of the chiefs superintending it. In these stories, which often gave me palpitation of the heart, not a shadow of hatred or rancour could be detected; they laughed at what they had suffered like children.

It was not the same, however, with M—tçki, when he told me of his punishment. As he was not a noble, he had been sentenced to be flogged. He had never spoken to me of it, and when I asked him if it were true, he replied affirmatively in two brief words, but with evident suffering, and without looking at me. He at the same time turned red, and when he raised his eyes, I saw flames burning in them, while his lips trembled with indignation. I felt that he would not forget, that he could never forget this page of his history. Our companions generally on the other hand (though theirs might have been exceptions), looked upon their adventures with quite another eye. It is impossible, I sometimes thought, that they can be conscious of their guilt, and not acknowledge the justice of their punishment; above all, when their offences were against their companions and not against some chief. The greater part of them did not acknowledge their guilt. I have already said that I never observed in them the least remorse, even when the crime had been committed against people of their own station. As for the crimes committed against a chief, they did not even speak of them. It seems to me that for those cases, they had special views of their own. They looked upon them as accidents caused by destiny, by fatality, into which they had fallen unconsciously as the result of some extraordinary impulse. The convict always justifies the crimes he has committed against his chief; he does not trouble himself about the matter. But he admits that the chief cannot share his view, and consequently, that he must naturally be punished, and then he will be quits with him.

The struggle between the administration and the prisoner is of the severest character on both sides. What in a great measure justifies the criminal in his own eyes, is his conviction that the people among whom he has been born and has lived will acquit him. He is certain that the common people will not look upon him as a lost man, unless, indeed, his crime has bean committed against persons of his own class, against his brethren. He is quite calm about that; supported by his conscience, he will not lose his moral tranquillity, and that is the principal thing. He feels himself on firm ground, and has no particular hatred for the knout, when once it has been administered to him. He knows that it was inevitable, and consoles himself by thinking that he was neither the first nor the last to receive it. Does the soldier detest the Turk whom he fights? Not in the least! yet he sabres him, hacks him to pieces, kills him.

It must not be thought, moreover, that all of these stories were told with indifference and in cold blood.

When the name of Jerebiatnikof was mentioned, it was always with indignation. I made the acquaintance of this officer during my first stay in the hospital—only by the convicts' stories, it must be understood. I afterwards saw him one day when he was commanding the guard at the convict prison; he was about thirty years old, very stout and very strong, with red cheeks hanging down on each side, white teeth, and a formidable laugh. One could see in a moment that he was in no way given to reflection. He took the greatest pleasure in whipping and flogging, when he had to superintend the punishment. I must hasten to say that the other officers looked upon Jerebiatnikof as a monster, and the convicts did the same. This was in the good old time, which is not very very far off, but in which it is already difficult to believe executioners delighted in their office. But, generally speaking, the strokes were administered without enthusiasm.

This lieutenant was an exception, and he took a real pleasure and delight in punishment. He had a passion for it, and liked it for its own sake; he looked to this art for unnatural delights in order to tickle and excite his base soul. A prisoner is conducted to the place of punishment. Jerebiatnikof is the officer superintending the execution. Arranging a long line of soldiers, armed with heavy rods, he walks along the front with a satisfied air, and encourages each one to do his duty, conscientiously or otherwise—the soldiers know before what "otherwise" means. The criminal is brought out. If he does not yet know Jerebiatnikof, if he is not in the secret of the mystery, the Lieutenant plays him the following trick—one of the inventions of Jerebiatnikof, very ingenious in this style of thing. The prisoner, whose back has been bared, and whom the non-commissioned officers have fastened to the butt end of a musket in order to drag him afterwards through the whole length of the "Green Street." He begs the officer in charge, with a plaintive and tearful voice, not to have him struck too hard, not to double the punishment by any undue severity.

"Your nobility!" cries the unhappy wretch, "have pity on me, treat me fraternally, so that I may pray God throughout my life for you. Do not destroy me, show mercy!"

Jerebiatnikof had waited for this. He now suspended the execution, and engaged the prisoner in conversation, speaking to him in a sentimental, compassionate tone.

"But, my good fellow," he would say, "what am I to do? It is the law that punishes you—it is the law."

"Your nobility! You can make it everything; have pity upon me."

"Do you really think that I have no pity on you? Do you think it is any pleasure to me to see you whipped? I am a man, am I not? Answer me, am I not a man?"

"Certainly, your nobility. We know that the officers are our fathers and we their children. Be to me a venerable father," the prisoner would cry, seeing some possibility of escaping punishment.

"Then, my friend, judge for yourself. You have a brain to think with, you know I am human, I ought to take compassion on you, sinner though you be."

"Your nobility says the absolute truth."

"Yes, I ought to be merciful to you however guilty you may be. But it is not I who punish you, it is the law. I serve God and my country, and consequently I commit a grave sin if I mitigate the punishment fixed by the law. Only think of that!"

"Your nobility!"

"Well, what am I to do? Only think, I know that I am doing wrong, but it shall be as you wish; I will have mercy upon you, you shall be punished lightly. But if I really do this on one occasion, if I show mercy, if I punish you lightly, you will think that at another time I shall be merciful, and you will recommence your follies. What do you say to that?"

"Your nobility, preserve me! Before the throne of the heavenly Creator, I——"

"No, no; you swear that you will behave yourself."

"May the Lord cause me to die this moment and in the next world."

"Do not swear in that way, it is a sin; I shall believe you if you will give me your word."

"Your nobility."

"Well, listen, I will have mercy on you on account of your tears, your orphan's tears, for you are an orphan, are you not?"

"Orphan on both sides, your nobility, I am alone in the world."

"Well, on account of your orphan's tears I have pity on you," he added, in a voice so full of emotion, that the prisoner could not sufficiently thank God for having sent him so good an officer.

The procession went out, the drum rolled, the soldiers brandished their arms. "Flog him," Jerebiatnikof would roar from the bottom of his lungs, "flog him! burn him! skin him alive! Harder! harder! Give it harder to this orphan! Give it him, the rogue."

The soldiers lay on the strokes with all their might on the back of the unhappy wretch, whose eyes dart fire, and who howls while Jerebiatnikof runs after him in front of the line, holding his sides with laughter—he puffs and blows so that he can scarcely hold himself upright. He is happy. He thinks it droll. From time to time his formidable resonant laugh is heard, as he keeps on repeating, "Flog him! thrash him! this brigand! this orphan!"

He had composed variation on this motive. The prisoner has been brought to undergo his punishment. He begs the lieutenant to have pity on him. This time Jerebiatnikof does not play the hypocrite; he is frank with the prisoner.

"Look, my dear fellow, I will punish you as you deserve, but I can show you one act of mercy. I will not attach you to the butt end of the musket, you shall go along in a new style, you have only to run as hard as you can along the front, each rod will strike you as a matter of course, but it will be over sooner. What do you say to that, will you try?"

The prisoner, who has listened, full of mistrust and doubt, says to himself: Perhaps this way will not be so bad as the other. If I run with all my might, it will not last quite so long, and perhaps all the rods will not touch me.

"Well, your nobility, I consent."

"I also consent. Come, mind your business," cries the lieutenant to the soldiers. He knew beforehand that not one rod would spare the back of the unfortunate wretch; the soldier who failed to hit him would know what to expect.

The convict tries to run along the "Green Street," but he does not go beyond fifteen men before the rods rain upon his poor spine like hail; so that the unfortunate man shrieks out, and falls as if he had been struck by a bullet.

"No, your nobility, I prefer to be flogged in the ordinary way," he says, managing to get up, pale and frightened. While Jerebiatnikof, who knew beforehand how this affair would end, held his sides and burst into a laugh.

But I cannot relate all the diversions invented by him, and all that was told about him.

My companions also spoke of a Lieutenant Smekaloff, who fulfilled the functions of Commandant before the arrival of our present Major. They spoke of Jerebiatnikof with indifference, without hatred, but also without exalting his high achievements. They did not praise him, they simply despised him, whilst at the name of Smekaloff the whole prison burst into a chorus of laudation. The Lieutenant was by no means fond of administering the rods; there was nothing in him of Jerebiatnikof's disposition. How did it happen that the convicts remembered his punishments, severe as they were, with sweet satisfaction. How did he manage to please them. How did he gain the popularity he certainly enjoyed?

Our companions, like Russian people in general, were ready to forget their tortures if a kind word was said to them; I speak of the effect itself without analysing or examining it. It is not difficult, then, to gain the affections of such a people and become popular. Lieutenant Smekaloff had gained such popularity, and when the punishments he had directed were spoken of, they were always mentioned with a certain sympathy.

"He was as kind as a father," the convicts would sometimes say, as, with a sigh, they compared him with their present chief, the Major who had replaced him.

He was a simple-minded man, and kind in a manner. There are chiefs who are naturally kind and merciful, but who are not at all liked and are laughed at; whereas, Smekaloff had so managed that all the prisoners had a special regard for him; this was due to innate qualities, which those who possess them do not understand. Strange thing! There are men who are far from being kind, and who have yet the talent of making themselves popular; they do not despise the people who are beneath their rule. That, I think, is the cause of this popularity. They do not give themselves lordly airs; they have no feeling of "caste;" they have a certain odour of the people; they are men of birth, and the people at once sniff it. They will do anything for such men; they will gladly change the mildest and most humane man for a very severe chief, if the latter possesses this sort of odour, and especially if the man is also genial in his way. Oh! then he is beyond price.

Lieutenant Smekaloff, as I have said, ordered sometimes very severe punishments. But he seemed to inflict them in such a way, that the prisoners felt no rancour against him. On the contrary, they recalled his whipping affairs with laughter; he did not punish frequently, for he had no artistic imagination. He had invented only one practical joke, a single one which amused him for nearly a year in our convict prison. This joke was dear to him, probably, because it was his only one, and it was not without humour.

Smekaloff assisted himself at the executions, joking all the time, and laughing at the prisoner as he questioned him about the most out-of-the-way things, such, for instance, as his private affairs. He did this without any bad motive, and simply because he really wished to know something about the man's affairs. A chair was brought to him, together with the rods which were to be used for chastising the prisoner. The Lieutenant sat down and lighted his long pipe; the prisoner implored him.

"No, comrade, lie down. What is the matter with you?"

The convict stretched himself on the ground with a sigh.

"Can you read fluently?"

"Of course, your nobility; I am baptized, and I was taught to read when I was a child."

"Then read this."

The convict knows beforehand what he is to read, and knows how the reading will end, because this joke has been repeated more than thirty times; but Smekaloff knows also that the convict is not his dupe any more than the soldier who now holds the rods suspended over the back of the unhappy victim. The convict begins to read; the soldiers armed with the rods await motionless. Smekaloff ceases even to smoke, raises his hand, and waits for a word fixed upon beforehand. At the word, which from some double meaning might be interpreted as the order to start, the Lieutenant raises his hand, and the flogging begins. The officer bursts into a laugh, and the soldiers around him also laugh; the man who is whipping laughs, and the man who is being whipped also.

CHAPTER III. THE HOSPITAL (*continued*).

I have spoken here of punishments and of those who have administered them, because I got a very clear idea on the subject during my stay in the hospital. Until then I knew of them only by general report. In our room were confined all the prisoners from the battalion who were to receive the spitzruten , as well as those from the military establishment in our town and in the district surrounding it.

During my first few days I looked at all that surrounded me with such greedy eyes that these strange manners, these men who had just been flogged or were about to be flogged, left upon me a terrible impression. I was agitated, frightened.

As I listened to the conversation or narratives of the other prisoners on this subject, I put to myself questions which I endeavoured in vain to solve. I wished to know all the degrees of the sentences; the punishments, and their shades; and to learn the opinion of the convicts themselves. I tried to represent to myself the psychological condition of the men flogged.

It rarely happened, as I have already said, that the prisoner approached the fatal moment in cold blood, even if he had been beaten several times before. The condemned man experiences a fear which is very terrible, but purely physical—an unconscious fear which upsets his moral nature.

During my several years' stay in the convict prison I was able to study at leisure the prisoners who wished to leave the hospital, where they had remained some time to have their damaged backs cured before receiving the second half of their punishment. This interruption in the punishment is always called for by the doctor who assists at the execution.

If the number of strokes to be received is too great for them to be administered all at once, it is divided according to advice given by the doctor on the spot. It is for him to see if the prisoner is in a condition to undergo the whole of his punishment, or if his life is in danger.

Five hundred, one thousand, and even one thousand five hundred strokes with the stick are administered at once. But if it is two or three thousand the punishment is divided into two or three doses.

Those whose back had been cured after the first administration, and who are to undergo a second, were sad, sombre and silent the day they went out, and the evening before. They were almost in a state of torpor. They engaged in no conversation, and remained perfectly silent.

It is worthy of remark that the prisoners avoid addressing those who are about to be punished, and, above all, never make any allusion to the subject, neither in consolation nor in superfluous words. No attention whatever is paid to them, which is certainly the best thing for the prisoner.

There are exceptions, however.

The convict Orloff, of whom I have already spoken, was sorry that his back did not get more quickly cured, for he was anxious to get his leave-ticket in order that he might take the rest of his flogging, and then be assigned to a convoy of prisoners, when he meant to escape during the journey. He had a passionate, ardent nature, and with only that object in view.

A cunning rascal, he seemed very pleased when he first came; but he was in a state of abnormal excitement, though he endeavoured to conceal it. He had been afraid of being left on the ground, and dying before half of his punishment had been undergone. He had heard steps taken in his case, by the authorities, when he was still being tried, and he thought he could not survive the punishment. But when he had received his first dose he recovered his courage.

When he came to the hospital I had never seen such wounds as his; but he was in the best spirits. He now hoped to be able to live. The stories which had reached him were untrue, or the execution would not have been interrupted.

He now began to think of a long Siberian journey, possibly of escaping to liberty, fields, and forests.

Two days after he had left the hospital he came back to die—on the very couch which he had occupied during my stay there.

He had been unable to support the second half of his punishment; but I have already spoken of this man.

All the prisoners without exception, even the most pusillanimous, even those who were beforehand tormented night and day, supported it courageously when it came. I scarcely ever heard groans during the night following the execution; our people, as a rule, knew how to endure pain.

I questioned my companion often in reference to this pain, that I might know to what kind of suffering it might be compared. It was no idle curiosity which urged me. I repeat that I was moved and frightened; but it was in vain, I could get no satisfactory reply.

"It burns like fire!" was the general answer; they all said the same thing.

First I tried to question M—tski. "It burns like fire! like hell! It seems as if one's back were in a furnace."

I made one day a strange observation, which may or may not have been well founded, although the opinion of the convicts themselves confirms my views; namely, that the rods are the most terrible punishment in use among us.

At first it seems absurd, impossible, yet five hundred strokes of the rods, four hundred even, are enough to kill a man. Beyond five hundred death is almost certain; the most robust man will be unable to support a thousand rods, whereas five hundred sticks are endured without much inconvenience, and without the least risk in the world of losing one's life. A man of ordinary build supports a thousand sticks without danger; even two thousand sticks will not kill a man of ordinary strength and constitution. All the convicts declared that rods were worse than sticks or ramrods.

"Rods hurt more and torture more!" they said.

They must torture more than sticks, that is certain, that is evident; for they irritate much more forcibly the nervous system, which they excite beyond measure. I do not know whether any person still exists, but such did a short time ago, to whom the whipping of a victim procured a delight which recalls the Marquis de Sade and the Marchioness Brinvilliers. I think this delight must consist in the sinking of the heart, and that these nobles must have experienced pain and delight at the same time.

There are people who, like tigers, are greedy for blood. Those who have possessed unlimited power over the flesh, blood, and soul of their fellow-creatures, of their brethren according to the law of Christ, those who have possessed this power and who have been able to degrade with a supreme degradation, another being made in the image of God; these men are incapable of resisting their desires and their thirst for sensations. Tyranny is a habit capable of being developed, and at last becomes a disease. I declare that the best man in the world can become hardened and brutified to such a point, that nothing will distinguish him from a wild beast. Blood and power intoxicate; they aid the development of callousness and debauchery; the mind then becomes capable of the most abnormal cruelty in the form of pleasure; the man and the citizen disappear for ever in the tyrant; and then a return to human dignity, repentance, moral resurrection, becomes almost impossible.

That the possibility of such license has a contagious effect on the whole of society there is no doubt. A society which looks upon such things with an indifferent eye, is already infected to the marrow. In a word, the right granted to a man to inflict corporal punishment on his fellow-men, is one of the plague-spots of our society. It is the means of annihilating all civic spirit. Such a right contains in germ the elements of inevitable, imminent decomposition.

Society despises an executioner by trade, but not a lordly executioner. Every manufacturer, every master of works, must feel an irritating pleasure when he reflects that the workman he has beneath his orders is dependent upon him with the whole of his family. A generation does not, I am sure, extirpate so quickly what is hereditary in it. A man cannot renounce what is in his blood, what has been transmitted to him with his mother's milk; these revolutions are not accomplished so quickly. It is not enough to confess one's fault. That is very little! Very little indeed! It must be rooted out, and that is not done so quickly.

I have spoken of the executioners. The instincts of an executioner are in germ in nearly every one of our contemporaries; but the animal instincts of the man have not developed themselves in a uniform manner. When they stifle all other faculties, the man becomes a hideous monster.

There are two kinds of executioners, those who of their own will are executioners and those who are executioners by duty, by reason of office. He who, by his own will, is an executioner, is in all respects below the salaried executioner, whom, however, the people look upon with repugnance, and who inspires them with disgust, with instinctive mystical fear. Whence comes this almost superstitious horror for the latter, when one is only indifferent and indulgent to the former?

I know strange examples of honourable men, kind, esteemed by all their friends, who found it necessary that a culprit should be whipped until he would implore and beg for mercy; it seemed to them a natural thing, a thing recognised as indispensable. If the victim did not choose to cry out, his executioner, whom in other respects I should consider a good man, looked upon it as a personal offence; he meant, in the first instance, to inflict only a light punishment, but directly he failed to hear the habitual supplications, "Your nobility!" "Have mercy!" "Be a father to me!" "Let me thank God all my life!" he became furious, and ordered that fifty more blows should be administered, hoping thus, at last, to obtain the necessary cries and supplications; and at last they came.

"Impossible! he is too insolent," cried the man in question, very seriously.

As for the executioner by office, he is a convict who has been chosen for this function. He passes an apprenticeship with an old hand, and as soon as he knows his trade remains in the convict prison, where he lives by himself. He has a room, which he shares with no one. Sometimes, indeed, he has a separate establishment, but he is always under guard. A man is not a machine. Although he whips by virtue of his office, he sometimes becomes furious, and beats with a certain pleasure. Notwithstanding he has no hatred for his victim, a desire to show his skill in the art of whipping may sharpen his vanity. He works as an artist; he knows well that he is a reprobate, and that he excites everywhere superstitious dread. It is impossible that this should exercise no influence upon him, and not irritate his brutal instincts.

Even little children say that this man has neither father nor mother. Strange thing!

All the executioners I have known were intelligent men, possessing a certain degree of conceit. This conceit became developed in them through the contempt which they everywhere met with, and was strengthened, perhaps, by the consciousness of the fear with which they inspired their victims, and of the power over unfortunate wretches.

The theatrical paraphernalia surrounding them developed, perhaps, in them a certain arrogance. I had for some time an opportunity of meeting and observing at close quarters an ordinary executioner. He was a man about forty, muscular, dry, with an agreeable, intelligent face, surrounded by long curly hair. His manners were quiet and grave, his general demeanour becoming. He replied clearly and sensibly to all questions put to him, but with a sort of condescension as if he were in some way my superior. The officers of the guard spoke to him with a certain respect, which he fully appreciated, for which reason, in presence of his chiefs, he became polite, and more dignified than ever.

He never departed from the most refined politeness. I am sure that, when I was speaking to him, he felt incomparably superior to the man who was addressing him. I could read that in his countenance. Sometimes he was sent under escort, in summer, when it was very hot, to kill the dogs of the town with a long, very thin spear. These wandering dogs increased in numbers with such prodigious rapidity, and became so dangerous during the dog days, that, by the decision of the authorities, the executioner was ordered to destroy them. This degrading duty did not in any way humiliate him. It should have been seen with what gravity he walked through the streets of the town, accompanied by a soldier escorting him; how, with a single glance, he frightened the women and children; and how, from the height of his grandeur, he looked down upon the passers-by generally.

Executioners live at their ease. They have money to travel comfortably, and drink vodka. They derive most of their income from presents which the prisoners condemned to be flogged slip into their hands before the execution. When they have to do with convicts who are rich, they then fix a sum to be paid in proportion to the means of the victim. They will exact thirty roubles, sometimes more. The executioner has no right to spare his victim; and he does so at the risk of his own back. But for a suitable present he agrees not to strike too hard. People almost always give what he asks; should they in any case refuse, he would strike like a savage; and it is in his power to do so. He sometimes exacts a heavy sum from a man who is very poor. Then all the relations of the victim are put in movement. They bargain, try and beat him down, supplicate him; but it will not be well if they do not succeed in satisfying him. In such a case the superstitious fear inspired by the executioner stands them in good part. I had been told the most wonderful things—that at one blow the executioner can kill his man.

"Is this your experience?" I asked.

Perhaps so. Who knows? Their tone seemed to decide, if there could be any doubt about it. They also told me that he can strike a criminal in such a way that he will not feel the least pain, and without leaving a scar.

Even when the executioner receives a present not to whip too severely, he gives the first blow with all his strength. It is the custom! Then he administers the other blows with less severity, above all if he has been well paid.

I do not know why this is done. Is it to prepare the victim for the succeeding blows, which will appear less painful after the first cruel one; or do they want to frighten the criminal, so that he may know with whom he has to deal; or do they simply wish to display their vigour from vanity? In any case the executioner is slightly excited before the execution, and he is conscious of his strength and of his power. He is acting at the time; the public admires him, and is filled with terror. Accordingly, it is not without satisfaction that he cries out to his victim, "Look out! you are going to have it!"—customary and fatal words which precede the first blow.

It is difficult to imagine a human being degraded to such a point.

The first day of my stay at the hospital I listened attentively to the stories of the convicts, which broke the monotony of the long days.

In the morning, the doctor's visit was the first diversion. Then came dinner, which it will be believed was the most important affair of our daily life. The portions were different according to the nature of the illness: some of the prisoners received nothing but broth with groats in it; others nothing but gruel; others a kind of semolina, which was much liked. The convicts ended by becoming effeminate and fastidious. The convalescents received a piece of boiled beef. The best food, which was reserved for the scorbutic patients, consisted of roast beef with onions, horseradish, and sometimes a small glass of spirits. The bread was, according to the illness, black or brown; the precision preserved in distributing the rations would make the patients laugh.

There were some who took absolutely nothing; the portions were exchanged in such a way that the food intended for one patient was eaten by another: those who were being kept on low diet, who received only small rations, bought those of the scorbutic patients; others would give any price for meat. There were some who ate two entire portions; it cost them a good deal, for they were generally sold at five kopecks each. If one had no meat to sell in our room the warder was sent to another section, and if he could not find any there he was asked to get some from the military "infirmary"—the free infirmary, as we called it.

There were always patients ready to sell their rations; poverty was general, and those who possessed a few kopecks used to send out to buy cakes and white bread, or other delicacies, at the market. Warders executed these commissions in a disinterested manner. The most painful moment was that which followed the dinner; some went to sleep, if they had no other way of passing their time; others either wrangled or told stories in a loud voice.

When no new patients were brought in, everything became very dull. The arrival of a new patient caused always a certain excitement, above all, if no one knew anything about him; he was questioned about his past life.

The most interesting ones were the birds of passage: they had always something to tell.

Of course they never spoke of their own little faults. If the prisoner did not enter upon this subject himself, no one questioned him about it.

The only thing he was asked was, what quarter he came from? who were with him on the road? what state the road was in? where he was being taken to? etc. Stimulated by the stories of the new comers, our comrades in their turn began to tell what they had seen and done; what was most talked about was the convoys, those in command of them, the men who carried the sentences into execution.

About this time, too, towards evening, the convicts who had been scourged came up; they always made a rather strong impression, as I have said; but it was not every day that any of these were brought to us, and everybody was bored to extinction, when nothing happened to give a fillip to the general relaxed and indolent state of feeling. It seemed, then, as though the sick themselves were exasperated at the very sight of those near them. Sometimes they squabbled violently.

Our convicts were in high glee when a madman was taken off for medical examination; sometimes those who were sentenced to be scourged, feigned insanity that they might get off. The trick was found out, or it would sometimes be that they voluntarily gave up the pretence. Prisoners, who during two or three days had done all sorts of wild things, suddenly became steady and sensible people, quieted down, and, with a gloomy smile, asked to be taken out of the hospital. Neither the other convicts nor the doctors said a word of remonstrance to them about the deceit, or brought up the subject of their mad pranks. Their names were put down on a list without a word being said, and they were simply taken elsewhere; after the lapse of some days they came back to us with their backs all wounds and blood.

On the other hand, the arrival of a genuine lunatic was a miserable thing to see all through the place. Those of the mentally unsound who were gay, lively, who uttered cries, danced, sang, were greeted at first with enthusiasm by the convicts.

"Here's fun!" said they, as they looked on the grins and contortions of the unfortunates. But the sight was horribly painful and sad. I have never been able to look upon the mad calmly or with indifference. There was one who was kept three weeks in our room: we would have hidden ourselves, had there been any place to do it. When things were at the worst they brought in another. This one affected me very powerfully.

In the first year, or, to be more exact, during the first month of my exile, I went to work with a gang of kiln men to the tileries situate at two versts from our prison. We were set to repairing the kiln in which the bricks were baked in summer. That morning, in which M—tski and B. made me acquainted with the non-commissioned officer, superintendent of the works. This was a Pole already well on in life, sixty years old at least, of high stature, lean, of decent and even somewhat imposing exterior. He had been a long time in service in Siberia, and although he belonged to the lower orders he had been a soldier, and in the rising of 1830—M—tski and B. loved and esteemed him. He was always reading the Vulgate. I spoke to him; his talk was agreeable and intelligent; he told a story in a most interesting way; he was straightforward and of excellent temper. For two years I never saw him again, all I heard was that he had become a "case," and that they were inquiring into it; and then one fine day they brought him into our room; he had gone quite mad.

He came in yelling, uttering shouts of laughter, and began to dance in the middle of the room with indecent gestures which recalled the dance known as Kamarinskaïa.

The convicts were wild with enthusiasm; but, for my part, account for it as you will, I felt utterly miserable. Three days after, we were all of us upset with it; he got into violent disputes with everybody, fought, groaned, sang in the dead of the night; his aberrations were so inordinate and disgusting as to bring our very stomachs up.

He feared nobody. They put the strait-waistcoat on him; but we were no whit better off for it, for he went on quarreling and fighting all round. At the end of three weeks, the room put up an unanimous entreaty to the head doctor that he might be removed to the other apartment reserved for the convicts. But after two days, at the request of the sick people in that other room, they brought him back to our infirmary. As we had two madmen there at once, both rooms kept sending them back and forward, and ended by taking one or the other of the two lunatics, turn and turn about. Everybody breathed more freely when they took them away from us, a good way off, somewhere or other.

There was another lunatic whom I remember—a very remarkable creature. They had brought in, during the summer, a man under sentence, who looked like a solid and vigorous fellow enough, of about forty-five years. His face was sombre and sad, pitted with small-pox, with little red and swollen eyes. He sat down by my side. He was extremely quiet; spoke to nobody, and seemed utterly absorbed in his own deep reflections.

Night fell; then he addressed me, and, without a word of preface, told me in a hurried and excited way—as if it were a mighty secret he were confiding—that he was to have two thousand strokes with the rod; but that he had nothing to fear, as the daughter of Colonel G—— was taking steps on his behalf.

I looked at him with surprise, and observed that, as I saw the affair, the daughter of a Colonel could be of little use in such a case. I had not yet guessed what sort of person I had to do with, for they had brought him to the hospital as a bodily sick person, not mentally. I then asked him what illness he was suffering from.

He answered that he knew nothing about it; that he had been sent among us for something or other; but that he was in good health, and that the Colonel's daughter had fallen in love with him. Two weeks before she had passed in a carriage before the guard-house, where he was looking through the barred window, and she had gone head over ears in love at the mere sight of him.

After that important moment she had come three times to the guard-house on different pretexts. The first time with her father, ostensibly to visit her brother, who was the officer on service; the second with her mother, to distribute alms to the prisoners. As she passed in front of him she had muttered that she loved him and would get him out of prison.

He told me all this nonsense with minute and exact details; all of it pure figment of his poor disordered head. He believed devoutly and implicitly that his punishment would be graciously remitted. He spoke very calmly, and with all assurance of the passionate love he had inspired in this young lady.

This odd and romantic delusion about the love of quite a young girl of good breeding, for a man nearly fifty years and afflicted with a face so disfigured and gloomy, simply showed the fearful effect produced by the fear of the punishment he was to have, upon the poor, timid creature.

It may be that he had really seen some one through the bars of the window, and the insanity, germinating under excess of fear, had found shape and form in the delusion in question.

This unfortunate soldier, who, it may be warranted, had never given a thought to young ladies, had got this romance into his diseased fancy, and clung convulsively to this wild hope. I heard him in silence, and then told the story to the other convicts. When these questioned him in their natural curiosity, he preserved a chastely discreet silence.

Next day the doctor examined him. As the madman averred that he was not ill, he was put down on the list as qualified to be sent out. We learned that the physician had scribbled "*Sanat. est*" on the page, when it was quite too late to give him warning. Besides, we were ourselves not by any means sure what was really the matter with the man.

The error was with the authorities who had sent him to us, without specifying for what reason it was thought necessary to have him come into the hospital—which was unpardonable negligence.

However, two days later the unhappy creature was taken out to be scourged. We understood that he was dumbfounded by finding, contrary to his fixed expectation, that he really was to have the punishment. To the last moment he thought he would be pardoned, and when conducted to the front of the battalion, he began to cry for help.

As there was no room or bedding-place now in our apartment they sent him to the infirmary. I heard that for eight entire days he did not utter a single word, and remained in stupid and misery-stricken mental confusion. When his back was cured they took him off. I never heard a single further word about him.

As to the treatment of the sick and the remedies prescribed, those who were but slightly indisposed paid no attention whatever to the directions of the doctors, and never took their medicines; while, speaking generally, those really ill were very careful in following the doctor's orders; they took their mixtures and powders; they took all the possible care they could of themselves; but they preferred external to internal remedies.

Cupping-glasses, leeches, cataplasms, blood-lettings—in all which things the populace has so blind a confidence—were held in high honour in our hospital. Inflictions of that sort were regarded with satisfaction.

There was one thing quite strange, and to me interesting. Fellows, who stood without a murmur the frightful tortures caused by the rods and scourges, howled, and grinned, and moaned for the least little ailment. Whether it was all pretence or not, I really cannot say.

We had cuppings of a quite peculiar kind. The machine with which instantaneous incisions in the skin are produced, was all out of order, so they had to use the lancet.

For a cupping, twelve incisions are necessary; with a machine these are not painful at all, for it makes them instantaneously; with the lancet it is a different affair altogether—that cuts slowly, and makes the patient suffer. If you have to make ten openings there will be about one hundred and twenty pricks, and these very painful. I had to undergo it myself; besides the pain itself, it caused great nervous irritation; but the suffering was not so great that one could not contain himself from groaning if he tried.

It was laughable to see great, hulking fellows wriggling and howling. One couldn't help comparing them to some men, firm and calm enough in really serious circumstances, but all ill-temper or caprice in the bosom of their families for nothing at all; if dinner is late or the like, then they'll scold and swear; everything puts them out; they go wrong with everybody; the more comfortable they really are, the more troublesome are they to other people. Characters of this sort, common enough among the lower orders, were but too numerous in our prison, by reason of our company being forced on one another.

Sometimes the prisoners chaffed or insulted the thin-skins I speak of, and then they would leave off complaining directly; as if they only wanted to be insulted to make them hold their tongues.

Oustiantsef was no friend of grimacings of this kind, and never let slip an opportunity of bringing that sort of delinquent to his bearings. Besides, he was fond of scolding; it was a sort of necessity with him, engendered by illness and also his stupidity. He would first fix his gaze upon you for some time, and then treat you to a long speech of threatening and warning, and a tone of calm and impartial conviction. It looked as though he thought his function in this world was to watch over order and morality in general.

"He must poke his nose into everything," the prisoners with a laugh used to say; for they pitied, and did what they could to avoid conflicts with him.

"Has he chattered enough? Three waggons wouldn't be too much to carry away all his talk."

"Why need you put your oar in? One is not going to put himself about for a mere idiot. What's there to cry out about at a mere touch of a lancet?"

"What harm in the world do you fancy *that* is going to do you?"

"No, comrades," a prisoner strikes in, "the cuppings are a mere nothing. I know the taste of them. But the most horrid thing is when they pull your ears for a long time together. That just shuts you up."

All the prisoners burst out laughing.

"Have you had them pulled?"

"By Jove, yes, I should think he had."

"That's why they stick upright, like hop-poles."

This convict, Chapkin by name, really had long and quite erect ears. He had long led a vagabond life, was still quite young, intelligent, and quiet, and used to talk with a dry sort of humour with much seriousness on the surface, which made his stories very comical.

"How in the world was I to know you had had your ears pulled and lengthened, brainless idiot?" began Oustiantsef, once more wrathfully addressing Chapkin, who, however, vouchsafed no attention to his companion's obliging apostrophe.

"Well, who did pull your ears for you?" some one asked.

"Why, the police superintendent, by Jove, comrades! Our offence was wandering about without fixed place of abode. We had just got into K——, I and another tramp, Eptinie; he had no family name, that fellow. On the way we had fixed ourselves up a little in the hamlet of Tolmina; yes, there is a hamlet that's got just that name—Tolmina. Well, we get to the town, and are just looking about us a little to see if there's a good stroke of tramp-business to do, after which we mean to flit. You know, out in the open country you're as free as air; but it's not exactly the same thing in the town. First thing, we go into a public-house; as we open the door we give a sharp look all round. What's there? A sunburnt fellow in a German coat all out at elbows, walks right up to us. One thing and another comes up, when he says to us:

"'Pray excuse me for asking if you have any papers with you?'

"'No, we haven't.'

"'Nor have we either. I have two comrades besides these with me who are in the service of General Cuckoo . We have been seeing life a bit, and just now haven't a penny to bless ourselves with. May I take the liberty of requesting you to be so obliging as to order a quart of brandy?'

"'With the greatest pleasure,' that's what we say to him. So we drink together. Then they tell us of a place where there's a real good stroke of business to be done—a house at the end of the town belonging to a wealthy merchant fellow; lots of good things there, so we make up our minds to try the job during the night; five of us, and the very moment we are going at it they pounce on us, take us to the station-house, and then before the head of the police. He says, 'I shall examine them myself.' Out he goes with his pipe, and they bring in for him a cup of tea; a sturdy fellow it was, with whiskers. Besides us five, there were three other tramps, just brought in. You know, comrades, that there's nothing in this world more funny than a tramp, because he always forgets everything he's done. You may thump his head till you're tired with a cudgel; all the same, you'll get but one answer, that he has forgotten all about everything.

"The police superintendent then turns to me and asks me squarely,

"'Who may you be?'

"I answer just like all the rest of them:

"'I've forgotten all about it, your worship.'

"'Just you wait; I've a word or two more to say to you. I know your phiz.'

"Then he gives me a good long stare. But I hadn't seen him anywhere before, that's a fact.

"Then he asks another of them, 'Who are you?'

"'Mizzle-and-scud, your worship.'

"'They call you Mizzle-and-scud?'

"'Precisely that, your worship.'

"'Well and good, you're Mizzle-and-scud! And you?' to a third.

"'Along-of-him, your worship.'

"'But what's your name—your name?'

"'Me? I'm called Along-of-him, your worship.'

"'Who gave you that name, hound?'

"'Very worthy people, your worship. There are lots of worthy people about; nobody knows that better than your worship.'

"'And who may these "worthy people" be?'

"'Oh, Lord, it has slipped my memory, your worship. Do be so kind and gracious as to overlook it.'

"'So you've forgotten them, all of them, these "worthy people"?'

"'Every mother's son of them, your worship.'

"'But you must have had relations—a father, a mother. Do you remember them?'

"'I suppose I must have had, your worship; but I've forgotten about 'em, my memory is so bad. Now I come to think about it, I'm sure I had some, your worship.'

"'But where have you been living till now?'

"'In the woods, your worship.'

"'Always in the woods?'

"'Always in the woods!'

"'Winter too?'

"'Never saw any winter, your worship.'

"'Get along with you! And you—what's your name?'

"'Hatchets-and-axes, your worship.'

"'And yours?'

"'Sharp-and-mum, your worship.'

"'And you?'

"'Keen-and-spry, your worship.'

"'And not a soul of you remembers anything that ever happened to you.'

"'Not a mother's son of us anything whatever.'

"He couldn't help it; he laughed out loud. All the rest began to laugh at seeing him laugh! But the thing does not always go off like that. Sometimes they lay about them, these police, with their fists, till you get every tooth in your jaw smashed. Devilish big and strong these fellows, I can tell you.

"'Take them off to the lock-up,' said he. 'I'll see to them in a bit. As for you, stop here!'

"That's me.

"'Just you go and sit down there.'

"Where he pointed to there was paper, a pen, and ink; so thinks I, 'What's he up to now?'

"'Sit down,' he says again; 'take the pen and write.'

"And then he goes and clutches at my ear and gives it a good pull. I looked at him in the sort of way the devil may look at a priest.

"'I can't write, your worship.'

"'Write, write!'

"'Have mercy on me, your worship!'

"'Write your best; write, write!'

"And all the while he keeps pulling my ear, pulling and twisting. Pals, I'd rather have had three hundred strokes of the cat; I tell you it was hell.

"'Write, write!' that was all he said."

"Had the fellow gone mad? What the mischief was it?

"Bless us, no! A little while before, a secretary had done a stroke of business at Tobolsk: he had robbed the local treasury and gone off with the money; he had very big ears, just as I have. They had sent the fact all over the country. I answered to that description; that's why he tormented me with his 'Write, write!' He wanted to find out if I could write, and to see my hand.

"'A regular sharp chap that! Did it hurt?'

"'Oh, Lord, don't say a word about it, I beg.'

"Everybody burst out laughing.

"'Well, you did write?'

"'What the deuce was there to write? I set my pen going over the paper, and did it to such good account that he left off torturing me. He just gave me a dozen thumps, regulation allowance, and then let me go about my business: to prison, that is.'

"'Do you really know how to write?'

"'Of course I did. What d'ye mean? Used to very well; forgotten the whole blessed thing, though, ever since they began to use pens for it.'"

Thanks to the gossip talk of the convicts who filled the hospital, time was somewhat quickened for us. But still, Almighty God, how wearied and bored we were! Long, long were the days, suffocating in their monotony, one absolutely the same as another. If only I had had a single book.

For all that I went often to the infirmary, especially in the early days of my banishment, either because I was ill or because I needed rest, just to get out of the worse parts of the prison. In those life was indeed made a burden to us, worse even than in the hospital, especially as regards the effect upon moral sentiment and good feeling. We of the nobility were the never-ceasing objects of envious dislike, quarrels picked with us all the time, something done every moment to put us in the wrong, looks filled with menacing hatred unceasingly directed on us! Here, in the sick-rooms, one lived on a sort of footing of equality, there was something of comradeship.

The most melancholy moment of the twenty-four hours was evening, when night set in. We went to bed very early. A smoky lamp just gave us one point of light at the very end of the room, near the door. In our corner we were almost in complete darkness. The air was pestilential, stifling. Some of the sick people could not get to sleep, would rise up, and remain sitting for an hour together on their beds, with their heads bent, as though they were in deep reflection. These I would look at steadily, trying to guess what they might be thinking of; thus I tried to kill time. Then I became lost in my own reveries; the past came up to me again, showing itself to my imagination in large powerful outlines filled with high lights and massive shadows, details that at any other time would have remained in oblivion, presented themselves in vivid force, making on me an impression impossible under any other circumstances.

Then I would begin to muse dreamily on the future. When shall I leave this place of restraint, this dreadful prison? Whither betake myself? What will then befall me? Shall I return to the place of my birth? So I brood, and brood, until hope lives once again in my soul.

Another time I would begin to count, one, two, three, etc., to see if sleep could be won that way. I would set sometimes as far as three thousand, and was as wakeful as ever. Then somebody would turn in his bed.

Then there's Oustiantsef coughing, that cough of the hopelessly-gone consumptive, and then he would groan feebly, and stammer, "My God, I've sinned, I've sinned!"

How frightful it was, that voice of the sick man, that broken, dying voice, in the midst of that silence so dead and complete! In a corner there are some sick people not yet asleep, talking in a low voice, stretched on their pallets. One of them is telling the story of his life, all about things infinitely far off; things that have fled for ever; he is talking of his trampings through the world, of his children, his wife, the old ways of his life. And the very accent of the man's voice tells you that all those things are for ever over for him, that he is as a limb cut off from the world of men, cut off, thrown aside; there is another, listening intently to what he is saying. A weak, feeble sort of muttering and murmuring comes to one's ear from far-off in the dreary room, a sound as of far-off water flowing somewhere.... I remember that one time, during a winter night that seemed as if it would never end, I heard a story which at first seemed as if it were the stammerings of a creature in nightmare, or the delirium of fever. Here it is:

FOOTNOTE:

What I relate about corporal punishment took place during my time. Now, as I am told, everything is changed, and is changing still.

CHAPTER IV. THE HUSBAND OF AKOULKA

It was late at night, about eleven o'clock. I had been sleeping some time and woke up with a start. The wan and weak light of the distant lamp barely lit the room. Nearly everybody was fast asleep, even Oustiantsef; in the quiet of the night I heard his difficult breathing, and the rattlings in his throat with every respiration. In the ante-chamber sounded the heavy and distant footsteps of the patrol as the men came up. The butt of a gun struck the floor with its low and heavy sound.

The door of the room was opened, and the corporal counted the sick, stepping softly about the place. After a minute or so he closed the door again, leaving a fresh sentinel there; the patrol went off, silence reigned again. It was only then that I observed two prisoners, not far from me, who were not sleeping, and who seemed to be holding a muttered conversation. Sometimes, in fact, it would happen that a couple of sick people, whose beds adjoined and who had not exchanged a word for weeks, would all of a sudden break out into conversation with one another, in the middle of the night, and one of them would tell the other his history.

Probably they had been speaking for some considerable time. I did not hear the beginning of it, and could not at first seize upon their words, but little by little I got familiar with the muttered sounds, and understood all that was going on. I had not the least desire for sleep on me, so what could I do but listen.

One of them was telling his story with some warmth, half-lying on his bed, with his head lifted and stretched towards his companion. He was plainly excited to no little degree; the necessity of speech was on him.

The man listening was sitting up on his pallet, with a gloomy and indifferent air, his legs stretched out flat on the mattress, and now and again murmured some words in reply, more out of politeness than interest, and kept stuffing his nose with snuff from a horn box. This was the soldier Techérévin, one of the company of discipline; a morose, cold-reasoning pedant, an idiot full of *amour propre*; while the narrator was Chichkof, about thirty years old; this was a civilian convict, whom up to that time I had not at all observed; and during the whole time I was at the prison I never could get up the smallest interest in him, for he was a conceited, heady fellow.

Sometimes he would hold his tongue for weeks together, and look sulky and brutal enough for anything; then all of a sudden he would strike into anything that was going on, behave insufferably, go into a white heat about nothing at all, and tell you long stories with nothing in them whatever about one barrack or another, blowing abuse on all the world, and acting like a man beside himself. Then some one would give him a hiding, and he would have another fit of silence. He was a mean and cowardly fellow, and the object of general contempt. His stature was low, he had little flesh on him, he had wandering eyes, though they sometimes got mixed and seemed filled with a stupid sort of thinking. When he told you anything he worked himself into a fever, gesticulated wildly, suddenly broke off and went to another subject, lost himself in fresh details, and at last forgot altogether what he was talking about. He often got into squabbles, this Chichkof, and when he poured insult on his adversary, he spoke with a sentimental whine and was affected nearly to tears. He was not a bad hand at playing the *balalaika*, and had a weakness for it; on fête days he would show you his dancing powers when others set him at it, and he danced by no means badly. You could easily enough make him do what you wanted ... not that he was of a complying turn, but he liked to please and to get intimate with fellows.

For some considerable time I couldn't understand the story Chichkoff was telling; that night I mean. It seemed to me as though he were constantly rambling from the point to talk of something else. Perhaps he had observed that Tchérévine was paying little attention to the narrative, but I fancy that he was minded to overlook this indifference, so as not to take offence.

"When he went out on business," he continued, "every one saluted him politely, paid him every respect ... a fellow with money that."

"You say that he was in some trade or other."

"Yes; trade indeed! The trading class in my country is wretchedly ill-off; just poverty-stricken. The women go to the river and fetch water from ever such a distance to water their gardens. They wear themselves to the very bone, and, for all that, when winter comes, they haven't got enough to make a mere cabbage soup. I tell you it's starvation. But that fellow had a good lump of land, which his labourers cultivated; he had three. Then he had hives, and sold his honey; he was a cattle-dealer too; a much respected man in our parts. He was very old and quite gray, his seventy years lay heavy on his old bones. When he came to the market-place with his fox-skin pelisse, everybody saluted him.

"'Good-day, daddy Aukoudim Trophimtych!'

"'Good-day,' he'd return.

"'How are you getting along;' he never looked down on any one.

"'God keep you, Aukoudim Trophimtych!'

"'How goes business with you?'

"'Business is as good as tallow's white with me; and how's yours, daddy?'

"'We've just got enough of a livelihood to pay the price of sin; always sweating over our bit of land.'

"'Lord preserve you, Aukoudim Trophimtych!'

"He never looked down on anybody. All his advice was always worth having; every one of his words was worth a rouble. A great reader he was, quite a man of learning; but he stuck to religious books. He would call his old wife and say to her, 'Listen, woman, take well in what I say;' then he would explain things. His old Marie Stépanovna was not exactly an old woman, if you please; it was his second wife; he had married her to have children, his first wife had not brought him any. He had two boys still quite young, for the second of them was born when his father was close on sixty; Akoulka, his daughter, was eighteen years old, she was the eldest."

"Your wife? Isn't it so?"

"Wait a bit, wait. Then Philka Marosof begins to kick up a row. Says he to Aukoudim: 'Let's split the difference. Give me back my four hundred roubles. I'm not your beast of burden; I don't want to do any more business with you, and I don't want to marry your Akoulka. I want to have my fling now that my parents are dead. I'll liquor away my money, then I'll engage myself, 'list for a soldier; and in ten years I'll come back here a field-marshal!' Aukoudim gave him back his money—all he had of his. You see he and Philka's father had both put in money and done business together.

"'You're a lost man,' that's what he said to Philka.

"'Whether I'm a lost man or not, old gray-beard, you're the biggest cheat I know. You'd try to screw a fortune out of four farthings, and pick up all the dirt about to do it with. I spit upon it. There you are piling up here, digging deep there, the devil only knows why. I've got a will of my own, I tell you. All the same I won't take your Akoulka; I've slept with her already.'

"'How dare you insult a respectable father—a respectable girl? When did you sleep with her, you spawn of the sucker, you dog, you hound, you——?' said Aukoudim shaking with passion. (Philka told us all this later).

"'I'll not only not marry your daughter, but I'll take good care that nobody marries her, not even Mikita Grigoritch, for she's a disreputable girl. We had a fine time together, she and I, all last autumn. I don't want her at any price. All the money in the world wouldn't make me take her.'

"Then the fellow went and had high jinks for a while. All the town was as one man in sending up a cry against him. He got a lot of other fellows round him, for he had a heap of money. Three months he had of it. Such recklessness as you never heard of. Every penny went.

"'I want to see the end of this money. I'll sell the house; everything; then I'll 'list or go on the tramp.'

"He was drunk from morning to evening, and went about with a carriage and pair.

"The girls liked him well, I tell you, for he played the guitar very nicely."

"Then it is true that he had been too well with this Akoulka?"

"Wait, wait, can't you? I had just buried my father. My mother lived by baking gingerbread. We got our livelihood by working for Aukoudim; barely enough to eat, a precious hard life it was. We had a bit of land the other side of the woods, and grew corn there; but when my father died I went on a spree. I made my mother give me money; but I had to give her a good hiding first."

"You were very wrong to beat her; a great sin that?"

"Sometimes I was drunk the whole blessed day. We had a house that was just tumbling to pieces with dry rot, still it was our own; we were as near famished as could be; for weeks together we had nothing but rags to chew. Mother nearly killed me with one stupid trick or another, but I didn't care a curse. Philka Marosof and I were always together day and night. 'Play the guitar to me,' he'd say, 'and I'll lie in bed the while. I'll throw money to you, for I'm the richest chap in the world!' The fellow could not speak without lying. There was only one thing. He wouldn't touch a thing if it had been stolen. 'I'm no thief, I'm an honest man. Let's go and daub Akoulka's door with pitch, for I won't have her marry Mikita Grigoritch, I'll stick to that.'

"The old man had long meant to give his daughter to this Mikita Grigoritch. He was a man well on in life, in trade too, and wore spectacles. When he heard the story of Akoulka's bad conduct, he said to the old father, 'That would be a terrible disgrace for me, Aukoudim Trophimtych; on the whole, I've made up my mind not to marry; it's to late.'

"So we went and daubed Akoulka's door all over with pitch. When we'd done that her folks beat her so that they nearly killed her.

"Her mother, Marie Stépanovna, cried, 'I shall die of it,' while the old man said, 'If we were in the days of the patriarchs, I'd have hacked her to pieces on a block. But now everything is rottenness and corruption in this world.' Sometimes the neighbours from one end of the street to the other heard Akoulka's screams. She was whipped from morning to evening, and Philka would cry out in the market-place before everybody:

"Akoulka's a jolly girl to get drunk with. I've given it those people between the eyes, they won't forget me in a hurry.'

"Well, one day, I met Akoulka, she was going for water with her bucket, so I cried out to her: 'A fine morning, pet Akoulka Koudimovna! you're the girl who knows how to please fellows. Who's living with you now, and where do you get your money for your finery?' That's just what I said to her; she opened her eyes as wide as you please. No more flesh on her than on a log of wood. She had only just given me a look, but her mother thought she was larking with me, and cried from her door-step, 'Impudent hussy, what do you mean by talking with that fellow?' And from that moment they began to beat her again. Sometimes they hided her for an hour together. The mother said, 'I give her the whip because she isn't my daughter any more.'"

"She was then as bad as they said?"

"Now you just listen to my story, nunky, will you? Well, we used to get drunk all the time with Philka. One day when I was abed, mother comes and says:

"'What d'ye mean by lying in bed, you hound, you thief!' She abused me for some time, then she said, 'Marry Akoulka. They'll be glad to give her to you, and they'll give three hundred roubles with her.'

"'But,' says I, 'all the world knows that she's a bad girl——'

"'Hist, the marriage ceremony cures all that; besides, she'll always be in fear of her life from you, so you'll be in clover together. Their money would make us comfortable; I've spoken about the marriage already to Marie Stépanovna, we're of one mind about it.'

"So I say, 'Let's have twenty roubles down on the spot, and I'll have her.'

"Well, you needn't believe it unless you please, but I was drunk right up to the wedding-day. Then Philka Marosof kept threatening me all the time.

"'I'll break every bone in your body, a nice fellow you to be engaged, and to Akoulka; if I like I'll sleep every blessed night with her when she's your wife.'

"'You're a hound, and a liar,' that's what I said to him. But he insulted me so in the street, before everybody, that I ran to Aukoudim's and said, 'I won't marry her unless I have fifty roubles down this moment.'"

"And they really did give her to you in marriage?"

"Me? Why not, I should like to know? We were respectable people enough. Father had been ruined by a fire a little before he died; he had been a richer man than Aukoudim Trophimtych.

"'A fellow without a shirt to his back like you ought to be only too happy to marry my daughter;' that's what old Aukoudim said.

"'Just you think of your door, and the pitch that went on it,' I said to him.

"'Stuff and nonsense,' said he, 'there's no proof whatever that the girl's gone wrong.'

"'Please yourself. There's the door, and you can go about your business; but give back the money you've had!'

"Then Philka Marosof and I settled it together to send Mitri Bykoff to Father Aukoudim to tell him that we'd insult him to his face before everybody. Well, I had my skin as full as it could hold right up to the wedding-day. I wasn't sober till I got into the church. When they took us home after church the girl's uncle, Mitrophone Stépanytch, said:

"'This isn't a nice business; but it's over and done now.'

"Old Aukoudim was sitting there crying, the tears rolled down on his gray beard. Comrade, I'll tell you what I had done: I had put a whip into my pocket before we went to church, and I'd made up my mind to have it out of her with that, so that all the world might know how I'd been swindled into the marriage, and not think me a bigger fool than I am."

"I see, and you wanted her to know what was in store for her. Ah, was——?"

"Quiet, nunky, quiet! Among our people I'll tell you how it is; directly after the marriage ceremony they take the couple to a room apart, and the others remain drinking till they return. So I'm left alone with Akoulka; she was pale, not a bit of colour on her cheeks; frightened out of her wits. She had fine hair, supple and bright as flax, and great big eyes. She scarcely ever was known to speak; you might have thought she was dumb; an odd creature, Akoulka, if ever there was one. Well, you can just imagine the scene. My whip was ready on the bed. Well, she was as pure a girl as ever was, not a word of it all was true."

"Impossible!"

"True, I swear; as good a girl as any good family might wish."

"Then, brother, why—why—why had she had to undergo all that torture? Why had Philka Marosof slandered her so?"

"Yes, why, indeed?"

"Well, I got down from the bed, and went on my knees before her, and put my hands together as if I were praying, and just said to her, 'Little mother, pet, Akoulka Koudimovna, forgive me for having been such an idiot as to believe all that slander; forgive me. I'm a hound!'

"She was seated on the bed, and gazed at me fixedly. She put her two hands on my shoulders and began to laugh; but the tears were running all down her cheeks. She sobbed and laughed all at once.

"Then I went out and said to the people in the other room, 'Let Philka Marosof look to himself. If I come across him he won't be long for this world.'

"The old people were beside themselves with delight. Akoulka's mother was ready to throw herself at her daughter's feet, and sobbed.

"Then the old man said, 'If we had known really how it was, my dearest child, we wouldn't have given you a husband of that sort.'

"You ought to have seen how we were dressed the first Sunday after our marriage—when we left church! I'd got a long coat of fine cloth, a fur cap, with plush breeches. She had a pelisse of hareskin, quite new, and a silk kerchief on her head. One was as fine as the other. Everybody admired us. I must say I looked well, and pet Akoulka did too. One oughtn't to boast, but one oughtn't to sing small. I tell you people like us are not turned out by the dozen."

"Not a doubt about it."

"Just you listen, I tell you. The day after my marriage I ran off from my guests, drunk as I was, and went about the streets crying, 'Where's that scoundrel of a Philka Marosof? Just let him come near me, the hound, that's all!' I went all over the market-place yelling that out. I was as drunk as a man could be, and stand.

"They went after me and caught me close to Vlassof's place. It took three men to get me back again to the house.

"Well, nothing else was spoken about all over the village. The girls said, when they met in the market-place, 'Well, you've heard the news—Akoulka was all right!'

"A little while after I do come across Philka Marosof, who said to me before everybody, strangers to the place, too, 'Sell your wife, and spend the money on drink. Jackka the soldier only married for that; he didn't sleep one night with his wife; but he got enough to keep his skin full for three years.'

"I answered him, 'Hound!'

"'But,' says he, 'you're an idiot! You didn't know what you were about when you married—you were drunk. How could you tell all about it?'

"So off I went to the house, and cried out to them 'You married me when I was drunk.'

"Akoulka's mother tried to fasten herself on me; but I cried, 'Mother, you don't know about anything but money. You bring me Akoulka!'

"And didn't I beat her! I tell you I beat her for two hours running, till I rolled on the floor myself with fatigue. She couldn't leave her bed for three weeks."

"It's a dead sure thing," said Tchérévine phlegmatically; "if you don't beat them they—— Did you find her with her lover?"

"No; to tell the truth, I never actually caught her," said Chichkoff after a pause, speaking with effort; "but I was hurt, a good deal hurt, for every one made fun of me. The cause of it all was Philka. 'Your wife is just made for everybody to look at,' said he.

"One day he invited us to see him, and then he went at it. 'Do just look what a good little wife he has! Isn't she tender, fine, nicely brought up, affectionate, full of kindness for all the world? I say, my lad, have you forgotten how we daubed their door with pitch?' I was full at that moment, drunk as may be; then he seized me by the hair and had me down upon the ground before I knew where I was. 'Come along—dance; aren't you Akoulka's husband? I'll hold your hair for you, and you shall dance; it will be good fun.' 'Dog!' said I to him. 'I'll bring some jolly fellows to your house,' said he, 'and I'll whip your Akoulka before your very eyes just as long as I please.' Would you believe it? For a whole month I daren't go out of the house, I was so afraid he'd come to us and drag my wife through the dirt. And how I did beat her for it!"

"What was the use of beating her? You can tie a woman's hands, but not her tongue. You oughtn't to give them a hiding too often. Beat 'em a bit, then scold 'em well, then fondle 'em; that's what a woman is made for."

Chichkoff remained quite silent for a few moments.

"I was very much hurt," he went on; "I began it again just as before. I beat her from morning till night for nothing; because she didn't get up from her seat the way I liked; because she didn't walk to suit me. When I wasn't hiding her, time hung heavy on my hands. Sometimes she sat by the window crying silently—it hurt my feelings sometimes to see her cry, but I beat her all the same. Sometimes her mother abused me for it: 'You're a scoundrel, a gallows-bird!' 'Don't say a word or I'll kill you; you made me marry her when I was drunk, you swindled me.' Old Aukoudim wanted at first to have his finger in the pie. Said he to me one day: 'Look here, you're not such a tremendous fellow that one can't put you down;' but he didn't get far on that track. Marie Stépanovna had become as sweet as milk. One day she came to me crying her eyes out and said: 'My heart is almost broken, Ivan Semionytch; what I'm going to ask of you is a little thing for you, but it is a good deal to me; let her go, let her leave you, daddy Ivan.' Then she throws herself at my feet. 'Do give up being so angry! Wicked people slander her; you know quite well she was good when you married her.' Then she threw herself at my feet again and cried. But I was as hard as nails. 'I won't hear a word you have to say; what I choose to do, I do, to you or anybody, for I'm crazed with it all. As to Philka Marosof, he's my best and dearest friend.'"

"You'd begun to play your pranks together again, you and he?"

"No, by Jove! He was out of the way by this time; he was killing himself with drink, nothing less. He had spent all he had on drink, and had 'listed for a soldier, as substitute for a citizen body in the town. In our parts, when a lad makes up his mind to be substitute for another, he is master of that house and everybody there till he's called to the ranks. He gets the sum agreed on the day he goes off, but up to then he lives in the house of the man who buys him, sometimes six whole months, and there isn't a horror in the whole world those fellows are not guilty of. It's enough to make folks take the holy images out of the house. From the moment he consents to be substitute for the son of the family then he considers himself their patron and benefactor, and makes them dance as he pipes, or else he goes off the bargain.

"So Philka Marosof played the very mischief at the home of this townsman. He slept with the daughter, pulled the master of the house by the beard after dinner, did anything that came into his head. They had to heat the bath for him every day, and, what's more, give him brandy fumes with the steam of the bath; and he would have the women lead him by the arms to the bath room.

"When he came back to the man's house after a revel elsewhere, he would stop right in the middle of the road and cry out:

"'I won't go in by the door; pull down the fence!'

"And they actually *had* to pull down the fence, though there was the door right at it to let him in. That all came to an end though, the day they took him to the regiment. That day he was sobered sufficiently. The crowd gathered all through the street.

"'They're taking off Philka Marosof!'

"He made a salute on all sides, right and left. Just at that moment Akoulka was returning from the kitchen-garden. Directly Philka saw her he cried out to her:

"'Stop!' and down he jumped from the cart and threw himself down at her feet.

"'My soul, my sweet little strawberry, I've loved you two years long. Now they're taking me off to the regiment with the band playing. Forgive me, good honest girl of a good honest father, for I'm nothing but a hound, and all you've gone through is my fault.'

"Then he flings himself down before her a second time. At first Akoulka was exceedingly frightened; but she made him a great bow, which nearly bent her double.

"'Forgive me, too, my good lad; but I am really not at all angry with you.'

"As she went into the house I was at her heels.

"'What did you say to him, you she-devil, you?'

"Now you may believe it or not as you like, but she looked at me as bold as you please, and answered:

"'I love him better than anything or anybody in this world.'

"'I say!'

"That day I didn't utter one single word. Only towards evening I said to her: 'Akoulka, I'm going to kill you now.' I didn't close an eye the whole night. I went into the little room leading to ours and drank kwass. At daybreak I went into the house again. 'Akoulka, get ready and come into the fields.' I had arranged to go there before; my wife knew it.

"'You are right,' said she. 'It's quite time to begin reaping. I've heard that our labourer is ill and doesn't work a bit.'

"I put to the cart without saying a word. As you go out of the town there's a forest fifteen versts in length. At the end of it is our field. When we had gone about three versts through the wood I stopped the horse.

"'Come, get up, Akoulka; your end is come.'

"She looked at me all in a fright, and got up without a word.

"'You've tormented me enough. Say your prayers.'

"I seized her by the hair—she had long, thick tresses—I rolled them round my arm. I held her between my knees; took out my knife; threw her head back, and cut her throat. She screamed; the blood spurted out. Then I threw away my knife. I pressed her with all my might in my arms. I put her on the ground and embraced her, yelling with all my might. She screamed; I yelled; she struggled and struggled. The blood—her blood—splashed my face, my hands. It was stronger than I was—stronger. Then I took fright. I left her—left my horse and began to run; ran back to the house.

"I went in the back way, and hid myself in the old ramshackle bath-house, which we never used now. I lay myself down under the seat, and remained hid till the dead of the night."

"And Akoulka?"

"She got up to come back to the house; they found her later, a hundred steps from the place."

"So you hadn't finished her?"

"No." Chichkoff stopped a while.

"Yes," said Tchérévine, "there's a vein; if you don't cut it at the first the man will go on struggling; the blood may flow fast enough, but he won't die."

"But she was dead all the same. They found her in the evening, and she was cold. They told the police, and hunted me up. They found me in the night in the old bath.

"And there you have it. I've been four years here already," added he, after a pause.

"Yes, if you don't beat 'em you make no way at all," said Tchérévine sententiously, taking out his snuff-box once more. He took his pinches very slowly, with long pauses. "For all that, my lad, you behaved like a fool. Why, I myself—I came upon my wife with a lover. I made her come into the shed, and then I doubled up a halter and said to her:

"'To whom did you swear to be faithful?—to whom did you swear it in church? Tell me that?'

"And then I gave it her with my halter—beat her and beat her for an hour and a half; till at last she was quite spent, and cried out:

"'I'll wash your feet and drink the water afterwards.'

"Her name was Crodotia."

FOOTNOTES:

Daubing the door of a house, where a young girl lives, is done to show that she is dishonoured.

A mark of respect paid in Russia formerly, now disused.

CHAPTER V. THE SUMMER SEASON

April is come; Holy Week is not far off. We set about our summer tasks. The sun becomes hotter and more brilliant every day; the atmosphere has the spring in it, and acts upon our nervous system powerfully. The convict, in his chains, feels the trembling influence of the lovely days like any other creature; they rouse desires in him, inexpressible longings for his home, and many other things. I think that he misses his liberty, yearns for freedom more when the day is filled with sunlight than during the rainy and melancholy days of autumn and winter. You may observe this positively among convicts; if they *do* feel a little joy on a beautiful clear day, they have a reaction into greater impatience and irritability.

I noticed that in spring there was much more squabbling in our prison; there was more noise, the yelling was greater, there were more fights; during the working hours we would see a man sometimes fixed in a meditative gaze, which seemed lost in the blue distance somewhere, the other side of the Irtych, where stretched the boundless plain, with its flight of hundreds of versts, the free Kirghiz Steppe. Long-drawn sighs came to one's ear, sighs breathed from the depths of the chest; it might seem that the air of those wide and free regions, haunted by their thought, forced the convicts to draw deep respirations, and was a sort of solace to their crushed and fettered souls.

"Ah!" cries at last the poor prisoner all at once, with a long, sighing cry; then he seizes his pick furiously, or picks up the bricks, which he has to carry from one place to another. But after a brief minute he seems to forget the passing impression, and begins laughing, or insulting people near, so fitful is his humour; then he attacks the work he has to do with unusual fire, labours with might and main, as if trying to stifle by fatigue the grief that has him by the throat. You see they are fellows of unimpaired vigour, all in the very flower of life, with all their physical and other strength about them.

How heavy the irons are during this season! All this is not sentimentality, it is the report of rigorous observation. During the hot season, under a fiery sun, when all one's being, all one's soul, is vividly conscious of, and intimately feels, the unspeakably strong resurrection of nature going on everywhere, it is more difficult to support the confinement, the perpetual surveillance, the tyranny of a will other than one's own.

Besides this, it is in spring with the first song of the lark that throughout all Siberia and Russia men set out on the tramp; God's creatures, if they can, break their prison and escape into the woods. After the stifling ditch where they work, after the boats, the irons, the rods and whips, they go vagabondizing where they please, wherever they can make it out best; they eat and drink what they can get, 'tis all the time pot-luck with them; and by night they sleep undisturbed in the woods or in a field, without a care, without the agony of knowing themselves in prison, as if they were God's own birds; their "good-night" is said to the stars, and the eye that watches them is the eye of God. Not altogether a rosy life, by any means; sometimes hunger and fatigue are heavy on them "in the service of General Cuckoo." Often enough the wanderers have not a morsel of bread to keep their teeth going for days and days. They have to hide from everybody, run to earth like marmots; sometimes they are driven to robbery, pillage—nay, even murder.

"Send a man there and he becomes a child, and just throws himself on all he sees"; that is what people say of those transported to Siberia. This saying may be applied even more fitly to the tramps. They are almost all brigands and thieves, by necessity rather than inclination. Many of them are hardened to the life, irreclaimable; there are convicts who go off after having served their time, even after they have been put on some land as their own. They ought to be happy in their new state, with their daily bread assured them. Well, it is not so; an irresistible impulse sends them wandering off.

This life in the woods, wretched and fearful as it is, but still free and adventurous, has a mysterious seduction for those who have experienced it; among these fugitives you may find to your surprise, people of good habit of mind, peaceable temper, who had shown every promise of becoming settled creatures—good tillers of the land. A convict will marry, have children, live for five years in the same place, then all of a sudden he will disappear one fine morning, abandoning wife and children, to the stupefaction of his family and the whole neighbourhood.

One day, I was shown at the convict establishment one of these deserters of the family hearthstone. He had committed no crime—at least, he was under suspicion of none—but all through his life he had been a deserter, a deserter from every post. He had been to the southern frontier of the empire, the other side of the Danube, in the Kirghiz Steppe, in Eastern Siberia, the Caucasus, in a word, everywhere. Who knows? under other conditions this man might have been a Robinson Crusoe, with the passion of travel so on him. These details I have from other convicts, for he did not like talk, and never opened his mouth except when absolutely necessary. He was a peasant, of quite small size, of some fifty years, very quiet in demeanour, with a face so still as to seem quite without any sort of meaning, impassive almost to idiotcy. His delight was to sit for hours in the sun humming a sort of song between his teeth so softly, that five steps off he was inaudible. His features were, so to speak, petrified; he ate little, principally black bread; he never bought white bread or spirits; my belief is, he never had had any money, and that he couldn't have counted it if he had. He was indifferent to everything. Sometimes he fed the prison dogs with his own hand, a thing no one else was known to do; (speaking generally, Russians don't like giving dogs things to eat from the hand). People said that he had been married, twice even, and that he had children somewhere. Why he had been sent as a convict, I have not the least idea. We fellows were always fancying that he would escape; but his hour did not come, or perhaps had come and gone; anyhow, he went through with his punishment without resistance. He seemed an element quite foreign to the medium wherein he had his being, an alien, self-concentrated creature. Still, there was nothing in this deep surface calm which could be trusted; yet, after all, what good would it have been to him to escape from the place?

Compared with life at the convict prison, the vagabond age of the forests is as the joys of Paradise. The tramp's lot is wretched enough, but at least free. So it is that every prisoner all over the soil of Russia, becomes restless with the first rays of the smiling spring.

Comparatively few form any settled plan for flight, they fear the hindrances in the way and the punishment that may ensue; only one in a hundred, not more, make up his mind to it, but how to do it is a thought that never ceases to haunt the minds of the ninety-nine others. Filled as they are with this longing, anything that looks like giving a chance of success is a comfort to them; then they set about comparing the facts with cases of successful escape. I speak only of prisoners after and under sentence, for prisoners not yet tried and condemned, are much more ready to try at an escape. And those who have been sentenced, rarely get away unless they attempt it in early days. When they have spent two or three years of their time, they put them to a sort of credit-account in their minds, and conclude that it is better to finish with the law and be put on land as a free man, rather than forfeit that time if they fail in escaping, which is always a possibility. Certainly not more than one convict in ten succeeds in *changing his lot*. Those who do, are nearly always men sentenced to an extremely long punishment, or for life. Fifteen, twenty years seem like an eternity to them. Then there is the branding, which is a great difficulty in the way of complete escape.

Changing your lot is a technical expression. When a convict is caught trying to escape, he is subjected to formal interrogatory, and will say he wanted to *change his lot*. This somewhat literary formula exactly represents the act in question. No escaped prisoner ever hopes to become a perfectly free man, for he knows that it is nearly impossible; what he looks for is to be sent to some other convict establishment, or to be put on the land, or to be tried again for some offence committed when on the tramp; in a word, to be sent anywhere else, it matters not where, so that he get out of his present prison which has become insufferable to him. All these fugitives, unless they find some unexpected shelter for the winter, unless they meet some one interested in concealing them, or if—last resort—they cannot procure—and sometimes a murder does it—the legal document, which enables them to go about unmolested everywhere; all these fugitives present themselves in crowds, during the autumn, in the towns and at the prisons; they confess themselves to be escaped tramps, pass the winter in jail, and live in the secret hope of getting away the following summer.

On me, as well as others, the spring exercised its influence. Well do I remember the avidity with which my gaze fed upon the horizon through the gaps in the palisades; long, long did I stand with my head glued to the pickets, obstinately and insatiably gazing on the grass greening in the ditch surrounding the fortress, and at the blue of the distant sky as it grew denser and denser. My anguish, my melancholy, were heavier on me; as each day wore away the jail became odious, detestable. Hatred for me, as a man of the nobility, filled the hearts of the convicts during these first years, and this feeling of theirs simply poisoned my life for me. Often did I ask to be sent to the hospital, when there was no need of it, merely to be out of the punishment part of the place, to feel myself out of the range of this unrelenting and implacable hostility.

"You nobles have beaks of iron, and you tore us to pieces with your beaks when we were serfs," is what the convicts used to say to us. How I envied the people of the lower class who came into the place as prisoners! It was different with them, they were in comradeship with all there from the very first moment. So was it that in the spring, Freedom showing herself as a sort of phantom of the season, the joy diffused throughout all Nature, translated themselves within my soul into a more than doubled melancholy and nervous irritability.

As the sixth week of Lent came I had to go through my religious exercises, for the convicts were divided by the sub-superintendent into seven sections—answering to the weeks in Lent—and these had to attend to their devotions according to this roster. Each section was composed of about thirty men. This week was a great solace to me; we went two or three times a day to the church, which was close to the prison. I had not been in church for a long time. The Lenten services, familiar to me from early childhood in my father's house, the solemn prayers, the prostrations—all stirred in me the fibres of the memory of things long, long past, and woke my earliest impressions to fresh life. Well do I remember how happy I was when at morn we went into God's house, treading the ground which had frozen in the night, under the escort of soldiers with loaded guns; the escort remained outside the church.

Once within we were massed close to the door so that we could scarcely hear anything except the deep voice of the ministering deacon; now and again we caught a glimpse of a black chasuble or the bare head of the priest. Then it came into my mind how, when a child, I used to look at the common people who formed a compact mass at the door, and how they would step back in a servile way before some important epauletted fellow, or some nobleman with a big paunch, some lady splendidly dressed and of high devotion who, in a hurry to get at the front benches, and ready for a row if there was any difficulty as to their being honoured with the best of places. As it seemed to me then, it was only *there*, near the church door, not far from the entry, that prayer was put up with genuine fervour and humility, only there that, when people did prostrate themselves on the floor it was done with real abasement of self and full sense of unworthiness.

And now I myself was in that place of the common people, no, not in their place, for we who were there were in chains and degradation. Everybody kept himself at a distance from us. We were feared, and alms were put in our hands as if we were beggars; I remember that all this gave me the strange sensation of a refined and subtle pleasure. "Let it even be so!" such was my thought. The convicts prayed with deep fervour; every one of them had with him his poor farthing for a little candle, or for their collection for the church expenses. "I too, I am a man," each one of them perhaps said, as he made his offering; "before God we are all equal."

After the six o'clock mass we went up to communion. When the priest, *ciforium* in hand, recited the words, "Have mercy on me as Thou hadst on the thief whom Thou didst save," nearly all the convicts prostrated themselves, and their chains clanked; I think they took these words literally as applied to themselves, and not as being in Scripture.

Holy Week came. The authorities presented each of us with an Easter egg, and a small piece of wheaten bread. The townspeople loaded us with benevolences. As at Christmas there was the priest's visitation with the cross, inspecting visit of the heads of departments, larded cabbage, general enlargement of soul, and unlimited lounging, the only difference being, that one could now walk about in the court-yard, and warm oneself in the sun. Everything seemed filled with more light, larger than in the winter, but also more fraught with sadness. The long, endless, summer days seemed peculiarly unbearable on Church holidays. Work days were at least shortened to our sense by the fatigue of work.

Our summer labours were much more trying than the winter tasks; our business was principally that of carrying out engineering works. The convicts were set to building, digging, bricklaying, or repairing Government buildings, locksmith's work, or carpentering, or painting. Others went into the brick-fields, and that was looked upon by us as the hardest of all we had laid on us. The brick-fields were situated about four versts from the fortress; through all the summer they sent there, every morning at six o'clock, a gang of fifty convicts. For this gang they used to pick out workmen who had learned no trade in particular. The convicts took with them their bread for the day, the distance was too great for them to come back, eight useless versts, for dinner with the others, so they had a meal when they returned in the evening.

Work was assigned to each for the day, but there was so much of it that it was all a man could do, nay, more, to get to the end of it. First, we had to dig and carry the clay, moisten it, and mould it in the ditch, and then make a goodly quantity of bricks, two hundred or so, sometimes fifty more than that. I was only twice sent to the brick-field. The convicts sent to this labour came back in the evening dead tired, and every one of them complained of the others, that he had had the worst of the work put on him. I believe that reproaches of this kind were a pleasure, a consolation to them. Some of them, however, liked the brick-field work, because they got away from the town, and to the banks of the Irtych into open, agreeable country, with the sky overhead; the surroundings were more agreeable than those frightful Government buildings. They were allowed to smoke there in all freedom, and to remain lying down for half-an-hour or so, which was a great pleasure.

As for me, I was sent to one of the shops, or else to pound up alabaster, or to carry bricks, which last job I had for two months together. I had to take my tale of bricks from the banks of the Irtych to a distance of about 140 yards, and to pass the ditch of the fortress before getting to the barrack which they were putting up. This work suited me well enough, although the cord with which I carried my bricks sawed my shoulders; what particularly pleased me was that my strength increased sensibly. At the outset I could not carry more than eight bricks at once; each of them weighed about twelve pounds. I got to be able to carry twelve, or even fifteen, which delighted me much. You wanted physical as well as moral strength to be able to bear all the discomforts of that accursed life.

There was this, too: I wanted, when I left the place, really to live, not to be half-dead. I took pleasure in carrying my bricks, then; it was not merely that this labour strengthened my body, but because it took me always to the banks of the Irtych. I speak often of this spot, it was the only one where we saw God's *own* world, a pure and bright horizon, the free desert steppes, whose bareness always produced a strange impression on me. All the other workyards were in the fortress itself, or in its neighbourhood; and the fortress, from the earliest days I was there, was the object of my hatred, and, above all, its appurtenant buildings. The house of the Major Commandant seemed to me a repulsive, accursed place. I never could pass it without casting upon it a look of detestation; while at the river-bank I could forget my miserable self as I sent my gaze over the immense desert space, just as a prisoner may when he looks at the world of freedom through the barred casement of his dungeon. Everything in that place was dear and gracious to my eyes; the sun shining in the infinite blue of heaven, the distant song of the Kirghiz that came from the opposite bank.

Sometimes I would fix my sight for a long while upon the poor smoky cabin of some *baïgouch*; I would study the bluish smoke as it curled in the air, the Kirghiz woman busy with her two sheep.... The things I saw were wild, savage, poverty-stricken; but they were free. I would follow the flight of a bird threading its way in the pure transparent air; now it skims the water, now disappears in the azure sky, now suddenly comes to view again, a mere point in space. Even the poor wee floweret fading in a cleft of the bank, which would show itself when spring began, fixed my attention and would draw my tears.... The melancholy of this first year of convict life and hard labour was unendurable, too much for my strength. The anguish of it was so great, I could not notice my immediate surroundings at all; I merely shut my eyes and would not see. Among the creatures with spoiled lives with whom I had to live, I did not yet note those who were capable of thinking and feeling, in spite of their external repulsiveness. There came not to my ears (or if there did I knew it not) one word of kindliness in the midst of the rain of poisonous talk that came down all the time. Still one such utterance there was, simple, straightforward, of pure motive, and it came from the heart of a man who had suffered and endured more than myself. But it is useless to enlarge on this.

The great fatigue I underwent was a source of satisfaction, it gave me hope of sound sleep. During the summer sleep was torment, more intolerable than the closeness and infection winter brought with it. Some of the nights were certainly very beautiful. The sun, which had not ceased to inundate the court-yard all the day, hid itself at last. The air freshened, and the night, the night of the steppe, became comparatively cold. The convicts, until shut up in their barracks, walked about in groups, especially on the kitchen side; for that was the place where questions of general interest were by preference discussed, and comments were made upon the rumours from without, often absurd indeed, but always keenly exciting to these men cut off from the world. For example, we suddenly learn that our Major had been roughly dismissed from his post. Convicts are as credulous as children; they know the news to be false, or most unlikely, and that the fellow who brings it is a past master in the art of lying, Kvassoff; for all that they clutch at the nonsensical story, go into high delight over it, are much consoled, and at last quite ashamed to have been duped by a Kvassoff.

"I should like to know who'll show *him* the door?" cries one convict; "don't you fear, he's a fellow who knows how to stick on."

"But," says another, "he has his superiors over him." This one is a warm controversialist, and has seen the world.

"Wolves don't feed on one another," says a third gloomily, half to himself. *This* one is an old fellow, growing gray, and he always takes his sour cabbage soup into a corner, and eats it there.

"Do you think his superiors will take *your* advice whether they shall show him the door or not?" adds a fourth, who doesn't seem to care about it at all, giving a stroke to his balalaïka.

"Well, why not?" replies the second angrily; "if you *are* asked, answer what's in your mind. But no, with us fellows it's all mere cry, and when you ought to go at things with a will, everybody sneaks out."

"That's *so!*" says the one playing with the balalaïka. "Hard labour and prison are just the things to cause *that.*"

"It was like that the other day," says the second one, without hearing the remark made to him. "There was a little wheat left, sweepings, a mere nothing; there was some idea of turning the refuse into money; well, look here, they took it to him, and he confiscated it. All economy, you see. Was that *so*, and was it right—yes or no?"

"But whom can you complain to?"

"To whom? Why, the 'spector (*Inspector*) who's coming."

"What 'spector?"

"It's true, pals, a 'spector is coming soon," said a youthful convict, who had got some sort of knowledge, had read the "Duchesse de la Vallière," or some book of that sort, and who had been Quartermaster in a regiment; a bit of a wag, whom, as a man of information, the convicts held in a sort of respect. Without paying the least attention to the exciting debate, he goes straight to the cook, and asks him for some liver. Our cooks often deal in victuals of that kind; they used to buy a whole liver, cut it in pieces, and sell it to the other convicts.

"Two kopecks' worth, or four?" asks cook.

"A four-kopeck cut; I'll eat, the others shall look on and long," says this convict. "Yes, pals, a general, a real general, is coming from Petersburg to 'spect all Siberia; it's so, heard it at the Governor's place."

This news produces an extraordinary effect. For a quarter of an hour they ask each other who this General can be? what's his title? whether his grade is higher than that of the Generals of our town? The convicts delight in discussing ranks and degrees, in finding out who's at the head of things, who can make the other officials crook their backs, and to whom he crooks his own; so they get up an argument and quarrel about their Generals, and rude words fly about, all in honour of these high officers—fights, too, sometimes. What interest can *they* possibly have in it? When one hears convicts speaking of Generals and high officials one gets a measure of their intelligence as they were while still in the world before the prison days. It cannot be concealed that among our people, even in much higher circles, talk about generals and high officials is looked upon as the most serious and refined conversation.

"Well, you see, they *have* sent our Major to the right about, don't ye?" observes Kvassoff, a little, rubicund, choleric, small-brained fellow, the same who had announced the supersession of the Major.

"We'll just grease their palm for them," this, in staccato tones from the morose old fellow in the corner who had finished his sour cabbage soup.

"I should think he would grease their palms, by Jove," says another; "he has stolen money enough, the brigand. And, only think, he was only a regimental Major before he came here. He's feathered his nest. Why, a little while ago he was engaged to the head priest's daughter."

"But he didn't get married; they turned him off, and that shows he's poor. A pretty sort of fellow to get engaged! He's got nothing but the coat on his back; last year, Easter time, he lost all he had at cards. Fedka told me so."

"Well, well, pals, I've been married myself, but it's a bad thing for a poor devil; taking a wife is soon done, but the fun of it is more like an inch than a mile," observes Skouratoff, who had just joined in the general talk.

"Do you fancy we're going to amuse ourselves by discussing *you*?" says the ex-quartermaster in a superior manner. "Kvassoff, I tell you you're a big idiot! If you fancy that the Major can grease the palm of an Inspector-General you've got things finely muddled; d'ye fancy they send a man from Petersburg just to inspect your Major? You're a precious dolt, my lad; take it from me that it is so."

"And you fancy because he's a General he doesn't take what's offered?" said some one in the crowd in a sceptical tone.

"I should think he did indeed, and plenty of it whenever he can."

"A dead sure thing that; gets bigger, and more, and worse, the higher the rank."

"A General *always* has his palm greased," says Kvassoff, sententiously.

"Did *you* ever give them money, as you're so sure of it?" asks Baklouchin, suddenly striking in, in a tone of contempt; "come, now, did you ever see a General in all your life?"

"Yes."

"Liar!"

"Liar, yourself!"

"Well, boys, as he *has* seen a General, let him say *which*. Come, quick about it; I know 'em all, every man jack."

"I've seen General Zibert," says Kvassoff in tones far from sure.

"Zibert! There's no General of that name. That's the General, perhaps, who was looking at your back when they gave you the cat. This Zibert was, perhaps, a Lieutenant-Colonel; but you were in such a fright just then, you took him for a General."

"No! Just hear me," cries Skouratoff, "for I've got a wife. There was really a General of that name, a German, but a Russian subject. He confessed to the Pope, every year, all about his peccadilloes with gay women, and drank water like a duck, at least forty glasses of Moskva water one after the other; that was the way he got cured of some disease. I had it from his valet."

"I say! And the carp didn't swim in his belly?" this from the convict with the balalaïka.

"Be quiet, fellows, can't you—one's talking seriously, and there they are beginning their nonsense again. Who's the 'spector that's coming?" This was put by a convict who always seemed full of business, Martinof, an old man who had been in the Hussars.

"Set of lying fellows!" said one of the doubters. "Lord knows where they get it all from; it's all empty talk."

"It's nothing of the sort," observes Koulikoff, majestically silent hitherto, in dogmatic tones. "The man coming is big and fat, about fifty years, with regular features, and proud, contemptuous manners, on which he prides himself."

Koulikoff is a Tsigan, a sort of veterinary surgeon, makes money by treating horses in town, and sells wine in our prison. He's no fool, plenty of brain, memory well stocked, lets his words fall as carefully as if every one of 'em was worth a rouble.

"It's true," he went on very calmly, "I heard of it only last week; it's a General with bigger epaulettes than most, and he's going to inspect all Siberia. They grease his palm well for him, that's sure enough; but not our Major with his eight eyes in his head. He won't dare to creep in about *him*, for you see, pals, there are Generals and Generals, as there are fagots and fagots. It's just this, and you may take it from me, our Major will remain where he is. *We're* fellows with no tongue, we've no right to speak; and as to our chiefs here, they're not going to say a word against him. The 'spector will come into our jail, give a look round, and go off at once; he'll say it was all right."

"Yes, but the Major's in a fright; he's been drunk since morning."

"And this evening he had two van-loads of things taken away; Fedka says so."

"You may scrub a nigger, he'll never be white. Is it the first time you've seen him drunk, hey?"

"No! It will be a devil of a shame if the General does nothing to him," said the convicts, who began to get highly excited.

The news of the arrival of the Inspector went through the prison. The prisoners went everywhere about the court-yard retailing the important fact. Some held their tongues and kept cool, trying to look important; some were really indifferent to it. Some of the convicts sat down on the steps of the doors to play the balalaïka, while some went on with their gossip. Some groups were singing in a drawling voice, but the whole court-yard was upset and excited generally.

About nine o'clock they counted us, and quartered us in our barracks, which were closed for the night. A short summer night it was, so we were roused up at five o'clock in the morning, yet nobody had managed to sleep before eleven, for up to that hour there was conversation and all sort of movement was going on; sometimes, too, games of cards were made up, as in winter. The heat was intolerable, stifling. True, the open window let in some of the cool night air, but the convicts kept tossing themselves on their wooden beds as if delirious.

Fleas countless. There were enough of them in winter; but when spring came they multiplied in proportions so formidable that I couldn't believe it before I had to endure them. And as the summer went on the worse it was with them. I found out that one *could* get used to fleas; but for all that, the torment of them is so great that it throws you into a fever; even when you get slumber you quite feel it is not sleep, you are half delirious, and know it.

At last, towards morning, when the enemy is tired and you are deliciously asleep in the freshness of the early hours, suddenly sounds the pitiless morning drum-call. How you curse as you hear them, those sharp, quick strokes; you cower in your semi-pelisse, and then—you can't help it—comes the thought that it will be so to-morrow, the day after, for many, many years, till you are set at liberty. When *will* it come, this freedom, freedom? Where *is* it in this world? *Where* is it hiding? You *have* to get up, they are walking about you in all directions. The usual noisy row begins. The convicts dress, and hurry to their work. It's true you have an hour you can spend in sleep at noon.

What we had been told about the Inspector was really true. The reports were more confirmed every day; and at last it became certain that a General, high in office, was coming from Petersburg to inspect all Siberia, that he was already at Tobolsk. Every day we learned something fresh about it. These rumours came from the town. They told us that there was alarm in all quarters, and that everybody was making preparations to show himself in as favourable a light as might be. The authorities were organising receptions, balls, fêtes of every kind. Gangs of convicts were sent to level the ways in the fortress, smooth away hummocks in the ground, paint the palings and other wood-work, to plaster, do up, and generally repair everything that was conspicuous.

Our prisoners perfectly well understood the object of this labour, and their discussions became all the more animated and excited. Their imaginations passed all bounds. They even set about formulating some demands to be set before the General on his arrival, but that did not prevent their going on with their quarrels and violent speeches. Our Major was on hot coals. He came continually to visit the jail, shouted, and threw himself angrily on the fellows more than usual, sent them to the guard-room and punishment for a mere nothing, and watched very severely over the cleanliness and good order of the barracks. Just then, there occurred a little event which did not at all painfully affect this officer as one might have expected, but, on the contrary, caused him a lively satisfaction. One of the convicts struck another with an awl right in the chest, in a place quite near the heart.

The delinquent's name was Lomof; the name the victim was known by in the jail was Gavrilka. He was one of those seasoned tramps I've spoken about earlier. Whether he had any other name, I don't know; I never heard any attributed to him, except that one, Gavrilka.

Lomof had been a peasant comfortably off in the Government of T——, and district of K——. There were five of them living together, two brothers Lomof, and three sons. They were quite rich peasants; the talk throughout the district was that they had more than 300,000 roubles in paper money. They worked at currying and tanning; but their chief business was usury, harbouring tramps, and receiving stolen goods; all sorts of petty irregular doings. Half the peasants of their district owed them money, and so were in their clutches. They passed for being intelligent and full of cunning, and gave themselves very great airs. A great personage of their province had stopped on his way once at the father Lomof's house, and this official had taken a fancy to him, because of his hardy and unscrupulous talk. Then they took it in their heads they might do exactly as they pleased, and mixed themselves up more and more with illegal doings. Everybody had a grievance against them, and would like to have seen them a hundred feet under the ground; but they got bolder and bolder every day. They were not afraid of the local police or the district tribunals.

At last fortune betrayed them; their ruin came, not out of their secret crimes, but from an accusation which was all calumny and falsehood. Ten versts from their hamlet they had a farm where six Kirghiz labourers, long since brought down by them to be no better than slaves, used to pass the autumn. One fine day these Kirghiz were found murdered. An inquiry was set on foot that lasted long, thanks to which no end of atrocious things were brought to light. The Lomofs were accused of having assassinated their workmen. They had themselves told their story to the convicts, all the jail knew it perfectly; they were suspected of owing a great deal of money to the Kirghiz, and, as they were full of greed and avarice in spite of their large fortunes, it was believed they had paid the debt by taking the lives of the poor fellows. While the inquiry and trial went on, their property melted away utterly. The father died, the sons were transported; one of these, with the uncle, was condemned to fifteen years of hard labour.

Now, they were perfectly innocent of the crime imputed to them. One fine day Gavrilka, a thorough-paced rascal, known as a tramp, but of very gay and lively turn, avowed himself the author of the crime. As a matter of fact I don't know whether he actually made this avowal himself, but what is sure is that the convicts held him to be the murderer of the Kirghiz.

This Gavrilka, while still tramping about, had been mixed up in some way with the Lomofs (his confinement in one jail was for quite a short sentence, for desertion from the army and tramping). He had cut the throats of the Kirghiz—three other marauding fellows had been in it with him—in the hope of setting themselves up a bit with the plunder of the farm.

The Lomofs were no favourites with us, I really don't know why. One of them, the nephew, was a sturdy fellow, intelligent and sociable; but his uncle, the one that struck Gavrilka with the awl, was a choleric, stupid rustic, always quarrelling with the convicts, who knocked him about like plaster. All the jail liked Gavrilka for his gaiety and good-humour. The Lomofs got to know, like the rest, that he was the man who committed the crime they were condemned for; but they never got into any quarrel with him. Gavrilka paid no attention whatever to them.

The row with Uncle Lomof began about some disgusting girl they had quarrelled over. Gavrilka had boasted of the favour she had shown him. The peasant, mad with jealousy, ended by driving an awl into his chest.

Although the Lomofs had been ruined by their trial and sentence, they passed in the jail for being very rich. They had money, a samovar, and drank tea. Our Major knew all about it, and hated the two Lomofs, sparing them no vexation. The victims of his hate explained it by a desire to have them grease his palm well, but they could not, or would not, bring themselves to do it.

If Uncle Lomof had struck his awl one hair's breadth further in Gavrilka's breast he would certainly have killed him; as it was, the wound did not much signify. The affair was reported to the Major. I think I see him now as he came up out of breath, but with visible satisfaction. He addressed Gavrilka in an affable, fatherly way:

"Tell me, lad, can you walk to the hospital or must they carry you there? No, I think it will be better to have a horse; let them put a horse to this moment!" he cried out to the sub-officer with a gasp.

"But I don't feel it at all, your worship; he's only given me a bit of a prick, your worship."

"You don't know, my dear fellow, you don't know; you'll see. A nasty place he's struck you in. All depends upon the place. He has given it you just below the heart, the scoundrel. Wait, wait!" he howled to Lomof. "I've got you tight; take him to the guard-house."

He kept his promise. Lomof was tried, and, though the wound was slight, there was plainly malice aforethought; his sentence of hard labour was extended for several years, and they gave him a thousand strokes with the rod. The Major was delighted.

The Inspector arrived at last.

The day after he reached the town, he came to the convict establishment to make his inspection. It was a regular fête-day. For some days everything had been brilliantly clean, washed with great precision. The convicts were all just shaven, their linen quite white and without a stain. (According to the regulations, they wore in summer waistcoats and pantaloons of canvas. Every one had a round black piece sown in at the back, eight centimetres in diameter.) For a whole hour the prisoners had been drilled as to what they should answer, the very words to be used, particularly if the high functionary should take any notice of them.

There had been even regular rehearsals. The Major seemed to have lost his head. An hour before the coming in of the Inspector, all the convicts were at their posts, as stiff as statues, with their little fingers on the seams of their pantaloons. At last, just about one o'clock the Inspector made his entry. He was a General, with a most self-sufficing bearing, so much so, that the mere sight of it must have sent a tremor into the hearts of all the officials of West Siberia.

He came in with a stern and majestic air, followed by a crowd of Generals and Colonels doing service in our town. There was a civilian, too, of high stature and regular features, in frock-coat and shoes. This personage bore himself very independently and airily, and the General addressed him every moment with exquisite politeness. This civilian also had come from Petersburg. All the convicts were terribly curious as to who he could be, such an important General showing him such deference? We learned who he was and what his office later, but he was a good deal talked about before we knew.

Our Major, all spick and span, with orange-coloured collar, made no too favourable impression upon the General; the blood-shot eyes and fiery rubicund complexion plainly told their own story. Out of respect for his superior he had taken off his spectacles, and stood some way off, as straight as a dart, in feverish expectation that something would be asked of him, that he might run and carry out His Excellency's wishes; but no particular need of his services seemed to be felt.

The General went all through the barracks without saying a word, threw a glance into the kitchen, where he tasted the sour cabbage soup. They pointed me out to him, telling him that I was an ex-nobleman, who had done this, that, and the other.

"Ah!" answered the General. "And how does he conduct himself?"

"Satisfactorily for the time being, your Excellency, satisfactorily."

The General nodded, and left the jail in a couple of minutes more. The convicts were dazzled and disappointed, and did not know what to be at. As to laying complaints against the Major, that was quite over, could not be thought of. He had, no doubt, been quite well assured as to this beforehand.

CHAPTER VI. THE ANIMALS AT THE CONVICT ESTABLISHMENT

Gniedko, a bay horse, was bought a little while afterwards, and the event furnished a much more agreeable and interesting diversion to the convicts than the visit of the high personage I have been talking about. We required a horse at the jail for carrying water, refuse matter, etc. He was given to a convict to take care of and use; this man drove him, under escort, of course. Our horse had plenty to do morning and night; it was a worthy sort of beast, but a good deal worn, and had been in service for a long time already.

One fine morning, the eve of St. Peter's Day, Gniedko, our bay, who was dragging a barrel of water, fell all of a heap, and gave up the ghost in a few minutes. He was much regretted, so all the convicts gathered round him to discuss his death. Those who had served in the cavalry, the Tsigans, the veterinary fellows, and others, showed a profound knowledge of horses in general and fiercely argued the question; but all that did not bring our bay horse to life again; there he was stretched out and dead, with his belly all swollen. Every one thought it incumbent on him to feel about the poor thing with his hands; finally the Major was informed of what Providence had done in the horse's case, and it was decided that another should be bought at once.

St. Peter's Day, quite early after mass, all the convicts being together, horses that were on sale were brought in. It was left to the prisoners to choose an animal, for there were some thorough experts among them, and it would have been difficult to take in 250 men, with whom horse-dealing had been a speciality. Tsigans, Lesghians, professional horse-dealers, townsmen, came in to deal. The convicts were exceedingly eager about the matter as each fresh horse was brought up, and were as amused as children about it all. It seemed to tickle their fancy very much, that they had to buy a horse like free men, just as if it was for themselves and the money was to come out of their own pockets. Three horses were brought and taken away before purchase; the fourth was settled on. The horse-dealers seemed astonished and a little awed at the soldiers of the escort who watched the business. Two hundred men, clean shaven, branded as they were, with chains on their feet, were well calculated to inspire respect, all the more as they were in their own place, at home so to speak, in their own convict's den, where nobody was ever allowed to come.

Our fellows seemed to be up to no end of tricks for finding out the real value of a horse brought up; they carefully examined it, handled it with the most serious demeanour, went on as if the welfare of the establishment was bound up with the purchase of this beast. The Circassians took the liberty of jumping upon his back: their eyes shone wildly, they chatted rapidly in their incomprehensible dialect, showed their white teeth, dilating the nostrils of their hooked copper-coloured noses. There were some Russians who paid the most lively attention to their discussion, and seemed ready to jump down their throats; they did not understand a word, but it was plain they did what they could to gather from the expression of the eyes of the fellows whether the horse was good or not. But what could it matter to a convict, especially to some of them, who were creatures altogether down and done for, who never ventured to utter a single word to the others? What *could* it matter to such as these, whether one horse or another was bought? Yet it seemed as if it did. The Circassians appeared to be most relied on for their opinion, and besides these a foremost place in the discussion was given to the Tsigans, and those who had formerly been horse-dealers.

There was a regular sort of duel between two convicts—the Tsigan Koulikoff, who had been a horse-dealer and stealer, and another who had been a professional veterinary, a tricky Siberian peasant, who had been at the establishment and at hard labour for some time, and who had succeeded in getting all Koulikoff's practice in the town. I ought to mention that the veterinary practitioners at the prison, though without diploma, were very much sought after, and that not only the townspeople and tradespeople, but high officials in the city, took their advice when their horses fell ill, rather than that of several regularly diplomatised veterinaries who were at the place.

Till Jolkin came, the Siberian peasant Koulikoff had had plenty of clients from whom he had had fees in good hard cash. He was looked on as quite at the head of his business. He was a Tsigan all over in his doings, liar and cheat, and not at all the master of his art he boasted of being. The income he made had raised him to be a sort of aristocrat among our convicts; he was listened to and obeyed, but he spoke little, and expressed an opinion only in great emergencies. He blew his own trumpet loudly, but he really was a fellow of great energy; he was of ripe age, and of quite marked intelligence. When he spoke to us of the nobility, he did so with exquisite politeness and perfect dignity. I am sure that if he had been suitably dressed, and introduced into a club at the capital with the title of Count, he would have lived up to it; played whist, talked to admiration like a man used to command, and one who knew when to hold his tongue. I am sure that the whole evening would have passed without any one guessing that the "Count" was nothing but a vagabond. He had very probably had a very large and varied experience in life; as to his past, it was quite unknown to us. They kept him among the convicts who formed a special section reserved from the others.

But no sooner had Jolkin come—he was a simple peasant, one of the "old believers," but just as tricky as it was possible for a moujik to be—the veterinary glory of Koulikoff paled sensibly. In less than two months the Siberian had got from him all his town practice, for he cured in a very short time horses Koulikoff had declared incurable, and which had been given up by the regular veterinaries. This peasant had been condemned and sent to hard labour for coining. It is an odd thing he should ever have been tempted to go into that line of business. He told us all about it himself, and joked about their wanting three coins of genuine gold to make one false.

Koulikoff was not a little put out at this peasant's success, while his own glory so rapidly declined. There was he who had had a mistress in the suburbs, who used to wear a plush jacket and top-boots, and here he was now obliged to turn tavern-keeper; so everybody looked out for a regular row when the new horse was bought. The thing was very interesting, each of them had his partisans; the more eager among them got to angry words about it on the spot. The cunning face of Jolkin was all wrinkled into a sarcastic smile; but it turned out quite differently from what was expected. Koulikoff had not the least desire for argument or dispute, he managed cunningly without that. At first he gave way on every point, and listened deferentially to his rival's criticisms, then he caught him up sharply on some remark or other, and pointed out to him modestly but firmly that he was all wrong. In a word, Jolkin was utterly discomfited in a surprisingly clever way, so Koulikoff's side was quite well pleased.

"I say, boys, it's no use talking; you can't trip *him* up. He knows what he is about," said some.

"Jolkin knows more about the matter than he does," said others; not offensively, however. Both sides were ready to make concessions.

"Then, he's got a lighter hand, besides having more in his head. I tell you that when it comes to stock, horses, or anything else, Koulikoff needn't duck under to anybody."

"Nor need Jolkin, I tell you."

"There's nobody like Koulikoff."

The new horse was selected and bought. It was a capital gelding—young, vigorous, and handsome; an irreproachable beast altogether. The bargaining began. The owner asked thirty roubles; the convicts wouldn't give more than twenty-five. The higgling went on long and hotly. At length the convicts began laughing.

"Does the money come out of your own purse?" said some. "What's the good of all this?"

"Do you want to save for the Government cashbox?" cried others.

"But it's money that belongs to us all, pals," said one.

"Us all! It's plain enough that you needn't trouble to grow idiots, they'll come up of themselves without it."

At last the business was settled at twenty-eight roubles. The Major was informed, the purchase sanctioned. Bread and salt were brought at once, and the new boarder led in triumph into the jail. There was not one of the convicts, I think, that did not pat his neck or caress his head.

The day we got him he was at once put to fetching water. All the convicts gazed on him curiously as he pulled at his barrel.

Our waterman, the convict Roman, kept his eyes on the beast with a stupid sort of satisfaction. He was formerly a peasant, about fifty years of age, serious and silent, like all the Russian coachmen, whose behaviour would really seem to acquire some extra gravity by reason of their being always with horses.

Roman was a quiet creature, affable all round, said little, took snuff from a box. He had taken care of the horses at the jail for some time before that. The one just bought was the third given into his charge since he came to the place.

The coachman's office fell, as a matter of course, to Roman; nobody would have dreamed of contesting his right to it. When the bay horse dropped and died, nobody dreamed of accusing Roman of imprudence, not even the Major. It was the will of God, that was all; as to Roman, he knew his business.

That bay horse had become the pet of the jail at once. The convicts were not particularly tender fellows; but they could not help coming to pet him often.

Sometimes when Roman, returning from the river, shut the great gate which the sub-officer had opened, Gniedko would stand quite still waiting for his driver, and turning to him as for orders.

"Get along, you know the way," Roman would cry to him. Then Gniedko would go off peaceably to the kitchen and stop there, and the cooks and other servants of the place would fill their buckets with water, which Gniedko seemed to know all about.

"Gniedko, you're a trump! He's brought his water-barrel himself. He's a delight to see!" they would cry to him.

"That's true; he's only a beast, but he knows all that's said to him."

"No end of a horse is our Gniedko!"

Then the horse shook his head and snorted, just as if he really understood all about his being praised; then some one would bring him bread and salt; and when he had finished with them he would shake his head again, as if to say, "I know you; I know you. I'm a good horse, and you're a good fellow."

I was quite fond of regaling Gniedko with bread. It was quite a pleasure to me to look at his nice mouth, and to feel his warm, moist lips licking up the crumbs from the palm of my hand.

Our convicts were fond of live things, and if they had been allowed would have filled the barracks with birds and domestic animals. What could possibly have been better than attending to such creatures for raising and softening the wild temper of the prisoners? But it was not permitted; it was not in the regulations; and, truth to say, there was no room there for many creatures.

However, in my time some animals had established themselves in the jail. Besides Gniedko, we had some dogs, geese, a he-goat—Vaska—and an eagle, which remained only a short time.

I think I have said before that *our* dog was called Bull, and that he and I had struck up a friendship; but as the lower orders regard dogs as impure animals undeserving of attention, nobody minded him. He lived in the jail itself; slept in the court-yard; ate the leavings of the kitchen, and had no hold whatever on the sympathy of the convicts; all of whom he knew, however, and regarded as masters and owners. When the men assigned to work came back to the jail, at the cry of "Corporal," he used to run to the great gate and gaily welcome the gang, wagging his tail and looking into every man's eyes, as though he expected a caress. But for several years his little ways were as useless as they were engaging. Nobody but myself did caress him; so I was the one he preferred to all others. Somehow—I don't know in what way—we got another dog. Snow he was called. As to the third, Koultiapka, I brought him myself to the place when he was but a pup.

Our Snow was a strange creature. A telega had gone over him and driven in his spine, so that it made a curve inside him. When you saw him running at a distance, he looked like twin-dogs born with a ligament. He was very mangy, too, with bleary eyes, and his tail was hairless, and always hanging between his legs.

Victim of ill-fate as he was, he seemed to have made up his mind to be always as impassive as possible; so he never barked at anybody, for he seemed to be afraid of getting into some fresh trouble. He was nearly always lurking at the back of the buildings; and if anybody came near he rolled on his back at once, as though he meant to say, "Do what you like with me; I've not the least idea of resisting you." And every convict, when the dog upset himself like that, would give him a passing obligatory kick, with "Ouh! the dirty brute!" But Snow dared not so much as give a groan; and if he was too much hurt, would only utter a little, dull, strangled yelp. He threw himself down just the same way before Bull or any other dog when he came to try his luck at the kitchen; and he would stretch himself out flat if a mastiff or any other big dog came barking at him. Dogs like submission and humility in other dogs; so the angry brute quieted down at once, and stopped short reflectively before the poor, humble beast, and then sniffed him curiously all over.

I wonder what poor Snow, trembling with fright, used to think at such moments. "Is this brigand of a fellow going to bite me?"—no doubt something like that. When he had sniffed enough at him, the big brute left him at once, having probably discovered nothing in particular. Snow used then to jump to his feet, and join a lot of four-footed fellows like him who were running down some yutchka or other.

Snow knew quite well that no yutchka would ever condescend to the like of him, that she was too proud for that, but it was some consolation to him in his troubles to limp after her. As to decent behaviour, he had but a very vague notion of any such thing. Being totally without any hope in his future, his highest aim was to get a bellyful of victuals, and he was cynical enough in showing that it was so.

Once I tried to caress him. This was such an unexpected and new thing to him that he plumped down on the ground quite helplessly, and quivered and whined in his delight. As I was really sorry for him I used to caress him often, so as soon as he caught sight of me he began to whine in a plaintive, tearful way. He came to his end at the back of the jail, in the ditch; some dogs tore him to pieces.

Koultiapka was quite a different style of dog. I don't know why I brought him in from one of the workshops, where he was just born; but it gave me pleasure to feed him, and see him grow big. Bull took Koultiapka under his protection, and slept with him. When the young dog began to grow up, Bull was remarkably complaisant with him. He allowed the pup to bite his ears, and pull his skin with his teeth; he played with him as mature dogs are in the habit of doing with the youngsters. It was a strange thing, but Koultiapka never grew in height at all, only in length and breadth. His hide was fluffy and mouse-coloured; one of his ears hung down, while the other was always cocked up. He was, like all young dogs, ardent and enthusiastic, yelping with pleasure when he saw his master, and jumping up to lick his face precisely as if he said: "As long as he sees how delighted I am, I don't care; let etiquette go to the devil!"

Wherever I was, at my call, "Koultiapka," out he came from some corner, dashing towards me with noisy satisfaction, making a ball of himself, and rolling over and over. I was exceedingly fond of the little wretch, and I used to fancy that destiny had reserved for him nothing but joy and pleasure in this world of ours; but one fine day the convict Neustroief, who made women's shoes and prepared skins, cast his eye on him; something had evidently struck him, for he called Koultiapka, felt his skin, and turned him over on the ground in a friendly way. The unsuspicious dog barked with pleasure, but next day he was nowhere to be found. I hunted for him for some time, but in vain; at last, after two weeks, all was explained. Koultiapka's natural cloak had been too much for Neustroief, who had flayed him to make up with the skin some boots of fur-trimmed velvet ordered by the young wife of some official. He showed them me when they were done, their inside lining was magnificent; all Koultiapka, poor fellow!

A good many convicts worked at tanning, and often brought with them to the jail dogs with a nice skin, which soon were seen no more. They stole them or bought them. I remember one day I saw a couple of convicts behind the kitchens laying their heads together. One of them held in a leash a very fine black dog of particularly good breed. A scamp of a footman had stolen it from his master, and sold it to our shoemakers for thirty kopecks. They were going to hang it; that was their way of disposing of them; then they took the skin off, and threw the body into a ditch used for *ejecta*, which was in the most distant corner of the court, and which stank most horribly during the summer heats, for it was rarely seen to.

I think the poor beast understood the fate in store for him. It looked at us one after another in a distressed, scrutinising way; at intervals it gave a timid little wag with its bushy tail between its legs, as though trying to reach our hearts by showing us every confidence. I hastened away from the convicts, who finished their vile work without hindrance.

As to the geese of the establishment, they had established themselves there quite fortuitously. Who took care of them? To whom did they belong? I really don't know; but they were a huge delight to our convicts, and acquired a certain fame throughout the town.

They had been hatched in the convict establishment somewhere, and their head-quarters was the kitchen, whence they emerged in gangs of their own, when the gangs of convicts went out to their work. But as soon as the drum beat and the prisoners massed themselves at the great gate, out ran the geese after them, cackling and flapping their wings, then they jumped one after the other over the elevated threshold of the gateway; while the convicts were at their work, the geese pecked about at a little distance from them. As soon as they had done and set out for the jail, again the geese joined the procession, and people who passed by would cry out, "I say, there are the prisoners with their friends, the geese!" "How did you teach them to follow you?" some one would ask. "Here's some money for your geese," another said, putting his hand in his pocket. In spite of their devotion to the convicts they had their necks twisted to make a feast at the end of the Lent of some year, I forget which.

Nobody would ever have made up his mind to kill our goat Vaska, unless something particular had happened; as it did. I don't know how it got into our prison, or who had brought it. It was a white kid, and very pretty. After some days it had won all hearts, it was diverting and winning. As some excuse was needed for keeping it in the jail, it was given out that it was quite necessary to have a goat in the stables; but he didn't live there, but in the kitchen principally; and after a while he roamed about all over the place. The creature was full of grace and as playful as could be, jumped on the tables, wrestled with the convicts, came when it was called, and was always full of spirits and fun.

One evening, the Lesghian Babaï, who was seated on the stone steps at the doors of the barracks among a crowd of other convicts, took it into his head to have a wrestling bout with Vaska, whose horns were pretty long.

They butted their foreheads against one another—that was the way the convicts amused themselves with him—when all of a sudden Vaska jumped on the highest step, lifted himself up on his hind legs, drew his fore-feet to him and managed to strike the Lesghian on the back of the neck with all his might, and with such effect that Babaï went headlong down the steps to the great delight of all who were by as well as of Babaï himself.

In a word, we all adored our Vaska. When he attained the age of puberty, a general and serious consultation was held, as the result of which, he was subjected to an operation which one of the prison veterinaries executed in a masterly manner.

"Well," said the prisoners, "he won't have any goat-smell about him, that's one comfort."

Vaska then began to lay on fat in the most surprising way. I must say that we fed him quite unconscionably. He became a most beautiful fellow, with magnificent horns, corpulent beyond anything. Sometimes as he walked, he rolled over on the ground heavily out of sheer fatness. He went with us out to work too, which was very diverting to the convicts and all others who saw; and everybody got to know Vaska, the jailbird.

When they worked at the river bank, the prisoners used to cut willow branches and other foliage, and gather flowers in the ditches to ornament Vaska. They used to twine the branches and flowers round his horns and decorate his body with garlands. Vaska then came back at the head of the gang in a splendid state of ornamentation, and we all came after in high pride at seeing him such a beauty.

This love for our goat went so far that prisoners raised the question, not a very wise one, whether Vaska ought not to have his horns gilded. It was a vain idea; nothing came of it. I asked Akim Akimitch, the best gilder in the jail, whether you really could gild a goat's horns. He examined Vaska's quite closely, thought a bit, and then said that it could be done, but that it would not last, and would be quite useless. So nothing came of it. Vaska would have lived for many years more, and, no doubt, have died of asthma at last, if, one day as he returned from work at the head of the convicts, his path had not been crossed by the Major, who was seated in his carriage. Vaska was in particularly gorgeous array.

"Halt!" yelled the Major. "Whose goat is that?"

They told him.

"What! a goat in the prison! and that without my leave? Sub-officer!"

The sub-officer received orders to kill the goat without a moment's delay; flay him, and sell his skin; and put the proceeds to the prisoners' account. As to the meat, he ordered it to be cooked with the convicts' cabbage soup.

The occurrence was much discussed; the goat was much mourned; but nobody dared to disobey the Major. Vaska was put to death close to the ditch I spoke of just now. One of the convicts bought the carcase, paying a rouble and fifty kopecks. With this money white bread was bought for everybody. The man who had bought the goat sold him at retail in a roasted state. The meat was delicious.

We had also, during some time, in our prison a steppe eagle; a quite small species. A convict brought it in, wounded, half-dead. Everybody came flocking around it; it could not fly, its right wing being quite powerless; one of its legs was badly hurt. It gazed on the curious crowd wrathfully, and opened its crooked beak, as if prepared to sell its life dearly. When we had looked at him long enough, and the crowd dispersed, the lamed bird went off, hopping on one paw and flapping his wing, and hid himself in the most distant part of the place he could find; there he huddled himself in a corner against the palings.

During the three months that he remained in our court-yard he never came out of his corner. At first we went to look at him pretty often, and sometimes they set Bull at him, who threw himself forward with fury, but was frightened to go too near, which mightily amused the convicts. "A wild chap that! He won't stand any nonsense!" But Bull after a while got over his fright, and began to worry him. When he was roused to it, the dog would catch hold of the bird's bad wing, and the creature defended itself with beak and claws, and then got up closer into his corner with a proud, savage sort of demeanour, like a wounded king, fixing his eyes steadily on the fellows looking at his misery.

They tired of the sport after a while, and the eagle seemed quite forgotten; but there was some one who, every day, put close to him a bit of fresh meat and a vessel with some water. At first, and for several days, the eagle would eat nothing; at last, he made up his mind to take what was left for him, but he never could be got to take anything from the hand, or in public. Sometimes I succeeded in watching his proceedings at some distance.

When he saw nobody, and thought he was alone, he ventured upon leaving his corner and limping along the palisade for a dozen steps or so, then went back; and so forwards and backwards, precisely as if he were taking exercise for his health under medical orders. As soon as ever he caught sight of me he made for his corner as quickly as he possibly could, limping and hopping. Then he threw his head back, opened his mouth, ruffled himself, and seemed to make ready for fight.

In vain I tried to caress him. He bit and struggled as soon as he was touched. Not once did he take the meat I offered him, and all the time I remained by him he kept his wicked, piercing eye upon me. Lonely and revengeful he waited for death, defying, refusing to be reconciled with everything and everybody.

At last the convicts remembered him, after two months of complete forgetfulness, and then they showed a sympathy I did not expect of them. It was unanimously agreed to carry him out.

"Let him die, but let him die in freedom," said the prisoners.

"Sure enough, a free and independent bird like that will never get used to the prison," added others.

"He's not like us," said some one.

"Oh well, he's a bird, and we're human beings."

"The eagle, pals, is the king of the woods," began Skouratof; but that day nobody paid any attention to him.

85

One afternoon, when the drum beat for beginning work, they took the eagle, tied his beak (for he struck a desperate attitude), and took him out of the prison on to the ramparts. The twelve convicts of the gang were extremely anxious to know where he would go to. It was a strange thing: they all seemed as happy as though they had themselves got their freedom.

"Oh, the wretched brute. One wants to do him a kindness, and he tears your hand for you by way of thanks," said the man who held him, looking almost lovingly at the spiteful bird.

"Let him fly off, Mikitka!"

"It doesn't suit *him* being a prisoner; give him his freedom, his jolly freedom."

They threw him from the ramparts on to the steppe. It was just at the end of autumn, a gray, cold day. The wind whistled on the bare steppe and went groaning through the yellow dried-up grass. The eagle made off directly, flapping his wounded wing, as if in a hurry to quit us and get himself a shelter from our piercing eyes. The convicts watched him intently as he went along with his head just above the grass.

"Do you see him, hey?" said one very pensively.

"He doesn't look round," said another; "he hasn't looked behind once."

"Did you happen to fancy he'd come back to thank us?" said a third.

"Sure enough, he's free; he feels it. It's *freedom*!"

"Yes, freedom."

"You won't see him any more, pals."

"What are you about sticking there? March, march!" cried the escort, and all went slowly to their work.

CHAPTER VII. GRIEVANCES

At the outset of this chapter, the editor of the "Recollections" of the late Alexander Petrovitch Goriantchikoff thinks it his duty to communicate what follows to his readers.

"In the first chapter of the 'Recollections of the House of the Dead,' something was said about a parricide, of noble birth, who was put forward as an instance of the insensibility with which the convicts speak of the crimes they have committed. It was also stated that he refused altogether to confess to the authorities and the court; but that, thanks to the statements of persons who knew all the details of his case and history, his guilt was put beyond all doubt. These persons had informed the author of the 'Recollections,' that the criminal had been of dissolute life and overwhelmed with debts, and that he had murdered his father to come into the property. Besides, the whole town where this parricide was imprisoned told his story in precisely the same way, a fact of which the editor of these 'Recollections' has fully satisfied himself. It was further stated that this murderer, even when in the jail, was of quite a joyous and cheerful frame of mind, a sort of inconsiderate giddy-pated person, although intelligent, and that the author of the 'Recollections' had never observed any particular signs of cruelty about him, to which he added, 'So I, for my part, never could bring myself to believe him guilty.'

"Some time ago the editor of the 'Recollections of the House of the Dead,' had intelligence from Siberia of the discovery of the innocence of this 'parricide,' and that he had undergone ten years of the imprisonment with hard labour for nothing; this was recognised and avowed by the authorities. The real criminals had been discovered and had confessed, and the unfortunate man in question set at liberty. All this stands upon unimpeachable and authoritative grounds."

To say more would be useless. The tragical facts speak too clearly for themselves. All words are weak in such a case, where a life has been ruined by such an accusation. Such mistakes as these are among the dreadful possibilities of life, and such possibilities impart a keener and more vivid interest to the "Recollections of the House of the Dead," which dreadful place we see may contain innocent as well as guilty men.

To continue. I have said that I became at last, in some sense, accustomed, if not reconciled, to the conditions of convict life; but it was a long and dreadful time before I was. It took me nearly a year to get used to the prison, and I shall always regard this year as the most dreadful of my life, it is graven deep in my memory, down to the very least details. I think that I could minutely recall the events and feelings of each successive hour in it.

I have said that the other prisoners, too, found it as difficult as I did to get used to the life they had to lead. During the whole of this first year, I used to ask myself whether they were really as calm as they seemed to be. Questions of this kind pressed themselves upon me. As I have mentioned before, all the convicts felt themselves in an alien element to which they could not reconcile themselves. The sense of home was an impossibility; they felt as if they were staying, as a stage upon a journey, in an evil sort of inn. These men, exiles for and from life, seemed either in a perpetual smouldering agitation, or else in deep depression; but there was not one who had not his ordinary ideas of one thing or another. This restlessness, which, if it did not come to the surface, was still unmistakable; those vague hopes of the poor creatures which existed in spite of themselves, hopes so ill-founded that they were more like the promptings of incipient insanity than aught else; all this stamped the place with a character, an originality, peculiarly its own. One could not but feel when one went there that there was nothing like it anywhere else in the whole world. There everybody went about in a sort of waking dream; nor was there anything to relieve or qualify the impressions the place made on the system of every man; so that all seemed to suffer from a sort of hyperæsthetic neurosis, and this dreaming of impossibilities gave to the majority of the convicts a sombre and morose aspect, for which the word morbid is not strong enough. Nearly all were taciturn and irascible, preferring to keep to themselves the hopes they secretly and vainly cherished. The result was, that anything like ingenuousness or frank statement was the object of general contempt. Precisely because these wild hopings were impossible, and, despite themselves, were felt to be so, confessed to their more lucid selves to be so, they kept them jealously concealed in the most secret recesses of their souls; while to renounce them was beyond their powers of self-control. It may be they were ashamed of their imagination. God knows. The Russian character is, in its normal conditions, so positive and sober in its way of looking at life, so pitiless in criticism of its own weaknesses.

Perhaps it was this inward misery of self-dissatisfaction which was at the bottom of the impatience and intolerance the convicts showed among themselves, and of the cruel biting things they said to each other. If one of them, more naïve or impartial than the rest, put into words what every one of them had in his mind, painted his castles in the air, told his dreams of liberty, or plans of escape, they shut him up with brutal promptitude, and made the poor fellow's life a burden to him with their sarcasms and jests. And I think those did it most unscrupulously who had perhaps themselves gone furthest in cherishing futile hopes, and indulging in senseless expectations. I have said, more than once, that those among them who were marked by simplicity and candour were looked on rather as being stupid and idiotic; there was nothing but contempt for them. The convicts were so soured and, in the wrong sense, sensitive, that they positively hated anything like amiability or unselfishness. I should be disposed to classify them all broadly, as either good or bad men, morose or cheerful, putting by themselves, as a sort of separate creatures, the ingenious fellows who could not hold their tongues. But the sour-tempered were in far the greatest majority; some of these were talkative, but these were usually of slanderous and envious disposition, always poking their noses into other people's business, though they took good care not to let anybody have a glimpse of the secret thoughts of their *own* souls; that would have been against the fashions and conventions of this strange, little world. As to the fellows who were really good—very few indeed were they—these were always very quiet and peaceable, and buried their hopes, if they had any, in strict silence; but more of real faith went with their hopes than was the case with the gloomy-minded among the convicts. Stay, there was one category further among our convicts, which ought not to be forgotten; the men who had lost all hope, who were despairing and desperate, like the old man of Starodoub; but these were very few indeed.

The old man of Starodoub! This was a very subdued, quiet, old man; but there were some indications of what went on in him, which he could not help giving, and from which, I could not help seeing, that his inward life was one of intolerable horror; still he had *something* to fall back upon for help and consolation—prayer, and the notion that he was a martyr. The convict who was always reading the Bible, of whom I spoke earlier, the one that went mad and threw himself, brick in hand, upon the Major, was also probably one of those whom hope had altogether abandoned; and, as it is perfectly impossible to go on living without hope of some sort, he threw away his life as a sort of voluntary sacrifice. He declared that he attacked the Major though he had no grievance in particular; all he wanted was to have some torments inflicted on himself.

Now, what sort of psychological operation had been going on in *that* man's soul? No man lives, can live, without having *some* object in view, and making efforts to attain that object. But when object there is none, and hope is entirely fled, anguish often turns a man into a monster. The object *we* all had in view was liberty, and getting out of our place of confinement and hard labour.

So I try to place our convicts in separately-defined classes and categories; but it cannot well be done. Reality is a thing of infinite diversity, and defies the most ingenious deductions and definitions of abstract thought, nay, abhors the clear and precise classifications we so delight in. Reality tends to infinite subdivision of things, and truth is a matter of infinite shadings and differentiations. Every one of us who were there had his own peculiar, interior, strictly personal life, which lay altogether outside of the world of regulations and our official superintendence.

But, as I have said before, I could not penetrate the depths of this interior life in the early part of my prison career, for everything that met my eyes, or challenged my attention in any way, filled me with a sadness for which there are no words. Sometimes I felt nothing short of hatred for poor creatures whose martyrdom was at least as great as mine. In those first days I envied them, because they were among persons of their own sort, and understood one another; so I thought, but the truth was that their enforced companionship, the comradeship where the word of command went with the whip or the rod, was as much an object of aversion to them as it was to myself, and every one of them tried to keep himself as much to himself as possible. This envious hatred of them, which came to me in moments of irritation, was not without its reasonable cause, for those who tell you so confidently that a cultivated man of the higher class does not suffer as a mere peasant does, are utterly in the wrong. That is a thing I have often heard said, and read too. In the abstract, the notion seems correct, and it is founded in generous sentiment, for all convicts are human beings alike; but in reality it is different. In the real living facts of the problem there come in a quantity of practical complications, and only experience can pronounce upon these: experience which I have had. I do not mean to lay it down peremptorily, that the nobleman and the man of culture feel more acutely, sensitively, deeply, because of their more highly developed conditions of being. On the other hand, it is impossible to bring all souls to one common level or standard; neither the grade of education, nor any other thing, furnishes a standard according to which punishment can be meted out.

It is a great satisfaction to me to be able to say that among these dreadful sufferers, in a state of things so barbarous and abject, I found abundant proof that the elements of moral development were not wanting. In our convict establishment there were men whom I was familiar with for several years, and whom I looked upon as wild beasts and abhorred as such; well, all of a sudden, when I least expected it, these very men would exhibit such an abundance of feeling of the best kind, so keen a comprehension of the sufferings of others, seen in the light of the consciousness of their own, that one might almost fancy scales had fallen from their eyes. So sudden was it as to cause stupefaction; one could scarcely believe one's eyes or ears. Sometimes it was just the other way: educated men, well brought up, would occasionally display a savage, cynical brutality which nearly turned one's stomach, conduct of a kind impossible to excuse or justify, however much you might be charitably inclined to do so.

I lay no stress on the entire change in the habits of life, the food, etc., as to which there come in points where the man of the higher classes suffers so much more keenly than the peasant or working man, who often goes hungry when free, while he always has his stomach-full in prison. We will leave all that out. Let it be admitted that for a man with some force of character these external things are a trifle in comparison with privations of a quite different kind; for all that, such total change of material conditions and habits is neither an easy nor a slight thing. But in the convict's *status* there are elements of horror before which all other horrors pale, even the mud and filth everywhere about, the scantiness and uncleanness of the food, the irons on your limbs, the suffocating sense of being always held tight, as in a vice.

The capital, the most important point of all is, that after a couple of hours or so, every new-comer to a convict establishment, who is of the lower class, shakes down into equality with the rest; he is *at home* among them, he has his "freedom" of this city of the enslaved, this community of convicted scoundrels, in which one man is superficially like every other man; he understands and is understood, he is looked upon by everybody as *one of themselves*. Now all this is *not* so in the case of the nobleman. However kindly, just-minded, intelligent a man of the higher class may be, every soul there will hate and despise him during long years; they will neither understand nor believe in him, not one whit. He will be neither friend nor comrade in their eyes; if he can get them to stop insulting him it will be as much as he can do, but he will be alien to them from the first to the last, he will have to feel the grief of a ceaseless, hopeless, causeless solitude and sequestration. Sometimes it is the case that sheer ill-will on the part of the prisoners has nothing to do with bringing about this state of things, it simply cannot be helped; the nobleman is not one of the gang, and there's the whole secret.

There is nothing more horrible than to live out of the social sphere to which you properly belong. The peasant, transported from Taganrog to Petropavlosk, finds there Russian peasants like himself; between him and them there can be mutual intelligence; in an hour they will be friends, and live comfortably together in the same izba or the same barrack. With the nobleman it is wholly otherwise; a bottomless abyss separates him from the lower classes, *how* deep and impassable is only seen when a nobleman forfeits his position and becomes as one of the populace himself. You may be your whole life in daily relations with the peasant, forty years you may do business with him regularly as the day comes—let us suppose it so, at all events—by the calls of official position or administrative duty; you may be his benefactor, all but a father to him—well, you'll never know what is at the bottom of the man's mind or heart. You may think you know something about him, but it is all optical illusion, nothing more. My readers will charge me with exaggeration, but I am convinced I am quite right. I don't go on theory or book-reading in this; in my case the realities of life have given me only too ample time and opportunity for reviewing and correcting my theoretic convictions, which, as to this, are now fixed. Perhaps everybody will some day learn how well founded I am in what I say about this.

All this was theory when I first went into the convict establishment, but events, and things observed, soon came to confirm me in such views, and what I experienced so affected my system as to undermine its health. During the first summer I wandered about the place, so far as I was free to move, a solitary, friendless man. My moral situation was such that I could not distinguish those among the convicts who, in the sequel, managed to care for me a little in spite of the distance that always remained between us. There *were* there men of my own position, ex-nobles like myself, but their companionship was repugnant to me.

Here is one of the incidents which obliged me to see at the outset, how solitary a creature I was, and all the strangeness of my position at the place. One day in August, a fine warm day, about one o'clock in the afternoon, a time when, as a rule, everybody took a nap before resuming work, the convicts rose as one man and massed themselves in the court-yard. I had not the slightest idea, up to that moment, that anything was going on. So deeply had I been sunk in my own thoughts, that I saw nearly nothing of what was happening about me of any kind. But it seems that the convicts had been in a smouldering sort of unusual agitation for three days. Perhaps it had begun sooner; so I thought later when I remembered stray remarks, bits of talk that had come to my ears, the palpable increase of ill-humour among the prisoners, their unusual irritability for some time past. I had attributed it all to the trying summer work, the insufferably long days; to their dreamings about the woods, and freedom, which the season brought up; to the nights too short for rest. It may be that all these things came together to form a mass of discontent, that only wanted a tolerably good reason for exploding; it was found in the food.

For several days the convicts had not concealed their dissatisfaction with it in open talk in their barracks, and they showed it plainly when assembled for dinner or supper; one of the cooks had been changed, but, after a couple of days, the new comer was sent to the right-about, and the old one brought back. The restlessness and ill-humour were general; mischief was brewing.

"Here are we slaving to death, and they give us nothing but filth to eat," grumbled one in the kitchen.

"If you don't like it, why don't you order jellies and blanc-mange?" said another.

"Sour cabbage soup, why, that's *good*. I delight in it; there's nothing more juicy," exclaimed a third.

"Well, if they gave you nothing but beef, beef, beef, for ever and ever, would you like *that*?"

"Yes, yes; they ought to give us meat," said a fourth; "one's almost killed at the workshops; and, by heaven! when one has got through with work there one's hungry, hungry; and you don't get anything to satisfy your hunger."

"It's true, the victuals are simply damnable."

"He fills his pockets, don't you fear!"

"It isn't your business."

"Whose business is it? My belly's my own. If we were all to make a row about it together, you'd soon see."

"Yes."

"Haven't we been beaten enough for complaining, dolt that you are?"

"True enough! What's done in a hurry is never well done. And how would you set about making a raid over it, tell me that?"

"I'll tell you, by God! If everybody will go, I'll go too, for I'm just dying of hunger. It's all very well for those who eat at a better table, apart, to keep quiet; but those who eat the regulation food——"

"There's a fellow with eyes that do their work, bursting with envy *he* is. Don't his eyes glisten when he sees something that doesn't belong to him?"

"Well, pals, why don't we make up our minds? Have we gone through enough? They flay us, the brigands! Let's go at them."

"What's the good? I tell you ye must chew what they give you, and stuff your mouth full of it. Look at the fellow, he wants people to chew his food for him. We're in prison, and have got to stand it."

"Yes, that's it; we're in prison."

"That's it always; the people die of hunger, and the Government fills its belly."

"That's true. Our eight-eyes (*the Major*) has got finely fat over it; he's bought a pair of gray horses."

"He don't like his glass at all, that fellow," said a convict ironically.

"He had a bout at cards a little while ago with the vet; for two hours he played without a half-penny in his pocket. Fedka told me so."

"That's why we get cabbage soup that's fit for nothing."

"You're all idiots! It doesn't matter; *nothing* matters."

"I tell you if we all join in complaining we shall see what he has to say for himself. Let's make up our minds."

"*Say* for himself? You'll get his fist on your pate; that's just all."

"I tell you they'll have him up, and try him."

All the prisoners were in great agitation; the truth is, the food was execrable. The general anguish, suffering, and suspense seemed to be coming to a head. Convicts are, by disposition, or, as such, quarrelsome and rebellious; but a general revolt is rare, for they can never agree upon it; we all of us felt that since there was, as a rule, more violent talk than doing.

This time, however, the agitation did not fall to the ground. The men gathered in groups in their barracks, talking things over in a violent way, and going over all the particulars of the Major's misdoings, and trying to get to the bottom of them. In all affairs of that sort there are ringleaders and firebrands. The ringleaders on such occasions are generally rather remarkable fellows, not only in convict establishments, but among all large organisations of workmen, military detachments, etc. They are always people of a peculiar type, enthusiastic men, who have a thirst for justice, very naïve, simple, and strong, convinced that their desires are fully capable of realisation; they have as much sense as other people; some are of high intelligence; but they are too full of warmth and zeal to measure their acts. When you come across people who really do know how to direct the masses, and get what they want, you find a quite different sort of popular leaders, and one excessively rare among us Russians. The more usual type of leader, the one I first alluded to, does certainly in some sense accomplish their object, so far as bringing about a rising is concerned; but it all ends in filling up the prisons and convict establishments. Thanks to their impetuosity they always come off second-best; but it is this impetuosity that gives them their influences over the masses; their ardent, honest indignation does its work, and draws in the more irresolute. Their blind confidence of success seduces even the most hardened sceptics, although this confidence is generally based on such uncertain, childish reasons that it is wonderful how people can put faith in them.

The secret of their influence is that they put themselves at the head, and *go* ahead, without flinching. They dash forward, heads down, often without the least knowledge worth the name of what they are about, and have nothing about them of the jesuitical practical faculty by dint of which a vile and worthless man often hits his mark and comes uppermost, and will sometimes come all white out of a tub of ink. They *must* dash their skulls against stone walls. Under ordinary circumstances these people are bilious, irascible, intolerant, contemptuous, often very warm, which really after all is part of the secret of their strength. The deplorable thing is that they never go at what is the essential, the vital part of their task, they always go off at once into details instead of going straight to their mark, and this is their ruin. But they and the mob understand one another; that makes them formidable.

I must say a few words about this word "grievance."

Some of the convicts had been transported in connection with a "grievance;" these were the most excited among them, notably a certain Martinoff, who had formerly served in the Hussars, an eager, restless, and choleric, but a worthy and truthful, fellow. Another, Vassili Antonoff, could work himself up into anger coolly and collectedly; he had a generally impudent expression, and a sarcastic smile, but he, too, was honest, and a man of his word, and of no little education. I won't enumerate; there were plenty of them. Petroff went about in a hurried way from one group to another. He spoke few words, but he was quite as highly excited as any one there, for he was the first to spring out of the barrack when the others massed themselves in the court-yard.

Our sergeant, who acted as sergeant-major, came up very soon in quite a fright. The convicts got into rank, and politely begged him to tell the Major that they wanted to speak with him and put him a few questions. Behind the sergeant came all the invalids, who ranked themselves in face of the convicts. What they asked the sergeant to do frightened the man out of his wits almost, but he dared not refuse to go and report to the Major, for if the convicts mutinied, God only knows what might happen. All the men set over us showed themselves great poltroons in handling the prisoners; then, even if nothing further worse happened, if the convicts thought better of it and dispersed, the sub-officer was still in duty bound to inform the authorities of what had been going on. Pale, and trembling with fright, he went headlong to the Major, without even an effort to bring the convicts to reason. He saw that they were not minded to put up with any of his talk, no doubt.

Without the least idea of what was going on, I went into rank myself (it was only later that I heard the earlier details of the story). I thought that the muster-roll was to be called, but I did not see the soldiers who verify the lists, so I was surprised, and began to look about me a little. The men's faces were working with emotion, and some were ghostly pale. They were sternly silent, and seemed to be thinking of what they should say to the Major. I observed that many of the convicts seemed to wonder at seeing me among them, but they turned their glances away from me. No doubt they thought it strange that I should come into the ranks with them, and join in their remonstrances, and could not quite believe it. Then they turned round to me again in a questioning sort of way.

"What are you doing here?" said Vassili Antonoff, in a loud, rude voice; he happened to be close to me, and a little way from the rest; the man had always hitherto been scrupulously polite to me.

I looked at him in perplexity, trying to understand what he meant by it; I began to see that something extraordinary was up in our prison.

"Yes, indeed, what are you about here? Go off into the barrack," said a young fellow, a soldier-convict, whom I did not know till then, and who was a good, quiet lad, "this is none of *your* business."

"Have we not fallen into rank," I answered, "aren't we going to be mustered?"

"Why, *he's* come, too," cried one of them.

"Iron-nose," said another.

"Fly-killer," added a third, with inexpressible contempt for me in his tone. This new nickname caused a general burst of laughter.

"These fellows are in clover everywhere. We are in prison, with hard labour, I rather fancy; they get wheat-bread and sucking-pig, like great lords as they are. Don't you get your victuals by yourself? What are you doing here?"

"Your place is not here," said Koulikoff to me brusquely, taking me by the hand and leading me out of the ranks.

He was himself very pale; his dark eyes sparkled with fire, he had bitten his under lip till the blood came; he wasn't one of those who expected the Major without losing self-possession.

I liked to look at Koulikoff when he was in trying circumstances like these; then he showed himself just what he was in his strong points and weak. He attitudinised, but he knew how to act, too. I think he would have gone to his death with a certain affected elegance. While everybody was insulting me in words and tones, his politeness was greater than ever; but he spoke in a firm and resolved tone which admitted of no reply.

"We are here on business of our own, Alexander Petrovitch, and you've got to keep out of it. Go where you like and wait till it's over ... here, your people are in the kitchens, go there."

"They're in hot quarters down there."

I did in fact see our Poles at the open window of the kitchen, in company with a good many other convicts. I did not well know what to be at; but went there followed by laughter, insulting remarks, and that sort of muttered growling which is the prison substitute for the hissings and cat-calls of the world of freedom.

"He doesn't like it at all! Chu, chu, chu! Seize him!"

I had never been so bitterly insulted since I was in the place. It was a very painful moment, but just what was to be expected in the excessive excitement the men were labouring under. In the ante-room I met T—vski, a young nobleman of not much information, but of firm, generous character; the convicts excepted him from the hatred they felt for the convicts of noble birth; they were almost fond of him; every one of his gestures denoted the brave and energetic man.

"What are you about, Goriantchikoff?" he cried to me; "come here, come here!"

"But what is *it* all about?"

"They are going to make a formal complaint, don't you know it? It won't do them a bit of good; who'll pay any attention to convicts? They'll try to find out the ringleaders, and if we are among them they'll lay it all on us. Just remember what we have been transported for. They'll only get a whipping, but we shall be put regularly to trial. The Major detests us all, and will be only too happy to ruin us; all his sins will fall on our shoulders."

"The convicts would tie us hands and feet and sell us directly," added M—tski, when we got into the kitchen.

"They'll never have mercy on *us*," added T—vski.

Besides the nobles there were in the kitchen about thirty other prisoners who did not want to join in the general complaints, some because they were afraid, others because of their conviction that the whole proceeding would prove quite useless. Akim Akimitch, who was a decided opponent of everything that savoured of complaint, or that could interfere with discipline and the usual routine, waited with great phlegm to see the end of the business, about which he did not care a jot. He was perfectly convinced that the authorities would put it all down immediately.

Isaiah Fomitch's nose drooped visibly as he listened in a sort of frightened curiosity to what we said about the affair; he was much disturbed. With the Polish nobles were some inferior persons of the same nation, as well as some Russians, timid, dull, silent fellows, who had not dared to join the rest, and who waited in a melancholy way to see what the issue would be. There were also some morose, discontented convicts, who remained in the kitchen, not because they were afraid, but that they thought this half-revolt an absurdity which could not succeed; it seemed to me that these were not a little disturbed, and their faces were quite unsteady. They saw clearly that they were in the right, and that the issue of the movement would be what they had foretold, but they had a sort of feeling that they were traitors who had sold their comrades to the Major. Jolkin—the long-headed Siberian peasant sent to hard labour for coining, the man who got Koulikoff's town practice from him—was there also, as well as the old man of Starodoub. None of the cooks had left their post, perhaps because they looked upon themselves as belonging specially to the authorities of the place, whom it would be unbecoming, therefore, to join in opposing.

"For all that," said I to M—tski, "except these fellows, all the convicts are in it," and no doubt I said it in a way that showed misgivings.

"I wonder what in the world *we* have to do with it?" growled B——.

"We should have risked a good deal more than they had we gone with them; and why? *Je hais ces brigands.* Why, do you think that they'll bring themselves up to the scratch after all? I can't see what they want putting their heads in the lion's mouth, the fools."

"It'll all come to nothing," said some one, an obstinate, sour-tempered old fellow. Almazoff, who was with us too, agreed heartily in this.

"Some fifty of them will get a good beating, and that's all the good they'll all get out of it."

"Here's the Major!" cried one; everybody ran to the windows.

The Major had come up, spectacles and all, looking as wicked as might be, towering with passion, red as a turkey-cock. He came on without a word, and in a determined manner, right up to the line of the convicts. In conjunctures of this sort he showed uncommon pluck and presence of mind; but it ought not to be overlooked that he was nearly always half-seas over. Just then his greasy cap, with its yellow border, and his tarnished silver epaulettes, gave him a Mephistophelic look in my excited fancy. Behind him came the quartermaster, Diatloff, who was quite a personage in the establishment, for he was really at the bottom of all the authorities did. He was an exceedingly capable and cunning fellow, and wielded great influence with the Major. He was not by any means a bad sort of man, and the convicts were, in a general way, not ill-inclined towards him. Our sergeant followed him with three or four soldiers, no more; he had already had a tremendous wigging, and there was plenty more of the same to come, if he knew it. The convicts, who had remained uncovered, cap in hand, from the moment they sent for the Major, stiffened themselves, every man shifting his weight to the other leg; then they remained motionless, and waited for the first word, or the first shout rather, to come from him.

They had not long to wait. Before he had got more than one word out, the Major began to shout at the top of his voice; he was beside himself with rage. We saw him from the windows running all along the line of convicts, dashing at them here and there with angry questions. As we were a pretty good distance off, we could not hear what he said or their replies. We only heard his shouts, or rather what seemed shouting, groaning, and grunting beautifully mingled.

"Scoundrels! mutineers! to the cat with ye! Whips and sticks! The ringleaders? *You're* one of the ringleaders!" throwing himself on one of them.

We did not hear the answer; but a minute after we saw this convict leave the ranks and make for the guard-house.

Another followed, then a third.

"I'll have you up, every man of you. I'll—— Who's in the kitchen there?" he bawled, as he saw us at the open windows. "Here with all of you! Drive 'em all out, every man!"

Diatloff, the quartermaster, came towards the kitchens. When we had told him that *we* were not complaining of any grievance, he returned, and reported to the Major at once.

"Ah, those fellows are not in it," said he, lowering his tone a bit, and much pleased. "Never mind, bring them along here."

We left the kitchen. I could not help feeling humiliation; all of us went along with our heads down.

"Ah, Prokofief! Jolkin too; and you, Almazof! Here, come here, all the lump of you!" cried the Major to us, with a gasp; but he was somewhat softened, his tone was even obliging. "M—tski, you're here too?... Take down the names. Diatloff, take down all the names, the grumblers in one list and the contented ones in another—all, without exception; you'll give me the list. I'll have you all before the Committee of Superintendence.... I'll ... brigands!"

This word "*list*" told.

"We've nothing to complain of!" cried one of the malcontents, in a half-strangled sort of voice.

"Ah, you've nothing to complain of! *Who's* that? Let all those who have nothing to complain of step out of the ranks."

"All of us, all of us!" came from some others.

"Ah, the food is all right, then? You've been put up to it. Ringleaders, mutineers, eh? So much the worse for them."

"But, what do you mean by that?" came from a voice in the crowd.

"Where is the fellow that said that?" roared the Major, throwing himself to where the voice came from. "It was you, Rastorgouïef, you; to the guard-house with you."

Rastorgouïef, a young, chubby fellow of high stature, left the ranks and went with slow steps to the guard-house. It was not he who had said it, but, as he was called out, he did not venture to contradict.

"You fellows are too fat, that's what makes you unruly!" shouted the Major. "You wait, you hulking rascal, in three days you'd—— Wait! I'll have it out with you all. Let all those who have nothing to complain of come out of the ranks, I say——"

"We're not complaining of anything, your worship," said some of the convicts with a sombre air; the rest preserved an obstinate silence. But the Major wanted nothing further; it was his interest to stop the thing with as little friction as might be.

"Ah, *now* I see! *Nobody* has anything to complain of," said he. "I knew it, I saw it all. It's ringleaders, there are ringleaders, by God," he went on, speaking to Diatloff. "We must lay our hands on them, every man of them. And now—now—it's time to go to your work. Drummer, there; drummer, a roll!"

He told them off himself in small detachments. The convicts dispersed sadly and silently, only too glad to get out of his sight. Immediately after the gangs went off, the Major betook himself to the guard-house, where he began to make his dispositions as to the "ringleaders," but he did not push matters far. It was easy to see that he wanted to be done with the whole business as soon as possible. One of the men charged told us later that he had begged for forgiveness, and that the officer had let him go immediately. There can be no doubt that our Major did not feel firm in the saddle; he had had a fright, I fancy, for a mutiny is always a ticklish thing, and although this complaint of the convicts about the food did not amount really to mutiny (only the Major had been reported to about it, and the Governor himself), yet it was an uncomfortable and dangerous affair. What gave him most anxiety was that the prisoners had been unanimous in their movement, so their discontent had to be got over somehow, at any price. The ringleaders were soon set free. Next day the food was passable, but this improvement did not last long; on the days ensuing the disturbance, the Major went about the prison much more than usual, and always found something irregular to be stopped and punished. Our sergeant came and went in a puzzled, dazed sort of way, as if he could not get over his stupefaction at what had happened. As to the convicts, it took long for them to quiet down again, but their agitation seemed to wear quite a different character; they were restless and perplexed. Some went about with their heads down, without saying a word; others discussed the event in a grumbling, helpless kind of way. A good many said biting things about their own proceedings as though they were quite out of conceit with themselves.

"I say, pal, take and eat!" said one.

"Where's the mouse that was so ready to bell the cat?"

"Let's think ourselves lucky that he did not have us all well beaten."

"It would be a good deal better if you thought more and chattered less."

"What do *you* mean by lecturing me? Are you schoolmaster here, I'd like to know?"

"Oh, you want putting to the right-about."

"Who are you, I'd like to know?"

"I'm a man! What are you?"

"A man! You're——"

"You're——"

"I say! Shut up, do! What's the good of all this row?" was the cry from all sides.

On the evening of the day the "mutiny" took place, I met Petroff behind the barracks after the day's work. He was looking for me. As he came near me, I heard him exclaim something, which I didn't understand, in a muttering sort of way; then he said no more, and walked by my side in a listless, mechanical fashion.

"I say, Petroff, your fellows are not vexed with us, are they?"

"Who's vexed?" he asked, as if coming to himself.

"The convicts with us—with us nobles."

"Why should they be vexed?"

"Well, because we did not back them up."

"Oh, why should you have kicked up a dust?" he answered, as if trying to enter into my meaning: "you have a table to yourselves, you fellows."

"Oh, well, there are some of you, not nobles, who don't eat the regulation food, and who went in with you. We ought to back you up, we're in the same place; we ought to be comrades."

"Oh, I *say*. Are you our comrades?" he asked, with unfeigned astonishment.

I looked at him; it was clear that he had not the least comprehension of my meaning; but I, on the other hand, entered only too thoroughly into his. I saw now, quite thoroughly, something of which I had before only a confused idea; what I had before guessed at was now sad certainty.

It was forced on my perceptions that any sort of real fellowship between the convicts and myself could never be; not even were I to remain in the place as long as life should last. I was a convict of the "special section," a creature for ever apart. The expression of Petroff when he said, "are we comrades, how can that be?" remains, and will always remain before my eyes. There was a look of such frank, naïve surprise in it, such ingenuous astonishment that I could not help asking myself if there was not some lurking irony in the man, just a little spiteful mockery. Not at all, it was simply meant. I was not their comrade, and could not be; that was all. Go you to the right, we'll go to the left! your business is yours, ours is ours.

I really fancied that, after the mutiny, they would attack us mercilessly so far as they dared and could, and that our life would become a hell. But nothing of the sort happened; we did not hear the slightest reproach, there was not even an unpleasant allusion to what had happened, it was all simply passed over. They went on teasing us as before when opportunity served, no more. Nobody seemed to bear malice against those who would not join in, but remained in the kitchens, or against those who were the first to cry out that they had nothing to complain of. It was all passed over without a word, to my exceeding astonishment.

FOOTNOTES:

An insulting phrase which is untranslatable.

French in the original Russian.

CHAPTER VIII. MY COMPANIONS

As will be understood, those to whom I was most drawn were people of my own sort, that is, those of "noble" birth, especially in the early days; but of the three ex-nobles in the place, who were Russians, I knew and spoke to but one, Akim Akimitch; the other two were the spy A——n, and the supposed parricide. Even with Akim I never exchanged a word except when in extremity, in moments when the melancholy on me was simply unendurable, and when I thought I really never should have the chance of getting close to any other human being again.

In the last chapter I have tried to show that the convicts were of different types, and tried to classify them; but when I think of Akim Akimitch I don't know how to place him, he was quite *sui generis*, so far as I could observe, in that establishment.

There may be, elsewhere, men like him, to whom it seemed as absolutely a matter of indifference whether he was a free man, or in jail at hard labour; at that place he stood alone in this curious impartiality of temperament. He had settled down in the jail as if he was going to pass his whole life, and didn't mind it at all. All his belongings, mattress, cushions, utensils, were so ordered as to give the impression that he was living in a furnished house of his own; there was nothing provisional, temporary, bivouac-like, about him, or his words, or his habits. He had a good many years still to spend in punishment, but I much doubt whether he ever gave a thought to the time when he would get out. He was entirely reconciled to his condition, not because he had made any effort to be so, but simply out of natural submissiveness; but, as far as his comfort went, it came to the same thing. He was not at all a bad fellow, and in the early days his advice and help were quite useful to me; but sometimes, I can't help saying it, his peculiarities deepened my natural melancholy until it became almost intolerable anguish.

When I became desperate with silence and solitude of soul, I would get into talk with him; I wanted to hear, and reply to *some* words falling from a living soul, and the more filled with gall and hatred with all our surroundings they had been, the more would they have been in sympathy with my wretched mood; but he would just barely talk, quietly go on sizing his lanterns, and then begin to tell me some story as to how he had been at a review of troops in 18—, that their general of division was so-and-so, that the manœuvring had been very pretty, that there had been a change in the skirmisher's system of signalling, and the like; all of it in level imperturbable tones, like water falling drop by drop. He did not put any life into them even when he told me of a sharp affair in which he had been, in the Caucasus, for which his sword had got the decoration of the Riband of St. Anne. The only difference was, that his voice became a little more measured and grave; he lowered his tones when he pronounced the name "St. Anne," as though he were telling a great secret, and then, for three minutes at least, did not utter a word, but only looked solemn.

During all that first year I had strange passages of feeling, in which I hated Akim Akimitch with a bitter hatred, I am sure I cannot say why, moments when I would despairingly curse the fate which made him my next neighbour on my camp-bed, so close indeed that our heads nearly touched. An hour afterwards I bitterly reproached myself for such extravagance. It was, however, only during my first year of confinement that these violent feelings overpowered me. As time went on, I got used to Akim Akimitch's singular character, and was ashamed of my former explosions. I don't remember that he and I ever got into anything like an open quarrel.

Besides the three Russian nobles of whom I have spoken, there were eight others there during my time; with some of whom I came to be on a footing of intimate friendship. Even the best of them were morbid in mind, exclusive, and intolerant to the very last degree; with two of them I was obliged to discontinue all spoken intercourse. There were only three who had any education, B—ski, M—tski, and the old man, J—ski, who had formerly been a professor of mathematics, an excellent fellow, highly eccentric, and of very narrow mental horizon in spite of his learning. M—tski and B—ski were of a mould quite different from his. Between M—tski and myself there was an excellent understanding from the first set-off. He and I never once got into any sort of dispute; I respected him highly, but could never become sincerely attached to him, though I tried to. He was sour, embittered, and mistrustful, with much self-control; this was quite antipathetic to me; the man had a closed soul, closed to everybody, and he made you feel it. I felt it so strongly that perhaps I was wrong about it. After all, his character, I must say, was stamped with both nobleness and strength. His inveterate scepticism made him very prudent in his relations with everybody about him, and in conducting these he gave proof of remarkable tact and skill. Sceptic as he was, there was another and a reverse side in his nature, for in some things he was a profound and unalterable believer with faith and hope unshakable. In spite of his tact in dealing with men, he got into open hostilities with B—ski and his friend T—ski.

The first of these, B—ski, was a man of infirm health, of consumptive tendency, irascible, and of a weak, nervous system; but a good and generous man. His nervous irritability went so far that he was as capricious as a child; a temperament of that kind was too much for me there, so I soon saw as little of B—ski as I could possibly help, though I never ceased to like him much. It was just the other way so far as M—tski was concerned; with him I always was on easy terms, though I did not like him at all. When I edged away from B—ski, I had to break also, more or less, with T—ski, of whom I spoke in the last chapter, which I much regretted, for, though of little education, he had an excellent heart; a worthy, very spiritual man. He loved and respected B—ski so much that those who broke with that friend of his he regarded as his personal enemies. He quarrelled with M—tski on account of B—ski, and they kept up the difference a long while. All these people were as bilious as they could be, humoursome, mistrustful, the victims of a moral and physical supersensitiveness. It is not to be wondered at; their position was trying indeed, much more so than ours; they were all exiled, transported, for ten or twelve years; and what made their sojourn in the prison most distressing to them was their rooted, ingrained prejudice, especially their unfortunate way of regarding the convicts, which they could not get over; in their eyes the unhappy fellows were mere wild beasts, without a single recognisable human quality. Everything in their previous career and their present circumstances combined to produce this unhappy feeling in them.

Their life at the jail was perpetual torment to them. They were kindly and conversible with the Circassians, with the Tartars, with Isaiah Fomitch; but for the other prisoners they had nothing but contempt and aversion. The only one they had any real respect for was the aged "old believer." For all this, during all the time I spent at the convict establishment, I never knew a single prisoner to reproach them with either their birth, or religious opinions, or convictions, as is so usual with our common people in their relations with people of different condition, especially if these happen to be foreigners. The fact is, they cannot take the foreigner seriously; to the Russian common people he seems a merely grotesque, comical creature. Our convicts had and showed much more respect for the Polish nobles than for us Russians, but I don't think the Poles cared about the matter, or took any notice of the difference.

I spoke just now of T—ski, and have something more to say of him. When he had with his friend to leave the first place assigned to them as residence in their banishment to come to our fortress, he carried his friend B—— nearly the whole way. B—— was of quite a weak frame, and in bad health, and became exhausted before half of the first march was accomplished. They had first been banished to Y—gorsk, where they lived in tolerable comfort; life was much less hard there than in our fortress. But in consequence of a correspondence with the exiles in one of the other towns—a quite innocent exchange of letters—it was thought necessary to remove them to our jail to be under the more direct surveillance of the government. Until they came M—tski had been quite alone, and dreadful must have been his sufferings in that first year of his banishment.

J—ski was the old man always deep in prayer, of whom I spoke a little earlier. All the political convicts were quite young men while J—ski was at least fifty years old. He was a worthy, gentlemanlike person, if eccentric. T—ski and B—ski detested him, and never spoke to him; they insisted upon it that he was too obstinate and troublesome to put up with, and I was obliged to admit it was so. I believe that at a convict establishment—as in every place where people have to be together, whether they like it or not—people are more ready to quarrel with and detest one another than under other circumstances. Many causes contributed to the squabbles that were, unfortunately, always going on. J—ski was really disagreeable and narrow-minded; not one of those about him was on good terms with him. He and I did not come to a rupture, but we were never on a really friendly footing. I fancy that he was a strong mathematician. One day he explained to me in his half-Russian, half-Polish jargon, a system of astronomy of his own; I have been told that he had written a work upon the subject which the learned world had received with derision; I fancy his reasonings on some things had got twisted. He used to be on his knees praying for a whole day sometimes, which made the convicts respect him exceedingly during the remnant of life he had to pass there; he died under my eyes at the jail after a very trying illness. He had won the consideration of the prisoners, from the first moment of his coming in, on account of what had happened with the Major and him. When they were brought afoot from Y—gorsk to our fortress, they were not shaved on the road at all, their hair and beards had grown to great lengths when they were brought before the Major. That worthy foamed like a madman; he was wild with indignation at such infraction of discipline, though it was none of their fault.

"My God! did you ever see anything like it?" he roared; "they are vagabonds, brigands."

J—ski knew very little Russian, and fancied that he was asking them if they were brigands or vagabonds, so he answered:

"We are political prisoners, not rogues and vagabonds."

"So-o-o! You mean impudence! Clod!" howled the Major. "To the guard-house with him; a hundred strokes of the rod at once, this instant, I say!"

They gave the old man the punishment; he lay flat on the ground under the strokes without the slightest resistance, kept his hand in his teeth, and bore it all without a murmur, and without moving a muscle. B—ski and T—ski arrived at the jail as this was all going on, and M—ski was waiting for them at the principal gate, knowing that they were just coming in; he threw himself on their neck, although he had never seen them before. Utterly disgusted at the way the Major had received them, they told M—ski all about the cruel business that had just occurred. M—ski told me later that he was quite beside himself with rage when he heard it.

"I could not contain myself for passion," he said, "I shook as though with ague. I waited for J—ski at the great gate, for he would come straight that way from the guard-house after his punishment. The gate was opened, and there I saw pass before me J—ski, his lips all white and trembling, his face pale as death; he did not look at a single person, and passed through the groups of convicts assembled in the court-yard—they knew a noble had just been subjected to punishment—went into the barrack, went straight to his place, and, without a word, dropped down on his knees for prayer. The prisoners were surprised and even affected. When I saw this old man with white hairs, who had left behind him at home a wife and children, kneeling and praying after that scandalous treatment, I rushed away from the barrack, and for a couple of hours felt as if I had gone stark, staring, raving mad, or blind drunk.... From that first moment the convicts were full of deference and consideration for J—ski; what particularly pleased them, was that he did not utter a cry when undergoing the punishment."

But one must be fair and tell the truth about this sort of thing; this sad story is not an instance of what frequently occurs in the treatment by the authorities of transported noblemen, Russian or Polish; and this isolated case affords no basis for passing judgment upon that treatment. My anecdote merely shows that you may light upon a bad man anywhere and everywhere. And if it happen that such a one is in absolute command of a jail, and if he happen to have a grudge against one of the prisoners, the lot of such a one will be indeed very far from enviable. But the administrative chiefs who regulate and supervise convict labour in Siberia, and from whom subordinates take their tone as well as their orders, are careful to exercise a discriminating treatment in the case of persons of noble birth, and, in some cases, grant them special indulgences as compared with the lot of convicts of lower condition. There are obvious reasons for this; these heads of departments are nobles themselves, they know that men of that class must not be driven to extremity; cases have been known where nobles have refused to submit to corporal punishment, and flung themselves desperately on their tormentors with very grave and serious consequences indeed; moreover—and this, I think, is the leading cause of the good treatment—some time ago, thirty-five years at least, there were transported to Siberia quite a crowd of noblemen; these were of such correct and irreproachable demeanour, and held themselves so high, that the heads of departments fell into the way, which they never afterwards left, of regarding criminals of noble birth and ordinary convicts in quite a different manner; and men in lower place took their cue from them.

Many of these, no doubt, were little pleased with that disposition in their superiors; such persons were pleased enough when they could do exactly as they liked in the matter, but this did not often happen, they were kept well within bounds; I have reason to be satisfied of this and I will say why. I was put in the second category, a classification of those condemned to hard labour, which was primarily and principally composed of convicts who had been serfs, under military superintendence; now this second category, or class, was much harder than the first (of the mines) or the third (manufacturing work). It was harder, not only for the nobles but for the other convicts too, because the governing and administrative methods and *personnel* in it were wholly military, and were pretty much the same in type as those of the convict establishments in Russia. The men in official position were severer, the general treatment more rigorous than in the two other classes; the men were never out of irons, an escort of soldiers was always present, you were always, or nearly so, within stone walls; and things were quite different in the other classes, at least so the convicts said, and there were those among them who had every reason to know. They would all have gladly gone off to the mines, which the law classified as the worst and last punishment, it was their constant dream and desire to do so. All those who had been in the Russian convict establishments spoke with horror of them, and declared that there was no hell like them, that Siberia was a paradise compared with confinement in the fortresses in Russia.

If, then, it is the case that we nobles were treated with special consideration in the establishment I was confined in, which was under direct control of the Governor-General, and administered entirely on military principles, there must have been some greater kindliness in the treatment of the convicts of the first and third category or class. I think I can speak with some authority about what went on throughout Siberia in these respects, and I based my views, as to this, upon all that I heard from convicts of these classes. We, in our prison, were under much more rigorous surveillance than was elsewhere practised; we were favoured with no sort of exemptions from the ordinary rules as regards work and confinement, and the wearing of chains; we could not do anything for ourselves to get immunity from the rules, for I, at least, knew quite well that, *in the good old time which was quite of yesterday*, there had been so much intriguing to undermine the credit of officials that the authorities were greatly afraid of informers, and that, as things stood, to show indulgence to a convict was regarded as a crime. Everybody, therefore, authorities and convicts alike, was in fear of what might happen; we of the nobles were thus quite down to the level of the other convicts; the only point we were favoured in was in regard to corporal punishment—but I think that we should have had even that inflicted on us had we done anything for which it was prescribed, for equality as to punishment was strictly enjoined or practised; what I mean is, that we were not wantonly, causelessly, mishandled like the other prisoners.

When the Governor got to know of the punishment inflicted on J—ski, he was seriously angry with the Major, and ordered him to be more careful for the future. The thing got very generally known. We learned also that the Governor-General, who had great confidence in our Major, and who liked him because of his exact observance of legal bounds, and thought highly of his qualities in the service, gave him a sharp scolding. And our Major took the lesson to heart. I have no doubt it was this prevented his having M—ski beaten, which he would much have liked to do, being much influenced by the slanderous things A—f said about M——; but the Major could never get a fair pretext for doing so, however much he persecuted and set spies upon his proposed victim; so he had to deny himself that pleasure. The J—ski affair became known all through the town, and public opinion condemned the Major; some persons reproached him openly for what he had done, and some even insulted him.

The first occasion on which the man crossed my path may as well be mentioned. We had alarming things reported to us—to me and another nobleman under sentence—about the abominable character of this man, while we were still at Tobolsk. Men who had been sentenced a long while back to twenty-five years of the misery, nobles as we were, and who had visited us so kindly during our provisional sojourn in the first prison, had warned us what sort of man we were to be under; they had also promised to do all they could for us with their friends to see that he hurt us as little as possible. And, in fact, they did write to the three daughters of the Governor-General, who, I believe, interceded on our behalf with their father. But what could he do? No more, of course, than tell the Major to be fair in applying the rules and regulations to our case. It was about three in the afternoon that my companion and myself arrived in the town; our escort took us at once to our tyrant. We remained waiting for him in the ante-chamber while they went to find the next-in-command at the prison. As soon as the latter had come, in walked the Major. We saw an inflamed scarlet face that boded no good, and affected us quite painfully; he seemed like a sort of spider about to throw itself on a poor fly wriggling in its web.

"What's your name, man?" said he to my companion. He spoke with a harsh, jerky voice, as if he wanted to overawe us.

My friend gave his name.

"And you?" said he, turning to me and glaring at me behind his spectacles.

I gave mine.

"Sergeant! take 'em to the prison, and let 'em be shaved at the guard-house, civilian-fashion, hair off half their skulls, and let 'em be put in irons to-morrow. Why, what sort of cloaks have you got there?" said he brutally, when he saw the gray cloaks with yellow sewn at the back which they had given to us at Tobolsk. "Why, that's a new uniform, begad—a new uniform! They're always getting up something or other. That's a Petersburg trick," he said, as he inspected us one after the other. "Got anything with them?" he said abruptly to the gendarme who escorted us.

"They've got their own clothes, your worship," replied he; and the man carried arms, just as if on parade, not without a nervous tremor. Everybody knew the fellow, and was afraid of him.

"Take their clothes away from them. They can't keep anything but their linen, their white things; take away all their coloured things if they've got any, and sell them off at the next sale, and put the money to the prison account. A convict has no property," said he, looking severely at us. "Hark ye! Behave prettily; don't let me have any complaining. If I do—cat-o'-nine-tails! The smallest offence, and to the sticks you go!"

This way of receiving me, so different from anything I had ever known, made me nearly ill that night. It was a frightful thing to happen at the very moment of entering the infernal place. But I have already told that part of my story.

Thus we had no sort of exemption or immunity from any of the miseries inflicted there, no lightening of our labours when with the other convicts; but friends tried to help us by getting us sent for three months, B—ski and me, to the bureau of the Engineers, to do copying work. This was done quietly, and as much as possible kept from being talked about or observed. This piece of kindness was done for us by the head engineers, during the short time that Lieutenant-Colonel G—kof was Governor at our prison. This gentleman had command there only for six short months, for he soon went back to Russia. He really seemed to us all like an angel of goodness sent from heaven, and the feeling for him among the convicts was of the strongest kind; it was not mere love, it was something like adoration. I cannot help saying so. How he did it I don't know, but their hearts went out to him from the moment they first set eyes on him.

"He's more like a father than anything else," the prisoners kept continually saying during all the time he was there at the head of the engineering department. He was a brilliant, joyous fellow. He was of low stature, with a bold, confident expression, and he was all gracious kindness to the convicts, for whom he really did seem to entertain a fatherly sort of affection. How was it he was so fond of them? It is hard to say, but he seemed never to be able to pass a prisoner without a bit of pleasant talk and a little laughing and joking together. There was nothing that smacked of authority in his pleasantries, nothing that reminded them of his position over them. He behaved just as if he was one of themselves. In spite of this kind condescension, I don't remember any one of the convicts ever failing in respect to him or taking the slightest liberty—quite the other way. The convict's face would light up in a wonderful, sudden way when he met the Governor; it was odd to see how the face smiled all over, and the hand went to the cap, when the Governor was seen in the distance making for the poor man. A word from him was regarded as a signal honour. There are some people like that, who know how to win all hearts.

G—kof had a bold, jaunty air, walked with long strides, holding himself very straight; "a regular eagle," the convicts used to call him. He could not do much to lighten their lot materially, for his office was that of superintending the engineering work, which had to be done in ways and quantities, settled absolutely and unalterably by the regulations. But if he happened to come across a gang of convicts who had actually got through their work, he allowed them to go back to quarters before beat of drum, without waiting for the regulation moment. The prisoners loved him for the confidence he showed in them, and because of his aversion for all mean, trifling interferences with them, which are so irritating when prison superiors are addicted to that sort of thing. I am absolutely certain that if he had lost a thousand roubles in notes, there was not a thief in the prison, however hardened, who would not have brought them to him, if the man lit on them. I am sure of it.

How the prisoners all felt for him, and with him when they learned that he was at daggers drawn with our detested Major. That came about a month after his arrival. Their delight knew no bounds. The Major had formerly served with him in the same detachment; so, when they met, after a long separation, they were at first boon companions, but the intimacy could not and did not last. They came to blows—figuratively—and G—kof became the Major's sworn enemy. Some would have it that it was *more* than figuratively, that they came to actual fisticuffs, a likely thing enough as far as the Major was concerned, for the man had no objection to a scrimmage.

When the convicts heard of the quarrel they really could not contain their delight.

"Old Eight-eyes and the Commandant get on finely together! *He's* an eagle; but the other's a *bad 'un*!"

Those who believed in the fight were mighty curious to know which of the two had had the worst of it, and got a good drubbing. If it had been proved there had been no fighting our convicts, I think, would have been bitterly disappointed.

"The Commandant gave him fits, you may bet your life on it," said they; "he's a little 'un, but as bold as a lion; the other one got into a blue funk, and hid under the bed from him."

But G—kof went away only too soon, and keenly was he regretted in the prison.

Our engineers were all most excellent fellows; we had three or four fresh batches of them while I was there.

"Our eagles never remain very long with us," said the prisoners; "especially when they are good and kind fellows."

It was this G—kof who sent B—ski and myself to work in his bureau, for he was partial to exiled nobles. When he left, our condition was still fairly endurable, for there was another engineer there who showed us much sympathy and friendship. We copied reports for some time, and our handwriting was getting to be very good, when an order came from the authorities that we were to be sent back to hard labour as before; some spiteful person had been at work. At bottom we were rather pleased, for we were quite tired of copying.

For two whole years I worked in company with B—ski, all the time in the shops, and many a gossip did we have about our hopes for the future and our notions and convictions. Good B—ski had a very odd mind, which worked in a strange, exceptional way. There are some people of great intelligence who indulge in paradox unconscionably; but when they have undergone great and constant sufferings for their ideas and made great sacrifices for them, you can't drive their notions out of their heads, and it is cruel to try it. When you objected something to B—ski's propositions, he was really hurt, and gave you a violent answer. He was, perhaps, more in the right than I was as to some things wherein we differed, but we were obliged to give one another up, very much to my regret, for we had many thoughts in common.

As years went on M—tski became more and more sombre and melancholy; he became a prey to despair. During the earliest part of my imprisonment he was communicative enough, and let us see what was going on in him. When I arrived at the prison he had just finished his second year. At first he took a lively interest in the news I brought, for he knew nothing of what had been going on in the outer world; he put questions to me, listened eagerly, showed emotion, but, bit by bit, his reserve grew on him and there was no getting at his thoughts. The glowing coals were all covered up with ashes. Yet it was plain that his temper grew sourer and sourer. "*Je hais ces brigands*," he would say, speaking of convicts I had got to know something of; I never could make him see any good in them. He really did not seem to fully enter into the meaning of anything I said on their behalf, though he would sometimes seem to agree in a listless sort of way. Next day it was just as before: "*je hais ces brigands*." (We used often to speak French with him; so one of the overseers of the works, the soldier, Dranichnikof, used always to call us *aides chirurgiens*, God knows why!) M—tski never seemed to shake off his usual apathy except when he spoke of his mother.

"She is old and infirm," he said; "she loves me better than anything in the world, and I don't even know if she's still living. If she learns that I've been whipped——"

M—tski was not a noble, and had been whipped before he was transported. When the recollection of this came up in his mind he gnashed his teeth, and could not look anybody in the face. In the latest days of his imprisonment he used to walk to and fro, quite alone for the most part. One day, at noon, he was summoned to the Governor, who received him with a smile on his lips.

"Well, M—tski, what were your dreams last night?" asked the Governor.

Said M—tski to me later, "When he said that to me a shudder ran through me; I felt struck at the heart."

His answer was, "I dreamed that I had a letter from my mother."

"Better than that, better!" replied the Governor. "You are free; your mother has petitioned the Emperor, and he has granted her prayer. Here, here's her letter, and the order for your dismissal. You are to leave the jail without delay."

He came to us pale, scarcely able to believe in his good fortune.

We congratulated him. He pressed our hands with his own, which were quite cold, and trembled violently. Many of the convicts wished him joy; they were really glad to see his happiness.

He settled in Siberia, establishing himself in our town, where a little after that they gave him a place. He used often to come to the jail to bring us news, and tell us all that was going on, as often as he could talk with us. It was political news that interested him chiefly.

Besides the four Poles, the political convicts of whom I spoke just now, there were two others of that nation, who were sentenced for very short periods; they had not much education, but were good, simple, straightforward fellows. There was another, A—tchoukooski, quite a colourless person; one more I must mention, B—in, a man well on in years, who impressed us all very unfavourably indeed. I don't know what he had been sentenced for, although he used to tell us some story or other about it pretty frequently. He was a person of a vulgar, mean type, with the coarse manner of an enriched shopkeeper. He was quite without education, and seemed to take interest in nothing except what concerned his trade, which was that of a painter, a sort of scene-painter he was; he showed a good deal of talent in his work, and the authorities of the prison soon came to know about his abilities, so he got employment all through the town in decorating walls and ceilings. In two years he beautified the rooms of nearly all the prison officials, who remunerated him handsomely, so he lived pretty comfortably. He was sent to work with three other prisoners, two of whom learned the business thoroughly; one of these, T—jwoski, painted nearly as well as B—in himself. Our Major, who had rooms in one of the government buildings, sent for B—in, and gave him a commission to decorate the walls and ceilings there, which he did so effectively, that the suite of rooms of the Governor-General were quite put out of countenance by those of the Major. The house itself was a ramshackle old place, while the interior, thanks to B—in, was as gay as a palace. Our worthy Major was hugely delighted, went about rubbing his hands, and told everybody that he should look out for a wife at once, "a fellow *can't* remain single when he lives in a place like that;" he was quite serious about it. The Major's satisfaction with B—in and his assistants went on increasing. They occupied a month in the work at the Major's house. During those memorable days the Major seemed to get into a different frame of mind about us, and began to be quite kind to us political prisoners. One day he sent for J—ski.

"J—ski," said he, "I've done you wrong; I had you beaten for nothing. I'm very sorry. Do you understand? I'm very sorry. I, Major ——"

J—ski answered that he understood perfectly.

"Do you understand? I, who am set over you, I have sent for you to ask your pardon. You can hardly realise it, I suppose. What are you to me, fellow? A worm, less than a crawling worm; you're a convict, while I, by God's grace, am a Major; Major ——, *do* you understand?"

J—ski answered that he quite well understood it all.

"Well, I want to be friends with you. But can you appreciate what I'm doing? Can you feel the greatness of soul I'm showing—feel and appreciate it? Just think of it; I, I, the Major!" etc. etc.

J—ski told me of this scene. There was, then, some human feeling left in this drunken, unruly, and tormenting brute. Allowing for the man's notions of things, and feeble faculties, one cannot deny that this was a generous proceeding on his part. Perhaps he was a little less drunk than usual, perhaps more; who can tell?

The Major's glorious idea of marrying came to nothing; the rooms got all their bravery, but the wife was not forthcoming. Instead of going to the altar in that agreeable way, he was pulled up before the authorities and sent to trial. He received orders to send in his resignation. Some of his old sins had found him out, it seems; things done when he had been superintendent of police in our town. This crushing blow came down upon him without notice, quite suddenly. All the convicts were greatly rejoiced when they heard the great news; it was high day and holiday all through the jail. The story went abroad that the Major sobbed, and cried, and howled like an old woman. But he was helpless in the matter. He was obliged to leave his place, sell his two gray horses, and everything he had in the world; and he fell into complete destitution. We came across him occasionally afterwards in civilian, threadbare clothes, and wearing a cap with a cockade; he glanced at us convicts as spitefully and maliciously as you please. But without his Major's uniform, all the man's glory was gone. While placed over us, he gave himself the airs of a being higher than human, who had got into coat and breeches; now it was all over, he looked like the lackey he was, and a disgraced lackey to boot.

With fellows of this sort, the uniform is the only saving grace; that gone, all's gone.

FOOTNOTES:

The Decembrists.

French in the original Russian.

Our Major was not the only officer who spoke of himself in that lofty way; a good many officers did the same, men who had risen from the ranks chiefly.

CHAPTER IX. THE ESCAPE

A little while after the Major resigned, our prison was subjected to a thorough reorganization. The "hard labour" hitherto inflicted, and the other regulations, were abolished, and the place put upon the footing of the military convict establishments of Russia. As a result of this, prisoners of the second category were no longer sent there; this class was, for the future, to be composed of prisoners who were regarded as still on the military footing, that is to say, men who, in spite of sentence, did not forfeit for ever their civic *status*. They were soldiers still, but had undergone corporal punishment; they were sentenced for comparatively short periods, six years at most; when they had served their time, or in case of pardon, they went into the ranks again, as before. Men guilty of a second offence were sentenced to twenty years of imprisonment. Up to the time I speak of, we had a section of soldier-prisoners among us, but only because they did not know where else to dispose of them. Now the place was to be occupied by soldiers exclusively. As to the civilian convicts, who were stripped of all civic rights, branded, cropped, and shaven, these were to remain in the fortress to finish their time; but as no fresh prisoners of this class were to come in, and those there would get their discharge successively, at the end of ten years there would be no civilian convicts left in the place, according to the arrangements. The line of division between the classes of prisoners there was maintained; from time to time there came in other military criminals of high position, sent to our place for security, before being forwarded to Eastern Siberia, for the more aggravated penalties that awaited them there.

There was no change in our general way of life. The work we had to do and the discipline observed were the same as before; but the administrative system was entirely altered, and made more complex. An officer, commandant of companies, was assigned to be at the head of the prison; he had under his orders four subaltern officers who mounted guard by turns. The "invalids" were superseded by twelve non-commissioned officers, and an arsenal superintendent. The convicts were divided into sections of ten, and corporals chosen among them; the power of these over the others was, as may be supposed, nominal. As might be expected, Akim Akimitch got this promotion.

All these new arrangements were confided to the Governor to carry out, who remained in superior command over the whole establishment. The changes did not go further than this. At first the convicts were not a little excited by this movement, and discussed their new guardians a good deal among themselves, trying to make out what sort of fellows they were; but when they saw that everything went on pretty much as usual they quieted down, and things resumed their ordinary course. We had got rid of the Major, and that was something; everybody took fresh breath and fresh courage. The fear that was in all hearts grew less; we had some assurance that in case of need we could go to our superiors and lodge our complaint, and that a man could not be punished without cause, and would not, unless by mistake.

Brandy was brought in as before, although we had subaltern officers now where "invalids" were before. These subalterns were all worthy, careful men, who knew their place and business. There were some among them who had the idea that they might give themselves grand airs, and treat us like common soldiers, but they soon gave it up and behaved like the others. Those who did not seem to be well able to get into their heads what the ways of our prison really were, had sharp lessons about it from the convicts themselves, which led to some lively scenes. One sub-officer was confronted with brandy, which was of course too much for him; when he was sober again we had a little explanation with him; we pointed out that he had been drinking with the prisoners, and that, accordingly, etc. etc.; he became quite tractable. The end of it was that the subalterns closed their eyes to the brandy business. They went to market for us, just as the invalids used to, and brought the prisoners white bread, meat, anything that could be got in without too much risk. So I never could understand why they had gone to the trouble of turning the place into a military prison. The change was made two years before I left the place; I had two years to bear of it still.

I see little use in recording all I saw and went through later at the convict establishment day by day. If I were to tell it all, all the daily and hourly occurrences, I might write twice or thrice as many chapters as this book ought to contain, but I should simply tire the reader and myself. Substantially all that I might write has been already embodied in the narrative as it stands so far; and the reader has had the opportunity of getting a tolerable idea of what the life of a convict of the second class really was. My wish has been to portray the state of things at the establishment, and as it affected myself, accurately and yet forcibly; whether I have done so others must judge. I cannot pronounce upon my own work, but I think I may well draw it to a close; as I move among these recollections of a dreadful past, the old suffering comes up again and all but strangles me.

Besides, I cannot be sure of my memory as to all I saw in these last years, for the faculty seems blunted as regards the later compared with the earlier period of my imprisonment, there is a good deal I am sure I have quite forgotten. But I remember only too well how very, very slow these last two years were, how very sad, how the days seemed as if they never would come to evening, something like water falling drop by drop. I remember, too, that I was filled with a mighty longing for my resurrection from that grave which gave me strength to bear up, to wait, and to hope. And so I got to be hardened and enduring; I lived on expectation, I counted every passing day; if there were a thousand more of them to pass at the prison I found satisfaction in thinking that one of them was gone, and only nine hundred and ninety-nine to come. I remember, too, that though I had round me a hundred persons in like case, I felt myself more and more solitary, and though the solitude was awful I came to love it. Isolated thus among the convict-crowd I went over all my earlier life, analysing its events and thoughts minutely; I passed my former doings in review, and sometimes was pitiless in condemnation of myself; sometimes I went so far as to be grateful to fate for the privilege of such loneliness, for only that could have caused me so severely to scrutinise my past, so searchingly to examine its inner and outer life. What strong and strange new germs of hope came in those memorable hours up in my soul! I weighed and decided all sorts of issues, I entered into a compact with myself to avoid the errors of former years, and the rocks on which I had been wrecked; I laid down a programme for my future, and vowed that I would stick to it; I had a sort of blind and complete conviction that, once away from that place, I should be able to carry out everything I made my mind up to; I looked for my freedom with transports of eager desire; I wanted to try my strength in a renewed struggle with life; sometimes I was clutched, as by fangs, by an impatience which rose to fever heat. It is painful to go back to these things, most painful; nobody, I know, can care much about it at all except myself; but I write because I think people will understand, and because there are those who have been, those who yet will be, like myself, condemned, imprisoned, cut off from life, in the flower of their age, and in the full possession of all their strength.

But all this is useless. Let me end my memoirs with a narrative of something interesting, for I must not close them too abruptly.

What shall it be? Well, it may occur to some to ask whether it was quite impossible to escape from the jail, and if during the time I spent there no attempt of the kind was made. I have already said that a prisoner who has got through two or three years thinks a good deal of it, and, as a rule, concludes that it is best to finish his time without running more risks, so that he may get his settlement, on the land or otherwise, when set at liberty. But those who reckon in this way are convicts sentenced for comparatively short times; those who have many years to serve are always ready to run some chances. For all that the attempts at escape were quite infrequent. Whether that was attributable to the want of spirit in the convicts, the severity of the military discipline enforced, or, after all, to the situation of the town, little favourable to escapes, for it was in the midst of the open steppe, I really cannot say. All these motives no doubt contributed to give pause. It was difficult enough to get out of the prison at all; in my time two convicts tried it; they were criminals of importance.

When our Major had been got rid of, A—v, the spy, was quite alone with nobody to back him up. He was still quite young, but his character grew in force with every year; he was a bold, self-asserting fellow, of considerable intelligence. I think if they had set him at liberty he would have gone on spying and getting money in every sort of shameful way, but I don't think he would have let himself be caught again; he would have turned his experiences as a convict to far too much good for that. One trick he practised was that of forging passports, at least so I heard from some of the convicts. I think this fellow was ready to risk everything for a change in his position. Circumstances gave me the opportunity of getting to the bottom of this man's disposition and seeing how ugly it was; he was simply revolting in his cold, deep wickedness, and my disgust with him was more than I could get over. I do believe that if he wanted a drink of brandy, and could only have got it by killing some one, he would not have hesitated one moment if it was pretty certain the crime would not come out. He had learned there, in that jail, to look on everything in the coolest calculating way. It was on him that the choice of Koulikoff—of the special section—fell, as we are to see.

I have spoken before of Koulikoff. He was no longer young, but full of ardour, life, and vigour, and endowed with extraordinary faculties. He felt his strength, and wanted still to have a life of his own; there are some men who long to live in a rich, abounding life, even when old age has got hold of them. I should have been a good deal surprised if Koulikoff had *not* tried to escape; but he did. Which of the two, Koulikoff and A—v, had the greater influence over the other I really cannot say; they were a goodly couple, and suited each other to a hair, so they soon became as thick as possible. I fancy that Koulikoff reckoned on A—v to forge a passport for him; besides, the latter was of the noble class, belonged to good society, a circumstance out of which a good deal could be made if they managed to get back into Russia. Heaven only knows what compacts they made, or what plans and hopes they formed; if they got as far as Russia they would at all events leave behind them Siberia and vagabondage. Koulikoff was a versatile man, capable of playing many a part on the stage of life, and had plenty of ability to go upon, whatever direction his efforts took. To such persons the jail is strangulation and suffocation. So the two set about plotting their escape.

But to get away without a soldier to act as escort was impossible; so a soldier had to be won. In one of the battalions stationed at our fortress was a Pole of middle life—an energetic fellow worthy of a better fate—serious, courageous. When he arrived first in Siberia, quite young, he had deserted, for he could not stand his sufferings from nostalgia. He was captured and whipped. During two years he formed part of the disciplinary companies to which offenders are sent; then he rejoined his battalion, and, showing himself zealous in the service, had been rewarded by promotion to the rank of corporal. He had a good deal of self-love, and spoke like a man who had no small conceit of himself.

I took particular notice of the man sometimes when he was among the soldiers who had charge of us, for the Poles had spoken to me about him; and I got the idea that his longing for his native country had taken the form of a chill, fixed, deadly hatred for those who kept him away from it. He was the sort of man to stick at nothing, and Koulikoff showed that his scent was good, when he pitched on this man to be an accomplice in his flight. This corporal's name was Kohler. Koulikoff and he settled their plans and fixed the day. It was the month of June, the hottest of the year. The climate of our town and neighbourhood was pretty equable, especially in summer, which is a very good thing for tramps and vagabonds. To make off far after leaving the fortress was quite out of the question, it being situated on rising ground and in uncovered country, for though surrounded by woods, these are a considerable distance away. A disguise was indispensable, and to procure it they must manage to get into the outskirts of the town, where Koulikoff had taken care some time before to prepare a den of some sort. I don't know whether his worthy friends in that part of the town were in the secret. It may be presumed they were, though there is no evidence. That year, however, a young woman who led a gay life and was very pretty, settled down in a nook of that same part of the city, near the county. This young person attracted a good deal of notice, and her career promised to be something quite remarkable; her nickname was "Fire and Flame." I think that she and the fugitives concerted the plans of escape together, for Koulikoff had lavished a good deal of attention and money on her for more than a year. When the gangs were formed each morning, the two fellows, Koulikoff and A—v, managed to get themselves sent out with the convict Chilkin, whose trade was that of stove-maker and plasterer, to do up the empty barracks when the soldiers went into camp. A—v and Koulikoff were to help in carrying the necessary materials. Kohler got himself put into the escort on the occasion; as the rules required three soldiers to act as escort for two prisoners, they gave him a young recruit whom he was doing corporal's duty upon, drilling and training him. Our fugitives must have exercised a great deal of influence over Kohler to deceive him, to cast his lot in with them, serious, intelligent, and reflective man as he was, with so few more years of service to pass in the army.

They arrived at the barracks about six o'clock in the morning; there was nobody with them. After having worked about an hour, Koulikoff and A—v told Chilkin that they were going to the workshop to see some one, and fetch a tool they wanted. They had to go carefully to work with Chilkin, and speak in as natural a tone as they could. The man was from Moscow, by trade a stove-maker, sharp and cunning, keen-sighted, not talkative, fragile in appearance, with little flesh on his bones. He was the sort of person who might have been expected to pass his life in honest working dress, in some Moscow shop, yet here he was in the "special section," after many wanderings and transfers among the most formidable military criminals; so fate had ordered.

What had he done to deserve such severe punishment? I had not the least idea; he never showed the least resentment or sour feeling, and went on in a quiet, inoffensive way; now and then he got as drunk as a lord; but, apart from that, his conduct was perfectly good. Of course he was not in the secret, so he had to be thrown off the scent. Koulikoff told him, with a wink, that they were going to get some brandy, which had been hidden the day before in the workshop, which suited Chilkin's book perfectly; he had not the least notion of what was up, and remained alone with the young recruit, while Koulikoff, A—v, and Kohler betook themselves to the suburbs of the town.

Half-an-hour passed; the men did not come back. Chilkin began to think, and the truth dawned upon him. He remembered that Koulikoff had not seemed at all like himself, that he had seen him whispering and winking to A—v; he was sure of that, and the whole thing seemed suspicious to him. Kohler's behaviour had struck him, too; when he went off with the two convicts, the corporal had given the recruit orders what he was to do in his absence, which he had never known him do before. The more Chilkin thought over the matter the less he liked it. Time went on; the convicts did not return; his anxiety was great; for he saw that the authorities would suspect him of connivance with the fugitives, so that his own skin was in danger. If he made any delay in giving information of what had occurred, suspicion of himself would grow into conviction that he knew what the men intended when they left him, and he would be dealt with as their accomplice. There was no time to lose.

It came into his mind, then, that Koulikoff and A—v had become markedly intimate for some time, and that they had been often seen laying their heads together behind the barracks, by themselves. He remembered, too, that he had more than once fancied that they were up to something together.

He looked attentively at the soldier with him as escort; the fellow was yawning, leaning on his gun, and scratching his nose in the most innocent manner imaginable; so Chilkin did not think it necessary to speak of his anxieties to this man: he told him simply to come with him to the engineers' workshops. His object was to ask if anybody there had seen his companions; but nobody there had, so Chilkin's suspicions grew stronger and stronger. If only he could think that they had gone to get drunk and have a spree in the outskirts of the town, as Koulikoff often did. No, thought Chilkin, that was *not* so. They would have told him, for there was no need to make a mystery of that. Chilkin left his work, and went straight back to the jail.

It was about nine o'clock when he reached the sergeant-major, to whom he mentioned his suspicions. That officer was frightened, and at first could not believe there was anything in it all. Chilkin had, in fact, expressed no more than a vague misgiving that all was not as it should be. The sergeant-major ran to the Major, who in his turn ran to the Governor. In a quarter-of-an-hour all necessary measures were taken. The Governor-General was communicated with. As the convicts in question were persons of importance, it might be expected that the matter would be seriously viewed at St. Petersburg. A——v was classed among political prisoners, by a somewhat random official proceeding, it would seem; Koulikoff was a convict of the "special section," that is to say, as a criminal of the blackest dye, and, what was worse, was an ex-soldier. It was then brought to notice that according to the regulations each convict of the "special section" ought to have two soldiers assigned as escort when he went to work; the regulations had not been observed as to this, so that everybody was exposed to serious trouble. Expresses were sent off to all the district offices of the municipality, and all the little neighbouring towns, to warn the authorities of the escape of the two convicts, and a full description furnished of their persons. Cossacks were sent out to hunt them up, letters sent to the authorities of all adjoining Governmental districts. And everybody was frightened to death.

The excitement was quite as great all through the prison; as the convicts returned from work, they heard the tremendous news, which spread rapidly from man to man; all received it with deep, though secret satisfaction. Their emotion was as natural as it was great. The affair broke the monotony of their lives, and gave them something to think of; but, above all, it was an escape, and as such, something to sympathise with deeply, and stirred fibres in the poor fellows which had long been without any exciting stimulus; something like hope and a disposition to confront their fate set their hearts beating, for the incident seemed to show that their hard lot was not hopelessly unchangeable.

"Well, you see they've got off in spite of them! Why shouldn't we?"

The thought came into every man's mind, and made him stiffen his back and look at his neighbours in a defiant sort of way. All the convicts seemed to grow an inch taller on the strength of it, and to look down a bit upon the sub-officers. The heads of the place soon came running up, as you may imagine. The Governor now arrived in person. We fellows looked at them all with some assurance, with a touch of contempt, and with a very set expression of face, as though to say: "Well, you there? We can get out of your clutches when we've a mind to."

All the men were quite sure there would be a general searching of everything and everybody; so everything that was at all contraband was carefully hidden; for the authorities would want to show that precious wisdom of theirs which may be reckoned on after the event. The expectation was verified; there was a mighty turning of everything upside down and topsy-turvy, a general rummage, with the discovery of exactly nothing, as they might have known.

When the time came for going out to work after dinner the usual escorts were doubled. When night came, the officers and sub-officers on service came pouncing on us at every moment to see if we were off our guard, and if anything could be got out of us; the lists were gone over once more than the usual number of times, which extra mustering only gave more trouble for nothing; we were hunted out of the court-yard that our names might be gone through again. Then, when in barrack, they reckoned us up another time, as if they never could be done with the exercise.

The convicts were not at all disturbed by all this bustling absurdity. They put on a very unconcerned demeanour, and, as is always the case in such a conjuncture, behaved in the prettiest manner all that evening and night. "We won't give them any handle anyhow," was the general feeling. The question with the authorities was whether some among us were not in complicity with those who had got away, so a careful watch was kept over our doings, and a careful ear for our conversations; but nothing came of it.

"Not such fools, those fellows, as to leave anybody behind who was in the secret!"

"When you go at that sort of thing you lie low and play low!"

"Koulikoff and A——v know enough to have covered up their tracks. They've done the trick in first-rate style, keeping things to themselves; they've mizzled, the rascals; clever chaps, those, they could get through shut doors!"

The glory of Koulikoff and A——v had grown a hundred cubits higher than it was. Everybody was proud of them. Their exploit, it was felt, would be handed down to the most distant posterity, and outlive the jail itself.

"Rattling fellows, those!" said one.

"Can't get away from here, eh? *That's* their notion, is it? Just look at those chaps!"

"Yes," said a third, looking very superior, "but who *is* it that has got away? Tip-top fellows. *You* can't hold a candle to them."

At any other time the man to whom anything of that sort was said would have replied angrily enough, and defended himself; now the observation was met with modest silence.

"True enough," was said. "Everybody's not a Koulikoff or an A——v, you've got to show what you're made of before you've a right to speak."

"I say, pals, after all, why do we remain in the place?" struck in a prisoner seated by the kitchen window; he spoke drawlingly, but the man, you could see, enjoyed it all; he slowly rubbed his cheek with the palm of his hand. "Why do we stop? It's no life at all, we've been buried, though we're alive and kicking. Now *isn't* it so?"

"Oh, curse it, you can't get out of prison as easy as shaking off an old boot. I tell you it sticks to your calves. What's the good of pulling a long face over it?"

"But, look here; there is Koulikoff now," began one of the most eager, a mere lad.

"Koulikoff!" exclaimed another, looking askance at the young fellow. "Koulikoff! They don't turn out Koulikoffs by the dozen."

"And A——v, pals, there's a lad for you!"

"Aye, aye, he'll get Koulikoff just where he wants him, as often as he wants him. He's up to everything, he is."

"I wonder how far they've got; that's what *I* want to know," said one.

Then the talk went off into details: Had they got far from the town? What direction did they go off in? *Which* gave them the best chance? Then they discussed distances, and as there were convicts who knew the neighbourhood well, these were attentively listened to.

Next, they talked over the inhabitants of the neighbouring villages, of whom they seemed to think as badly as possible. There was nobody in the neighbourhood, the convicts believed, who would hesitate at all as to the course to be pursued; nothing would induce them to help the runaways; quite the other way, these people would hunt them down.

"If you only knew what bad fellows these peasants are! Rascally brutes!"

"Peasants, indeed! Worthless scamps!"

"These Siberians are as bad as bad can be. They think nothing of killing a man."

"Oh, well, our fellows——"

"Yes, that's it, they may come off second best. Our fellows are as plucky as plucky can be."

"Well, if we live long enough, we shall hear something about them soon."

"Well, now, what do you *think*? Do you think they really will get clean away?"

"I am sure, as I live, that they'll never be caught," said one of the most excited, giving the table a great blow with his fist.

"Hm! That's as things turn out."

"I'll tell you what, friends," said Skouratof, "if I once got out, I'd stake my life they'd never get me again."

"*You?*"

Everybody burst out laughing. They would hardly condescend to listen to him; but Skouratof was not to be put down.

"I tell you I'd stake my life on it!" with great energy. "Why, I made my mind up to *that* long ago. I'd find means of going through a key-hole rather than let them lay hands on me."

"Oh, don't you fear, when your belly got empty you'd just go creeping to a peasant and ask him for a morsel of something."

Fresh laughter.

"I ask him for victuals? You're a liar!"

"Hold your jaw, can't you? We know what you were sent here for. You and your Uncle Vacia killed some peasant for bewitching your cattle."

More laughter. The more serious among them seemed very angry and indignant.

"You're a liar," cried Skouratof; "it's Mikitka who told you that; I wasn't in that at all, it was Uncle Vacia; don't you mix my name up in it. I'm a Moscow man, and I've been on the tramp ever since I was a very small thing. Look here, when the priest taught me to read the liturgy, he used to pinch my ears, and say, 'Repeat this after me: Have pity on me, Lord, out of Thy great goodness;' and he used to make me say with him, 'They've taken me up and brought me to the police-station out of Thy great goodness,' and the like. I tell you that went on when I was quite a little fellow."

All laughed heartily again; that was what Skouratof wanted; he liked playing clown. Soon the talk became serious again, especially among the older men and those who knew a good deal about escapes. Those among the younger convicts who could keep themselves quiet enough to listen, seemed highly delighted. A great crowd was assembled in and about the kitchen. There were none of the warders about; so everybody could give vent to his feelings in talk or otherwise. One man I noticed who was particularly enjoying himself, a Tartar, a little fellow with high cheek-bones, and a remarkably droll face. His name was Mametka, he could scarcely speak Russian at all, but it was odd to see the way he craned his neck forward into the crowd, and the childish delight he showed.

"Well, Mametka, my lad, *iakchi*."

"*Iakchi, ouk, iakchi!*" said Mametka as well as he could, shaking his grotesque head. "*Iakchi.*"

"They'll never catch them, eh? *Iok.*"

"*Iok, iok!*" and Mametka waggled his head and threw his arms about.

"You're a liar, then, and I don't know what you're talking about. Hey!"

"That's it, that's it, *iakchi*!" answered poor Mametka.

"All right, good, *iakchi* it is!"

Skouratof gave him a thump on the head, which sent his cap down over his eyes, and went out in high glee, and Mametka was quite chapfallen.

For a week or so a very tight hand was kept on everybody in the jail, and the whole neighbourhood was repeatedly and carefully searched. How they managed it I cannot tell, but the prisoners always seemed to know all about the measures taken by the authorities for recovering the runaways. For some days, according to all we heard, things went very favourably for them; no traces whatever of them could be found. Our convicts made very light of all the authorities were about, and were quite at their ease about their friends, and kept saying that nothing would ever be found out about them.

All the peasants round about were roused, we were told, and watching all the likely places, woods, ravines, etc.

"Stuff and nonsense!" said our fellows, who had a grin on their faces most of the time, "they're hidden at somebody's place who's a friend."

"That's certain; they're not the fellows to chance things, they've made all sure."

The general idea was, in fact, that they were still concealed in the suburbs of the town, in a cellar, waiting till the hue and cry was over, and for their hair to grow; that they would remain there perhaps six months at least, and then quietly go off. All the prisoners were in the most fanciful and romantic state of mind about the things. Suddenly, eight days after the escape, a rumour spread that the authorities were on their track. This rumour was at first treated with contempt, but towards evening there seemed to be more in it. The convicts became much excited. Next morning it was said in the town that the runaways had been caught, and were being brought back. After dinner there were further details; the story was that they had been seized at a hamlet, seventy versts away from the town. At last we had fully confirmed tidings. The sergeant-major positively asserted, immediately after an interview with the Major, that they would be brought into the guard-house that very night. They were taken; there could be no doubt of it.

It is difficult to convey an adequate idea of the way the convicts were affected by the news. At first their rage was great, then they were deeply dejected. Then they began to be bitter and sarcastic, pouring all their scorn, not on the authorities, but on the runaways who had been such fools as to get caught. A few began this, then nearly all joined, except a small number of the more serious, thoughtful ones, who held their tongues, and seemed to regard the thoughtless fellows with great contempt.

Poor Koulikoff and A—v were now just as heartily abused as they had been glorified before; the men seemed to take a delight in running them down, as though in being caught they had done something wantonly offensive to their mates. It was said, with high contempt, that the fellows had probably got hungry and couldn't stand it, and had gone into a village to ask bread of the peasants, which, according to tramp etiquette, it appears, is to come down very low in the world indeed. In this supposition the men turned out to be quite mistaken; for what had happened was that the tracks of the runaways out of the town were discovered and followed up; they were ascertained to have got into a wood, which was surrounded, so that the fugitives had no recourse but to give themselves up.

They were brought in that night, tied hands and feet, under armed escort. All the convicts ran hastily to the palisades to see what would be done with them; but they saw nothing except the carriages of the Governor and the Major, which were waiting in front of the guard-house. The fugitives were ironed and locked up separately, their punishment being adjourned till the next day. The prisoners began all to sympathise with the unhappy fellows when they heard how they had been taken, and learned that they could not help themselves, and the anxiety about the issue was keen.

"They'll get a thousand at least."

"A thousand, is it? I tell you they'll have it till the life is beaten out of them. A—v may get off with a thousand, but the other they'll kill; why, he's in the 'special section.'"

They were wrong. A—v was sentenced to five hundred strokes, his previous good conduct told in his favour, and this was his first prison offence. Koulikoff, I believe, had fifteen hundred. The punishment, upon the whole, was mild rather than severe.

The two men showed good sense and feeling, for they gave nobody's name as having helped them, and positively declared that they had made straight for the woods without going into anybody's house. I was very sorry for Koulikoff; to say nothing of the heavy beating he got; he had thrown away all his chances of having his lot as a prisoner lightened. Later he was sent to another convict establishment. A—v did not get all he was sentenced to; the physicians interfered, and he was let off. But as soon as he was safe in the hospital he began blowing his trumpet again, and said he would stick at nothing now, and that they should soon see what he would do. Koulikoff was not changed a bit, as decorous as ever, and gave himself just the same airs as ever; manner or words to show that he had had such an adventure. But the convicts looked on him quite differently; he seemed to have come down a good deal in their estimation, and now to be on their own level every way, instead of being a superior creature. So it was that poor Koulikoff's star paled; success is everything in this world.

FOOTNOTE:

The expression of the original is untranslatable; literally "you killed a cattle-kill." This phrase means murder of a peasant, male or female, supposed to bewitch cattle. We had in our jail a murderer who had done this cattle-kill.—Dostoïeffsky's Note.

CHAPTER X. FREEDOM!

This incident occurred during my last year of imprisonment. My recollection of what occurred this last year is as keen as of the events of the first years; but I have gone into detail enough. In spite of my impatience to be out, this year was the least trying of all the years I spent there. I had now many friends and acquaintances among the convicts, who had by this time made up their minds very much in my favour. Many of them, indeed, had come to feel a sincere and genuine affection for me. The soldier who was assigned to accompany my friend and myself—simultaneously discharged—out of the prison, very nearly cried when the time for leaving came. And when we were at last in full freedom, staying in the rooms of the Government building placed at our disposal for the month we still spent in the town, this man came nearly every day to see us. But there were some men whom I could never soften or win any regard from—God knows why—and who showed just the same hard aversion for me at the last as at the first; something we could not get over stood between us.

I had more indulgences during the last year. I found among the military functionaries of our town old acquaintances, and even some old schoolfellows, and the renewal of these relations helped me. Thanks to them I got permission to have some money, to write to my family, and even to have some books. For some years I had not had a single volume, and words would fail to tell the strange, deep emotion and excitement which the first book I read at the jail caused me. I began to devour it at night, when the doors were closed, and read it till the break of day. It was a number of a review, and it seemed to me like a messenger from the other world. As I read, my life before the prison days seemed to rise up before me in sharp definition, as of some existence independent of my own, which another soul had had. Then I tried to get some clear idea of my relation to current events and things; whether my arrears of knowledge and experience were too great to make up; whether the men and women out of doors had lived and gone through many things and great during the time I was away from them; and great was my desire to thoroughly understand what was *now* going on, *now* that I could know something about it all at last. All the words I read were as palpable things, which I wanted rather to feel sensibly than get mere meaning out of; I tried to see more in the text than *could* be there. I imagined some mysterious meanings that *must* be in them, and tried at every page to see allusions to the past, with which my mind was familiar, whether they were there or not; at every turn of the leaf I sought for traces of what had deeply moved people before the days of my bondage; and deep was my dejection when it was forced on my mind that a new state of things had arisen; a new life, among my kind, which was alien to my knowledge and my sentiments. I felt as if I was a straggler, left behind and lost in the onward march of mankind.

Yes, there were indeed arrears, if the word is not too weak.

For the truth is, that another generation had come up, and I knew it not, and it knew not me. At the foot of one article I saw the name of one who had been dear to me; with what avidity I flung myself on *that* paper! But the other names were nearly all new to me; new workers had come upon the scene, and I was eager to know their doings and themselves. It made me feel nearly desperate to have so few books, and to know how hard it would be to get more. At an earlier date, in the old Major's time, it was a dangerous thing indeed to bring books into the jail. If one was found when the whole place was searched, as was regularly done, great was the disturbance, and no efforts were spared to find out how they got in, and who had helped in the offence. I did not want to be subjected to insulting scrutiny, and, if I had, it would have been useless. I *had* to live without books, and did, shut up in myself, tormenting myself with many a question and problem on which I had no means of throwing any light. But I can *never* tell it all.

It was in winter that I came in, so in winter I was to leave, on the anniversary-day. Oh, with what impatience did I look forward to the thrice-blessed winter! How gladly did I see the summer die out, the leaves turn yellow on the trees, the grass turn dry over the wide steppe! Summer is gone at last! the winds of autumn howl and groan, the first snow falls in whirling flakes. The winter, so long, long-prayed for, is come, come at last. Oh, how the heart beats with the thought that freedom was really, at last, at last, close at hand. Yet it was strange, as the time of times, the day of days, grew nearer and nearer, so did my soul grow quieter and quieter. I was annoyed at myself, reproached myself even with being cold, indifferent. Many of the convicts, as I met them in the court-yard when the day's work was done, used to get out, and talk with me to wish me joy.

"Ah, little Father Alexander Petrovitch, you'll soon be out now! And here you'll leave us poor devils behind!"

"Well, Mertynof, have you long to wait still?" I asked the man who spoke.

"I! Oh, good Lord, I've seven years of it yet to weary through."

Then the man sighed with a far-away, wandering look, as if he was gazing into those intolerable days to come.... Yes, many of my companions congratulated me in a way that showed they really felt what they said. I saw, too, that there was more disposition to meet me as man to man, they drew nearer to me as I was to leave them; the halo of freedom began to surround me, and caring for that they cared more for me. It was in this spirit they bade me farewell.

K—schniski, a young Polish noble, a sweet and amiable person, was very fond, about this time, of walking in the court-yard with me. The stifling nights in the barracks did him much harm, so he tried his best to keep his health by getting all the exercise and fresh air he could.

"I am looking forward impatiently to the day when *you* will be set free," he said with a smile one day, "for when you go I shall *realise* that I have just one year more of it to undergo."

Need I say what I can yet not help saying, that freedom in idea always seemed to us who were there something *more* free than it ever can be in reality? That was because our fancy was always dwelling upon it. Prisoners always exaggerate when they think of freedom and look on a free man; we did certainly; the poorest servant of one of the officers there seemed a sort of king to us, everything we could imagine in a free man, compared with ourselves at least; he had no irons on his limbs, his head was not shaven, he could go where and when he liked, with no soldiers to watch and escort him.

The day before I was set free, as night fell I went *for the last time* all through and all round the prison. How many a thousand times had I made the circuit of those palisades during those ten years! There, at the rear of the barracks, had I gone to and fro during the whole of that first year, a solitary, despairing man. I remember how I used to reckon up the days I had still to pass there—thousands, thousands! God! how long ago it seemed. There's the corner where the poor prisoned eagle wasted away; Petroff used often to come to me at that place. It seemed as if the man would never leave my side now; he would place himself by my side and walk along without ever saying a word, as though he knew all my thoughts as well as myself, and there was always a strange, inexplicable sort of wondering look on the man's face.

How many a mental farewell did I take of the black, squared beams in our barracks! Ah, me! How much joyless youth, how much strength for which use there was none, was buried, lost in those walls!—youth and strength of which the world might surely have made *some* use. For I must speak my thoughts as to this: the hapless fellows there were perhaps the strongest, and, in one way or another, the most gifted of our people. There was all that strength of body and of mind lost, hopelessly lost. Whose fault is that?

Yes; whose fault *is* that?

The next day, at an early hour, before the men were mustered for work, I went through all the barracks to bid the men a last farewell. Many a vigorous, horny hand was held out to me with right good-will. Some grasped and shook my hand as though all their hearts went with the act; but these were the more generous souls. Most of the poor fellows seemed so much to feel that, for them, I was already a man changed by what was coming, that they could feel scarce anything else. They knew that I had friends in the town, that I was going away at once to *gentlemen*, that I should sit at their table as their equal. This the poor fellows felt; and, although they did their best as they took my hand, that hand could not be the hand of an equal. No; I, too, was a gentleman now. Some turned their backs on me, and made no reply to my parting words. I think, too, that I saw looks of aversion on some faces.

The drum beat; all the convicts went to their work; and I was left to myself. Souchiloff had got up before everybody that morning, and now set himself tremblingly to the task of getting ready for me a last cup of tea. Poor Souchiloff! How he cried when I gave him my clothes, my shirts, my trouser-straps, and some money.

"'Tain't that, 'tain't that," he said, and he bit his trembling lips, "it's that I am going to lose you, Alexander Petrovitch! What *shall* I do without you?"

There was Akim Akimitch, too; him, also, I bade farewell.

"Your turn to go will come soon, I pray," said I.

"Ah, no! I shall remain here long, long, very long yet," he just managed to say, as he pressed my hand. I threw myself on his neck; we kissed.

Ten minutes after the convicts had gone out, my companion and myself left the jail *for ever*. We went to the blacksmith's shop, where our irons were struck off. We had no armed escort, we went there attended by a single sub-officer. It was convicts who struck off our irons in the engineers' workshop. I let them do it for my friend first, then went to the anvil myself. The smiths made me turn round, seized my leg, and stretched it on the anvil. Then they went about the business methodically, as though they wanted to make a very neat job of it indeed.

"The rivet, man, turn the rivet first," I heard the master smith say; "there, so, so. Now, a stroke of the hammer!"

The irons fell. I lifted them up. Some strange impulse made me long to have them in my hands for one last time. I couldn't realise that, only a moment before, they had been on my limbs.

"Good-bye! Good-bye! Good-bye!" said the convicts in their broken voices; but they seemed pleased as they said it.

Yes, farewell!

Liberty! New life! Resurrection from the dead!

Unspeakable moment!

THE END